Praise for *Tho...*

'*Those Above* is a clever book, sh[...]
dry humour and steady world bu[...]
well-created and beautifully created [...], which also happen
to be both darkly comic and devastatingly grim, will find
themselves swiftly addicted.'
Starburst

'Gripping . . . Polansky has pulled off a polished fantasy thriller
that's very much in the George RR Martin/Joe Abercrombie
vein, but has still given the book its own distinctive style and
voice, alongside plenty of evocative world-building. The *Empty
Throne* (series) looks set to be fascinating and provocative'
SFX

'Prepare yourself to be blown away . . . the only problem
being the wait for book two!'
The Bibliophile Chronicles

'A cracking good adventure. There's politics and plotting, war
and adventure, conquest, invasion, flirtation, assassination, big
magic swords, tawdry affairs, murder, blackmail, burglary,
mountaintop duels and (why not?) an airship. As brilliantly
as *Those Above* delivers its big, thematic vision, it is also
gloriously entertaining – as any great epic fantasy should be.
Those Above is *I, Claudius* – by way of Tolkien and filtered
through Chandler. That is to say, really damn good.'
Pornokitsch

'A brilliant start to what is sure to be one of the fantasy epics
of all time, *Those Above* is the work of an author at the top of
his game and brings with it the promise of a lot more to come.'
Reader Dad

'*Those Above* is an excellent new series from an author that has
gone from strength to strength. Dark, epic and a eloquent,
Those Above is a delight to read.'
Mithril Wisdom

Daniel Polansky was born in Baltimore, Maryland. He can be found in Brooklyn, when he isn't somewhere else. This is his first epic fantasy.

The Low Town Novels

The Straight Razor Cure
Tomorrow, the Killing
She Who Waits

Those Above

Book 1 of The Empty Throne

DANIEL POLANSKY

HODDER

First published in Great Britain in 2015 by
Hodder & Stoughton
An Hachette UK company

First published in paperback in 2016

1

A CIP catalogue record for this title is
available from the British Library

ISBN 978 1 444 77991 2

Typeset in Sabon MT by Palimpsest Book Production Ltd, Falkirk, Stirlingshire

Printed and bound by CPI Group (UK) Ltd, Croydon, CR0 4YY

Hodder & Stoughton policy is to use papers that are natural,
renewable and recyclable products and made from wood grown in sustainable
forests. The logging and manufacturing processes are expected to
conform to the environmental regulations of the country of origin.

Hodder & Stoughton Ltd
Carmelite House
50 Victoria Embankment
London EC4Y 0DZ

www.hodder.co.uk

To Julian – the world awaits.

PROLOGUE

S een from the view of a bird, or of a god – which of course are not the same thing – the landscape might have been beautiful. A clear day in early summer, stalks high in the fields, the scattered currant bushes crowned with small red flowers. Far to the east a river ran fast and clear, a translucent snake of blue churning south-west towards the bay and the sea beyond. In half an hour it would be so thick with blood as to choke the perch, bubble the salmon to the surface.

To the west many thousands of men stood in tightly packed ranks, the sunlight off the tips of their spears and the straight hard lines of their swords blinding, a small mass of cavalry on each wing. Further west, towards the low foothills of the mountains, you would have seen the whole vast apparatus that had facilitated their progress, tents and wagons and great stocks of supplies. You would likely not have been able to hear the buzz of anticipation, the muttered oaths and curses, but you might have been able to sense it, the way the skin tingles before a hard rain.

Facing them to the east was a smaller coterie of heavy cavalry, still and silent, the only flicker of movement coming from their coloured banners and the trailing of gossamer streamers that the wind stretched out behind them. From such a height you might have made the mistake of thinking them the same species as their foes – but this would have been a very great mistake indeed, and a closer perspective would swiftly have disabused you of such foolishness. They wore closed helms with visages strange and terrible, chimerical amalgamations of animals and monsters, exquisite craftsmanship put to the service of inducing fear. They carried pronged lances the length of a young elm tree, jewelled great axes of improbable size, tapered swords and multi-headed flails, an arsenal varied and dazzling.

Neither sound nor signal heralded their charge, only the sudden rapid beat of hooves, the particoloured host of cavalry surging forward in perfect unison, as a skein of geese wheel in flight, as a hawk descends upon a marmot. The distance between the two sides narrowed and narrowed until there was nothing between them.

Then it would have been impossible not to hear the screams of the men and the horses, a caterwaul of fear and pain and despair. A disharmonious chorus, for the things which were not quite men remained mute, silent even when skewered on the end of a pike or hacked apart like cordwood, dying without noise or complaint. For a moment the contest seemed in some doubt, as if the vast weight of metal and flesh might balance into equilibrium, and then the heavy cavalry continued on, the infantry giving way like wheat, or water.

Had you been a vulture you would have crowed joyously at the feast. And had you been a god? Who can say? The gods give little credence to the deaths of men, or of those other things so like them.

I

Bas could not remember a time when it didn't hurt to wake.

Age alone would have been enough to make it an exercise in misery, but well before sprouting its first grey hairs his body had been a catalogue of injury. Those halcyon days before pain had ended after he had taken an arrow in the knee during a skirmish in Dycia, and that was closer to twenty years past than fifteen. Bas had preferred a possible future on two legs over a certain existence on one, and though he'd had to threaten the sawbones with his boot knife, and to refuse water for fear it had been drugged, Bas had had his way. Bas was a man who often had his way. The knee still pained him when it rained, and when he stood, and when it was dry, and when he sat, but he got around on it well enough.

That had been the first serious injury, but far from the last. A Marcher had crushed two fingers of his left hand some years back, and this time after a look at the ruptured flesh

Bas had allowed the doctor to go ahead with his hacksaw. Sometimes they ached, the ghosts of these digits, though Bas did not understand why their absence would be a source of pain. There were others, many others: a scar on his chest from where a hand axe had cut through his armour, another just below his hip where a disgruntled subordinate had tried to make good on some real or perceived slight, an array of nicks and gouges and half-healed contusions the source, even the existence, of which Bas had all but forgotten. Bas was not one to waste time on rumination.

Nor did his injuries noticeably affect his comportment. From the first words of his attendant – from before really, from when he had heard the folds of his tent being opened – the Legatus had been fully cognisant, or close to it. A short moment and he rolled up from his mat, prepared to face another day.

He had slept in a long shirt and thick wool trousers. Winter came early here on the plains, and summer was no great joy either. The rain had died off before dawn but left behind a thick patina of mist that carried the cold inside the tent and inside Bas's bones. He turned to the corner and took a long, slow piss into a tin bedpan, taking his time with it, the only luxury he'd be allowed that day. Then he washed his face in the basin of fresh rainwater, paying no more mind to the cold than he had to the ache in his knee. 'Any movement?'

'A few more may have trickled in. Nothing that will affect the balance.'

'And our emissary?' Bas had told Isaac to send out a rider to the Marchers' camp at first light. It was a mark of respect for his subordinate that he hadn't bothered to enquire whether it had been done, simply assumed it and moved on to the resolution.

'Still out.'

Bas pulled on his armour, supple leather overlaid with strong chain links – good against a blade or arrow, all but useless for the chill. Over the top he belted a long dirk and a short war hammer. Leaning against the wall, covered with a scarred leather scabbard and a thick layer of cloth, was a long blade. He swung the baldric over his shoulder, an awkward motion accomplished without thought or strain. 'Best have a look,' he said.

Issac had worked as Bas's number two for near on fifteen years. Whether his character had fitted itself to the position from the start or whether he had moulded himself to it Bas couldn't quite remember. He was short and dark and hard as the knob of an oak tree. His eyes were flat and brown and roamed about like a stray dog, searching for a loose strap or a broken catch or a man out of position. Looking at him straight on it took a few seconds to realise that his head was off-kilter, his features strangely unbalanced, though you'd have needed to have viewed him in profile to see the raw red mess of his cropped ears. What exactly Isaac had done to mandate not only his mutilation but also a lifetime of service in the outermost hellhole of the Aelerian Commonwealth Bas had never asked, and Isaac never volunteered. 'At your command,' he said now, holding open the folds of his tent.

Bas nodded, then dipped out of what passed for his home and into the structured chaos of camp.

The bivouac of the Western Army, consisting of the Eleventh and Thirteenth Themas, was a city on the move, a whirling, clanging, all-consuming metropolis of flesh and steel that had crossed half a continent to take up residence in the very heart of enemy territory. They came from the Aelerian heartland, a month's hard ride east; from the coast and the border cities, whose independence had only been finally eclipsed in the years just after Bas's birth; and from more recently subjugated territories as well, slingers from the Baleferic Isles, archers from Old Dycia. Twenty thousand men and two thousand horses, three hundred wagons, a dozen mobile foundries and a herd of cattle large enough to keep everyone fed. These were only the official numbers, didn't take into account the perhaps only slightly smaller mob of merchants, con-artists, camp-followers and beggars who had decided the financial benefits of attaching themselves to Bas's wandering nation outweighed whatever risks the Marchers posed.

Bas stood in the centre of it. Was the centre of it, the camp radiating out around him like the spokes of a wheel. The ranking officers down to the chiliarchs had pitched their tents nearest to Bas. The remainder, with the hoplitai themselves, were packed closer to the walls. The scavengers took up position wherever they could, brightly painted wagons advertising drink and flesh and food. It was Aeleria made manifest. Tomorrow it might well be ashes. Today it was the largest city that the March had ever seen.

There was a fire in front of Bas's tent, and a cauldron of coffee boiling over it. Bas poured himself a cup, drank it and pretended not to see the boy staring. When that didn't work he turned his dark brown eyes over to him, only for a moment, but long enough.

'Legatus,' Theophilus said, belatedly realising his attentions had been noticed, and snapped a quick salute.

Bas would have found it difficult to hate Theophilus even if Theophilus hadn't been so obviously infatuated with him. In fact, this last was the only thing Bas really disliked about the youth, though he had been well prepared to find more when the boy had shown up six months earlier, escorted by a troop of cavalrymen. He was the son of a senator and looked it: dark hair cropped short, piercing blue eyes, sallow skin over loose muscles. Of course a half-year on the plains had done its work, levelled out some of his boyishness. It had been a surprise, the speed with which he had taken to the tasks required of every soldier who served on the frontier, for out here there were no servants, and the chores of all but the highest-ranking officers included the menial. Many of the senators Bas had met were courageous, in their way – could wield a blade and didn't shirk from doing so. Far fewer would have put up their tent without complaint, or chiselled a stone from the shoe of a horse, as Theophilus had been doing until he noticed Bas approaching.

'It will be today, then?' he asked.

'Sharpen your sword,' Bas said.

Theophilus swallowed his smile, but not before it lit up his face. Though he had taken part in any number of skirmishes since his arrival on the plains, chasing rogue bands of barbarians further into the endless waste, this would be his first real engagement. Bas tried to remember if he had been the same way at the boy's age. He wasn't sure. He couldn't even quite recall the circumstances of his first real battle. It would have been in Salucia, during the long series of conflicts that had anticipated the war against the Others, but that was as far as Bas could say. It had become part of his legend long since – born on the battlefield, bastard son of a camp-follower and an anonymous ranker, nursed by the themas, his first toy a dagger, the beloved son of Terjunta, god of war.

That he hadn't been born on a battlefield, but in a yurt like countless other of the Commonwealth's by-blows, was a moot point to the minstrels who had made his name common wherever Aelerian was spoken. Bas had the impression that, as a group, minstrels did not consider truthfulness so great a virtue.

The coffee had grown cool, and Bas tossed what was left of his cup in the fire. 'I'm going to take a walk,' he said, turning his back and starting off before Theophilus could answer.

The Western Army was not a popular posting. Far from the capital, half forgotten by the Senate, so far from civilisation it was all but impossible to find a competent whore or a decent flask of wine. And though the Marchers were brutal and cruel, deadly as the passing of time, their cities were mobile camps and their temples wooden, so a soldier couldn't even expect much in the way of plunder. You'd get something out of the slaves, but not much, as the Marcher men were rough and wild and the women considered uncomely. Bas's hoplitai were a cross section of the Commonwealth's poorest and least influential citizens – the third sons of tenant farmers, minor criminals offered the choice of a stint in the themas or the loss of a hand. Man for man they were dirty, cruel and infrequently sober. As a group they were the finest corps of fighting men the nation had to offer, at least as far as Bas was concerned, and there was no one more qualified to offer an opinion.

They had spent the previous afternoon and much of the evening putting up the camp, a task that the barbarians across from them wouldn't have been capable of completing to any degree of competence in a fortnight. Wood and water had been gathered, a long ditch had been dug at the perimeters, a set of sharpened stakes erected in front of them. Watchtowers had been built at regular intervals along the line – only forty or so links tall, three times the height of a man, but here on the plains you could see halfway to the capital from forty links up. Behind the palisades the rest of the camp had been cut out along classic lines, surveyors ensuring that each avenue was straight as any thoroughfare in the capital, hoplitai setting up their mass tents, quartermasters passing out provisions. The labour had continued until well after nightfall, and for many had been followed by long hours on watch, staring out into the endless night of the plains, piteously far from the bonfires around which their comrades hunkered.

Just the same, Bas's arrival in the south-east section of camp brought the men to their feet, and a cheer to their lips. The men of the Western Army, and particularly of the Thirteenth Thema, loved Bas, loved him with the curious and unselfconscious passion of children, loved him though he gave no speeches and never offered more than a curt nod. His presence was enough, brooding and unapproachable as it was. They preferred it that way, even – a god does not lower himself to speak with men, to laugh and curse and scratch himself, to feel fear or joy or despair. Let the Commonwealth's other soldiers, the men of the Fourth or the hated Seventh, enjoy a joke with their superiors, the good humour easy and inauthentic – the Western Army fought beneath the auspice of Death himself.

Bas passed among them, keen-eyed for any show of weakness or lack of discipline. He found little of either. The plains discouraged incompetence. A man who couldn't handle himself wouldn't last long enough to be chewed out by his pentarche, would be cut away by one of the roving bands of Marchers looking for stragglers, or lose his toes to frostbite, or find a reed-snake in his boots one morning. Though this would be the first major engagement they'd fought in nearly a year, even in peacetime skirmishes were the rule rather than the exception.

Satisfied, Bas returned to his fire, drank a second cup of coffee and ate three pieces of salted jerky with the methodical rhythm of a man attending to a task. He didn't say anything to anyone, and his officers made a point of not interrupting the silence. The commander was a man of ritual, of rote even. His daily routine had brought them success in the past – there was no point in disrupting it.

When Bas finished he unslung his weapon and checked the edge. It was threefold the size of the short swords common to the rest of the thema, though it weighed the same or less. The lack of heft had been one of the things Bas had taught himself to compensate for over long years of practice. The guard, in the fashion of the Others who loved all thing avian, was a hawk with wings extended. Or perhaps it was an eagle – falconry was one of the many arts of which Bas remained ignorant. Indeed, the hilt was not of any great interest to him, though it was beautifully rendered and the eyes sapphire. It was the blade that rendered the weapon priceless, sharper and stronger than even the finest human smith could craft. A few of the other hoplitai, veterans of the war against the Others, carried with them smaller blades of similar make, daggers and hand axes, but none could claim a treasure equal to his. Bas spent a few minutes sharpening the foreign metal, glimmering folds and vermillion hue, ever so slightly darker than that of human blood. In the twenty years since he had taken it off its last owner, it had rarely been out of his sight. It rested next to him when he slept, hung on the wall when he shat, lay beside the bed on those infrequent occasions when he felt the need for a fuck. In the strands of doggerel that grew around Bas like ivy, it was called Soulflame, or Endbringer, or Salvation, though if Bas had given it a name he had never yet let it passed his lips.

Bas knew the emissary had arrived before he could see him from the buzz coming off the south road. Not long after a man on horseback could be seen trotting towards the centre of camp, very conscious of his moment of glory.

'Legatus,' the emissary said, 'I return.'

Bas sheathed his sword, stood and approached the man. 'What news?'

'Hetman Mykhailo agrees to a meeting. Midway between the camps, in thirty minutes' time.'

Bas nodded, dismissed him and returned to the fire. The area had grown crowded with officers waiting to hear the news or just to bask in the glory of their leader.

'What's the word then, Legatus?' Hamilcar asked. The Dycian sat cross-legged on the ground, stringing his long, horn-sheathed bow. Hamilcar was tall and dark, dark even by the standards of his nation, with lively eyes that seemed to smile even when his mouth was a grim line. And indeed, his tone suggested that he found the threat of imminent violence a source of amusement. Everything seemed to be a source of amusement to Hamilcar, and though levity was a quality for which Bas had little regard, he found the Dycian's skill and cleverness nearly made up for it. 'Are we finally to finish chasing these mule-fuckers?' Hamilcar said.

'Make sure your people are ready,' Bas replied.

Hamilcar lifted one arse-cheek off the ground and let loose a wet fart. The expulsion failed to interrupt the work of his hands. 'My people are always ready.'

It had taken three themas five years to subdue the Dycians, a contest that had only ended with the capture and virtual destruction of their capital. Bas himself had been part of the force that had stormed the ramparts, could remember the mad rush as his soldiers had swarmed past the remaining defenders and into the great city itself. In part as a guarantee of their continued loyalty, in part because the Commonwealth always needed more killers, a force of three thousand were pressed into service as auxiliaries. The greater part of these had found themselves fighting on the Marches these last ten years, firing their arrows from beneath Aeleria's banner. Had Bas been a poet, this reversal of fortune might have offered him some fodder.

Bas was very much not a poet, though Hamilcar had some

pretensions in that regard. He liked to say that his tongue was sharper than his eye, before demonstrating the excellence of the latter with some extraordinary act of marksmanship, bringing down a bird on the wing or piercing a coin at a hundred paces. Hamilcar's men were less impressive manifestations of the ideal set by their leader, rough-bodied and cruel, good with a long knife and better with a bow; reckless in victory, brave in defeat. Loud, arrogant, dishonest, clever verging on untrustworthy. In short, excellent allies, so long as you kept a boot on their neck.

Hamilcar finished with his bow, slipped it gently back in the case at his side and took to stuffing his long clay pipe full of tobacco. 'When you die today, boy,' he asked Theophilus suddenly, 'will the Marchers be impressed enough with your bravery to give you a spot on their pyres? Or will they leave your corpse to be picked apart by the winter wolves?'

'I will labour not to dishonour my fathers,' Theophilus said, young enough for such seriousness to be forgiven.

'Then you think to see battle?'

'The Legatus said to keep my sword sharp.'

Hamilcar held a small branch in the fire till the tip turned red, then brought it to his pipe. 'The Legatus can only speak in orders. "Sharpen your sword." "Ready your people." When he lies with a woman, his first words are, "Moisten your cunt."'

Theophilus turned redder than the kindling. Isaac turned a chuckle into a cough. No one else in the camp, perhaps no one else in the Commonwealth, would have dared to make a joke at Bas's expense.

Bas pretended he hadn't heard the remark. In truth, his temper was not so fierce as was generally believed. He didn't find Hamilcar amusing, particularly – there was very little indeed that Bas found amusing – but neither was he so consumed by self-importance as to resent the occasional joke.

'If you talked as well as you fought,' Isaac said, 'I wouldn't have had the pleasure of raping your mother in front of your palace.'

'Wasn't my mother,' Hamilcar answered, taking a draw from

his pipe. 'Was my grandmother. She hadn't had a good roll for years, and you Aelerians are energetic, if fundamentally untalented.'

'Remember me to her in your letters,' Isaac said, taking his leather cap off and holding it to his chest for a moment. 'She was very tender.'

Hamilcar laughed, went to continue in that line, but Bas cut him off. 'Enough,' he said, standing. 'Hamilcar, you're with me. Isaac, the camp is yours.'

Hamilcar feigned a scowl, tapped out his half-smoked pipe and stood. It was a source of pride that Bas kept him in his counsels despite his foreign birth and former allegiance, that his intellect and ability was respected by the Legatus. In fact, Bas would have preferred to take Isaac, who was more reliable if less brilliant than the Dycian. But in the unlikely event that the Marchers decided to violate the flag of truce, Isaac would be required to lead the hoplitai in revenge of their fallen commander. Or, failing that, maintain a capable fighting retreat.

Bas grabbed a pair of bodyguards and his personal standard-bearer, and they walked quickly towards the stables. Bas did not count himself much of a horseman, and his opinion contained no weight of false modesty. To be a truly skilled rider requires empathy, the capacity to interpret and alter the moods and feelings of a dumb animal, and this was not a quality that Bas could justly claim. He worked best on two feet, or in the thick of battle where manoeuvre counted for little. Oat was the name of the horse he chose – a silly name, but Oat had been given it long before Bas had owned him and Bas had never cared enough to change it. Oat was a stallion, strong and mean. He obeyed Bas for the simple reason that Bas was stronger and meaner.

Though his people were little-regarded as riders, Hamilcar was a masterful horseman. It was what he did best, he claimed, after bending a bow and pleasuring a woman, and though Bas couldn't speak to the last, he had seen the Dycian feather enough men to recognise at least that much of the boast as truth. 'Shall we die today, then, Legatus?' Hamilcar asked, boosting himself into the saddle. 'Will Mykhailo do the wise thing, as my people should have done, and kill you as soon as he sees you?'

'If they kill me they'll kill you the same.'

'I'd die happy, knowing that Aeleria has lost the tip of her spear.' Hamilcar had been a servant of the Commonwealth for ten years, had signed up for a second term after his first had expired. In all that time he had never returned to Dycia, though he claimed three wives and a passel of lovers still wept his name into the night. Hamilcar would die in a foreign land, the victim of some quarrel in which he had no particular interest. He was as much a soldier now as Isaac; the talk was just posturing, and posturing was how he handled his nerves.

Everyone had a way, and Bas had seen most of them. Some yelled, some boasted, some prayed. Isaac was steady as a stone in the thick of things, but as soon as it was over he'd find the nearest flask and drink himself into oblivion. Jon the Sanguine, who had taught Bas everything he knew of war, used to piss himself before a hard scrap, a bloom of yellow spreading out through the crotch of his trousers – but despite the odour his orders were unfailingly correct, and in those few instances when his own life had been in danger he had fought like a man possessed, laughing and cutting flesh like spring flowers.

Bas put spurs to his beast by way of answer, and Hamilcar and the bodyguards followed after him. Down the south road leading out of camp, through the open gate and into the plains beyond. It was late summer and the March was striking if not quite beautiful, the grass high enough to hide a troop of soldiers, the land so flat that it extended out into the horizon, a sea of blue meeting with a sea of green.

Bas of course thought little of it, his attention taken up with the horde of men occupying the field some few cables distant. They seemed very large, as hordes of men tend to. The Marchers' camp looked haphazard by the elaborate standards of the Aelerians, but Bas knew that impression to be a false one. This was not a mass of raiders and bandits, brought together by the promise of booty. The confederation that lay across from him represented an extraordinary accomplishment of diplomacy, hundreds of man-hours spent by the counsel fires trying to convince a warlike people to put aside centuries of enmity, to forget their traditional freedoms and swear obedience to a single leader. That it existed at all was testament to the degree to which the Commonwealth was hated.

It was twenty minutes before Hamilcar made out the Hetman and his lifeguard riding out from the vast horde, and another five before Bas could do the same. Mykhailo had been a leader of the Marchers for thirty years, and a year to the plainsfolk meant six months shivering in their tents and six months making war on their neighbours. They had no notion of power as a hereditary gift, nor as an obligation. Success was what they honoured, the only acceptable currency – success in raids against the Aelerians and against their fellow barbarians, success that could only be achieved with a strong arm and a sharp eye. Mykhailo possessed all of these qualities in abundance, had demonstrated them for decades in an arena as brutal as could be found.

He was smaller than his reputation might have suggested, and age hung over him like a mantle. His face was strained as old leather, his eyes grey and small, his hair bone-white, hip-long and pulled back in a gaudy silver clasp. But his body was perfectly erect in the saddle, and his war lance equally steady, and he greeted his enemy without a tremor. 'Hail Bas, Killer of Gods. May death pass over you another day.'

It was what the Marchers called him. Even two thousand cables distant, among a people who had never seen an Other, Bas's great act of murder had elevated him above the common rung of men. 'Hail Mykhailo, son of Bohdan, who rode between the raindrops. May fate view your enemies with displeasure.'

Mykhailo had brought with him a half-dozen of his riders, young men, tall and fierce-looking, each mounted on a shaggy pony and carrying a steel weapon. 'Are you so sure you wish that, God-Killer? For my enemies to meet with misfortune?' He spoke Aelerian confidently, though with a harsh accent.

'We aren't yet enemies, Hetman. There's still time to avoid bloodshed.' But Bas knew better even as he said it. If Mykhailo had wanted peace, if this had been a show of force to sell a few more years of tranquillity for golden trinkets and Commonwealth-forged steel, he would have brought with him a yurt, one of the small horsehide tents that could be set up and taken down within the span of a few minutes. And they would have sat beneath it and drank the fermented mare's milk that the barbarians loved more than wine, and paid each other elaborate compliments, and the Legatus would promise the Hetman trade goods and coin, and the Hetman would promise not to kill anyone for a while, or at least not to kill any Aelerians.

Bas knew when Mykhailo didn't get off his horse that there was no chance of averting the coming battle. He had known before that, really, but he was sure then.

'Why do I find the son of Bohdan here, on territory the people long ago granted to the children of Aeleria?' Bas asked.

Mykhailo turned his head to one side and coughed over his shoulder. 'Who made you this grant? Mykhailo, who comes with the setting sun?'

'With the great Chief Longinus, whose banner you rode beneath.'

'Rode beneath for one summer, five years ago. I swore no oath to that flea-ridden cripple. He is no kin of mine, not by birth, nor suckling. If he is happy eating Aelerian bread, that is his burden to take to the ancestors. I am not content, and I have made no such promises. Better to ask the God-Killer what it is that brings him so far from his home, and his hearth?'

'Aeleria is wherever its people are. And wherever its people were. We've come east from Eilweid. The Commonwealth has seen the bodies of her citizens in half a dozen freeholds all the way up from the mouth of the Pau. The bodies and what were done to them.'

'The bodies of invaders, of trespassers well-warned.'

'Do invading armies bring with them their women and children?'

'Your kind do. They bring their families and they fence in the grass, and they build their foolish wooden houses that freeze in the winter and burn as soon as a torch is put to them. And then they come screaming to the God-Killer to save them from their own foolishness. Does it ever bother you, being the running dog of halfwits too weak to protect their own seed?'

Mykhailo was a fine speaker, even in his second tongue. Most of the plainsfolk were – the leaders anyway, skills honed over long winter fires in the communal yurts, telling jokes and false stories of their accomplishments. Bas wasn't a good speaker, had never wanted or tried to be so. 'I won't argue the rights and wrongs of it with you, Hetman. This is not the first time we've stood across from each other. I need not boast of the strength of my themas – you've watched your riders break against them more than once.'

Mykhailo smiled, brown-toothed but honest. 'Do I look so young as to bend knee for a few more years beneath the sky?'

'And your men? Are there none among them who would prefer life to death?' Bas pointed almost unconsciously to one of Mykhailo's bodyguards, a hulking brute who became furious at being singled out. He shook his lance and said something unfriendly to the Hetman. Mykhailo responded in his native tongue, too swiftly for Bas to make out, though he recognised the tone, each word like a lash. And indeed the bodyguard fell silent and turned his eyes away to hide his shame.

The conflict averted, or more accurately postponed, Mykhailo took a long time before answering. 'Better an honest death in battle than a dotage as protectorates of Aeleria. When first you came here, God-Killer, we rode free from the Salt Flats to the Pau River, and never saw a yurt or a cow that was not ours. Now the dark-skinned children of Aeleria plant wheat on the graves of my fathers, tell me where to ride and whom to kill. Your hunger is never-ending. You speak of peace, but what peace can be made with fire?' Mykhailo fell into a long coughing jag, spat a hunk of yellow into the wind. 'Enough, God-Killer – between us there is nothing but war. I will die this morning, or you will.'

Mykhailo had intended this to be the last word, was turning his pony back the way he had come when Bas reached out and grabbed his forearm. 'Think hard before refusing. If you find victory today you will not have long to enjoy it – by spring Aeleria will have sent another army to avenge me, and a third if that proves insufficient. And on the day that fortune turns against you, they will plant stakes from here to the wastes, and spike your men atop them, and sell your womenfolk into bondage. And there will be no one to remember your glory beside the fires, or carry your name onward. We do not make war for glory, or for captives.' Bas spread his free hand out over the empty plains around them. 'Aeleria will till these fields. If not this year, then the next.'

'I know how your kind make war,' Mykhailo said, tearing his arm away from Bas. A spark of fury uncoiled itself from the Hetman's soul and spread up into his eyes. Hamilcar shifted his hand to the hilt of the sabre that hung down his saddle, and a second later Bas's small lifeguard did the same.

But the Hetman's rage ended suddenly, becoming a drawn-out cough, followed by the hint of a smile. 'And there are no other men like you, God-Killer. You should have been born one of us. We would have had fine roaming together. If you die today, I will build a pyre six spans wide to send you on your way, and burn a dozen hoplitai alive on top of it, that you will not enter the next world unattended.'

As many men as he had sent to it, Bas had never spent much time thinking about the afterlife. Whether he would sit at the feet of Enkedri the Self-Formed as his native priests insisted; or ride endlessly across the skies, as the Marchers believed; or if he would sleep cold and ignorant beneath the unfeeling loam, Bas neither knew nor cared. If Mykhailo died today, Bas could offer the man no gallantries. He would go in the mass ditch the themas dug for all their enemies, to join his fellows in perpetual and unmourned anonymity. It was the custom of the Commonwealth, and Bas was not one to buck tradition.

'Then it seems the affair is settled,' Bas said.

'Not yet. But very soon, God-Killer. Very soon.' He turned on his nag and rode off. His followers did the same.

'What do you think?' Bas asked Hamilcar quietly, after their enemies had ranged out of earshot.

Hamilcar scratched black fingernails through a black beard. 'I think the ravens won't go hungry.'

'They rarely do.'

'I think that cough of the Hetman's will kill him before spring, and I think he knows it. I think the one next to him would have liked to try you right then, to test his strength against that of the God-Killer, to make his name atop your corpse. I think there are fifty thousand men on their side of the field that would like to do the same, and barely twenty on yours to keep them from doing so. I think their cavalry will come along your right flank sometime after noon, and I think they will come hard, very hard indeed. So the question is a simple one – will your line hold?'

'It held against you,' Bas answered, turning his horse and heading back to camp.

2

Domina Eudokia Sabina Aurelia, Revered Mother by the order of the Senate, awoke shortly after dawn, promptly and without preamble. Eudokia considered it a matter of pride that she never overslept, never stalled beneath the blankets, never spent an extra few moments ensconced in warmth. She had given five hours to repose and would allow not a moment more – there was simply too much to do.

On the other side of the cot, bunched in covers and drooling slightly, Heraclius moaned softly. Eudokia waited for him to return to slumber, not wanting to endure the sexual overture he would initiate on awaking, too busy to spare half an hour for pleasure. After a moment he pulled the blankets back up to his neck and returned to snoring. Eudokia slipped on the robe that hung above her bed and left.

In the small chamber that bordered her room, Eudokia made her morning obeisances to the household gods – represented on this plane by a pair of rather ill-formed wooden altars.

Siraph was given two joss sticks and a few drops of sour wine. Terjunta made do with an absolution of water mixed with honey. Eudokia could never remember a time when she had believed in either, nor a morning when she had not given her prayers to both. That a thing was not real did not mean that it could not have power.

Jahan stood outside the chamber door, as he did every morning. Not much taller than Eudokia herself, still he gave an impression of great bulk, of something bloated and distended. Each fragment of his body seemed oversized, from the bony protrusions of his shoulders to the trunk of his neck to a head the circumference of a globe. He had massive hands – fingers like summer squash, knuckles like the bark from an oak tree. His face was a fleshy oval, his nostrils upturned and wide as copper pennies, a jet-black moustache dovetailing beneath them. In short he was quite hideous, except for his skin, which was the hue of brown sugar, and his eyes, which were almond-shaped and feminine, though generally half hidden beneath heavy lids.

One other point in his favour was that he was a cold-blooded killer of the highest order, deadlier than the swamplands in summer. Such at least was what Phocas had told her, when he had presented Jahan on the occasion of their engagement. 'He was the best fighter in the grand arena of Kara,' Phocas had informed her. 'I paid a hundred solidus for him, after I saw him take on three Dycian whip-men and come away unblooded. He's kept me safe for four years. Gods willing, he'll do the same for you far longer.'

At the time all she had seen was a fat man with a corpselike languor and an odour that was less than fresh. It was two years before she could confirm Phocas's opinion, when a madman with a knife burst out from a crowd of petitioners one morning and Jahan had broken his neck quicker than Eudokia could draw breath, then gone immediately back into his torpor. Since then he had proved his worth a dozen times over, as a bodyguard and more than that. And if he moved slowly at times, it was her understanding that the crocodile was a beast renowned for its sloth as much as its bite. The smell still rankled, but then, one can't have everything.

He wore the costume of his native land, thin sheets of coloured silk overlapping. Impractical dress, given the climate of his adopted country, but if the cold bothered him he did not let it show. His only visible weapon was a talwar hanging loosely on his right hip. He slouched against the wall and breathed very slowly, as if hoarding his energy for some future effort.

'Mistress,' Eudokia heard Jahan say, though somehow without quite going to the effort of moving his lips.

'Slave,' Eudokia said. 'And what of the day?'

'It rises.'

Eudokia nodded agreement, then entered her toilet. Hot water steamed up from the marble bath, her handmaiden standing beside it.

'Good morning, Theodora.'

'Good morning, mistress.'

'Two drams of the blue salt. And a few drops of rosewater.'

'Right away, mistress.'

Eudokia spent fifteen minutes in the tub, fifteen minutes almost to the second. Then she stood, allowed Theodora to towel her off. While waiting she inspected herself in the mirror with a dispassionate eye, and what she saw she did not find altogether displeasing. She had already weathered time's first great sally, watched the beauty of her youth give way to middle age, ripe breasts gone saggy, thighs swelling. But she had kept herself trim, and her tummy was still flat, and her face little lined. Eudokia ran a hand through her hair, white since her fortieth year. She had never bothered to give it colour, and soon it had become the fashion at court. If you looked carefully you could see that half of the snowy-headed widows thronging the city's salons had brown at their roots.

Eudokia took another moment at the mirror. Soon age would return to finish what it had started, collapse her remaining defences, turn her from venerable to old. Eudokia did not dread this eventuality, though she still luxuriated in what beauty remained to her. There was no point in railing against time, the ever-victorious. Against all other enemies, however, Eudokia felt herself a fair match.

Her dress closet was large enough to serve as the living chamber of a middle-class home, though for a fraction of what she had spent filling it you could have bought a mansion near the harbour. In fact, Eudokia felt fairly little for her costumes – she had mastered fashion because it was one of the things it had become necessary for her to master, not because she had any great love for it in or of itself.

For the morning she chose a blue shift, accented with silver twine. Compared to her evening dress it was simple attire, though it still took Theodora twenty minutes to fasten the whole thing properly and another twenty minutes to apply her make-up and perfume. Eudokia aimed for a sort of clean simplicity, enhancement rather than adornment, though of course executing that competently was more laborious than throwing on a whore's mask.

She took one final moment to inspect herself in her mirror, conscious of every second stolen by vanity. It was not lost on Eudokia how much more she could accomplish if she wasn't required to give so much of her time and energy to her appearance. To the degree that she ever envied anyone anything, which as a rule she rarely did, she found herself jealous of the extra hour a day that the opposing sex was able to use on something other than their own dress. Finally satisfied, she gave Theodora a quick though not unfriendly dismissal before heading downstairs to breakfast.

Eudokia had moved into the mansion when she had married Phocas, and she had kept it after he died and for the long interval since. Her initial impression upon inspecting the place had been that they had better get to making children quite quickly, if there was ever to be any hope of filling the space. That hadn't happened, obviously, though they could have been breeding like rabbits and never needed to use more than a wing. Really it was an absurd edifice, more a statement than a domicile. What exactly that statement was, Eudokia had never been entirely clear, but she supposed it to have something to do with an abundance of money unconstrained by any reasonable notions of taste. Even her vast wealth couldn't serve to maintain the building in its entirety; at any given moment three-fifths of it was unused. Occasionally she would make a foray into one of these abandoned portions, an explorer penetrating deep into a jungle of outdated furniture and atrocious mosaics.

Off the stairwell to the right was the main dining room, but it was ludicrously oversized. Eudokia only used it a handful of times a year, during her least exclusive gatherings, when it seemed that half the gentry of the Commonwealth was in attendance. She took most of her meals at the smaller chamber attached to the kitchen, at an oak table large enough to comfortably seat a dozen.

On her way to it, Eudokia passed two house slaves cleaning the banisters. Marchers, recently acquired, barely a word of Aelerian between them. Eudokia made a point of remembering the name of every member of her staff – not as easy as it sounded, given the number. Galla and Gemma were the two thin, pale, simple-looking creatures who gave an awkward impression of a curtsy as Eudokia trailed down the steps. Not their real names, of course, but then Eudokia couldn't very well be stumbling over whatever mash of consonants their barbarian parents had bestowed upon them. Galla and Gemma were fine, simple names, better than their service merited, though Eudokia didn't exactly blame them for their incompetence. A lifetime spent in some ghastly leather tent, eating horsemeat and dressed in rags – well, Eudokia could appreciate the change of setting would be a source of confusion. She would try to remember that when she went upstairs that evening and found finger marks on the railings, as she was certain she would. It was a strange world, Eudokia thought, that could be put in order more easily than her own household.

Down the hallway and into the dining room, where Leon sat

at one corner of the dining table, spooning porridge into his mouth while engrossed in a heavy text.

'Nephew,' Eudokia said, taking the seat next to him.

'Auntie,' Leon responded, but without raising his head from the book.

Leon was her second cousin Nonia's child, or had been at least before the plague took her five years back. Scour her memory though she tried, Eudokia could remember almost nothing about poor Nonia — a meek, mousy, unprepossessing sort whom Eudokia had married to the similarly uninspired offspring of one of the appropriate families. He had been made governor of a southern province, died choking on a fishbone. It was Eudokia's feeling that very few great men ever died by choking on a fishbone, though whether that was because they took more care when eating fish, or that posterity refused to recognise the accomplishments of anyone who had expired in such a preposterous fashion, she wasn't sure.

Regardless, when Eudokia had learned that Nonia had gone the way of her husband, albeit with slightly greater dignity, Eudokia had arranged for her issue to take up residence in one of the many unused sections of the estate. Konstantinos had just left for the provinces, and the house felt a bit silent. Eudokia liked company, so long as it didn't make a nuisance of itself. And she liked the reputation for generosity that these acts of largesse afforded her.

Nor, in the years since he'd come to the mansion, had Leon given her cause to regret her magnanimity. He was clever but not loquacious, which was a combination one found rarely enough to take notice. Five years had turned him into a fine-looking youth, though he had inherited his mother's weak chin, and he could do with a bit more exercise of the physical rather than mental variety. His tutors all spoke well of him, which either meant that he was smart enough to satisfy their demands or strong-willed enough to bully them into submission. Eudokia suspected the former, which disappointed her slightly.

If she had one complaint against the boy, it was that he

seemed sometimes not that at all. At an age when most of his contemporaries couldn't see past the next whorehouse, Leon maintained a sense of learning and decorum that bordered on the severe. Bordered too closely, she thought. There was a certain sort of man who made a vice of virtue – fetishising austerity, turning their nose up at the compromises required of worldly activity, holding to a code of ethics that allowed them to do nothing and feel proud of it. They called themselves philosophers, or poets sometimes, two professions that Eudokia found to be beneath the dignity of a scion of the Aurelia family. How exactly she was to channel her charge into an existence worthy of his ancient line was not the least of Eudokia's current slate of concerns.

'And what use will you make of the sun?' Eudokia asked.

'Ionnes just sent over a book of his poetry. I've promised I'll give him my notes by tomorrow. After that I was thinking I might go down to the Senate. They're scheduled to debate the northern question – it's certain to generate some heat.'

'More than light, I imagine.'

'You underrate them. Senator Andronikos, in particular, has been making a compelling case for forgiving this recent unpleasantness with Salucia.'

'I don't suppose his interests in the sugar trade have anything to do with his position on the subject.'

'Cupidity? In the Senate?' Leon turned a page. 'I'm sure I have no idea what you're talking about.'

'And how are the other grandees taking to Senator Andronikos's latest bit of wisdom?'

'Hard to say. Manuel made a rather passionate speech in support of it yesterday afternoon, though there weren't many senators present to hear him make it.'

'Manuel feels passionately about everything, so I'm not sure that indicates much.'

'He's a man of strong principles.'

'And how he loves to let you know it.'

The door to the servants' quarters opened and a slave came

in with Eudokia's breakfast on a silver tray – a small cup of tea and a few slices of melon. Except on feast days, she rarely ate more. The wolf does not hunt on a full stomach.

'Andronikos is a reprobate,' Leon continued, 'Manuel a fanatic. One might get to thinking you lack faith in our governing body entirely.'

'Perish the very thought. Why, wherever would we be without that noble forum to give us guidance in these clouded and corrupt days?' Eudokia slipped a spoon of cream into her tea, let it rise to the top before mixing. 'Will you be attending Senator Valens' name-day gathering?'

'I hadn't planned on it. I quite loathe the senator, and hardly see the point in celebrating his managing to hold on to life for another year. Should he stage a funeral, on the other hand, you can be certain of my presence.'

'Your personal feelings towards the man notwithstanding,' Eudokia said, clamping down on a tickle of exasperation, 'high society anxiously awaits your arrival.'

'Drunken heiresses and half-witted grandees – they can wait a little longer.'

'Yes, quite the iconoclast. How proud we all are of this courageous stance you've taken against gaiety.' Eudokia rose from the table. 'Your time is yours to spend or waste, as you will. But if you've an interest in how the Commonwealth is actually run, you'd be better off spending an hour with the Valens' guests than a day observing the Senate. You'd also be far more likely to find someone to take home at the end of the evening.'

Leon blushed to the roots of his hair. It was a cheap means to victory, Eudokia realised – sharp as a blade when it came to politics, the boy all but shrivelled if you mentioned the bedchamber. Not for the first time, Eudokia wondered if his timorousness was cover for deviancy. She thought not – the Salucian vice was hardly unknown among the aristocracy, and certainly shouldn't have been cause for such exaggerated bashfulness.

Man or woman, though, he wouldn't find them sitting reading in his room. 'You're too young to be so boring,'

Eudokia said, patting the boy lightly on the cheek as she left the room.

Jahan was already waiting when she entered the study, standing near her desk, peeling an orange. He was the room's chief ornament, which was bare bordering on austere. A desk, a chair beneath it, one in the corner in the thus far unrealised possibility that Jahan might prefer to sit rather than stand. She had a large library of course, and often used it when entertaining. But this was where the real work took place.

For the next six hours Eudokia busied herself with the small mountain of correspondence that she had received in the twenty-four hours since she'd last emptied the pile. First came the personal correspondence, dull work but necessary, answering invitations to weddings and birth-celebrations and naming days. Most of these received a polite refusal, though the very important and particularly highly favoured would find their fetes graced by the first lady of the Commonwealth.

Next there were matters of business, the extensive enterprises which Eudokia had inherited and which her acumen had expanded upon in the long decades since reaching her majority. Huge plots of farmland throughout the Aelerian heartland, mineral and timber rights for vast swathes of territory in eastern reaches of the March, monopolies on wine and oil and salt from the recently conquered Baleferic isles. Eudokia's wealth endowed dozens of hospices, temples, schools and orphanages across the capital and the inner provinces, and simultaneously facilitated a hundred plots, stratagems and conspiracies, a massive engine which required constant stoking, stacks of gold solidus disappearing into the furnace.

Only when she had finished with these did Eudokia turn her attention to her real work. Missives from across the length and breadth of Aeleria, and from far outside it as well. From nobles and domestics, from army officers and tax-farmers, from Salucian merchant princes and Dycian shipping magnates. The greater portion of them had no idea to whom they were writing, left their news in dead-letter drops or had it filtered through some third party. Most were written so obliquely as to require outside knowledge to make any sense of them. The very sensitive were transposed to a code of Eudokia's own design, and when she came across these she would spend a quick few minutes deciphering them. The shrinking pile of letters represented what Eudokia felt confident was the finest intelligence system in the Commonwealth – in the Commonwealth at the very least. It was the product of long years of diligent labour, carefully cultivated over the course of most of a lifetime, all the more impressive because it had been grown from nothing.

At half past noon Eudokia drank a goblet of red wine mixed liberally with spring water. Then she walked the sack of letters to the furnace. Four separate trips it took, to rid herself of the information she had acquired that day. It was too hot for a fire, but comfort took second place to caution.

Next she took a brisk walk round the compound, Jahan trailing close behind. A handful of slaves were busy ensuring the continued health of the grounds, pruning and watering and a dozen other activities the purpose of which Eudokia was only vaguely clear on. Eudokia loved gardens but hated gardening, in truth disliked manual labour of any kind. It was a very good thing that Eudokia had been born to a station befitting her abilities, she often thought. Imagine a lifetime spent bending over and standing upright, over and upright, over and upright till finally you don't come upright any more. The gods had known what they were doing when they had made Eudokia who she was.

A shorter perambulation than she'd have preferred, and Eudokia was back to work. She kept open hours twice a month – an exhausting activity, granting audience to every trumped-up aristocrat and acquaintance's friend desperate for a favour – but among her intimate circle of supporters, it was well known that she was available most days in the early afternoon.

She took a spot in a large armchair, one of several that sat in the centre of the library. It was her favourite room in the house – Phocas had built it for her as a wedding present, though she had chosen the decor. It did not contain the largest collection of manuscripts in the capital; plenty of senators possessed entire wings demonstrating their erudition. But Eudokia's was large enough, and the titles were well chosen and had the added virtue of having actually been read.

From the small end table beside her she removed a ball of twine and sewing needle and continued her work on the tunic she had begun. Eudokia averaged two articles of outerwear a week, depending on size and complexity, two a week since she had been a young woman: a hill of trousers, a mountain of socks. It played well with the image she liked to portray, and it was a good way to buy a few seconds of time if a conversation turned awkward. Of course, her work was every bit as good as any professional seamstress. What Eudokia chose to do, she excelled at.

She'd barely got started on the sleeve when her steward knocked twice on the door, entered smoothly and announced a visitor.

'Revered Mother,' Irene said, adding a quick curtsy to the term of endearment. 'How does the afternoon find you?'

'Busy, Irene, as ever.'

Eudokia had taken Irene on as a handmaiden because her mother had been a childhood friend, or at least an acquaintance, and because a woman in Eudokia's position was expected to be surrounded by pretty young things, and because it occasionally gave her pleasure to gossip and play as if she were still a girl. Irene was only the latest in a long slate of women Eudokia had brought under her wing, tended and nurtured and married off.

She was stop-short beautiful. Her hair was a black so dark it seemed almost blue, her skin white as alabaster. She had sparkling eyes and a bosom that demanded attention, even when she wasn't wearing something cut to show it off, which she almost always was. Her one flaw – physically, at least, since morally the girl was very much as rotten as a sewer – was her tremulous, high-pitched voice, like a hinge begging for oil. Eudokia knew that she had never been so lovely as Irene, not even in the very prime of her youth, but at least when she baited a lover she didn't sound like a eunuch.

Not that Eudokia had any doubt as to whom the average man

would prefer. It was good practice, she found, trying not to hate Irene on general principle. Mostly, she even succeeded.

'How goes the day's work?'

'Well enough, dear child, well enough.'

Irene's gown had all the fabric of a hand towel, and when she took the seat across from Eudokia her chest strained the cloth. Overdone, Eudokia thought, particularly as she would return home and change before the evening's entertainment. 'I'll never understand,' Irene began, 'how you bear up under so heavy a load.'

Eudokia smiled. It wasn't that she enjoyed the flattery, particularly – true pride does not require affirmation – but she was a strict believer in upholding the hierarchy. Irene was her creature, and it was well that she gave frequent evidence of it. 'How was your evening?'

'Dull to the point of madness. Of course we had to make an appearance at the Hypatos's little amusement, and with him living out towards Broad Hill it took our palanquin an hour to get there and an hour to get back. By then there was nothing to do but stop in at the Second Consul's, and the Second Consul being the Second Consul he was less than sober and more than willing to try his hands with any girl foolish enough to let him.'

Irene continued in this fashion for a while, light gossip that Eudokia had long since ceased to cause but still enjoyed hearing. The surrogate sins of an adopted daughter, red meat for a mother now used to softer fare. Jahan leaned against the far wall, chewing betel nuts and groping the girl with his eyes. The Parthan lacked the most basic social graces, though Eudokia had no intention of improving them. It was the effect Irene had intended, after all, and a woman who could not deal with a man's attentions was no such thing at all.

Irene was midway through an amusing little piece of calumny when the steward interrupted her apologetically, announcing an arrival. Without anything being said, Irene stood, curtsied and left by the side exit. A moment later the main door opened and Gratian Eyconos, senator, walked in.

What was it that made a man powerful? Eudokia often wondered. Birth, first and foremost. Gratian came from a family that could trace itself back to the foundations of Aeleria, back to the first ships that had come north to the Tullus Coast hundreds of years prior. His ancestors had helped carve out a kingdom amidst the human nations that had long lived there, sheltered beneath the protection of the Others. And they had died in droves at the Lamentation, when the demons had ridden down Aeleria's last king and slaughtered his line, leaving the throne empty and giving birth to the Republic.

Apart from that, there wasn't much to recommend him. Whatever looks he'd once possessed had long retreated against an onslaught of working lunches and second helpings. He had a basic education, could quote the more popular poets and philosophers, though not understand them. He had never commanded a thema, and Eudokia felt confident in asserting that he was as lacking in physical courage as he was moral. He dressed well, and was a deft if unspectacular hand at cards. Eudokia didn't rank either of these qualities as relevant to being a leader of men, but then Eudokia was not a man.

All things considered, what had brought Gratian to the forefront of the Senate was that he spoke in a pleasing baritone and said what she told him to say. One would think, given the commonplace nature of these traits, Gratian would do everything possible not to cause her any undue difficulty. But in fact barely a week passed without him begging a concession or favour, assistance in erasing some self-created misfortune.

'Senator,' Eudokia said, presenting her cheek. 'How goes things among the great and good?'

'I'm not sure that the Senate is either of those things, Revered Mother,' he said ruefully, after planting a kiss a paper's breadth from her skin. 'But in a state of something close to chaos, regardless.'

Eudokia gestured to the opposite chair, 'You say that every time I see you.'

'And I'm right every time. The west seethes with rebellion – the

March lords will chase us back to the Pau River, for all the vaunted skill of the Caracal. The Salucians continue their programme of economic warfare, and every day we accept it we show ourselves unworthy of the duties of our fathers. And of course the Anamnesis draws close, with all its attendant concerns.'

'The Commonwealth can be grateful for your leadership in these times of woe.'

Gratian shook his fat face back and forth, rotund cheeks quivering for a half-second before falling still. 'This is my last term as a senator, I swear it by the Self-Formed. This time next year I'll be on my estate, free of the nattering of fools and ingrates.'

It would be a neat trick to escape himself, though Eudokia doubted the senator would attempt it. He aired the possibility of retirement with all the frequency of a refrain in a drinking song, but Gratian couldn't last half a month away from the fleshpots and eating houses of the capital. 'Then we can only be grateful for the time you're willing to spare us.'

Gratian took that as his due, barely seemed even to hear it, so caught up was he with the problem he was about to lay at Eudokia's feet. 'Though in truth, it's not politics that has brought me here today, but something more personal.'

That he imagined there was a distinction between these two realms was one of the many things that made Gratian a fool. 'Do continue.'

'You've heard, I imagine, that I have grown very . . . close to Helena Comatus, daughter of Zeno who was once Strategos?'

'If one paid attention to rumour, one would hardly have time to attend to anything else.'

'In this case the gossips have the truth of it.'

'She's a fine woman. I can only hope she brings you the joy you deserve.' In fact Helena was one of the single dullest people Eudokia had ever had the misfortune to be seated next to at a garden party, lacking in any virtue except for the cosmetic.

'An angel, I assure you. The most exquisite creature. To find, in these days, such a storied innocence, such taste, such refinement—'

This needed to be ended, or it would continue till sundown. 'And what might I do for this half-divine?'

'For her, nothing. For her cousin, however . . .'

'Cousin?'

'Justinian. She's terribly fond of him, you see. A fine young lad, though he's had some trouble finding his way in the world.'

Justinian Comatus had trouble finding his way in the world because he was virtually an imbecile – indeed a difficult burden to labour beneath. Rumour also suggested that he and Helena shared bonds more than cousinly, and though as a rule Eudokia did not believe any gossip so piquant, somehow this one smacked of truth. 'And what might I do for the young gentleman?'

'The elections for Consul are coming up next month, and Justinian is on the ballot.'

'Then your problem solves itself. Certainly the great esteem the people hold for his line should be sufficient to find him comfortably carrying the rod of office.'

'One would think that, but in fact it seems a long shot that he'll be called to serve.'

'I shall light a candle to Terjunta. Undoubtedly the Sun Lord will look with favour on a man so similar in bearing and conduct.'

Gratian exhaled a slow round of breath. 'I had hoped you might take a more direct hand.'

Eudokia smiled her empty smile. 'How so?'

'Please, Honoured Mother. With your connections, it would be a small thing to ensure Justinian's . . . many virtues are given their proper account. He seeks appointment in the Third District – I thought, perhaps . . .'

Eudokia waited for him to continue. Normally she preferred to smooth over the naked selfishness that lay at the heart of most of her relationships, but the sheer sordidness of Gratian's request had perturbed her. Justinian wasn't fit for any task more rigorous than cleaning out his asshole, and Gratian would have him made Consul, put in charge of maintaining order in the capital, ensuring the good behaviour of the rabble.

It was nearly enough to bring one to anger. Eudokia's smile remained bright and wide, and her stitching constant as ever.

After longer than it should have taken him, Gratian realised he wasn't to be let off the hook. 'If you could perhaps say a few words to your man there, explain how much benefit Justinian's leadership might have for the area.'

Narses was the man she had in the Third District, one of those civic leaders more thug than businessman. But between violence and the largesse his violence allowed him to offer, he could command enough votes to get a corpse elected to sit on the Empty Throne. Eudokia let Gratian's request hang in the air, watched him crumple in the face of it. 'Truly, you exaggerate my influence. My acquaintances have all forgotten me, an old woman, only steps from the cenotaph.' Gratian blanched, but she continued before he could turn to begging. 'Still, let it never be said that an Aurelia is forgetful of her friends. I'll make what efforts I can.'

Gratian was so overcome with emotion that he half stumbled getting out of his chair, had to right himself awkwardly before crossing to her seat and taking her hand. Helena must have riled him near to madness – how any man ever got anything accomplished, attached to that mad, desperate beast that was his cock, Eudokia could never fathom. Indeed, few overcame the handicap. 'Your kindness is as boundless as your beauty, Revered Mother. Your name will perpetually find praise on my lips, and be etched for ever on the innermost lining of my heart.'

Eudokia slipped her hand back from his, returned to her knitting. There was an awkward silence while Gratian tried to determine why he hadn't been dismissed yet. He sat back down finally, unsure of what else to do.

'My nephew tells me that Andronikos and his people have been quite active in the Senate of late,' Eudokia said.

Gratian licked his lips. 'Our misguided opposition. The noise they make is nothing but a cover for their lack of support, and a poor cover at that.'

'Still, though. It would be wise not to let their provocations go unanswered. Perhaps a strong display of reason is in order, to clarify the situation for those misguided unfortunates yet to swing round to our way of thinking.'

It took more than a few beats for Gratian to wrap himself round the subtext, but when that first gleam of enlightenment finally reached his eyes, he was quick to move on it. 'As it happens, I've been preparing a devastating brief in support of our eastern policies. I should be ready to present it any day now.'

'I anxiously await reports of its success.' She extended her hand for Gratian to kiss, which he did quickly and without embarrassment, then scampered to the exit.

Irene returned to take his spot shortly thereafter. 'What did the senator want?'

'To wet his dick, like every other member of his sex. Sometimes, dear, I despair over the fate of the Commonwealth, with such . . . tiny little men running it.'

'But they don't run it,' Irene said, smiling sweetly. 'You do.'

'Now, now,' Eudokia said, though she did not bother to contradict the girl.

3

Calla woke just past the hour of the Crake, as the night gave gradually before the dawn. She shifted aside the curtain of the window that hung above her bed, stared out at the water below. The descendant moon denuded the scene of pigment, grey waves breaking against grey rocks, the grey tower scraping the surface of a grey sky. Of course, Calla had been staring out of the window for her entire life, could repaint the panorama with the colours daylight would soon provide. She spent a moment toying with the luxurious blasphemy that she might not get up at all, sink back into her feather bed and return to sleep, rocked by the sounds of the waves she could hear far below, or imagine she could hear.

But only for a moment. Then the sheets were cast aside and she was up, moving smoothly but with speed through the dark. There was a steam chamber attached to her bedroom and here, more so than beneath her covers, she had to be careful not to allow five minutes to become ten, ten to become twenty, twenty to become a short eternity. Calla towelled herself free of damp and returned to her darkened bedroom, kindling the beeswax candles by her bed more from custom than necessity.

A timid knock at the door signalled the arrival of the day's troubles.

'Enter,' Calla said.

'I've come to wake you, mistress,' Tourmaline said. Tourmaline was twenty but looked five years younger, the product of having no chest to speak of and the haircut of a prepubescent boy. At half their size her eyes might have been fetching, but their current diameter overawed the rest of her features, gave one the unpleasant impression of staring at a giant insect.

In the three years since she had assumed the position of seneschal, Calla had never once required a wake-up call. It was a small source of pride to her, the discipline and self-control she maintained over her mind even while lost in the realm of slumber. Still, better certain than sorry, and it wasn't beyond the realm of possibility that one morning the aid of a human alarm would be needed. Knowing Tourmaline as she did, Calla felt that would be the one day the poor, stupid little thing would muck it up, falling asleep herself, or tripping down a staircase and breaking both legs.

'You're not here delivering dinner?'

Two blinks of blue eyes not far from idiocy. 'No, mistress. It's barely morning.'

Calla gave no outward sign of annoyance. 'Not everyone has your advantages,' her father used to tell her, after she had left one of the other children of the Keep in tears. 'And you ought not be so proud over something you had no hand in creating. You owe your mind to an accident of birth. As soon praise yourself for growing tall.' A wise man, her father, a good deal wiser than Calla knew herself to be.

Though she tried to follow the example he had left her. 'Thank you for your service, Tourmaline – you may return to your quarters now.'

'Thank you, mistress,' Tourmaline said, bowing and bowing

and then bowing again, as if Calla had saved her from the gibbet rather than sent her off to bed.

With the girl gone, Calla turned her full attention to her mirror. She had never taken any great pride in her beauty, though she couldn't help but recognise it. She had long legs and a flat stomach and a nose that mostly didn't even bother her any more. Strawberry-blonde locks curled down below her shoulders, shoulders that led into a round bosom. Starting at her wrist and ending just below her neck was her brand, a cast of hawks shadowing the noonday sun. All human residents of the Roost, apart from those unfortunates living on the lowest Rung, were marked at adolescence, though it was only here at the summit that tattooing had been elevated to an art. The markings of the lower Rungs were crude things, proof that the bearer was allowed to remain within a certain proximity to Those Above, each Rung and section of a Rung having different symbols – three variously sized stars, twisted lines on an oval. By contrast Calla's own brand was a minor masterpiece, the red sun a composite of garnet-based ink, the hawks outlined in gold leaf. At a glance, anyone living on the First Rung could tell by the colour scheme that she owed obedience to the Aubade, and from its intricacy that she was a servant of the highest rank. She hid it beneath blue robes that accentuated her features without drawing overmuch attention to them. Checking herself in the mirror one final time, Calla decided that she liked what she saw, or at least accepted it, and slipped on her house shoes as if to leave.

But before doing so she walked over to one of the bookcases and lifted a volume off the shelves. She took a long look around the room before she did so, knowing it was foolishness, that there were no peepholes hidden in the walls, that her sanctuary was inviolate. And even if someone had walked in on her, what would they have seen? Most of the rest of the servants were illiterate, or nearly so, and of course the Lord and his kind had no books, did not entirely understand their purpose even. Still, it paid to be careful – what she held in her hands might get her killed, and not swiftly. A quick flip through to make sure the words hadn't run away since the night before, then she buried the book back in with its siblings. For years she had kept it hidden beneath a loose stone in the floor, before realising it was far more conspicuous to constantly be moving two clove of stone than for one more tome to join her collection.

Satisfied, Calla opened the door and started briskly on her way.

She had ground to cover – there were towns in the hinterlands between Salucia and Aeleria that were smaller than the Red Keep, and cities far less impressive. Calla had never left the Roost, but her lack of experience, in this case at least, did not make her wrong. There was nowhere in the world to compete with the paradise Those Above had built, and one did not need to have visited every backwater burg to know that for a truth. One needed only to open one's eyes.

From Calla's room it was a twenty-minute walk to the kitchens, though of course if you were unfamiliar with the terrain it would have taken far longer. With most of the staff still asleep she felt the dignity of her office could survive a light jog, her footfalls muffled by finely woven carpets, down long corridors of red brick, windows overlooking the gardens or the bay itself. Once morning came, assuming it did not look like rain, the house servants would open the thousands and thousands of glass apertures, and the sun would flood over the intricate stonework, and the wind would carry in the fragrance of fresh flowers and salt water. But in the evenings and when the weather was foul the Lord preferred his own, carefully crafted scents, and in the predawn hours incense simmered in small bronze bowls hanging from the ceiling.

First, Calla paid a quick visit to the kitchens, making sure that everything was in readiness for the Lord's feast. He took a light breakfast by the standards of his kind: three courses of small plates, a round eighteen dishes in all, plus sherbet to cleanse the palate, tea and several different juices, depending upon what had been available at market the evening prior. Besides the head cook herself there was a specialist for the pastries, one for the meat, one to see to the beverages and a handful of other culinary adepts of whom the Lord made infrequent use, not to mention any number of half-chefs and assistants and attendants.

The head cook was an elderly, waspish woman, easily offended. In Calla's father's day the head cook had been a middle-aged waspish woman, though at least at the time she'd also been a thoroughly competent one. But the last year had seen a swift uptick in the woman's sense of bitterness, accompanied by a slightly less dramatic decrease in her skill. A month earlier she had left the custard tarts in too long, burned them an unsightly brown. The Lord was, of course, the noblest of spirits, his reputation for generosity and temperance literally a byword among the Roostborn – but all the same it didn't bear thinking about, what might have happened to the unfortunate woman, had Calla not caught the mistake in time to salvage the situation, rearranging the menu so that a replacement could be offered without causing the Lord offence. Of course, for her efforts Calla had earned nothing but an increase in the vitriol of which the cook seemed to possess an ever-increasing supply, and entering the kitchens Calla girded herself for battle.

Today, at least, all was in readiness; the fires were stoked, the pastries and sweetmeats soon to be set over them. The cook was busy berating one of the twenty-odd souls under her direct command, crowding him into a corner and banging her hand against a hanging pot to make her point. Unfortunate for the boy, but at least it gave Calla the opportunity to make a quick survey of the situation. By the time Calla was finished with her inspection the target of the cook's abuse had been reduced to tears and the cook herself, having momentarily exhausted her spleen, even managed a friendly wave to speed Calla on her way.

Calla left by a side corridor at a fast walk, checking one of the water clocks that were evenly spaced around the estate. Still some time before the hour of the Lark – Calla was on schedule, but the schedule was as tight as it was every other day. She double-timed it down hallways and through antechambers, every step of the maze long ingrained from memory into routine. One of the banisters running along the fourth stairwell in the far quarters had been inexpertly cleaned, not for the first time, and she made a mental note to chastise the maid responsible for that portion of the Keep. She wouldn't have an opportunity to do so until late in the afternoon, but Calla's mind was neat as a well-kept slate, and she wouldn't forget.

Calla exited the walls of the manor and walked swiftly to the east aviary, a walled area of wilderness that looked as if someone had snatched a square cable of old-growth forest, sawed it free from the earth, carried it with some giant hand and replanted it at the top of the Roost. Here, amidst the towering maples and redwood trees like turrets, the Lord's vast stable of raptors was situated, hawks and eagles and merlins and falcons and one huge, ugly, cruel-seeming condor. In the centre of the arboretum the caretaker and his two sons resided, and Calla spent some time ensuring that all was in readiness should the Lord, as he often did, wish to watch his killers in action. Next she checked on the smaller west aviary, where the other birds in the Lord's collection – the cassowaries and button-quails, the coots and turacos, were kept. Calla much preferred the west to the east, with its menagerie of tiny bright things singing sweet songs, and strutting false-winged avians staring about with good-natured confusion.

From there Calla visited the other menageries that it pleased the Lord to keep – the tanks of fish and waterfowl and aquatic mammals that held residence in the north garden, schools of creatures that had been found and hooked and transported halfway round the world to add colour and life to the Lord's estates. Much of the bottom floor of the manor was taken up with the Lord's workshop, a forge for making the steamwork mechanisms that were all the rage on the First Rung of the Roost. In truth the Lord was at best a competent craftsman, a fact of which he was well aware but which did not at all seem to affect his passion for the activity. The fortunes he had pissed away in that workshop, and for so little result!

Having seen to the Lord's needs, she then moved on to doing the same for the large staff of humans. Making sure that all was in readiness in the human kitchens, and the staff would have something to eat when the majority of them awoke within the next hour. Ensuring order amidst the various cadres of servants, pouring oil on the turbulent waters ever-present in any large group of people. Later in the day, if she could carve out some time, she'd take a look at yesterday's accounts, make sure all was in order, that the dozen-odd people deputised to visit the Perennial Exchange on the Third Rung and make purchases on the Lord's accounts had done so honestly and competently. Then she would check that the stockrooms were full, that they hadn't been crept into while an inattentive or corrupt quartermaster looked elsewhere. A year earlier she had discovered that the woman in charge of the staff's bedding had been selling off some of the reserve linens. How that foolish old bag had wept when she had been dismissed, losing her job and her home at one stroke, forced to move to one of the lower Rungs and scrape by doing whatever she could find, her brand scarred off with a heated iron. Imagine, throwing away generations of honest service to the Lord for a few coins! Sometimes, Calla had to admit, her own species was as much a source of mystery as the Eternal.

It was a busy morning, though not quite frantic. With the hour of the Lark drawing near, Calla arrived at the foot of the steam-powered elevator which would take her to the top of the Keep. She had just enough time to swallow one of the raisin buns she had snatched from the human kitchens before climbing inside and beginning her ascent.

There were many things that made the Red Keep magnificent – its size, its ingenious construction, the infinity of tiny but striking details present on the facades and the porticoes, on the stairwells and the ceilings and the floors. Most of these could be attributed to the brilliance of the Lord, or the Lord's ancestors, who had laboured diligently in its creation and upkeep. But for its placement at the absolute easternmost point of the Roost, jutting out over the water below, one could not rightly credit the Lord, nor his line – for that one needed to herald Providence, or the sheer wonders of nature itself. In the spring and summer the

Red Keep was the beneficiary of a strong wind that blew in the early mornings. As dawn rose over the endless blue abyss the breeze pulled the vast abundance of fluttering strands towards the bay, the ribbons and banners and particoloured kites – as if at any moment the Keep itself might detach from the city and float off into the ether, an island of its own, drifting east towards unknown lands.

Turning her back on the Bay of Eirann, Calla stared westward at the neighbouring manors – the Aurelian Abode, with its gilded towers higher even than the Red Keep, and beyond that to the House of the Blind Swallow, flowering vines bright over indigo walls. Rising gradually in the distance was the Source, the surging fountain at the apex of the city, the Roost's heart and centre. Further to the north and south and west the mountain began to slope downward away from the water, slowly and barely perceptibly. Indeed, a casual pedestrian might not have noticed the gradient until they had come to the barrier with the Second Rung, heavy stone walls running the length of the divide. The Second Rung, with its civil servants and wealthy merchants and the occasional artisan, was twice the size of the First Rung, and the Third Rung twice the size of the Second, expanding outward and downward until one came to the base of the mountain, to the Fifth Rung and the vast human population that lived there. Such was Calla's understanding, at least, though in point of fact she had never descended lower than the Third Rung, and she had been there rarely. Her knowledge of the First Rung was all but comprehensive – she could tell the Alabaster Haunt from the Calignous Citadel by the appearance of their minarets in the late evening, knew the name of every demesne by which the east estuary flowed – but dropped in the heart of the Fourth Rung she would have been as lost as a seagull in the desert.

For all that luxury reigned throughout the rest of the estate, the Lord's personal preserve was noteworthy for its simplicity, albeit a simplicity married to the highest taste. The silk hammock on which he slept was the sole piece of furniture in the cell that served as his bedchamber, a single room composed entirely of glass, naked to sunshine and moonbeam. Surrounding it was a surreal desert landscape, a kaleidoscope of hued sands that were combed and re-patterned daily. Dotting it were two half-boulders of ebony and crystal, eyes staring up into the sky. The sun was still struggling to break night's final grip, but in a few moments the entire tier would be flooded with light and colour. Calla found the trail the Lord had left in the prismatic sand, followed his footsteps towards the precipice.

The Aubade, twelfth scion of the Red Keep, perched motionlessly atop a tongue of granite jutting off the ramparts, perfectly naked, greeting the morning. His weight rested easily on the balls of his feet, his arms were outstretched, his eyes gazing out at the sea below and the sun just now reflecting off its waters. To maintain such a position without a tremor of movement, a human would have needed to be an exceptionally talented acrobat. To attempt to do so while resting precariously on a narrow length of stone set many cables above the sea, said human would have needed to be uncommonly foolish as well.

Calla was careful to make no sound that might disturb the Lord. Her silence was as much pleasure as duty – in truth she considered it one of the secret rewards of her position, that she was allowed to observe this moment in the Lord's schedule, two perfect things giving each other greeting.

Abruptly, for no reason which Calla could identify, the Lord broke free from his reverie, dropped his hands to his sides and descended from his perch with a motion that was more jagged than fluid. All her life she had observed them, and at times it still surprised her, the abrupt brokenness of their movements – each one perfect in itself, but strangely separated from that which preceded and followed it. Two long steps and he was standing in front of her, gazing down through unbroken aurous pools.

'Good morning, Calla,' the Lord said. 'I hope the sun finds you well.'

Broadly speaking the Eternal resembled Calla's own species – two legs and two feet, two eyes, a head where you'd expect one to be. But somehow what was similar about them seemed only to accentuate the differences. It was not just that they were taller and more robust than humans, limbs long and even and fine. Not that their hands ended in four digits rather than five. Not the oddly oval shape of their faces, not the tiny, hooked noses, not even their eyes, monochrome pools without sclera or iris. Not that they smelled different, though they did, a slightly sweet fragrance, something like dried cinnamon. Not their hair, which from a distance resembled a bundle of vines spilled backwards over their heads, but up close was soft and fuzzy as velvet. There was an ineffable otherness about them that seemed more than the sum of these relatively trivial variations, as if, despite being bipedal and roughly hominid, they had no more in common with Calla than a hawk, or a stone, or the sky.

Calla offered the traditional bow of greeting, dipping her head down to the level of his waist and bringing her hands palm-up behind her. 'May the light shine brightly on you today, my Lord,' she said, meaning it.

The Aubade was tall even for an Eternal, and more heavily muscled, though the extra weight did not seem to affect his grace and agility. His eyes were a pure and vivid gold. He was still young by the standards of his kind, and the thick strands of his white hair stretched from his waist back up to his forehead – except for a gap in the centre of his plumage, one tendril notably absent.

After breakfast they would begin the long grooming sessions required to prepare the Lord for his day. First the dyer, carefully choosing which colours would grace the Lord's hair that day, rich strands of ebony and crimson. Then on to his tailor, fifty years in service and his eyes were still as sharp as his sewing needle. They would consult on the day's patterns, and a half-dozen of the Lord's personal servants would help him don whatever costume he decided on. In his sense of personal fashion, as in everything he did, the Lord was perfect – but still, Calla had always thought him at his most exquisite before all that, in this moment of nakedness. A lifetime of observing him should have inured her to his charms, but it hadn't.

'Your meal awaits you, my Lord,' Calla said. His morning robe hung over the wall, and Calla took the liberty of handing it to him. He shifted himself into it in one swift movement, covering his hairless chest and his dangling member, and then he strutted off to take his repast without another comment.

His name, of course, was not the Aubade. But the High Tongue, a language of whistles with rapid changes in tempo and tune, was entirely indecipherable to humans – or at least it was said to be so. Like all the First he had been given a name in the common human speech, a sobriquet that had become colloquial from long usage. The Aubade had been the Aubade since dim antiquity, before Calla's grandfather's father had quickened, and those qualities that had earned him his sobriquet were as evident in the present as they had been a century earlier.

Calla followed the Lord to another corner of the garden, one set near an elevator that rose up from the kitchens, steam-powered and mostly silent, large enough to carry up a live bull, though admittedly that particular fare had never been offered. The Lord's table had been set moments before – there was a member of the staff whose sole job was to wait for Calla's arrival, and to take that as the signal to begin putting out the feast.

It was no small task, either. Breakfast for the day was dumplings filled with muskrat liver, candied quince in plum liquor, slow-roasted pork belly and numerous other delicacies, each plate arranged neatly on a swivelling circular platform raised just above the table. The Lord sat cross-legged on a green cushion in front of the feast and brought a bit of watercress to his mouth.

'And how went your evening's entertainment?' the Aubade asked, after sampling a few of the plates.

Calla had spent her one free evening that week having dinner with the head chef from the Estate of Gilded Stone. 'Well enough, my Lord.'

'But not splendidly?'

Calla smiled. 'Splendidly, my Lord.'

'What a high bar you set for your prospective mates, Calla.' He spent a moment in consideration. 'Not that you aren't worthy of excellence.'

'Thank you, my Lord,' she said. He did not acknowledge her

response and she had not expected him to. Those Above had no notion of flattery, nor of dissimulation generally. A thing was said because it was meant, not in hopes of eliciting a reaction.

The Aubade turned his attention back to his feast, though not with any great relish. He expected an elaborate table, but in truth the Lord seemed to take little excitement in it. Those pleasures which inspired his passion tended towards the more abstract. 'I had thought of visiting the courses today,' he said idly, forking a caramelised prawn.

'Of course, my Lord. Your ship awaits you.'

'And the Lord of the Sidereal Citadel sent me a message last night, insisting that he has hit upon a new design for an aerial that is unique in its conception.'

'The Lord of the Sidereal Citadel is a fine craftsman.'

'The finest, though why he imagines I'll be of any use in turning his conception into reality is utterly beyond me.' The Lord seemed to think the matter over for a moment, though Calla had been among the High long enough to know that you could never really say with any certainty what their pauses meant, or if they meant anything.

He brushed his mouth with a silk handkerchief and stood abruptly. 'Still, he always has some fine pieces of steamwork to display. Send a messenger to his estate, ask if I might call at the hour of the Starling.'

The food lay unfinished on the table, and there were six more dishes soon to be making their way up in the elevators. Now it would all be burned in the central fires of the Keep – nothing intended for the use or consumption of an Eternal could be wasted on a lesser species, be it it ant, dog or human.

'Of course, my Lord,' Calla said, bowing deeply. 'At your command.'

4

Thistle woke up well past the hour of the Eagle, the sun beating down shamelessly, though he didn't know the time at first and didn't care when he did.

He didn't know because his sleeping quarters were a windowless shack built atop the slum tenement he lived in with his mother, siblings and a dozen-odd other families. He didn't care because he had nothing to do, no labour to occupy the morning, no toil to carry him through until evening. So far as the world was concerned, he could have gone on sleeping until nightfall. Could well have never woken up.

The shack had been a pigeon coop. When he'd assumed residence in the spring, Thistle had spent three solid days – perhaps the only three days of work he'd put in over the sixteen years he'd drawn breath – removing the cages and various bric-a-brac, washing the floors over and over and over again. It hadn't done much good. He could still smell them, the dander from their wings, the thick white goo of their shit.

Thistle hated birds. He hated a lot of things, but he particularly hated birds.

Still, it was better than his mother's apartment, two rooms separated by a wall the width of his little finger, four children packed into the front, his mother and little Apple in the back. The coop was his at least, and there wasn't much else in the world he could lay sole claim to. In a few months it would be too cold to sleep there and he'd be back sharing a pallet on the floor. Best enjoy it while he could.

Thistle stretched, yawned, pulled himself up and out into the early-afternoon sun. He took a long piss off the side of the building, watched the stream of urine fall against the alleyway below. This time of day there was little chance of watering a passer-by, though Thistle held out hope.

He was about average height for a youth from the lowest stretches of the Roost, which would have made him short almost anywhere else on the continent. His face was coarse, his mouth brutish. The last year he'd grown a patchy bush of black hair thick around his neck and above his lip but sparse everywhere else, peach-fuzz unsure if it was ever to become a beard. He'd been an ugly child, become an ugly youth, and in all likelihood would end up an ugly man. His one distinguishing feature was his eyes, which were so dark a brown you could be forgiven for mistaking them as black. If you passed him you'd walk faster, and maybe take a quick backwards look once you were safely past.

Thistle lived in the Barrow, far down on the Fifth Rung, a short walk upslope from the docks. His building was the tallest in the neighbourhood, five storeys in crumbling red brick. To the east could be seen one of the great pumps leeching water from the bay and sending it on its long journey skyward. Of course it could be heard wherever you were , an unpleasant slurping sound like an old man farting. Didn't smell much different to that either, gave the whole Rung a strong whiff of mildew and worse. Sixteen years Thistle had lived in the echo of the suck – he figured he ought to have got used to it by now, but he never had.

As far as Thistle was concerned the world was the Roost, and the Roost was the Fifth and the Fifth was the Barrow and the few neighbourhoods surrounding it, east to the pumps, south to the harbour, upslope towards the Points. Beyond that, Thistle's perceptions of place grew hazy, vague impressions of privilege and soft silks.

Thistle pulled on his trousers, noticed the shaky job he'd done during his most recent repatching, told himself to borrow some thread from his mother and take care of it later that evening, knew he wouldn't get round to actually doing it. It is a curious fact that the less one has to do the less one does, a vicious cycle that if uninterrupted leads to torpor. He went back into his hutch and pulled up a loose stone from the back corner. From inside the alcove he removed a thin bit of pig-iron, one end sharpened into a point, the other shoved into a piece of cork. The shiv was worn and ill-made, but like anything else that might be used as a weapon it was strictly illegal – humans were forbidden to own any blade larger than a cooking knife, even the Cuckoos had to make do with their knobbed ferules. Thistle told himself he carried it for protection, in case a rival crew caught him alone in a back stairwell or an alley. This wasn't quite a lie, but it wasn't quite the truth either. Thistle liked holding the shiv in his hand, liked feeling its weight when he walked. He shoved it into the back of his trousers, pulled his belt tight around it, put on his boots and started out into the afternoon.

Down the crumbling stairs, jumping over the third step on the second landing, crumbling now for half a generation, a trap for the forgetful or foreign. He skirted the door of his own apartment, quickly and quietly as he could. Mother would be down at the water, doing the day's wash. Inside would be his sisters, Thyme and Shrub and little Ivy, three years come winter and still couldn't quite walk right. And of course Apple, sharing the back room with the small altar their mother kept to Siraph, coughing his life out against the thin walls. In truth it had been Apple that had led Thistle to taking up his spot on the roof, the ever-constant hack, an intake of breath and two sharp ejections of phlegm.

Thistle's shack was dirty and often damp and always smelly, but it beat listening to your brother dying all night, every night. Secretly Thistle sometimes found himself wishing that Apple would stop mucking around already and just get to it. What was it exactly he had to live for? Thistle wondered. What was the point of prolonging such a miserable existence?

But then that same question could be asked of everyone – at least everyone Thistle had ever met.

Outside the Barrow was busy as ever, lines of porters like ants carrying goods up from the ships, laden double with bolts of raw silk from Chazar or chicory from the Baleferic Isles or Dycian oranges. From the Source at the top of the First Rung a complex and elaborate series of canals ran down through the city and back to the bay. But only the Eternal could use them, and since no seed-pecker ever came down to the Fifth, the waterways were empty of anything but fallen leaves. What goods made their way from the docks were taken to their destinations on the back of one of the city's endless supply of human chattel. Most of the men on the Fifth that had jobs – a modest majority, if you were being kind – worked in such a fashion, unloading cargo from the huge caravels that floated into the harbour, hauling it upslope, back and forth from morning till nightfall.

Thistle found the boys at their usual spot, in a long-abandoned pumping station a few blocks towards the docks. It was a small stone building beneath one of the main pipes, an access hole leading down into the bowels of the mountain. As children they had dared each other to explore it, crawling into the dark with a candle nub for guidance, but when they had been eight little Crimson, Bandage's second cousin, had gone down and never come back up, and that had been the last of the game. Still, it made for a good place to kill time, if you could get past the smell and the dark. 'What's gospel?' Thistle asked.

Felspar was handsome and clever, but more handsome than he was clever, a truth that he ignored to his frequent misfortune. By Thistle's count, every third or fourth scrap they got into was on account of Felspar's not being able to keep his mouth shut, relying on Treble's size and Thistle's savagery to save him from trouble. But then, down here in the Barrow, belligerence was not considered an unpardonable sin, and Thistle wasn't the sort who minded a good brawl, or was particularly concerned as to what sparked one. What was the point of having boys if you couldn't use them to bail you out, now and again?

Treble was big and dim and loyal, though you could never be sure of the degree to which the last was a function of the second, whether he would have your back from virtue or simply because he couldn't imagine another option. Thistle didn't suppose it mattered much. Treble's character didn't seem to be spoiling, and as for his wit, well – there were even fewer signs of change in that department.

Rat was as far from Treble as you could get, dark and always smiling. He hadn't yet lost his baby fat. Thistle wondered at what point baby fat just became fat, suspected that Rat was fast approaching it. Rat wasn't born in the Barrow – his father had been a baker up on the Fourth Rung – but when he had died of the plague his mother had lost the shop and had to move downslope. Perhaps it was this early brush with prosperity that was the cause of the Rat's vague softness.

They were the core group, though you could add the Brothers Calc and a few others. Urn the Youngest, the third of his name still extant, had been a mainstay as well, but the previous winter he had humiliated himself in a dust-up with some boys from upslope, left Felspar to deal with three of them on his own, and so by the rough and reasonable code of conduct adhered to in the Barrow he was no better than a dog, his name unfit for mention.

'It's hot,' Treble said.

'That's news to you?' Thistle asked.

Treble shrugged. He'd done his best.

Between the four of them they had enough tobacco for two cigarettes, and they went ahead and rolled them, Felspar doing the honours. Thistle felt that he rolled better than Felspar but Felspar felt otherwise, and it was too hot to fight over it, Treble had got that much right. The sun brought a rolling sort of boil that made it impossible to do anything but rot. With a dozen Salucian pennies or even a few bronze nummus they could have bought a bottle of potato liquor and sipped their way into evening. But it was empty pockets all round, and nothing to do but stew.

'They're having a dig tonight up at the East Stay. Supposed to have a band and everything,' Rat said.

'Be three pennies a head, at least,' Felspar answered.

'We won't keep them, we try and march our way to the East Stay.'

'The coin, or our heads?'

An open question, not worth a response. Rat wasn't really suggesting they go to the East Stay, he was just talking because there wasn't anything else to do. There is a common misconception that poverty breeds crime, but in fact this skips a step. Poverty breeds boredom, and boredom leads to crime. Two hours of aimless waiting and Thistle and his boys were ready to pull a smash and grab just to relieve the monotony.

It took longer to figure out where to pull it, though. Couldn't do it in the Barrow; their faces were too well known. Try rolling someone in the neighbourhood and you end up getting a visit from a member of the Brotherhood Below, some ornery mother-fucker with a burn scar on his neck and a knife in his waistband. The Brotherhood was responsible for smuggling and prostitution and pretty much every other illegal activity on the Fifth, and they didn't like having their monopoly challenged by a pack of kids, and they weren't slow to make known their displeasure. Of course the docks were straight out, they were at open steel with the crew living there, wouldn't be heading that way just for the lark of it. That left Seven Points or the North Straits, and there was a fair bit of back and forth as to which. Thistle might be the leader, but they were an anarchic bunch, cajoled and threatened rather than led.

They settled on the Points. There weren't any particular troubles with the locals that way – that didn't mean they wouldn't find any, but it at least meant there wouldn't be a crew of them waiting in an alley with sharpened iron. Course, upslope meant more money and that meant more chance of running into the Cuckoos, but the Cuckoos didn't much concern Thistle – they were less of a concern than the other gangs, gods knew, that bunch of slow fat drunkards comfortable trading the hatred of their entire species for a gold eagle a season. And Seven Points was a good place to lose anyone following you, a handful of different pipes joining at one central location, hence the name.

Felspar was pushing for the Straits, but that was just because he was trying to bed a girl that lived there. 'I'm not walking all the way to Ell Street just so you can not have sex with someone,' Thistle said. 'If I wanted to watch you not have sex with someone, I could just stay here.'

'She's ready to pop,' Felspar insisted.

'Only thing you'll get out of that girl is a stiff cock.'

'Or the drip,' Rat added.

'He ain't smooth enough to get the drip,' Thistle said.

'Why you gotta be smooth to get the drip?' Treble asked.

Thistle bit his tongue and shook his head. You could forget how stupid Treble was so long as he was staring silently at a wall, but even Treble couldn't stare silently at a wall for ever, and once he opened his mouth it all came storming back at you.

Thistle dropped down from the crate he was sitting on and started off at the sort of speed that made it clear the conversation was over. The rest fell in behind him.

The broken pipe was the unofficial barrier of the neighbourhood, a length of metal tubing rising up from the mountain and over the road that had burst some generations previous and never been fixed. Of course it wasn't on any map, but anyone living there knew what walking past it meant, knew you better quicken your step, pull your coat tight, keep your eyes wary but don't get to staring at nobody. Past the border it was open season on you and anyone born in the Barrow, just as it was in the Barrow for anyone from anywhere else

Thistle wasn't over-worried; not in the middle of the day, not with Treble and the boys with him – but he noticed just the same. They all noticed, the stroll turning to a march, Treble taking point almost unconsciously, because even the fiercest thug would take a good long second thought before taking a swing at him.

They'd been walking for half an hour when Thistle stopped in front of a small general store just off the main thoroughfare. No one said anything, but then it was an old game for the four of them, their parts well rehearsed. Felspar would be the distraction, because he had an even smile and eyes that might seem innocent if you weren't looking closely, and if you were foolish enough to think there was still an innocent left on the Fifth. Rat and Treble would keep lookout, because they weren't suited for anything more. And Thistle would make the grab, because he never flinched, or at least hadn't yet. It was this last that Thistle supposed made him the leader. Treble was a better scrapper, and Felspar a louder speaker, which most of the world seemed to take as evidence of superior intellect. But Thistle did what needed to be done, did it without any trembling, of his hands or his conscience. That made him special, and despite what Felspar might croon to the halfwit slatterns who mooned after him, when something needed to be done he put his eyes on Thistle, like all the rest of them.

Felspar went in first. Thistle gave him thirty seconds and followed. It was a small market like any other you could find on the lower levels, the sort of place that sold anything and everything, goods uniform only in being overpriced and of poor quality.

'Mother needs beef marrow,' Felspar was saying to the man at the counter.

'Ain't got no beef marrow,' said the proprietor, who was north of forty, grey-haired, fat and friendly-looking.

'You're the fifth shop I've tried.'

'That may be the case,' the merchant said affably. 'But it doesn't change the fact that I don't have any beef marrow. Try Sickle's butcher shop, it's up two streets on your right.'

'I tried Sickle's,' Felspar pleaded. 'Sickle said to come here.'

Thistle had edged his way to the corner pantry, made like he was inspecting the stock. The trick with pocketing merchandise is that there isn't any such thing – just make the snatch and don't fuss around. It didn't help that Thistle looked like the sort of kid who'd be up for a lift, but there wasn't anything that could be done about that.

'But if you don't have beef marrow,' Felspar continued, 'and Sickle doesn't have beef marrow, then how am I going to get my mother any beef marrow?'

The owner leaned against his counter, somewhere between annoyed and bemused. 'I guess you'd better start looking for a cow.'

Thistle wedged the bottle into his front pocket, the owner all but ignorant of his presence, attention occupied with Felspar's quest for goose marrow. They were in the clear. All Thistle needed to do was keep his head down, walk out casual, pass the thing off to Rat. They'd be drunk and happy inside of an hour. At the very least they'd be drunk.

But then Felspar muffed it, caught Thistle's eyes as Thistle went to slip out the door, a second or two longer than he should have, long enough for something to click in the owner's mind. 'What are you doing there, boy?'

Thistle figured it was best not to wait around and discuss it, pushed past his bumbling confederate and made for the exit with all the speed he could manage. Felspar picked up a second behind him, almost knocked Thistle down coming out of the door, and the owner started to shout, and the whole thing went sideways.

That they'd been noticed at all was Felspar's fault. That there were two Cuckoos making their way upslope as Thistle came outside, strutting down the middle of the street just like they'd been waiting for him, that wasn't nothing but bad luck. Officially they were the custodians, though everyone on the Fifth, which is to say everyone Thistle knew, just called them the Cuckoos, after those treasonous avians known to lay eggs in the nests of other birds, which then hatch early and destroy their clutch-mates. You almost never saw one so far downslope – there were always plenty hanging out by the docks but they were just there to make sure everything went smoothly with their pay-off, not to hassle anyone. What in the hell reason they had for being in the Points that day, Thistle never did learn.

Nor did it matter. 'Bolt,' Thistle ordered Treble and Rat as soon as he'd stepped outside, and they didn't need him to say it twice.

As a breed the Cuckoos were not renowned for their competence, but then you hardly needed to be to notice four boys sprinting off in separate directions while a shop owner screamed at them. The first Cuckoo was old and fat, and Thistle didn't have any worries about losing him. But the second was young and trim, with the slicked-back hair that they wore on the upper Rungs, and Thistle thought he might prove more trouble. They were both dressed the same, of course, in simple blue robes, and carrying a stout wood ferule with a noisemaker at the end that gave off a croaking sound when it was twirled.

Thistle figured he still had a decent chance of it; the Cuckoos might decide to pounce on Rat or Treble, or they might just not give a shit at all – it wouldn't be the first time a Cuckoo had decided not to do his job, wouldn't be the first time by a long shot. And indeed, the fat one didn't seem in any great hurry to chase after anybody, made do with yelling warnings at Thistle's back. But the younger was all hell-bent on running after someone, and for whatever reason he seized on Thistle as quarry.

As soon as he was out of view Thistle tossed the bottle, heard the glass shatter and the hopes of an evening drink with it. Still he had a smile on his face and felt something close to euphoric. He buzzed through back alleys and ducked down side streets, till every heartbeat throbbed so hard it was like being punched in the chest. The Fifth was his, you could keep the rest of the Roost and the rest of the damn world. There wasn't no way in hell they'd catch him here, not if he had to run for the rest of the day and night. He knew it like the back of his hand, every side alley and brown-water canal, every pipe and every tenement.

Then he turned a corner and standing there was the fat Cuckoo, and closer up he seemed more stout than fat, especially when he gave Thistle an open-handed slap strong enough to land him on his arse.

It wasn't the force of the blow that put Thistle on the ground so much as the shock of the thing. The fat man was sharper than Thistle would have credited a Cuckoo, let alone a Cuckoo whose man-breasts heaved up and down at having jogged for three solid minutes. But in those three minutes he had managed to deduce Thistle's destination and cut him off without a breath of trouble.

'Where's the bottle?' the Cuckoo asked, in a languid sort of drawl, as if he weren't excited about the matter either way.

Thistle spat a stream of blood against the alley wall, leaned against it as he worked himself upright. 'Don't have no bottle,' he said. It would take more than a smack to loosen the truth.

'That a fact?'

'You can search me,' Thistle said, not remembering until he said it that he was still carrying his shiv. And for the first time that day Thistle knew real fear. Getting caught with the bottle wouldn't have meant more than a walk up to the Cuckoo's head-quarters and a good beating, and neither for the first time. But carrying a weapon, even Thistle's makeshift blade? That was a heavy piece of sin, as reckoned by the Cuckoos and their four-fingered overlords. Theft, vandalism, even a good assault – none of these the Cuckoos found very interesting, so long as the victim was another denizen of the Fifth. A weapon, on the other hand, was counted as a close cousin of rebellion, a crime against the Eternal, against the Roost itself.

He'd go underground for this, into the roots of the mountain. Down into the suck, hammering away at the pipes, hard labour to make sure the water kept running, in the dark until they let you out or you died. Most men it was the latter, and it didn't take so long. The hardest thug didn't talk about going below casually, and it was widely agreed that it was better to find a way to die before they took you underground, if you could manage it.

The younger Cuckoo had arrived finally, the store owner a few steps behind him, looking winded and furious. 'Where's the bottle?' he asked, after taking a few seconds remembering how to breathe.

'Says he doesn't have it,' the fat Cuckoo said.

'Time Below, he doesn't.'

'Check his pockets.'

'Screw that,' the younger Cuckoo replied. 'Probably end up with lice.'

Thistle's heart rose for a second, just long enough for the fat Cuckoo's next words to dash it. 'Up against the wall.'

Thistle looked back and forth between the two, but couldn't yet bring himself to move.

'Are you deaf?' the thin Cuckoo asked. 'He said get against the wall.'

They would find the knife, and they would take him before a magistrate, and they would put him below, and when he came out he wouldn't be fit for anything more than swatting at flies. All of these things would happen, at that moment Thistle was certain of it, as certain as he'd ever been of anything in his life. There was nothing he could do to change it, nothing that could alter or improve the situation. There was nothing left but to beg or sneer.

Thistle sneered for all he was worth. 'Fuck you and your mother, you bent-kneed turncoat son of a bitch.'

The fat Cuckoo shook his head back and forth, tired and less than thrilled at what was about to come. The thin Cuckoo smiled, excited by the prospect of injuring someone.

'Why exactly are you bothering my son?' a voice asked.

Thistle's father had been a porter who'd got drunk one night and fallen into the bay, come back out again fish-pecked and green, so Thistle was pretty certain whoever was speaking wasn't him.

The fat Cuckoo took a long time to answer. 'What?'

'I asked, why exactly are you bothering my son?' Thistle turned and took a quick look at the man. The first thing to notice was the outlandish dress, coarse brown trouser and a coarse brown shirt, the uniform of someone who had laboured below – but he was clean and well kept, which didn't square, not at all. Nor did his bass voice, nor his easy tone of command. His hair trailed down his head like a mane, white as snow though he couldn't have had forty-five years on him. Between that and his forehead, disproportionately broad, he gave the impression of some great resting feline.

'This one's your kid?'

The man who was not Thistle's father walked over and put one hand on Thistle's shoulder. His arms were thick and he had a brand on his wrist that marked him as being from one of the higher Rungs. 'That's what I said.'

The thin Cuckoo looked at the second, gained some courage from the reminder that he wasn't facing the situation by his lonesome. 'What's his name, then?'

'Spring,' the man said cleanly, with a swift disregard for truth that any street kid could appreciate.

The Cuckoos spent the next couple of seconds realising that they had no way of proving that one way or the other, and the merchant took the opportunity to break in. 'If he is your son, he's in a lot of trouble. He ripped me off on a bottle of rotgut, the little savage. Him and his pack of hoods, trying to scam me.'

The man looked down at Thistle for a moment, then back up at the merchant. He had a gaze as heavy as a porter's pack, and he seemed in no great hurry to speak. 'I'm afraid you're mistaken, friend. My son and I have been together the last three hours. I just sent him out a moment ago to pick up a few things for dinner.'

'Birdshit,' the younger Cuckoo said.

'I'll thank you to avoid profaning yourself while in my presence,' the man said stiffly.

'Awful dark to be your son,' the fat Cuckoo said.

'His mother was Dycian,' the man answered. 'And if you're done combing my family tree, perhaps we might get on with our business?' Thistle had done his fair share of lying to figures of authority, but he knew he couldn't have matched the stranger's easy duplicity, natural as a duck in water.

'Father or not,' the older Cuckoo said, 'this boy is in trouble. Theft, vandalism and evading arrest.'

'Where's the bottle?'

'What?'

'The bottle he snatched, where is it?'

The Cuckoos looked at each other, then at the merchant. 'I suppose he's thrown it away, hasn't he?'

'So you've no proof at all, to back up this absurd allegation.'

'I chased him half a cable!' the younger Cuckoo said. 'You think I don't recognise him?'

'I just went into your shop looking for some garlic, sir,' Thistle broke in, pitching his voice high. 'Then I realised Father hadn't given me any money, and I was going back to find him when everyone started yelling.'

'Why'd you run?'

Thistle shrugged, tried to make himself look as friendly as Rat and as dumb as Treble. 'Cause you were chasing me.'

'Wasn't talking so polite two minutes ago,' the fat Cuckoo said, but he seemed to have lost his enthusiasm for the proceedings. 'Are you sure this was the one that made the snatch?'

'I got a better look at the other one,' the shopkeeper admitted, staring hard at Thistle.

'I don't have time for this,' the man who was not Thistle's father snapped, and there was real weight in his voice, such that even the Cuckoos had to respond. 'And neither does my boy. You say you're short a bottle of liquor?' he asked, turning towards the merchant and counting out five bronze nummus from his purse. 'This should make good your losses, and you can add to it my apologies at your misfortune. All the same, it would be better in the future not to go blaming innocent children for your adversity.'

The owner looked at Thistle, looked at the man, looked at the coin in the man's hand. Wasn't no way he was foolish enough to believe this story, but putting Thistle below wouldn't pay him back for the bottle of liquor. And this was the Fifth after all, no one was in any hurry to send a boy into the mountain. 'I suppose I might be confusing him with his double.'

'Kind of thing could happen to anyone,' Thistle's saviour said, handing over the coin and turning to the two Cuckoos. 'Your good service is appreciated, but I think we'd all agree the situation has resolved itself.'

'This is birdshit,' the thin Cuckoo said again, still mostly out of breath and wanting someone to blame.

But the fat Cuckoo seemed less inclined to make an issue out of it, probably because he didn't feel like having to walk Thistle all the way up to the station. 'Sorry for the confusion,' he muttered finally before turning and heading back towards the main road.

'I've got my eye on you,' the thin one said, not because he really meant it but because it seemed like the thing to say.

The shop owner waited till the Cuckoos were out of earshot, then he turned down to Thistle. 'Don't ever come into my shop again,' he said, then gave a long, searching look to the man who had just saved Thistle from something akin to death, before toddling back upslope.

And then there were just the two of them, Thistle and the man who was not Thistle's father but had done him better service in five minutes than that old sack of shit had during his whole miserable existence. Thistle didn't say anything for a while, couldn't quite figure out anything to say. He had had sixteen years downslope, and in those sixteen years he'd learned pretty well how things ran, and they did not run this way – strangers did not put themselves out to help you, especially not when that help was extralegal and costly.

'Thanks,' Thistle said finally, lamely, with awareness of the latter.

The man didn't answer, just stared at Thistle without blinking. Thistle didn't blink either, though he very much wanted to. 'That man you stole that bottle of liquor from – he seem rich to you?'

'Not really,' Thistle said.

'He seem like he's making enough money that he can afford to lose some of it to a pack of miscreant children?'

Thistle shrugged. He didn't know what miscreant meant exactly, but he didn't like being called it. And of course, no youth likes to be reminded of their age.

'And what do you need a bottle of liquor for at mid-afternoon? You're a man, or nearly one. What kind of man is it gets drunk before the sun sets?'

Thistle shrugged again, but his eyes clouded over and he felt his hands tense at his side.

'My name is Edom, the First of His Line,' and the way he said it, it sounded like something worth being. 'What's yours?'

'Thistle,' though even to his ears it didn't seem to have much weight to it.

'Thistle is the name they gave you,' the man said.

Thistle didn't know what that meant.

'Ask yourself if this is what you want to be, boy they call Thistle,' the strange man said. Then he reached into his purse, took out a silver tertarum and handed it over. 'Ask yourself if this is everything that you want to be.'

With that, the man turned quickly and marched north.

Thistle watched him till he disappeared out of sight. He knew the answer, wanted to shout it at the man's back. Instead he closed his hand round the coin and started to walk downslope. Back to the Barrow, and the tenements, and his life.

5

The line held, but barely.

The Marchers attacked just before noon, though apart from that, Hamilcar's prediction had been correct. Bas had formed out the men shortly after returning to camp, two wings with Hamilcar's bowmen on either side and the small force of cavalry in the centre. Three hours had passed then, though the certainty of the conflict made it feel longer, even for Bas. Twice he gave the order for the water-boys to pass through the ranks, grateful soldiers filling their bellies, no few for the last time.

The sun was near its zenith when the Marchers began to buzz, loud enough that you could hear them from half a valley away. Masters of ambush, of cutting a line of horses from camp, of slipping a baggage train as easy as a cutpurse would a pocket, in open battle the Marchers had no notion of trickery and little more of tactics. Their leaders and holy men would work them into a frenzy, then send them hurtling forward like javelins. Bas

64

had seen it before, seen it and survived, which was more than most men could say.

A few small packs of horsemen broke away from the main body, crossed to just outside of arrow range and began to ride back and forth, hooting and hollering and taunting their opponents. It was a source of some curiosity to Bas how these unlettered half-children had managed such a competent grasp of Aelerian profanity. More than competent, elegant even. Bas had never known his mother, but sight unseen he doubted her capable of half the gymnastics the young Marchers attributed to her.

They were to die, most of them, perhaps all of them, and if they didn't die they would do their best to kill. But all the same they looked very fine in the midday sun, vital and amoral as a thunderstorm. One particularly dextrous youth managed to remove himself from his codpiece while straddling his mount, galloped down the lines with his cock dangling in view. An impressive feat, though not one that Bas imagined would be of much help in the coming battle.

Through it all, not a man of the thema broke from the position, not so much as wavered, though you could hear a titter of laughter go through them after a particularly good jibe. There would be no individual heroics, no squaring off of champions. Warfare was not a matter of personal glory. The thema was an engine that ate up men and spat out corpses – it had no time for gallantry.

Disappointed at their reception, the emissaries rode back to their countrymen, now very near to acting, a howling squall of hardened killers, long lances erect. Hanging from these last the sharp-eyed among the Aelerians could see off-white circular bands – the scalped remnants of some previous combatant. Their own end if they weren't lucky and careful.

Then they were off, not suddenly, because no group of men that size could possibly get moving in any particularly rapid fashion, but with the growing momentum that gave their charge its potency. A swift canter at first, then steadily faster, like a summer rain. The noise was more than deafening, it was almost physical, a gust of wind blowing through the valley. The hammering of hooves, the painted men screaming their hatred as if expelling poison.

The thema had no equivalent caterwaul. Their silence before battle was part of what made them unique, part of their mystique – that they were professionals, that war for them caused no flutter of agitation, any more than a smith gets excited when he walks to his forge. That was the ideal at least, though here and there Bas noticed a neophyte go weak-kneed, and even some of the veterans looked less than enthused about the day's work. Still, for men about to face death, their seeming indifference was remarkable.

When the mass of riders had come within range there was an abrupt humming sound, a half-thousand bows twanging in unison, a half-thousand arrows clouding the sky. Lost for a moment against the sun, then falling again, a grim and deadly parabola, Hamilcar and his people at their work. The plainsmen wore no armour, not even the chieftains, and where the arrows fell they found flesh awaiting them. Horses plunged to the ground, death screams shriller and longer than a man's. Marchers died by the tens and hundreds, choking on blood or thrown from their saddles and crushed beneath their mounts, but the charge continued all the same. Hamilcar's men fired off a second volley with less effect. The front ranks shifted their pikes horizontal, a bristling line of steel dropping like a curtain.

Bas waited.

Horses are not wise creatures, insofar as they would prefer to stand in a field all day, eating and rutting and going for the occasional run when the mood takes them, rather than put on clothes and travel thousands of cables to kill other members of their species. But they are not so foolish as to run full speed into an obvious physical impediment, regardless of what the man on their back pushes them to do. The success of cavalry against infantry does not rely on force or momentum *per se* – it is the moral factor that determines its efficacy. Should the infantry stand firm, keep their feet planted and their arms thrust forward, the charge is certain to fail. The riders will pull up at the last moment, break and search for another weakness in the line. All that needs to be done to ensure victory, in effect, is to stand firm.

Not so easily done when staring at a multitude of screaming plainsmen, bare-chested, trails of raven and owl feathers streaming from their headdresses and their war lances. A rolling wave of muscle and sharpened iron, a crest of rage hurling itself across the plains. And a charge, while destined to fail should its target maintain a unified, compact mass, is the ideal formation by which to spear a disordered mob of soldiers.

So Bas waited.

Here and there the line weakened, bent, where a particularly brave Marcher dared slip between the rows of pikes to skewer a hoplitai, or where a horse, mad and dying from its wounds, collapsed into the front rank, making a gap in the lines. But more often the Marchers were forced to shy away at the last moment, the unbroken line of steel impenetrable. And where the Aelerian line held the very momentum of their charge doomed many of the Marchers, as the back ranks of horsemen pressed closely against the front, making escape impossible, offering easy targets.

And now, with the charge stalled and the Marchers in confusion, the hoplitai made their own attack, surging forward to impale the horsemen, Aelerian steel sliding into the unprotected flesh of the Marchers' ponies or, better aimed, into the unprotected flesh of the Marchers themselves. Unable to flee, pushed onward by the men behind them, hand-to-hand combat was the only option. The Marchers were armed with war spears, pig-iron hatchets and bent swords, heirloom or cast-off. Stalled, they were no match against the Aelerians, who were cool and brutal and, above all, competent.

But Mykhailo had another quiver in his bow, had not yet given up the game. As the rolling tumult of Marchers streaked across the valley they had forked in two. The first contingent launched themselves at Bas's left, pinned them down, while the second half of the horde wheeled and struck against Bas's right, aiming to roll up his flank.

And this time it was a very close thing, very close indeed. From his vantage point Bas could see the right flank buckle, bend against the onslaught, the Marchers and their war lances taking their toll. No, not see – it was impossible to take into account the thousand tiny battles taking place on either side of the line, each a matter of desperate importance for the men involved in them, none of any particular weight on their own. 'Sensed' would be a better way to put it, like knowing rain is on its way though the sun is hot overhead, or how some men say they can feel a run of cards coming at the gambling table.

It was one of those peculiar moments of clarity that sometimes descend in the midst of chaos, when a single decision, executed firmly, can turn fortune's tide. A good tactician needs to have something of the savage in him, needs to have the same instinct for the kill as a hawk, needs to be able to seize on the emptiness between the seconds. All the might of the Marchers wasn't enough to break the Aelerian right, just to pin it into place. And with the balance of the plainsmen engaged in combat against each side, unable to conquer but equally incapable of retreat, Bas gave the order for his own cavalry to charge.

The strength of the Commonwealth was in its hoplitai – iron-clad, hardbitten, trained to move as a single organism. For cavalry, they had little use. The Marchers were far more skilled – better riders, superior lancers. And of course the Others were as far beyond the Marchers as the Marchers were the Aelerians, as they had proved more than once during the short but sanguinary conflict known as the Seventh Other War. But still, while inferior to the plainsmen in open battle, the weight of the Aelerian cata-phracts were enough to strike a decisive blow against the weakened Marchers, the last piece that would turn defeat into a rout.

Bas stayed in the centre of the charge, careful to take no chances with his own life. He had enough acts of bravery to his credit, and he had seen more than one army collapse from the death of its leader. The thema was far too disciplined for that, of course, but Bas was not one to take a needless chance. With the force of their charge lost, the Marchers were left rudderless, incapable any longer of collective action. Too closely packed to manoeuvre, too brave to break and run, they collapsed beneath the full impetus of the Aelerian cavalry, a thousand men in close ranks and heavy armour.

In front and alongside him the Aelerian cataphracts – veterans all, or all save Theophilus, and if he lived past today he could claim that distinction and have no man gainsay him – went about the savage business of their trade. Exhausted by the fighting they had already seen that day, unarmoured, their hand weapons as like to break against the chain hauberks of the Aelerians as they were to find purchase in flesh, the Marchers were in no position to make a serious defence. That they did so at all was testament to the extraordinary, if pointless, sense of valour that was their national inheritance.

Bas unsheathed his sword but had not yet seen the point in doing anything with it, the front ranks of the charge sweeping the enemy in front of them. He felt a dissonant moment of bliss, as if he were about nothing more than a midday ride, the weather warm for once, the sun pleasant rather than absent or brutal. The noise was so loud and had lasted for so long that he had ceased to be entirely cognisant of it, a coterminous drone not altogether dissimilar to silence. Thus it was only belatedly that Bas realised he had dropped from the middle of the pack to the tail, that his mount was running ragged, and later still that he discovered the cause of the injury, a tear along the beast's haunches made by axe or blade, one that made it impossible for him to keep pace with the charge.

A battle has only one certainty, and that is that at some point everything will descend into chaos, with no one individual capable of enforcing his will upon the whole. The day had reached that point. The Marchers were thinking of nothing more than escape, the Aelerians so fired by victory and bloodlust that they'd have sprinted over a cliff sooner than notice the orders of their commander. It was each man to his own, until exhaustion set in or night fell.

Bas was lost in the melee, the rest of his force striking against the fleeing Marchers. After a few moments his horse had dropped down to a canter, and then a walk, and then began to stumble.

Bas sheathed his sword and slipped down off Oat. The charge had carried him out into the hinterland between where the two armies had begun the day. In front of him the mass of plainsmen that had been able to flee were doing so, the cataphracts in fierce pursuit. Behind him those Marchers that were unable to break free from combat against the pikemen were dying in a fashion bloody and wholesale. On a battlefield of more than seventy thousand men, Bas found himself virtually alone.

Oat collapsed into the grass about the same time that Bas noticed a retreating Marcher wheel and turn to face him. His horse looked to be of decent stock but the war lance he carried was tipped black where it had been tempered in fire – his first battle, then, newly blooded and looking to make a name for himself. Bas could see in the boy's face the certainty of escape compete with the possibility of glory, and he knew which would win out. Bas had been fighting the Marchers since before this youth had been a dream of his mother's – prestige would always trump survival.

The boy whooped and charged.

Pain and fear are the two gifts with which the gods have provided man to ensure the propagation of the species. It is the purpose of discipline and routine to render a soldier ignorant of these two saving graces, to ignore the reasonable instinct that makes a man flee from death. Man for man, the barbarians were the superiors of the thema, a fact which was well recognised even in the Aelerian camp. A lifetime of hardship inured them to cold and hunger and toil, their first toys as children were smaller versions of the arms they carried into battle, their skill on horseback was remarkable. But the barbarians fought for personal glory, or perhaps for some grand sense of national destiny, which was equally unhelpful from a practical perspective.

A hoplitai fought because that was what he did, because it was his profession. He was not brave because of a personal sense of courage, because he hoped to gain glory or renown. He was

certainly not brave out of any love of country, the very suggestion of which would have got you mocked out of the mess tent.
He was brave because the men next to him demanded it – in
effect, the genius of the thema lay in replacing the fear of death
with the fear of contempt, a curious bit of chicanery that had
ensured their onward progress across a dozen-odd nations. But
alone, outmatched, without hope of assistance, even the fiercest
of men can find their skin growing cold and the breath in their
lungs slow to escape.

Bas's next action carried with it little in the way of courage,
if by courage one means the ability to overcome fear. Because
– and this was the one way in which the reputation he had gained
matched the reality of it – Bas was possessed of no such emotion,
had never known the presence of it, even so much as its shadow.
Fear is the bastard child of imagination – and Bas was the sort
of man who had no clear conception of what might be, only
what ought. It was his duty not to fall beneath the blade of the
plainsman, and Bas was never one to shirk a duty.

Some ten paces ahead Bas noticed a small indentation in the
ground, and he moved towards it as fast as his knee could carry
him. His sword whistled from his sheath as he moved, coming
to his hands almost unconsciously, as it had a thousand times
before. The Marcher took notice of the gleaming red blade,
realised to whom he was about to give battle, screamed louder
and spurred his horse onward.

But Bas had chosen his position well. In his excitement the
Marcher failed to notice the depression, and just as he was set
to make his killing strike his horse half-stumbled. The traditional
skill of the barbarians was enough to keep him upright, but he
had to drop his lance to do so.

With an Aelerian blade it wouldn't have worked; the steel
would have caught in the horse's sinew or turned against bone.
But Bas's Other-crafted sword carved through the equine's legs
like a knife through melted wax. The horse pitched forward,
mewling piteously, and the Marcher went with it, tumbling heels
over hands.

He was up quickly, one of the advantages of riding bareback. His lance had followed the horse to the ground, but from the soon-to-be corpse of his mount he pulled a hand axe and a battered Aelerian short blade. Neither weapon would be enough, not against the God-Killer, but if the Marcher realised it he didn't seem to care. He beat his breast twice with the hand holding the axe, and came against Bas in a low crouch.

Bas's buckler rested on the side of his dying steed, and so he held the sword two-handed, blade elevated slightly. A younger man, or one more desirous of glory, would have surged forward, secure in his strength and prowess, hoping to best the Marcher in single combat. But victory was all for Bas; he would no more risk his own life needlessly than he would that of one of his subordinates. He gave a step, then two, knowing time was on his side, that his men would return to help him soon enough.

But the youth was wise enough to realise the same, and decided to stake the outcome on one single moment rather than allow himself to be overtaken. The axe spun through the air, not at all a bad toss given that it had been hurled from his off hand, which is to say that it went well over Bas's head. But then, the Marcher hadn't intended to kill Bas with it, though he'd happily have accepted that outcome. The thrown hand axe was meant to distract Bas from his own movement, to create an opening behind which the Marcher could attack.

Bas was not easily distracted. Had he been more familiar with Bas, the Marcher might have kept a hold on the hatchet, known better than to try to shake the God-Killer. Had he been more familiar with Bas, the Marcher might never have turned his horse round, might have made for the horizon with everything he had left in him.

The end came quickly. Bas thrust his blade forward, the Marcher stumbled trying to stop his momentum, made a desperate parry. Bas turned his own blade in a little half-circle and the sword the Marcher held was gone, as was the hand that held it, and almost before the pain could register Bas had pivoted and planted half of his weapon into the man's chest. They were very close when he died, close enough that Bas could see his eyes go dim as his body collapsed around the metal, till Bas was the only thing keeping him up.

Bas let the corpse slide off his blade. He crushed a handful of the wild grass in his hands, stalks of which reached up nearly to his breast, and wiped clean the blood from his weapon. Then he went back to check on his mount, saw it was beyond help, ended its pain quickly and dispassionately. He spent a few moments trying to remove the saddle, an awkward task given that three hundred clove of dead horseflesh was lying on most of it. Finally he gave up and just cut the straps with his knife. It had long since ceased to astonish Bas, how many of life's problems could be solved with naked steel.

6

The Lord jumped smoothly from the gently rocking bow of his pleasure craft to the soft sand of the beach. Next came Calla, and then the three bearers, young gentlemen of the Keep chosen for their grace and beauty, carrying the gifts the Lord was to present. The setting sun shone gold on the boughs of the oak and willow hanging out over the water. A path of grey stone led deeper into the forest. Standing inside the first line of trees was a household servant, wearing a white robe that covered everything but a respectful smile. 'Welcome to the House of the Second Moon, my Lord of the Red Keep.' Atop his ebony tray were a hollow gourd resting on a silver stand and several small wooden cups. 'May I offer refreshment?'

The Lord took the gourd. Calla took one of the cups and thanked the man, who nodded in response. The concoction tasted of cinnamon and cream and clover, and she could feel the kick almost before she had set it down.

'The Prime awaits you in the central pavilion,' the servant continued, and gestured, wide-armed, further into the wood. 'If you please.'

The Eternal had no conception of hereditary nobility. All were equal before the code of law that had been created at the foundation and passed down unchanged in the millennium since. All could trace their line to that period as well, and often did so, an hour-long monologue that Calla had heard the Aubade perform on more than one occasion. Each was fabulously wealthy, heir to the income of the great farms surrounding the city as well as to a portion of the tithes presented to the Roost by the human nations of the continent – though, in general, money meant nothing to them, and in practice Calla herself was responsible for keeping track of the Aubade's finances.

Thus the Prime could not be said to rule exactly; she gave no orders, possessed no special powers or rights. It was her quality that imbued the rank with meaning, rather than the reverse. For even amongst this race of near-divines, there were none to match her – not in wealth, not in dignity, not in beauty nor in accomplishment. Her estate was the largest in the Roost, a sprawling thing that dwarfed even the Red Keep, itself one of the larger of the Eternal's estates. She was regarded as the greatest practitioner of all the arts that defined their culture – her incense was the subtlest and most pleasing, her brushwork finer than any other, her skill with harp and lute unparalleled. In the Conclave her counsel was regarded as much the wisest and most temperate, though in the last war against Aeleria she had been at the vanguard, and acquitted herself with noteworthy ferocity. Across the length and breadth of the First Rung, which was to say the Roost, which was to say the world, there was simply none to match her.

None but the Aubade – Calla had her pride, after all.

But even she could not pretend that there was anything in the Red Keep to compare with the grandeur of the Prime's estate. The woods they walked through made the east aviary seem positively diminutive by contrast. It had been three hundred years since the Lord's father had brought the first cuttings to the Red Keep, but the Lady's forest was far older, went back almost to the Founding. Each seedling had been carefully chosen, planted in some infinitely distant past, lovingly cultivated, pruned and shaped. It was a living masterpiece, a millennium of careful planning married to virtually unlimited resources.

The path got smaller before disappearing altogether a half-cable into the forest. Calla held her breath in expectation.

'They'll find us soon,' the Aubade said.

Calla blushed. 'Is my excitement so obvious, my Lord?'

He neglected to answer, continuing forward into the wood, seemingly without direction. Even with the path gone the walk was easy, the ground a soft carpet of moss, undisturbed by weed or prickly bush. The late-summer foliage would be gone within a week, and in defiance it seemed to throw itself into one last explosion of colour, fireweeds and flecks of white hellebore and bright yellow strands of trumpet vine. Threads of sunlight leaked through the canopy above, but it was difficult to make out anything much further ahead, beyond a general impression of beauty and of soft, green, living things.

The Lord noticed it first, of course, and waved in its direction, though it took a while for Calla to make it out amidst the camouflage of flowers. But after the first became clear she quickly noticed more, hiding among the trees, gazing at her shyly.

The personal bestiary of the Prime was as famous as the reserve that surrounded them, a menagerie of creatures unique to her demesne, cultivated by generations of her ancestors and the Lady herself. Foremost among them were the velvet deer, and Calla could see why. They were the size of large dogs, hornless and wide-eyed. Their coats were reddish purple, notable even at this distance for the fine quality that had given the animals their name.

Calla brought her hands up to her lips, as if to catch the escaping sigh.

One of the deer was trying to work up the nerve to approach, dancing forward a few steps, then back again. Calla laughed and clapped her hands, and the beast spurred away shyly. But by then the other deer had lost their inhibitions, and they began to arrange themselves around the Lord and his party. They evinced neither fear nor wariness, indeed seemed to be gazing at Calla with the same interest and wonder as she at them. After a moment one came forward and nestled itself against her. She laughed again.

'Oh, my Lord,' she said. 'How magnificent.'

'She is a wonder, the Prime.'

The herd had accepted them completely now, sniffing at the bearers and the packages they carried, blinking up at the Aubade. After a moment some of their number began to draw away, but slowly and with frequent backward looks.

'Best follow them,' he said, and proceeded to do so. Calla could barely bring herself to break away from the creature that was, even now, rubbing her softly with its long neck, as glorious and carefree as a sunbeam. But she managed it – there were other wonders yet to explore, she reminded herself.

Their escort frolicked circles around them as they walked, pausing to nibble at the flowers or drink from the little streams running through the grounds. These last were clear as crystal and babbled kindly and were dotted with wide, flat stones so one could cross without wetting one's feet. Running along the bank were brightly coloured clusters of giant mushrooms, thick-stalked things that came up to her knee, bright red caps flecked with white. The flickering sunlight weakened and withdrew, and as prelude to evening the bell crickets struck up their tune, each variant chirruping in a different pitch and rhythm, the resultant symphony as complex and subtle as anything that could be written with four fingers or five.

They began to see other parties in the distance. Each had begun their journey at a different quay, but the wiles of the velvet deer had ensured they progressed towards their final destination. By custom they were not to speak to each other until they had been greeted by the hostess, and so each group continued as if ignorant of the others.

The central pavilion had been built over a small lake, atop a floating wooden platform. An intricate net of walkways radiated out from the tent, the freshly painted banisters wrapped with vines and flowers. The pavilion itself looked like a large silk tent, coloured verdant green to match the forest, but Calla somehow felt certain there was more to it, and was eager to discover whether she was correct. It wasn't until she grew close that she realised the velvet deer had disappeared back into the forest, their purpose fulfilled. An unpleasant reminder that time continued its progress.

The Prime stood on the pathway leading into the floating web, greeting each guest in turn. She was dressed in a skintight gown that covered her completely from neck to ankle but somehow hid nothing. Her hair was shaped into a sphere fully nine links in diameter, stained jet black. Her face was painted with gold leaf. Her eyes were a blue so dark as to be nearly black. She did not smile, but had she, you'd have seen her teeth were white and straight and perfect. Beaming down from the apex of her comb was a diamond every bit the size of a fist – the fist of an Eternal, to clarify, not a human. It was the only outward signifier of her position.

'Prime,' the Lord said, performing the bow of greeting fluidly.

'My Lord of the Red Keep,' she said, returning the courtesy. 'I greet you on behalf of the Lord of the Ivory Towers and the Lady of the East Estate, on the occasion of their binding.'

Those Above consummated sexual relationships with the frequency and ritual of a bowel movement, but to commit oneself fully to another was as rare as a double moon, and one celebrated with all the extravagance of which the Eldest were capable. It meant not only that the participants were to adhere to the most rigid standards of monogamy, but also that the pair intended to reproduce, an event always rare among the Eternal and particularly so in the current age.

'I accept your greeting,' the Aubade said. 'And I hope that their union is a fertile one, that brings honour to the Roost and to their line.'

This was part of the formula, the same exchange that the Prime was waiting to perform with the rest of the guests in line behind them. No doubt there was more that they might have said to each other; but decorum reigned over everything in the life of the High, and anyway, the evening was far from over.

Calla followed the Aubade across the walkway, felt it sway faintly. The lake itself was marvelously clear, swarms of iridescent fish darting through the depths, ebullient and wondrous and forgotten as soon as she caught close sight of the pavilion. Twelve cells surrounded the main chamber, separated by pure silk walls of different colours and complementary patterns, doorways cut into it on each side. By some cunning contrivance each wall had been set to revolve in alternating directions and at slightly different speeds, and occasionally the openings would align and one could see deeper into the heart of the pavilion, at the pleasures awaiting therein. Whatever engine drove its revolutions was invisible, and made so little noise as to be drowned out by the partygoers and the soft music.

In the first chamber the walls were azure with gold trim, and a staff of humans awaited to take the slippers of the new arrivals, and to wash their feet in basins of heated water. In the second chamber the walls were orange with pink offsetting, and cool drinks and warm towels were presented to revive the guests after their journey. In the third the walls were crimson with sterling silver, and couches had been set up around bright crystalline water pipes. They continued like that, each room more fabulous than the next, and hard though Calla tried she would not be able to remember all of them afterwards.

Deeper into the pavilion a cell had been set aside for gifts, and the bearers who had accompanied Calla and the Lord were finally able to relieve themselves of their burdens. After doing so a member of the Prime's staff led them back the way they'd come, out of the pavilion and presumably to some sort of waiting area. Only the Eldest and their highest-ranking servants were allowed to enjoy the cornucopia of delights the Prime had prepared. If Calla did not give the three porters a second thought, it must be said in her defence that there was much for her to think of at that moment.

With the gifts delivered and the bearers gone, Calla was able to spend a few minutes exploring the pavilion on her own. Some of the High insisted on keeping their servants near them at all times, but the Aubade was not one to have his hand held. In a sea-blue chamber further towards the core Calla found Sandalwood inspecting one of the silk curtains, looking handsome in his long green robes, if not quite young. He had been the Seneschal for the Lord of the Sidereal Citadel for fifteen years, though she had known him far longer, since she was a small child. He had been like an elder brother to her, growing up. He had been more than that for a time. What they were now, it was hard to say. A friend, at the very least.

'The Pavilion is our work,' he began. 'It took my Lord a week to conceive of it, and us six months to build. It'll be destroyed come morning,' he continued, wistfully but not unhappily. The Lord of the Sidereal Citadel, known among the low-born as the Wright, was famed as the most brilliant and forward-thinking of all the steam workers who graced the First Rung.

'It is magnificent,' Calla said, because it was and because she wanted him to be happy. She wanted everyone to be happy, that night; and it even seemed like everyone might be.

'It was no small thing to get each cell to run opposite the next,' he said, shaking his head ruefully. Though in fact he was the sort of person who never seemed happier than when he was in the midst of solving some technical problem. 'Has there ever been anything like it?'

The floor, which in the rest of the pavilion consisted of woven reeds, was in this chamber alone formed of one unbroken plate of glass, offering unobstructed views of the lake below. Bobbing along beneath was an array of floating crystal lanterns, through some genius of construction inextinguishable. Prismatic carp swarmed around these bubbles of illumination, while shifting-hued octopods crawled along the lake floor. Moustachioed catfish, so fat and mean-looking that even the squid seemed uninterested in disturbing them, floated lazily through the water grasses, proud as any Eternal.

'No,' Calla said confidently. 'There has not.'

He smiled and trailed his hand down her back. She leaned into him, and they stood together silently for a few moments.

The Woodcock's hour chimed, signalling that it was time for the ceremony to begin. The guests, four- and five-fingered alike, found themselves filtering back outside, to the long circular platforms extending out from the main pavilion. Half of the Eternal in the Roost were crowded out along the floating deck, along with their human servants, and Calla could not find much of a view.

Although for once that evening, there was not very much to see. The Eldest had no gods to swear by, and there was no officiant to perform any ritual. The Lord of the Ivory Towers and the Lady of the East Estate, each dressed in traditional and elaborate finery, swore loyalty to each other, gave succinct but lovely promises of fidelity. Then Those Above gave a whistling cheer in their foreign tongue, the humans remaining silent, and the couple joined hands and walked deeper into the pavilion, and deeper still, the spinning sections quickly obscuring them from view. They would continue on to the heart of the tent, and there they would consummate the union, the blessings of their act shaking centrifugally out to all those in attendance.

With the departure of the couple, the festivities could begin in earnest. Drink flowed more freely, Those Above spoke louder; even the humans began to unwind, to flirt and chatter among themselves. Between the warm afternoon and the long walk over and, perhaps, the libations in which she had indulged, Calla found herself a touch overhot, was pleased to forsake the pleasures inside the pavilion for the cool evening air.

And by now it was well and truly evening, a fact reinforced by the arrival of the glow-bugs, whole flocks of them appearing as if by magic. Another product of the Lady's long breeding, each individual insect produced light in a different colour, though by some strange instinct those of a similar hue grouped together, swarming clouds of crimson and cerulean and heliotrope winking in and out of the firmament. Hanging from the boughs of the trees were open silver cages baited with some sort of sweet or scent that drew in the flickering creatures, creating a living source of illumination softer and clearer than any lantern.

White-robed servants brought trays of food and drink for Eldest and human alike. The edibles were as magnificent as everything else that evening, though Calla could not bring herself to eat more than a few nibbles. She felt as if she could subsist on nothing but the warmth of the evening, on the sounds coming from the forest, on the reflection of the moon against the lake, on beauty itself.

Tonight's festivities aside, the Wellborn saw sex as a pleasant indulgence and little more. In and of itself it indicated no particular passion, or even affection, nothing beyond a brief spark of lust. Like their other customs, this had filtered down to the humans who served them, and to the higher reaches of the Roost more generally. Calla noticed no few members of other households drag smiling eyes over her body; found herself doing the same, nakedly and without shame. And why not? If ever there was a time for love to stand triumphant, was it not tonight?

She could see the Wright and the Lady Sweet Blossom talking quietly, standing near the southern bridge, and then the next moment they were eloping into the foliage. Here and there the woods played echo to the faint sounds of lovemaking, another strand to be added to the chorus of bell crickets and nightbirds. Calla drank a second glass of the cinnamon liquor she had been given at the start of their journey, and could feel it in her stomach and her cheeks and in the tips of her hair.

Amidst the soft bustle of joy the Lord leaned over one of the rails, staring out at the lake and the night beyond. He had not moved in a long time, and so Calla had not moved either, standing silently a short way off. There was much that made the Lord unique, Calla thought, even among his own kind. It was not only that he excelled in swordsmanship, in the strange and subtle movements of their dance, in the even stranger and more subtle workings of their poetry – indeed, it was these things least of all. The Lord carried with him, in a way no other Eldest could be said to, an ineffable sense of destiny, or of tragedy, which are perhaps the same thing. It was this that set him apart from the run of his fellows – not that he was their superior, but that he did not seem to value that superiority.

Calla was not the only one to notice it. Household servants shot him sidelong glances, lost themselves in the perfection of his face, stumbled as they walked and looked away, blushing. Sandalwood, his obligations discharged now that his lord had retired for the evening, stood silently within earshot, though Calla had to admit the possibility that it was she whom his attentions had fixed on, rather than her lord.

Nor was it the Five-Fingered alone on whom the Aubade exerted such a pull. The Prime herself broke off a conversation to approach him, a pair of human servants in her train. 'Who could judge, between the moon and the Lord of the Red Keep?'

The Aubade took a long time to wrench free of his contemplation. 'The Lord of the Red Keep will not be here to look at tomorrow evening.'

'And how does that weigh the scales? Do we herald the Lord for his transience, or the moon for its fidelity?'

'Is a thing not more beautiful because we know it will end? Indeed, is its end not what makes it beautiful?'

'If past evenings are any indication,' the Prime continued, the peerless diamond above her forehead reflecting the light, 'the moon will leave us sometime before the morning. And we will have long hours to lament its absence, and to hope for its return. And when it blesses us again, what joy we will feel at its homecoming, how we will cherish its light, for ever constant in its inconstancy.'

'Of the moon one may speak of for ever,' the Aubade said. 'But we who stand beneath it mark time with the beating of our hearts. Eternity is no blessing to us, as impossible as it is unwanted.'

'Impossible, certainly – but unwanted?' She brought herself to stand directly in front of the Aubade and set two fingertips against his chest. 'Would it really be so terrible to spend an eternity in my arms?'

If the Lord thought so, he did not say it. They stood there, silhouetted against the evening, and Calla swelled with the beauty of it, of the night and of everything that she had seen over the last few hours. It all seemed so perfect that she thought just then of dying. And how wonderful the Aubade had been, and how glorious the Prime! And how much she hoped that they might perform the night's ceremony themselves during her short span, and imagine the festivities that would accompany such a union!

Calla sighed. Sandalwood looked up at her sharply, then back at the lake.

The two Eternal remained still for a moment, silhouetted against the night but somehow beyond it. And then the Lady took the Lord's hand and led him off the bridgework and further into the evening.

Calla held the cuff of her robe up to her eyes for a moment. Sandalwood, ever decorous, avoided noticing. When the Lord and Lady were well out of earshot, however, he leaned over and spoke quietly. 'You grow careless,' he said. 'It is not enough to be a mute observer, you must be a deaf one as well.'

'They must know that we understand *something*,' Calla responded.

'Who knows what they know? It was not so long ago that the Seneschal of the Iron Mistress was put to death for overhearing his lady.'

'It was a hundred years past.'

'How much time do you think that is to them?' Sandalwood put his hand atop hers. 'I wish you would heed my advice.'

And herein lay the rub, because first and foremost, Calla knew, he wished that she would heed his advice regarding the proposal of marriage that had been standing between them for the better part of five years. The first man she had ever loved, and she could remember why – older than her but still handsome, his cheeks sharp lines and his chest the same. Clever and wise, which were not at all the same thing, and kindly, or as much as you could expect from a man. But Sandalwood had been her father's protégé and best friend, and seemed bent on trying to fill his absence. Calla had loved her father, esteemed him immensely, missed him daily. But she did not think he required a replacement.

All the same it was such a beautiful night that there was no sense in feeling anything the least unpleasant, and by unspoken agreement the subject was dropped. The nightbirds had awoken to greet the rising moon, which was full in the clear sky. There was enough light to make out the skin of a lover, but not so much as to rob the evening of its secrets. Calla and Sandalwood sipped slowly from their drinks, and looked out over everything there was to see. And then, after a few minutes had passed, she took his hand as the Lady had taken the Lord's, and walked him deeper out into the gardens, and they nested down amidst the wonder.

7

The Fifth Rung would see blood that night. It was too hot for anything else.

At street parties and in taverns guys looked at guys looking at their girls (or girls they wanted to be their girls), started cracking their knuckles and drinking to get mean. Long-suffering mothers stared across dinner tables at their progeny and saw voracious ingrates swallowing every groat they had and whining for more, nasty little brats that would get what was coming to them, ought to have got it sooner. Fathers looked at their wives over bowls of burnt stew, and how could you burn stew, worst cook on the damn Rung but she ate enough of it, must have gained two clove in the last year. Long-simmering feuds broke out into open violence, friends became enemies, enemies became corpses. There would be work for the Cuckoos come the morrow, if the Cuckoos ever did any work. Since they didn't, there would be work for the gravediggers.

In the Barrow, Thistle and Felspar and Treble and Rat and the two Calc brothers and a couple of other hangers-on were getting drunk on black whiskey in the shadow of the pipes. The pumphouse had been out of use since before Thistle's father's father had been pushed out of Thistle's father's father's mother. Two generations of hardbitten Barrow kids had been using it as a squat ever since, and left behind ample evidence of their existence. A cenotaph of cigarettes, a sepulchre of broken bottles.

It was two months since they'd had a good scuffle with the kids down by the docks, during the high-summer festival, and they'd come off worse from it, driven back to the Barrow in a hail of cobblestones and broken bricks. Course the dockers had been a few boys up on them, and had got lucky, it was universally agreed by those present at the pumphouse that evening, and anyway tonight was the night when they'd even up the tally, even up and maybe go a few ahead.

Thistle had a half-bottle in him and stood twenty links tall. Would have if he'd been standing, at least, though in actual fact he was sitting on a step, letting Petal braid his hair. Petal had hit womanhood before her fourteenth birthday, shot up two links and gained weight in the sort of places a fellow might notice. At the time it had been a source of intimidation to the boys, who were indisputably still that and not men. But a few years down the line Thistle felt distinctly differently about the flesh that was straining its way out of the cheap cotton dress she wore.

'I don't see why you've got to go down there at all,' she was saying, hands threading Thistle's black hair deftly. 'Y'all just like to make trouble.' Amber and Button echoed agreement, the latter seated happily on Felspar's lap, the former wedged between the first and second Calc brothers. There might be some dispute over who was in charge among the males, but there was no such confusion for that equivalent portion of the Barrow's fairer sex. Petal's opinion was the law, and better than, because the Cuckoos didn't generally bother to come this far downslope and ensure it was upheld, while Petal had no problem cracking the whip should anyone get out of hand.

'You wouldn't understand,' Felspar said grandly, situating his hands midway between Button's ample buttocks and small breasts. 'We owe them for what they did to Rat.'

Rat stopped drinking long enough to buck up at the sound of his name. A month or so after the last big brawl he'd been caught by his lonesome somewhat too close to the water, got a pretty decent beating for his lack of caution. 'They owed,' Rat agreed.

Which was true as far as you figured it, but then, the Barrow boys had been owed for when Thistle had dropped a stone on one of the dockers from the third floor of an abandoned tenement. Been aiming for the boy's head but hadn't hit it – hit his leg, however. Which had been fun and all, but which you had to admit offered the crew downslope a legitimate grievance.

'It's a question of honour,' Felspar finished, reaching over and taking a pull from Rat's whiskey. They'd bought the liquor they were drinking using money Felspar had stolen from his mother's purse while she was visiting the outhouse, though if anyone noticed the contradiction they kept silent on it.

It was an old game, but a good one. Petal might pretend otherwise, but she was as hot for blood as Thistle or Felspar or Treble, more maybe, cause at the end of the day it wasn't her skin in the game. Petal was too much of everybody's girl to ever be altogether Thistle's, but she'd been seeing more of him this last month or two than she had anybody else. So far they hadn't more than necked, endless hours pressed tight against each other, hours that had long gone from exciting to routine to flat dull, his tongue tired from overwork and his cock sore as a broken thumb. But that wouldn't last much longer. She was ready, Thistle could feel it, the instinct of the species making up for his own personal ignorance. She'd preened herself before coming down to the pumphouse, and she'd manouevred Thistle's back into the hollow of her breasts. If he returned with a docker's blood slick on his fists she'd let him take her up to the roof and slide her dress up her legs and Thistle would finally get a shot at what he'd been dreaming of ever since he'd woken up one morning a few years back with sticky thighs. Come back from the docks a conqueror, and later that night he might even end up a man.

'The dockers ain't like us,' Felspar was saying, more because he liked to hear himself talk than because he thought what he was saying made sense. 'They're not real Roostborn.'

'The docks aren't part of the Roost?' Rat asked.

'Of course the docks are part of the Roost. But the kids who live there, they're all the bastard sons of whores and sailors, their blood is as foreign as a Dycian orange.'

'What kind of sense do you think that makes?' Rat asked. 'Don't none of us come from here, you go far back enough.'

'Birdshit!' Felspar pulled his hand off Button's arse and slapped it against his chest. 'My people go back since the Founding, since the Time Below.'

'So you've been a slave the longest?' Thistle growled. 'Congratulations.'

Thistle found the pretence that they had a real reason for walking down to the docks and breaking down anybody they found there, that they needed a real reason, nonsense. Thistle didn't have any true hate for the dockers, not hate like he had for the folk upslope, not hate like he had for the Cuckoos or the Four-Fingers. They weren't any different to him, when it came right down to it; if any of the dockers had been born half a cable upslope they'd have been his brother, as much as Treble or Rat. But a man needs something to die and kill over, that's what makes him a man – and if half a cable was all you had, then half a cable would have to do.

Been enough fucking talk, was what Thistle thought then, and he stood up from the step, grabbed the mostly empty bottle from out of Rat's hand, made it all the way empty and dashed it against the wall. 'Let's go.'

A spark dropped on dry grass. Treble was up first, Rat a close second. Felspar gave Button a quick kiss on the neck, then scooted her up off his lap. The Calc brothers both tried for the same, but either Amber hadn't made her mind up about which of the two she had it for, or she didn't have it for either, cause she danced off, laughing merrily.

Petal stood up also, and in the moment Thistle didn't notice her bad skin or the way her eye sort of drooped. He grabbed her by the back of the neck, pulled her into a firm kiss, pressed his mouth against hers, hard, too hard, heard her moan, pushed her away and started walking downslope, certain that he wouldn't be walking alone.

Lock your doors and hide your ladyfolk, the Barrow boys were on the march.

Treble took the lead as usual, but Thistle was right behind him. Felspar had picked up a little wicker switch, was hooting and swinging it back and forth. Rat stopped every fifteen seconds to howl at the moon, low in the sky but getting higher. The Calc brothers were holding up the rear and helping fill in Rat's chorus, hollering back and forth to each other.

The burnt-out house on the intersection of Garden Street and Fallow was widely considered the demarcation line between the two territories, and as they passed it Felspar scampered up a sidewall onto the little bit of the second floor that remained extant. He clutched a support beam with one hand and leaned himself out over the ether, screaming his challenge into the night.

Thistle was thinking maybe they'd have to march further downslope, smash a window or two, make enough trouble to draw the dockers into battle. But the weather down by the bay was as torrid as it was at the Bowery, and the mood was the same. Felspar hadn't been giving out their war-call for more than a minute or two when Thistle heard it being answered from out of the gloom, their rival pack spitting strands of doggerel as they came to offer combat.

They'd come with an extra soldier, but that was fine as far as Thistle was concerned – a man from the Bowery was worth a man and a half from anywhere else, and Treble you had to figure was worth at least two. Though they'd been born less than a cable from each other, Thistle had never met one of them outside of a street fight. Thistle supposed that had a stranger been unfortunate enough to walk through the docks that night, they wouldn't have seen much difference between the two packs of rowdy, badly dressed youths. Had that theoretical stranger been foolish enough to say anything to that effect, however, he'd have found his words had a conciliatory effect on the two parties, encouraging them to redirect their violence towards his person.

'What you trash coming round for?' one asked. Thistle had used to think of him as the cocksucker with the patchy beard, but after Thistle had dropped a stone on the boy, he had mentally switched nomenclature to that motherfucker who is lucky to just have a limp. Whatever his real name was, he seemed to be the head of his crew in the same rough sense that Thistle was the head of his. 'Didn't you get enough of us last summer?'

'No!' Treble stuttered, and not for the first time Thistle wished his friend was mute, or at least smart enough to pretend.

Felspar had slipped down from off his heights and taken up a spot near Thistle. 'Don't know what the hell you're talking about. The Barrow runs right down to Cooper Street. The question is, what the fuck are you doing out of your territory?'

'Fallow Street is the border,' the leader said. 'Always was.'

'How about we sprint for it?' Thistle asked quietly, and with an ugly smirk.

The boy who couldn't walk right any more shot Thistle a look of pure and violent hatred, something beyond the passions they were all about to exercise. He maybe had reason to, Thistle had to admit. Taking someone in a straight fight was one thing, even jumping an unlucky sucker with your boys – but what Thistle had done was out of bounds, out of bounds even by the loose and anarchic standards of the Fifth.

Ahh, fuck him. Fuck all of them, and fuck this parley nonsense altogether. There wasn't anything at stake in this conflict except blood and honour, and neither of those could be satisfied with talk. The only question was whether they were going to make the jump from fists to weapons, whether the losers would end up bruised or buried. So far the running feud between the two sides had stayed short of making corpses, but there was a first time for everything, wasn't there? Thistle had his blade stuffed into his waistband, and he knew Treble had one hidden somewhere as well. The younger Calc brother was still carrying one of the bottles, and that could be turned deadly without much effort. Thistle would be surprised to discover that the dockers hadn't come to the party with a similar set of favours. All he needed to do to set it off was reach down into his trousers and whip out the blade, and there would be corpses in the evening and weeping mothers come the morrow.

For some reason he didn't, though one of these nights he figured he probably would.

'You dockers reek more than a Parthan outhouse,' Felspar continued.

'You kiss your mother with that mouth?'

Felspar grabbed himself with his off hand. 'I fuck your mother with this dick.'

And then the two lines rushed together in a mad scrum, kicking and clawing and screaming and biting, and the whole thing devolved into a formless melee.

Thistle squared off against a pie-faced little cunt that he'd seen around but whose name he didn't know, not that he'd ever lower himself to know the name of a docker. The pie-faced cunt had a few links on Thistle but was filling those links with fat rather than muscle, and Thistle felt pretty confident he'd put the boy down but good. There was no technique to any of it, Thistle just bulled into the boy with his shoulder, tried to get him on the ground and finish him as soon as possible. Thistle worked best up close, where he could get his finger into an eye or latched against the inner pocket of a cheek, where he could claw and scratch and bite.

But the boy was faster than Thistle had expected and than his frame would suggest, shifted beneath the blow and gave one of his own, a short right that popped against Thistle's jaw. Gave another while Thistle was stunned, straight out against his nose, Thistle could feel it split and he stumbled backwards a step. The sight of Thistle's blood got the boy overeager, and he came strong at Thistle, hoping to end the whole thing quick. If he'd have known Thistle any better he'd have been more careful, because Thistle was never more dangerous than when he was on his back legs, and while the boy wound up for a finishing shot Thistle leaned in and tapped him on the chin hard enough to set him up on his arse.

Thistle was planning on making sure the boy didn't get up again, not for a while, but next to him Rat was coming off worse in a contest with a tan-skinned giant, some Aelerian-looking mother-fucker who might have given Treble a run for his groat, and loyalty took precedence over sadism. Thistle dived into the back of the boy's legs and they collapsed into a heap, a heap Rat was quick to throw himself atop. Even outnumbered and on the ground the boy proved almost more than they could handle, clipping Thistle in the chin with his elbow. But Thistle gave him a return blow that stunned the boy long enough for Rat to get a decent grip on him, pinning his arms together. Thistle had got back up to his feet and was just about ready to give the tan-skinned boy a reasonable hammering when a blow to the side of his head rocked him hard enough that his vision went blurry. Thistle rolled sideways with the force of the punch, trying to get out of range of any follow-up.

The fat boy had recovered more quickly than Thistle would have suspected, and if the bottom half of his face was starting to swell he was smiling through the purple, the shot he'd just offered to the back of Thistle's skull sufficient analgesic. And all of a sudden Rat and the Aelerian giant were forgotten. The rest of the combatants were forgotten, the evening and the sound of the pumps and the universal dock smell of salt water and sewage were forgotten. In all the world there was nothing but Thistle and this thing that had done him wrong.

Thistle screamed and charged.

And then he was pulled upward, arms pressed tight against his chest, and he was kicking back against whoever was doing it, trying to get free. Someone was saying something to him but they had to repeat it three or four times before he could make it out – 'Cool down, boy, cool down,' and even a few more times to realise that it was Rat speaking.

Thistle didn't listen, still trying to break free from the grip he was in and get back at the tattered thing that was lying on the ground before him. But whoever had him was too strong to break free of, and after a few more seconds of failure Thistle realised that it must be Treble, what with Rat being the one speaking, and he remembered distantly that Treble was his friend, or at least his ally, and he went slack.

When Treble finally dropped him, Thistle had largely threaded himself back into consciousness, though it took him a while longer to realise that the fighting had stopped, most of the dockers bailing once it was clear things had gone bad. Those who remained stood intermingled with Thistle's people, the rest of the conflict abnegated by this change of circumstance, and they were all staring at Thistle with the same look on their faces, something between fear and disgust.

The fat boy Thistle had been fighting was on the ground, and he had not moved in what seemed like a very long time. His face looked relatively little like a face.

He coughed finally, and rolled himself over to the side, and there was a collective gasp of relief on the part of the assembled party. Thistle didn't say anything, and if he was relieved to discover he wasn't a murderer you couldn't tell it by his manner. The boys from the docks that hadn't run off grabbed their injured comrade by the shoulders, pulled him to his feet and started to walk him back the way they'd come. Neither group said anything to the other; the truce was unofficial and temporary.

It was a victory, of sorts – at the very least the dockers wouldn't be calling the Barrow boys pussies for a while, maybe not ever again. But walking back upslope afterwards there was nothing of the air of conquering heroes about them, not in Rat who seemed like he might be sick, nor in Felspar who was likewise pale as a corpse. Even Treble's silence for once seemed to indicate more than just an inability to string together a sentence in its entirety.

For his part, Thistle spent the walk back trying to figure out how he felt about what he had done – whether he felt anything at all, whether he might have felt more if Treble hadn't stopped him from killing the boy whose name he didn't know.

8

It had been nearly two weeks, and Bas still wasn't rid of the smell of blood.

The day after the battle was spent in a riotous orgy of victory, fuelled by loot stripped from the dead Marchers and, Bas felt unpleasantly certain, the hoplitai themselves. It was nothing like what had been won during the war against Salucia, or on the day of Dycia's fall, but still, the weapons, jewellery and small money of twenty thousand men were more than enough to gorge the vast flock of scavengers that had been following the Western Army these last six months, to leave the liquor-sellers dry and the whores exhausted. The two days after that were spent burying corpses, taking their own to the communal pyres, dumping the vast heap of Marcher carrion into pits. Bas didn't do it personally, of course, that was one of the benefits of being Legatus, but you couldn't very well camp downwind of a charnel house four cables in diameter and think to avoid the stink. His time had been spent dealing with the remnants of the great

Marcher confederacy that had been wise enough to stay and accept Bas's terms, which were stark and non-negotiable.

On the fourth day Bas had taken his cavalry and started off after that smaller portion of the enemy army that had attempted to escape, and over the course of the next week he had fought two full engagements and any number of smaller skirmishes, cornering and shattering the fragments of the vast horde that only a few days earlier had hoped to unravel the entire western wing of the Commonwealth. The cataphracts only made up a small portion of Bas's forces, but the fleeing remnants of the Marcher forces were in no condition to fight, worked desperately to escape the Caracal and his men, died easy when escape proved impossible.

Mykhailo's confederation had ended that day on the battlefield, and Mykhailo along with it, ridden down during the final charge that had sealed the fate of his kinsmen. But the seeds of some future horde might grow from the remains of this one, the sinewy youths riding hard to the west on broken ponies returning some twenty years hence, their children and grandchildren in tow.

Bas was not a man to leave a job half done.

They had been chasing a band of soldiers from the Yellow Otter clan, the last significant force of free Marchers in existence. Chasing them and chasing them hard, for three days they'd been finding the corpses of ponies left behind in the wake of the retreat. Perhaps it was the brutal pace they had kept that made the Otter clan imagine they had escaped their pursuers. More likely they had simply been too tired to care any more, though even at the limits of exhaustion they should have known not to make camp without ensuring a line of retreat.

But they hadn't, and when Bas's forces had arrived around midnight they had blocked the one entrance into the canyon, eliminating any chance of escape. A scout had sneaked down just before dawn, come back with reports of women and children among the Marchers. Bas had sent a messenger out afterwards, his white flag bright in the opening light of day. 'Surrender before noon,' read the note he carried, 'and I will only claim the men.'

It was a half-hour before the allotted time, and they had yet to hear word. The cavalry was formed up, prepared to make good on the unspoken second half of the ultimatum. Bas and a few of his men were overlooking the bottleneck leading down into the gorge, watching for signs of movement.

'Why did they run, do you think?' Theophilus asked, the fresh scar running across his forehead an unappetising purplish-black. The result of a half-deflected war club, it was only the most obvious mark he had gained from the Battle of the Western Reaches, as it was already being called. Subtler, though in the long run more important, was a certain swagger to him in the days since, a roll in his step, a sneer on his lips, half forced but so what? Theophilus had acquitted himself well enough to deserve a modicum of bluster, been at the forefront of the charge that had shattered the Marcher centre. A certain amount of swagger was a good thing, anyhow. A certain amount of swagger kept a man alive. Too much swagger would kill him, of course, but Bas did not think Theophilus was in much danger of going in that direction.

Though Hamilcar swaggered more vigorously than any man Bas had ever met, and the gods had not yet seen fit to make him pay for it. The rest of his countrymen had stayed behind with the infantry, and in truth there was no good reason for their captain to be here without them. But Hamilcar could not be left out of anything, even a task as miserable and unglamorous as this. 'The Yellow Otter were a cousin tribe of Mykhailo's own,' he explained, after ten years as knowledgeable about the intricacies of the Marchers as any man not born among them could be.

'Mykhailo is dead and buried,' Theophilus said. 'Even the plainsfolk can't make so much of loyalty.'

'Never think yourself too certain of what goes on inside another's head,' Hamilcar responded. 'Though I doubt it was devotion that drove them to flee. More likely they supposed that having been so closely aligned with the hetman, they'd have a particularly bad go of it.'

Isaac leaned over off his horse, let a spiral of tobacco spit splash into the tall grass. 'It would have been better than what they're going to get now.'

No one had anything to add. The sun told Bas he had fifteen minutes before it would be time to lead his men down to the valley below, indiscriminately slaughtering anyone he found there. He pulled his sword out from its sheath, made sure it wouldn't catch on anything, put it back in its place.

'Will they surrender?' Theophilus asked.

'Better a sword than the stakes,' Hamilcar said.

'They'll surrender,' Isaac answered, sounding confident.

'We didn't,' Hamilcar said.

'And how did that work out?'

Bas was flexing his hand along the hilt of his sword, could feel that low hum in the pit of his stomach that he always got in the moments before it seemed he might have to kill something. It was something like nausea, though it never seemed to get bad enough for him to have to vomit.

'Three tertarum say they choose the stake,' Isaac said.

'You'd move so quickly to silver?' Hamilcar asked, the glint of money shining in his dark eyes and white smile. 'You must be awfully confident.'

'I'm three tertarum confident, as I said.'

'Certainty like that, a man ought to offer odds.'

'Two to three?'

'Three to five.'

Issac took his hand off the hilt of his weapon and offered it to Hamilcar, who pumped it happily.

Bas would have made good on his threat, if he'd been pushed to it. A volley or two from the small number of men with bows, just to soften them up, just to let them know there was no point, and then the mad rush of cavalry, the Marchers scattering most likely, and then riding them down against the cliff walls they had backed themselves into, the long, murderous game of hide-and-seek, mothers trying to silence their weeping children, old men dying with gallant futility. And then stripping the bodies of whatever bits of wealth they had on them, copper necklaces and semi-precious stones. He'd have done it, and he'd have collapsed on his bedroll later that night, exhausted by the day's events, and he'd have woken up the next morning and thought no more about it. Not much, at least.

But still, when Hamilcar shouted that he saw a lone rider approaching the path, Bas felt a twinge of something like happiness. It was no sort of a task, killing women and children, for all that he'd done it before.

The man they had sent to play chief had almost certainly not been that the day before the battle; just a youth who would never get the chance to grow older. His hand was bandaged, and he looked dirty and tired and miserable. But he did not look beaten, riding up the path with his back straight, and when he saw Bas his gaze did not quiver. 'You are the God-Killer?' the chief asked. He spoke Aelerian like he was trying to spit out some unpleasant-tasting food.

'Yes.'

'I am Yan. I speak for the rest.'

'And what do you say?'

'The women live?'

'We'll leave them the ponies and what food can be spared. They should be able to make their way over the river.'

'And the boy children?'

'What is a child?'

'Fifteen.'

Bas shook his head. A Marcher had two notches into his belt before he had reached ten and five. 'Twelve,' Bas said, though he didn't plan on inspecting each boy to make certain he wasn't twelve and six months.

The chief thought it over for a moment, then nodded. 'A half an hour,' he said next.

'Leave your weapons piled at the foot of the path,' Bas said. 'And lead your horses.'

The chief nodded. He looked the sort of tired from which you could imagine death might even be a release.

After he was out of earshot, Hamilcar broke into as elaborate and sustained a bout of cursing as Bas had seen in a lifetime spent among soldiers. It encompassed three different languages, and threatened acts of molestation against Isaac and his family that Bas thought excessively impractical.

Bas turned to Isaac, who was smiling from cropped ear to cropped ear. 'How soon can we send out a foraging party?'

'Ten minutes.'

'And how long before we'll have enough stakes?'

'There was a copse of trees towards the river. Two hours? Two and a half maybe?'

'Make it two,' Bas said.

Isaac nodded, saluted and went off to take care of the errand – but not before taking his three silver from Hamilcar.

Jon the Sanguine had won his sobriquet during the series of minor wars that had led to the absorption of the small nations bordering Aeleria and the March proper, after he had given his soldiers permission to sack a resisting town on a feast day. It was a name that dogged his step to the grave. 'The Blood-Letter', the Salucians called him, burned him in effigy from the walls of cities he was soon to capture, put a price on his head large enough to bankrupt a port town. But hate is a close cousin of fear, and few men had tried to collect. An officer Bas had once captured promised to tell everything he knew about the defences of his city so long as Bas did not hand him over to his superior to be eaten.

Eight years Bas had known Jon the Sanguine, and had never seen him partake of the flesh of a fellow human. He was a bitter, miserable, brutal sort, but he was neither cruel nor vindictive, took no exaggerated love of violence. The name was useful – the name was a weapon in and of itself. 'I would rather have my nickname,' Jon had told Bas once, in a rare display of intimacy, 'than half a thema in train.'

Bas had earned his title before he had ever met Jon, and he did not imagine any resident divinities were quaking in their celestial boots. But most of his life he had roamed the Marches – first as a child, then as a hoplitai, which was nearly the same thing, following on behind whatever halfwit the Senate had sent out to find creative ways of getting people killed. Later as a Komes, leading small forces of cataphracts into unsettled sections of the Marches, pouring oil on troubled waters or spilling out blood, case depending. And now these last few years as the Commonwealth's chief representative in the area, the seated arse on the Empty Throne, as far as the barbarians were concerned. If his name was not spoken with quite the reverence that Jon's was, still it was a heavy thing, a thing to take shelter beneath.

And what they said of him was this – the God-Killer did what was required. His word would not bend against you, nor in your favour. Mercy was as alien to him as cruelty. It wasn't exactly true, to Bas's mind, but he supposed it was close enough.

By the Aelerian way of thinking, the March lords had risen up in rebellion against the Empty Throne, had broken the oaths of fealty they had sworn. The punishment for rebellion was the stake, a sharpened piece of wood shoved from rectum to throat, the victim left to bleed out, though most died of shock before the operation was finished. This would be the lot of the starving men in the canyon below – quite the price to pay for the safety of their families.

Bas watched the young man they had made chief ride back towards the mass of his fellows, watched him deliver the news. They couldn't have hoped for anything else. Or perhaps they could – it was strange, the lies people believed. Regardless, there seemed to be no dispute among them, no contingent still wishing to fight.

It did not take long. Twenty minutes after Bas had spoken to their leader, the last free body of Marchers in the land approached the narrow defile that would lead to the end of their existence as an autonomous people. They walked willingly upslope, women first, then the soldiers – soldiers in theory, though you could barely call the band of stragglers that had managed to escape from Mykhailo's disaster that any more, bleary-eyed, beaten men showing more rib than their overworked horses. The women were worse off, or at least no better, skeletons in tattered dresses dragging children in their wake, or carrying babes still at suck. These last were the only ones that made any sound, a keen wailing that echoed loudly through the canyon, appropriate accompaniment to the scene.

Isaac and a troop of dismounted soldiers waited for them at the top of the slope, a larger force waiting to be called on if necessary, though it was obvious to anyone with eyes that the Marchers had no fight left in them. They seemed to have very little left of anything, too tired and beaten even to bid proper farewell to the womenfolk and children whose lives they were saving with their sacrifices. Husbands held their wives in tepid embraces, patted the heads of their sons and daughters but did not look at them. For their part, the fortunate survivors seemed bleary-eyed and exhausted beyond meaning, like fruit with all the flesh squeezed out. You could have mistaken it for stoicism, though in fact it was sheer exhaustion. It takes strength to mourn properly, and the Marchers were too tired to do anything but die.

The women and children were led to the rear, out of sight of what was to come. Bas's forces were travelling light, and had no excess of provisions, but they'd give what they could. With the disappearance of their families the mood among the men seemed to lighten. There was no one to keep a brave face on for any longer; the Marchers were free to make what terms with death they were able. Mostly they did not seem to fear its arrival. They looked more like drawings of people than people, or clay statues, as if whatever animating force was in them had already been extinguished. Isaac looked over at Bas, and Bas nodded, and Isaac led the captured Marchers to be slaughtered.

In a year, when the plainsfolk west of the river crossed to bring their cattle into the great Commonwealth-sanctioned fairs, they would ride past the rotting corpses of their cousins, a stark and horrifying foliage, the only forest within a thousand cables. And they would curse the name of the God-Killer, and the might of Aeleria, and they would keep their weapons sheathed.

If they looked very carefully, however, they would discover that this atrocity was half staged. To properly stake a man was an elaborate ritual, costly in time and effort. It took two men to tie the captive down, three if they fought, and of course they always did. And the act itself was not so simple either; even the bloodiest-minded of men took no great pleasure in it. Shoving a corpse on top of a stake, however, was a much simpler matter, and would have the same effect on any future passer-by. A dozen kneeling men, one hoplitai with a drawn dagger, and then the meat went on the stick. The act of butchering was an exhausting one, but as the executioner was given first pick of their victim's posses-sions, it was rarely necessary to assign anyone to it.

If the Marchers realised they had gained a reprieve – though perhaps reprieve was too strong a word – they gave no great signs of joy. They remained unfettered; there would have been no point in chaining them even if Bas had anything to chain them with, which of course he hadn't. Two weeks of misery, seeing the flower of their nation cut down, their hopes dashed against the rock like the skull of a newborn. They wanted it a little, Bas thought. But then, doesn't everyone?

Theophilus was vomiting into the roots of some nearby scrub-grass. Bas made a point of not looking at him as he spoke. 'You're relieved. Go find Isaac, make sure they've got enough men collecting stakes.'

'I'm fine, sir,' Theophilus insisted, though Bas could smell yesterday's dinner from ten steps away.

'That wasn't a suggestion,' Bas said, turning back towards the slaughter.

Theophilus nodded, too tired to argue, or be grateful. But as he slipped past Bas leaned over to him and said in a half-whisper, 'It gets easier.'

Theophilus looked up at him, white as a ghoul, and he nodded and walked back towards camp.

Bas had caught three hours of sleep in between arriving at the canyon and the first light of dawn, which brought the total for the last week to something like thirty. He could remember a time when he could spend days in the saddle without resting, as hard as any Marcher, or nearly so. But those days were gone, gone with the jet black of his hair. He had been carried through the course of the morning by the possibility that he would see combat before the end of it, but with that no longer a spur, exhaustion had returned. He had to fight to keep from blinking, each flicker of his eyelids offering slumber purchase against his waking mind. There was no particular reason to stay and watch this, it would continue just the same with him asleep on a bedroll. But Bas did not go to find one. It did not do to look away from these things. It did not do to forget what one was.

The yellowed grass, withered and dry after the long summer months, drank deeply. But then, the earth is never satiated, nor the things that walk above it.

It took an aide three calls to get his attention, and even then he managed to do little more than stare back at him irritably. 'What?'

'There's a messenger here to see you, sir. From the capital.'

That was unexpected enough to shake Bas out of his lethargy. He followed the aide away from the open-air abattoir he had created.

They were ten men strong, five from the army that Bas had left behind, the other five Imperial emissaries, to judge by their horses and how unhappy they looked to be here. A month ago you'd have to have been mad to come this close to the Pau River with only ten men, but after what the Marchers had endured Bas did not imagine banditry would be much of a problem, not for the next few years at least.

The man who greeted him was that brand of officer who had earned his post from being someone's nephew. You didn't see many of them out here on the Marches, presumably because most uncles don't have so much hate for their siblings' children. The man looked a little disappointed, and Bas couldn't blame him. He'd come to find the Caracal, a colossus of sharpened steel, eyes like a raging fire, a voice like the strike of lightning. All he'd found was a tired old man in a battered suit of chain.

'Legatus,' he said, striking a fist off his breastplate.

Bas returned the salute. 'You've a message?'

'From the Senate itself.' He nodded happily.

They stood there looking at each other.

'Are you going to give it to me?' Bas asked finally.

The man blushed, stammered some, reached into his purse and passed over a packet, along with a stream of apologies.

Bas ignored them and cracked open the seal. The parchment was soft vellum and still had the faint scent of perfume. It was dated a week back, just after word of the victory would have arrived by pigeon. The formal greetings took up half the first page, but Bas skipped past without really seeing any of it. What remained were three or four lines of intricately traced calligraphy that upended the world.

In recognition of the great and noble services you have provided to the Empty Throne, it is the privilege of the Senate to recognise you as Strategos. It is also the wish of the Senate that you return to the capital with all possible speed, that the state may thank you properly, and determine where in the Commonwealth your talents can be most effectively utilised. Legatus Alexios will take over your command.

Bas reached the end of the missive and went back to the beginning. When he had finished he repeated the exercise a third time.

The news that he had been promoted went through Bas's mind without triggering any hint of excitement, gratitude or even pleasure. It was no more than his due, given the recent victory – would have been a strange and deliberate slight had he not received it. It was the second part of the message that had struck him like a cudgel blow, left him confused and struggling with its obvious meaning.

Isaac had snuck up behind him, anxious to find out the news but trying not to show it. 'The foraging party has returned,' he said. 'Time to start planting some Marchers.'

Bas didn't answer, though after a moment he handed over the letter. His adjutant took it with some surprise. Bas watched his lips move silently for about a minute and a half, and then Isaac looked up at him blankly. 'We're going home?' he asked.

Bas shrugged. That was not the way Bas would have put it. That was not the way Bas would have put it at all.

9

Eudokia was in her bedroom, getting ready for the evening's festivities. In contrast to what most of the women attending the party would be wearing, Eudokia's outfit was distinctly traditional, even old-fashioned, though of course it made the best use of the figure that remained to her. When she'd been younger her tastes had run towards the innovative and occasionally the salacious, but in latter years she had cultivated a more conservative style. This enlightened simplicity was difficult to pull off, required fine attention, and Heraclius was making it no easier with his constant interruptions.

He was a scion of one of the lower bits of nobility, holding on to a name, a decaying manor in the provinces and very little else. He was big and strong and well formed, the muscles of his abdomen and arms clearly defined against the light. He never really did anything with all that meat, apart from occasionally carry her into bed, but then that was all she required of him. He was dressed in formal blue robes, which she had bought him some months back. Of course, he was never dressed in anything that she hadn't bought him, nor did he make use of anything for which she had not already paid. He had been her lover for two years now – no, Eudokia corrected herself, only a year and a half. That it seemed longer was not, to her thinking, a particularly good sign.

'Does the blue suit me, katkins?'

'I've told you before never to call me that,' Eudokia said, too involved in putting on her make-up to get properly angry.

'I can't help but think the green might go better with my eyes,' he said, not hearing or not listening.

'You look lovely as you are,' she said, which was true but which she also hoped would shut him up.

Quite the opposite effect, sad to say. 'Do I please my little katkins?' he asked, taking her by the arm and drawing her in nearer, reaching his other hand round to firmly grip her buttocks.

Eudokia wondered, as she had wondered many times in the past, why men suddenly grew engorged just when any attempt at serious affection were certain to set one's preparations back an hour. Presumably it was a veiled attempt at control, insistent that lust dominate any external considerations. Under different circumstances, Eudokia had no problem playing the submissive, even found it erotic. But, of course, that was play and tonight was mostly work. She pushed Heraclius away and went back to her make-up.

And he seemed to forget it quickly enough, returning to his dresser to continue his own preparations. 'Have you seen my gold chain?'

'Did you check your closet?'

'No.'

'Check your closet.'

Heraclius disappeared into said armoire, returned with a medal she had procured for him last year in recognition of a state service that he had never actually performed. 'It was in the closet,' he said, smiling that gorgeous smile that increasingly failed to hide the vacuity beneath.

'Next time,' Eudokia said, giving herself a final once-over before standing, 'check before asking me.'

He seemed dimly to recognise this as reproach.

'Now remember, dear. Wait forty minutes, then slip out the back door and come in through the front.'

Heraclius pouted, another affectation that he imagined to be ingratiating but which was really just insipid. 'Must we truly?'

'You'd rather we descend the main stairway arm in arm?'

'Who would object? You know as well as I do that once the Revered Mother commits an indiscretion the whole court adopts it as custom.'

This was more flattering than accurate, though it held a fair portion of honesty. In truth, Eudokia was little enough concerned about causing gossip. In matters political, there were still a handful of other players who imagined themselves her rival, but in the social arena, Eudokia's position was as secure as if she had been seated on a mountain of skulls.

'Well?' Heraclius asked, drawing close enough to her that she could smell through his perfume to the scent of his flesh beneath. 'Shall we throw caution to the winds and announce ourselves together? Why ever not?'

When at all possible, Eudokia preferred not to lie. A lie was an admission of weakness, evidence that you needed to fear the target of your dishonesty. Occasionally imperative, never preferable and, in this circumstance, happily unnecessary. Eudokia allowed herself to be pulled tighter, gave Heraclius a light kiss where his neck joined his shoulder. 'Because I don't want you stealing any of my shine, darling,' she said, retreating and smoothing out her dress. 'Forty minutes, no sooner.'

Eudokia left a sulking child in her bedchamber, though it did nothing to dampen her spirit.

The herald announced her just as she reached the top of the staircase, and she descended with the slow grace that had long since become second nature. The party was in full swing – the chamber musicians talented, the dancers beautiful, the food excellent, the decor bright and stylish. This all but went without saying

109

– it was her party, after all, and among her manifold other accomplishments, it was widely agreed by that swathe of Aelerian society whose opinion mattered that the Revered Mother had no close second when it came to playing host.

Eudokia could see Prisca making a beeline for her almost as soon as she had reached the floor, a small, plump, dark-haired girl dressed in a perfect reproduction of the moment's high fashion, though somehow without the personal style that would have rendered the costume complete. 'Revered Mother, please, do you have a moment?'

Prisca's eyes were magnificently bright, and between that and her pleasant if lopsided smile, she managed to slip just barely onto this side of pretty. 'Of course, darling. There's a seat in the corner I'd be happy to fill. These shoes were not meant for standing.'

Prisca so hummed with enthusiasm that it was a struggle for her to remain silent during the minute-long trek to the side alcove. When they arrived she all but flung herself into the cushions, began her chatter even before Eudokia was seated.

'I can't wait any longer, Mother, I swear, not another moment. He's all I think about, day and night.'

Eudokia made soothing sounds and scanned the gathering, keeping careful count of the faces, ensuring that the evening's actors had all arrived.

'Father's dead set against it of course.'

'Fathers are always against their daughters marrying,' Eudokia said, forcing her eyes back to the girl. 'It's the way of the world.'

'He says Galerius is only interested in our money, and that we haven't very much anyway, and that if I only wait a little while longer he'll make a match that will have me forget Galerius completely.'

'Your father is a wise man,' Eudokia half lied.

'He's a fool! I could never forget Galerius. As soon ask the flower to forget the sun!'

'Ask the flower to forget the sun' had been the refrain to one of the more grating of last season's popular ditties. Eudokia had forbidden it to be played in her presence, but the thing had taken off anyway. Likely Prisca didn't even realise she'd stolen the line.

'He's the noblest man in the whole kingdom,' she continued, 'and the handsomest!' Though Eudokia felt confident that it was the second that Prisca found more important. 'And his eyes, Mother, have you seen his eyes?'

'Both of them.'

'You mock me, Mother, and perhaps you are right to do so. I know I can sound like a girl, but my love is as true and honest as anyone ever felt for anyone.'

This was a rather definitive statement to be making of such a vast swathe of the world and its history, Eudokia thought. 'Your passion does you credit, but your father's will is iron. You know as well as I that his consent is necessary for your betrothal, and that he will not give it.'

'Revered Mother, surely there must be something that you could do?'

'Me?' Eudokia said it as if the idea had never occurred to her. 'It saddens me to say this, but the vagaries of fortune have placed your father and me in somewhat opposing camps. I don't imagine he'd take kindly to any suggestions on my part.'

Prisca said nothing for a time, her face flushing rose, trying to work up the courage to spit out her request. It was some way from fascinating, especially as Eudokia already knew the punch-line – had written the joke in its entirety, in point of fact. 'Revered Mother, if only Galerius had some government position, something that would prove his suitability, I'm sure I could convince my father to allow our marriage. Oh, Mother, you don't suppose . . . I don't suppose . . . you don't imagine . . .'

But even Eudokia had limits to her patience, and while she would have preferred Prisca to be the first one to raise the issue, she couldn't very well wait around all night for the girl to remember her words. 'That I might find an office befitting a man of Galerius's talent and ability?'

Prisca nodded frantically.

Eudokia struck her index finger against her cheekbone twice, in even rhythm. 'Voting for Second Consul is next month. I could put in a strong word for him among those electors who remain unaware of his quality.' Which would be the entirety of the population, Prisca excluded.

The girl was so beside herself with gratitude that she seemed on the verge of crying, a possibility that would only enmesh Eudokia further, and which she moved quickly to avoid. 'Think nothing of it, child, think nothing of it at all. To do my small part to bring together such a powerful love – well, I'm not so old as to have forgotten what youth was like.'

But that proved to be too much for Prisca, who succumbed completely to the tide of emotion, throwing her arms round Eudokia's shoulders and weeping salt water into her dress. Eudokia let her continue on like that for a few moments, somewhat less than thrilled, before pushing her away lightly. 'Find a bathroom, girl,' Eudokia said. 'Your make-up is all a-run.'

Prisca managed this task on her own, and Eudokia retreated to the main room. Irene was in the corner looking painfully beautiful, surrounded by a semicircle of men with ravenous eyes. Eudokia was slightly surprised to find Heraclius among the wolves. Presumably he imagined he was engendering some sense of jealousy by paying more attention to her handmaiden than to her, but in fact she was thrilled to have him out of her hair for a few hours, busy as she was. Irene gave Eudokia a little nod as she came in, then turned her attention back towards her suitors.

Konstantinos had arrived some time earlier, and the gala had predictably and gratifyingly celebrated his arrival with a sustained bout of applause, applause that he did a less than competent job of pretending he did not enjoy. There were moments when her adopted son looked so very much like her husband Phocas that it caught the breath in her throat. The same hair, dark as a clouded evening, the same brown eyes, at once jovial and vital, the same high cheekbones, the same shoulders. Phocas had been dead for almost three decades now, cut down at Scarlet Fields, the defining battle of the Seventh Other War, and still hardly a week passed that she didn't think of him. If he had lived, how different it all would have been.

Eudokia broke herself free from memory, went to save her stepson from his current predicament, cornered by the senatorial grandee of a rival faction.

'Our forefathers—' Manuel was pontificating, but Konstantinos was quick to take Eudokia's arrival as an opportunity to interrupt the senator, so Eudokia never enjoyed the benefit of whatever scintillating bit of wisdom the senator was about to bestow.

'Revered Mother,' Konstantinos said, greeting Eudokia with a quick kiss. Manuel settled for a stiff bow. The Incorruptible, they called him, though what vice could be found in exchanging basic pleasantries, Eudokia could not figure.

'Dearest child,' Eudokia returned. 'Senator.'

Manuel Ogust, senator and protector of the Empty Throne, was easy to spot, inevitably the worst-dressed person in a crowd. As part of his claim to an anachronistically rigid sense of morality, Manuel steadfastly refused to adhere to fashion, making do with an undyed robe of coarse cotton – the same style of dress that had been popular in the days when the Throne had been filled. Supposedly, at least, though Eudokia found it hard to imagine she had ever had an ancestor so lackwitted as to wear hemp when silk was available. The robes were a clever bit of political propaganda, but they'd have served as well had he worn the costume in public, and made do in private with some form of dress that did not hold odour as a jail does convicts.

Apart from his choice of wardrobe, there was little enough in the man of interest. He was a fine speaker, if you liked them loud and easy to understand – which for most people was the very height of genius. He had never taken a bribe in his life, or at least never been caught doing so. He ate simply, abstained from drink, eschewed luxuries of all kinds. The common folk considered his abstemiousness evidence of the most rigorous sort of morality, but Eudokia knew it to be nothing more than a fetish. That a man preferred sackcloth to silk was no evidence of moral genius, and if Manuel's vices weren't quite as obviously on display as his virtues, still they were clear enough if you looked.

Like everyone else, Eudokia had heard the rumour that beneath his robe of homespun cloth, he wore undergarments of the sort frowned on by the more decent type of whores. Eudokia had trouble imagining someone so boring could have such an interesting secret, though she liked believing it anyway.

'I was just warning your son on his latest victories,' Manuel said.

'Congratulating, I think you mean.'

'I choose my words with care,' Manuel said, eager to find offence in anything.

By Enkedri, it was like having a conversation with a rabid dog. 'Your eloquence, of course, is renowned throughout the furthest reaches of the Commonwealth,' Eudokia said, hoping to placate him.

Manuel swallowed the encomium smoothly and continued. 'Warned because victory is the bread of tyrants, as it is of fools. The people gorge themselves on easy successes – on the celebrations thrown in our honour, on the trains of foreign captives, on cheap wars of choice. They begin to think that all conflict is so inexpensive, and so fruitful, and they grow loud in their demands that it continue. Continue endlessly, without regard for the wisdom of the contest or the justness of the cause. A republic cannot be an empire.'

'The pirate-lords of the Baleferic Isles were a threat to all of our commerce in the south seas,' Konstantinos said. Manuel had snapped his gaze back onto the boy as soon as he had begun to speak, Eudokia forgotten entirely. 'We had no choice but to go to war against them.'

The war against the pirates had been nothing of the sort, but a punitive expedition against a weak and scattered force of bandits and renegades, leaderless, each island-despot leaping at the chance to avoid being executed by the vastly superior forces she had arranged for her stepson to command. That it was being touted as a victory of such importance by the common folk and even a few of the more foolish senators could be attributed to some combination of Eudokia's own machinations and the inherent gullibility of all people. More the latter than the former, most likely, but a fair deal of the former as well. She found the realisation that her propaganda had apparently been so effective as to seduce Konstantinos himself to be more disturbing than surprising. He had his father's shoulders, and eyes, and skill with a blade, and easy way with people. But the savage genius that had made her husband, even in the short time he had lived, one of the dominant men in the Commonwealth – that, sad to say, young Konstantinos would never possess.

That was fine, though. That was what Eudokia was there for, after all.

'We have been paying off the pirates since before I was sworn to office,' Manuel was saying. 'A thousand gold solidus each spring, and our merchants left free to ply their trade. Do you know what your little expedition cost? Thirty thousand solidus, and that's not including the upkeep on the garrisons. It's a strange victory that costs thirty times that of defeat. One wonders at the bargain.'

'No bargain at all, Senator,' Konstantinos began, gradually speaking louder in an attempt to be noticed without giving notice of it. 'The dignity of the Empty Throne is not for bargaining, not to be sold for twelve months of peace, not to be bartered away that we might save a few gold. Are we a nation of book-keepers, to prize riches above honour? Have we truly decayed so far from the nobility of our ancestors?'

Disadvantageous comparisons to the ancients were Manuel's stock-in-trade, and you could see that he did not appreciate being on the other side of the cliché. 'The dignity of the Empty Throne rests on the happiness of its people, on their commerce and on their labour. It took two thousand men to break the back of the pirates, two thousand souls who will never till a field or bring their crops to market, who will never dig foundations or erect a wall. The Empty Throne counts her children dearly, does not fritter them away for war's transient glory.'

'These dead men you speak of,' Konstantinos began, and one would have been hard pressed to argue that he had not broken into outright oratory by this point, 'they are not abstractions to me, not numbers to be charted on an abacus. These were my comrades, brothers in arms. If you think I take the loss of a single one of them lightly, Senator, than you have gravely mistaken me. The men who have fallen in my service, in the service of the Commonwealth, to keep her free and safe – they were no strangers. Nikephoros and Romanos who were lost when their ship went down with all hands, Basil of the laughing eyes, who stormed the last redoubt before being caught with an arrow. Their names are written on the inner-most fold of my heart, and I can assure you – not a one of them would wish to be back amidst the living, if being so meant tarnishing the honour of their beloved motherland.'

Konstantinos could add necromancy to his list of other talents, apparently, though Manuel was taken back by the sheer force of his personality. 'Forgive me, if my words have given offence.'

'No apology is necessary, Senator. You speak what you believe to be in the best interests of the Empty Throne – no one can fault you for your patriotism, though I believe in this particular regard, you are mistaken.' He gave an appropriately decorous bow. 'If you would excuse me, I'm afraid I need a word with my dear mother.' He took her by the arm and walked her casually away from the scene of his victory.

'Basil of the laughing eyes?' Eudokia asked, bringing her glass up to cover her lips. 'I'm afraid I never had the opportunity to meet the man. Who were his people, do remind me?'

'Not my best work,' Konstantinos admitted. 'But he seemed to lap it up easily enough.'

'You're halfway to a convert,' Eudokia agreed. 'I imagine if you were to allow him to see you without your trousers, he'd throw his hand in with us completely.'

'We aren't that desperate, are we?'

'Not quite yet.'

Irene had managed to position herself in the corner of their view and, was laughing with one of her less handsome friends, making good use of the long neck the gods had given her. She was there to be looked at, and Konstantinos did not fail to take the opportunity.

'Surely there must be someone at this party you can take home that isn't my handmaiden?'

Konstantinos laughed. 'You miss nothing, Revered Mother. Truly you miss nothing.'

'And don't forget it,' she said, only half kidding. 'She's not for you, child. Find a nice little lamb to play with, and leave off mating with lions.'

'You think me so easily overcome?'

'I think you've a better head for war than you do for women,' she said. 'If you so desire a dalliance, forge one with someone too low-born to have any notions of holding on to you permanently.'

'Surely you don't imagine Irene to be so ambitious?'

'Never underestimate the pretensions of a woman.'

'With your long example to draw upon? Believe me, I have no illusions as to the weakness of the weaker sex.'

Eudokia saw Galerius approaching from the corner of her eye, gave her stepson a quick peck on the cheek. 'Be good now,' she said, moving to intercept the man.

'One of us ought to,' Konstantinos offered by way of a parting shot.

'Revered Mother,' Galerius said, dropping so low to kiss her hand that his knees nearly touched the ground. It was clear what Prisca saw in him – the striking eyes, the high cheekbones, the sense of certainty that both had given him. It was equally clear, to Eudokia at least, that this represented the sum total of his quality.

'Galerius,' she said. 'Walk with me to the garden, I fancy a moment spent in the air.'

'An honour, a joy,' he said smoothly, taking her hand and walking out onto the verandah.

In fact the evening was chill and wet and altogether less than pleasant, and Eudokia supposed if she spent much time in it without a cover then she was apt to catch a cold. But this wouldn't take long – behind that sweet face was a mind as mercenary as a Chazar money-counter. 'You seem to have made quite an impression on our dear Prisca,' she said.

Galerius's smile contained more naked avarice than is traditionally found attractive. 'She's a magnificent creature,' he said. 'Alas . . .'

'Alas, without position at court she seems rather beyond your reach.'

'As always, Mother, you cut to the heart of it.'

'A problem easily solved. You will stand for Second Consul next month. I am confident with my assistance that the gentlemen of the Brewers' Association will recognise the good service you can provide for them.'

Galerius did a reasonable job of pretending that he hadn't known this was coming. Not excellent, but reasonable. 'You've been so kind to me, Mother,' he said. 'I wish only that there were some way I could repay you.'

'Nothing, nothing, nothing,' Eudokia said, waving away his thanks. 'To midwife so true a love, to watch it flower and grow unto a second generation, what more happiness could an old woman desire?'

Galerius would begin to cheat on Prisca almost immediately of course. One could hardly blame him for it – there was nothing else to him but his body and his fatuous charm; without it he was hollow as a gourd. And quickly enough his bride would discover her passion sated, because for all its intensity lust is a sentiment that never rests with one individual for any great length of time. Lying in bed afterwards, sticky with him, Prisca might come to wish she had chosen someone who could entertain her for longer than seven minutes at a stretch. She would turn to her children, or if she proved barren, to drink.

Everyone would get exactly what they wanted, and be miserable as salt in three years. Well – we dig our holes and then fall into them. All Eudokia had done was provide the shovel. 'Prisca is a special creature,' Eudokia said.

'Unique.'

'A woman like that deserves a lifestyle equal to her quality, and a dowry capable of maintaining it.'

Galerius licked his lips. 'No doubt.'

'Senator Andronikos is the most tight-fisted man in the Senate,' Eudokia said. 'And that's a post that merits competition. Remember to stand firm with him – this is the good of his daughter we are speaking of, after all.'

'Her needs must come first.'

Eudokia took him in a shallow embrace, held his wrists with her fingers and brought him close. 'Five thousand solidus,' she whispered into his ear, 'and not a penny less.'

Galerius kissed her hand and went off to find his soon-to-be-betrothed, all but walking on gold dust.

When he was gone Eudokia sat down in one of the outside chairs, though the weather hardly suited it. But she needed a moment on her own, to rest, free of interruption. There had been a time when she could dance until morning and rise the next day on three hours of sleep, when she could plot the movement of the Commonwealth between glasses of wine and sharp witticisms. But age is as resolute as stone, and Eudokia found herself considering the lateness of the hour, and gauging whether she might not slip away from her own party to her own bed. By the gods, there was nothing so exhausting as play.

She rejected the notion, of course. After a moment sitting peacefully in the gardens – and not a very long moment, either – she stood and returned to face the tumult, red lips smiling, eyes calm and cold and clear as ice.

IO

It was the natural way of humankind to give priority of rank to one's own nations, cities, families, persons. To perceive virtues that an unbiased eye would fail to notice, to see excellence where a neutral party would observe nothing but mediocrity. To imagine your home a palace and your neighbourhood paradise. In Calla's case, it was not hyperbole. The Roost was the most beautiful city in the world, and the First Rung the most beautiful place in the Roost. These were the simple facts of the matter.

The First Rung was beautiful throughout the year, in every season and at every time of day. It was beautiful in the late afternoon in high summer, when the trees bowed beneath their blossoms and the Eternal drifted past lazily on their pleasure crafts, through the canals and estuaries stemming out from the Source. It was beautiful in the midwinter evening, at the Nightjar's hour, when frost gathered along the path, and claws of ice spiralled down from beneath the great arched bridges, and the street lamps sparkled in the heavy mist. But it was most beautiful – again, not a feeling, not an opinion but an unbiased statement of fact – on that day in mid-autumn called the Anamnesis, when the inhabitants of the Roost celebrate the Founding.

Those lucky people, those happy people, those blessed people who called themselves Roostborn and who resided on the upper Rungs, had no holidays, claimed no sacred rituals, prayed to no gods. Like the Eternal they concerned themselves with the moment, with the smell of wood rot and the feel of the soft breeze on their skin. Calla was in one of the many public gardens that dotted the city, sitting in a red wicker chair and wearing a dress that showed her off to the sun and anyone else who cared to look. She was thinking seriously of getting up and finding a drink – though, as with any such momentous decision, she wanted to give it some consideration before committing.

It had been a long morning. The Eternal would spend the day congregated around the Source, receiving obeisances from the representatives of the surrounding human nations, recalling, in ritual, when their ancestors had first spread protection over the inferior species that dotted the land. Five men and five women from Salucia, Aeleria and all the other lands south and east would present themselves as offerings, along with the vast spoils of raw ore and foodstuffs that represented the subject land's true tithing. Preparing the Aubade for such an important occasion was a stressful and laborious task. Today more than any other was a day for Those Above to preen and primp, to ornament and garnish. For what seemed the first time in decades the Lord's tailor had proven less than competent, or at least less than exceptional, and they were forced to scuttle about the Lord's closet – needless to say, the size of a large house – for a headdress that matched the rest of his costume. But it was completed now, the Lord had left on his skiff, and she had the rest of the day to devote to merriment.

There would be a grand ball held outside the Source once evening fell, everyone from the First Rung and everyone who was anyone from the Second in attendance, dressed in pale imitation of their masters but beautifully none the less. There they would laugh and dance and drink and very likely find themselves walking home with someone they hadn't known before the evening had begun. In nine months a great many children would be born, a belated autumnal blossom.

But for the moment Calla was perfectly content to sit quietly and enjoy doing very little. The Jade Terraces were not one of the larger gardens on the First Rung, but they were Calla's favourite all the same. Nestled where the Canal of Bowed Branches split off from the East Isthmus, overlooking the House of Indefinite Solace and the Mansion of the Gilded Stars, ringed by the towers of more distant estates. The First Rung was made up of the great castles of the Eternal, one for each of the lines and a fair number that had fallen out of use, their owners having died without heirs.

A group of children from the neighbouring manors were laughing and playing loudly in the small copse of trees nearby. For a child the Anamnesis was a special and extraordinary delight, a time for tasting fine things and being allowed up past one's bedtime. Calla could vividly recall the first time she had been allowed to attend the evening's ball, dressed in beautiful if child-like finery, holding her mother's hand and wondering at all there was to see. It was the only strong memory she had of the woman who had birthed her. The next winter she had fallen asleep one evening and never woken up.

Calla's reverie was broken by the pack of children, who had been gradually edging closer to her and now had deigned to involve her directly in their play. The eldest, or at least the tallest, a dark-haired girl with thick shoulders and an imposing mien, stopped in front of her for a moment, making sure she had Calla's attention before speaking.

'I am the Prime,' she volunteered.

'How very lovely to see you again, my Lady,' Calla returned neatly.

The children all but collapsed in a fit of giggles, the less courageous retreating to the shelter of the trees.

'I am the Prime,' the girl repeated.

'Quite so,' Calla agreed.

'Because she is the most beautiful of all the High, and also the wisest. And everyone has to do what I say, because I am so very wise.' This last seemed to be aimed at the rest of the children first and foremost, and she stayed silent a moment for it to sink in. Pleased with her work, she turned back to Calla. 'Also I am the strongest and most fierce.'

A second child, tow-headed and short of a front tooth, shook his head vigorously. 'The Aubade is the strongest of the Eldest, everyone knows that. And I am the Aubade!' He had a stick in one hand and he wagged it at Calla. 'I am the best fighter in the whole world! And I have a horse that is tall as an oak tree, and my sword is as big as . . . a second oak tree!'

'Is it?'

''tis,' the young Lord insisted, confident on the point.

'Well then,' Calla said, rising up from her perch and performing the bow of greeting with a grace and solemnity that few with five fingers on their hand could hope to match. 'May the sun shine on the both of you this morning, my Lord and Lady.'

The Prime did her best to return the gesture, though her enthusiasm did not translate to success. Belying the qualities of his namesake, the false Aubade, made nervous by Calla's movement, turned and ran back to the safety of the trees.

A hand pulled at Calla's skirt and she looked down to notice a third child, brown-haired and dark-eyed and a bit plump. 'I am the Wright,' he said to her quietly, as if it remained something of a secret. 'He is the greatest of all of the smiths, and the most clever with his hands, and also, they say, a great musician. I am also clever with my hands, and my mother says that we look alike, the Wright and I. And she works in his kitchens, so she would know.'

'The resemblance,' Calla acknowledged, 'is as plain as the beak on a bird.'

The child nodded and smiled, then turned without saying anything and returned to making piles with dirt.

'I do not think that Tallow looks very much like the Wright at all,' the child Prime said, with a touch of her namesake's imperiousness.

'Have you seen the Wright, then?'

'No,' the girl admitted, 'but Tallow does not look like what I imagine the Wright looks like.'

'And who is he?' Calla asked, pointing at a child who had taken up residence in the lower branches of one of the trees and was scowling fiercely down at the rest.

'I am the Shrike,' he snapped, happy to be noticed, 'bloody-handed and cruel, and if you are smart you will be very afraid of me. Every night I sup on the eyes of naughty children, and I will do so to you, if you do not eat everything on your plate, and speak respectfully to your parents.'

'I shall take care and do both,' Calla assured him quickly. But this seemed insufficient assurance to the Shrike, who began to roar from his spot in the tree, as well as making fierce gestures with his hands.

'Ignore him,' the Prime said. 'He is not really the Shrike at all, but in fact my little brother, Cinnabar. Mother told him that story last week to try and get him to eat all his peas. But he did not eat his peas,' the girl lamented, 'and now he insists that everyone must call him the Shrike, and refuses otherwise to answer. It is getting quite embarrassing.'

'Little brothers can be embarrassing, I have been told with great confidence.'

'Whoever told you so spoke truthfully,' the Prime said, before running off to engage the rest of the troop in some new diversion.

Soon Calla left her red wicker chair and strolled towards a wine stall in the west corner of the park. It was little more than a counter beneath a silk awning, but it was perched on a small hill and gave a lovely if understated view of the canal and the southern portion of the First Rung. On other days she had sat there and watched the Eternal float by on their skiffs, intricate things of glass and silver and white wood that looked more like waterfowl than boats. The water was empty now, of course, with all of the Eldest at the Source, but still it was a far from unpleasant vantage point.

Calla was vaguely friendly with the girl running the stand, knew her by face but not name, and they chatted pleasantly, about what Calla would be wearing to that night's ball, and what sorts of food might be served to the humans, and what sorts of food might be served to the Wellborn. And then Calla decided to give her full attention to the wine, which was red and strong and a little bit sweet.

The man at the other end of the counter was olive-skinned, with kinked black hair tied into a knot atop his head. He was not quite handsome – his waistline bulged more than was absolutely necessary, and his cheeks were a bit too close to jowls for Calla's taste. But his eyes were a very rich brown, and his lips were full as a woman's and covered a line of even, smiling teeth. He was dressed in the robes of a Chazar, overlapping bands of coloured silk. Gold weighed down his earlobes, and a jewelled chain hung from his neck. At his wrist was an elaborate interlocking bracelet, an expensive passkey that allowed non-natives to ascend above the lowest Rung of the Roost. Calla watched him watching her from the corner of her eye, stretched her neck sideways to show off her profile. How fine a thing it was, she thought then, as she thought often, to be young and handsome enough to call the attention of a stranger.

She didn't need to wait very long. When she turned back to look at him he was nearly upon her, but he stopped short and executed a bow of greeting with skill, something even most Roostborn could only accomplish indifferently. 'May the sun shine long on you this day.'

'And you as well.'

'I am Bulan of Atil, child of Busir the poet.' He had a rich, deep voice, and his accent was slight and not at all unpleasant.

'I'm afraid I'm unacquainted with the man,' Calla said, sipping from her flute.

'You've missed little,' Bulan acknowledged. 'He was a sot, and his rhymes far from noteworthy. His son, however, is a gentleman of distinction and renown.'

'Your brother sounds indeed like a person worth meeting. Is he about somewhere?'

Bulan smiled, took a seat on the stool next to Calla. 'Weep for Bulan, as he has no siblings – no brother with whom to take refuge against the rain, no sister to give him succour from the cold.'

'Bulan seems to have done well enough for himself,' Calla said. Up close he smelled faintly of vetiver.

'Appearances can be deceiving. At the moment, Bulan lies skewered, a broken, hopeless man, who will remain so until he is redeemed from his fate.'

'And whatever could be done to redeem the good man from such misfortune?'

'You might offer him your name.'

'Calla, of the Red Keep.'

Bulan brought one hand swiftly to his chest, as if overtaken by the moment. 'Calla of the Red Keep,' he repeated, 'how shall I repay your kindness?'

Calla made as if she were thinking this over. 'Perhaps another glass?'

Bulan smiled and signalled towards the bar girl. 'If you are a member of the Red Keep, then you would serve the Aubade himself.'

'You're well informed, for a foreigner.'

'It is my business to know things – though in truth, one barely needs ears to have heard of the Aubade. The Roost rings with stories of his accomplishments, with the tales of his great deeds.'

'When you put it that way,' Calla agreed, 'it's not really so impressive at all.'

Bulan laughed, easily and without affect. 'And what is he like, the Aubade?'

Calla took a long time to form a response, not because she needed it but because she was conscious of Bulan's eyes on her, and of how fine she looked in profile, while gazing out into the distance. 'He's the most extraordinary being in all of creation,' she said, the definitive word on the subject.

Bulan brushed his hand lightly against hers. 'If I were a less polite man, I might be inclined to argue that point.'

Calla felt a blush form on her cheeks, smiled along with the bloom. 'And what is it you do, Bulan whose father was no very great poet?'

'I buy things cheaply and sell them dearly.'

'A lucrative industry.'

'There is quite a bit of competition, I am afraid.'

'Then you have recently arrived in the Roost?'

'I've been here since late summer, looking after various interests.' Amongst many other things, the Roost was the largest and richest trading port in all the world. Foreigners from across the seas came to trade at the Perennial Exchange on the Third Rung, which sold what scraps the Eldest were willing to part with, as well as acting as a clearing-house for the goods and products of the rest of the continent.

'The crafts of the Roost are second to none,' Calla said, as if this were a well-known fact.

Bulan shrugged. 'The clockwork mechanisms of the Eternal are indeed very fine,' he said. 'And their arms, though of course those are not sold. Apart from that?' He shrugged. 'The cloth is better in Dycia, the fruit better in the Baleferic Isles, and the slaves better in Partha.'

'I'm sorry you seem to find our city less than satisfying.'

'Bulan is never satisfied,' he said, brushing aside her censure. 'Though he might almost feel so, here atop the city, surrounded by such . . . beauty.' The First Rung was reserved for the Eternal and those who served them directly. Even the most lavishly prosperous merchant prince or highest-ranking custodian was forbidden to own property on the crest. For a foreigner to purchase the right to visit cost a small fortune, and the bracelet on his wrist suggested Bulan was being less than ingenuous about his wealth. 'Beautiful, and very curious.'

'And what is it that you find so peculiar?'

Bulan made a gesture with his hands that seemed to encompass everything in view, opened his mouth to speak but was driven back to silence by the arrival of the hour of the Eagle, announced by the many steamwork chronographs set about the First Rung.

Bulan waited for the chimes to end before continuing. 'To begin with, Bulan has travelled the length of the world, from Old Dycia to distant Partha. And for all the differences in those lands, in custom, clothing, cuisine – time, at least, has remained constant. Here alone I find myself at a loss.'

'Those Above divide the day into eight hours, starting at dawn – Lark, Starling, Eagle, Kite, Woodcock, Nightjar, Owl and Crake. We have just begun the hour of the Eagle, when the sun stands at its zenith and looks down upon the Roost with pleasure.'

'A discerning creature, the sun. Tell me also, Calla of the Red Keep, of the curious reverence the Eternal hold for all things avian? Truly, there seems nothing in this city not named after some winged creature or other.'

'Not reverence, sir,' Calla said, pursing her lips. 'Those Above feel kinship with the birds, appreciate their beauty and cruelty – but they worship nothing but themselves, and the world they have built.'

'And yet, I had the impression that today was a feast day. What is it exactly that we are celebrating?'

'Today is the anniversary of the Founding of the Roost. When the first drop of water flowed up from the Bay of Eirann and spouted from the Source, and Those Above renounced their wandering, and pledged to build a city that would be the envy of the world.'

'They were not unsuccessful.'

'It is also the day when the humans of the surrounding lands swore their allegiance to the Roost, entered into eternal fealty to Those Above.'

'This is why Bulan always reads a contract twice.'

'Here in the Roost,' Calla said, 'we hardly suppose ourselves to have got the worst end of the deal.'

'Perhaps not everywhere in the Roost,' Bulan said, but he said it quietly and while signalling for another glass of wine for himself. 'When was this exactly?'

Calla shrugged. 'Impossible to say. The High do not keep track of time in quite the way we do.'

'And the humans of the Roost? Do they not count the years, like other peoples?'

'The humans of the Roost take after their masters, in this regard.'

'It seems a strange way of doing things,' Bulan said.

'But then, we are not in your country,' Calla said, taking a sip of wine to disguise the faint curl of displeasure.

'True,' Bulan acknowledged. 'In Chazar, the women are not half so pretty.'

'Sad for Chazar.'

'Depends on how one views it. The paucity of our females drives our men from their homeland, forces them across the length and breadth of the world. If, growing up, my neighbour's daughter had been slender-waisted and dark-haired, rather than thick-thighed and lightly bearded, who knows but that I would have become a greengrocer? Sold fruit in the afternoons, gone home at night and worked on expanding the line of Busir.'

'Not such a terrible life, as you've described it.'

'But one inappropriate for a man such as Bulan. His path was meant to be a rocky one, the climb steep, the summit unparallelled.'

'And will Bulan's ambitions be satisfied?'

The bar girl came by with another glass of wine, but Bulan ignored it, his eyes firmly on Calla's. 'He very much hopes so.'

Calla laughed the laugh that she gave when she wanted to look pretty rather than express levity, but beneath it was happiness, real and unfeigned. And who would not be happy on such a day, and in such a place as the Roost?

II

Down at the Barrow the women had been cooking since before dawn. Big copper pots of red beans and ladies fingers simmered on stoves, freshly baked loaves of quick bread cooled on window ledges. In tenement apartments mothers and sisters and young daughters sat spooning spices into bubbling cauldrons of tripe stew, or battering oysters in cornmeal, or just laughing and gossiping. The younger children tried on their costumes, adding final dashes of colour to their ensemble, tried to convince their mothers to give them a lick from the sweet spoon, enjoyed the thick atmosphere of revelry even if they couldn't quite understand it.

The women had been cooking since daylight, and the men had started drinking not long after, lounging on the pipes and on white cobblestone stairs and on the edges of the canals and in the streets themselves, because why not? The boulevards would see no business today, no commerce whether honest or illicit. Anyone passing would be infected by the mood, grab on to one of the little kernels of celebration, drink a shot of apple liquor and laugh with a stranger. Today was the Anamnesis, and everywhere on the Fifth, from the boundaries to the docks, it seemed there was no soul unaffected by the spirit of the holiday.

Almost none. Thistle sat on the roof of his building, dangled his feet over the crowds milling below, thought seriously of dropping a stone. His hopes of sleeping until evening, or at least through the festivities, had been dashed by the crowds of people slipping molasses-slow down to the docks, but he still nurtured a vague hope of staying above the flood.

Hopes dashed by the footsteps he heard coming up the stairwell. He didn't bother to turn and see who was making them. Probably it was a sibling come to bother him about something, in which case he didn't see the point in making their job any easier.

And sure enough, the voice that interrupted him was as familiar and grating as a rash. 'You up here, Thistle?'

'You can see I am,' he said, turning to face the interloper. Shrub was seven, freckled and dark-haired, a girl, though so spindly you'd have to strip her to be certain. Thistle saw her constantly and thought about her near to never. She was part of the scenery, like the *drip-drip-drip* of the slurp, something that there was no point in feeling any way about since it wasn't going anywhere. In honour of the day she was wearing a worn brown frock, and her braids had been pleated with bright-coloured beads. Some of them, anyway. 'Ma says you got to help me with my costume,' she said.

'Who you supposed to be?'

Shrub had this way of looking at you, as if everything she saw was new and strange and fabulously complicated, and she was struggling to map the shapes and colours in front of her into a coherent whole. Shrub was looking at Thistle like that now, and Thistle very much wanted to slap her for it. 'Fink Jon,' she said finally.

'What you want?'

'Mum says you need to go get me some more beads,' she said. 'For my costume.'

'Can't she do it?'

'She's cooking.'

Thistle sighed, pulled himself upright. 'What am I buying them with?'

Shrub blinked for a while, sussing her way through the question. Then she recalled the weight she'd been holding in her left hand, opened it and revealed two Aelerian nummus. Thistle snatched them out of her palm as soon as he saw the glitter, stuffed them into his back pocket and made for the stairs.

'Those are for my beads,' Shrub reminded Thistle's back, but got no answer.

Out the front door and Thistle was in the midst of the mob of revellers, sharp elbows and hot sweat. From four storeys up he had found the mass irritating and somewhat shameful. Incorporated within their midst he felt both but more strongly – reeking, drunken fools clogging up the thoroughfares, only interrupting the consumption of food and liquor to stumble over to a canal and piss or vomit, maybe not even all the way to a canal, maybe just lean up against somebody's home and start leaking onto it.

The men of the Barrow were porters or bums, with a small smattering of shopkeepers and dockworkers thrown in for good measure. A bum will take any excuse for merriment, a sunny day or a half-full bottle of liquor. For the porters, the Anamnesis was one of the year's only opportunities for indulgence, an event to be anticipated and treasured upon its arrival. Up before dawn nine days out of ten, down to the docks to pick up whatever shipment of produce or poultry or silk had come in that day. Strap twenty clove worth of goods to your back and hoof it upslope a cable or two or five, standing in line at the gates to each new Rung, waiting for the Cuckoos to check your tattoo, hoping they won't decide to reject you because the shipowner didn't pay his requisite bribe, or out of sheer pique. Drop your load off at one of the mid-Rung markets, but don't think of waiting there too long, or, Founders forbid, of taking a moment to rest, because your kind aren't wanted upslope, only the things you can carry. Then the jaunt back down to the docks, legs aching, back crooked, two or three more trips before night falls and you can head back to your hovel, down a bowl of stew while your wife complains and your children screech, six hours on a lumpy bed so you can wake up the next day and do it all over again – you couldn't blame a fellow for taking advantage of an opportunity to drink himself into oblivion.

Perhaps you couldn't, but Thistle sure as hell did. He waded through at the fastest clip possible, ignoring the angry looks and occasional outright slurs caused by his brusqueness. Another time and Thistle might have found himself the recipient of a lesson on proper etiquette, and on the volatility of the rabble. But mostly everyone was in too good a mood for needless violence, so he managed to find his way across the thoroughfare without having his cheek repaid.

On the steps of an abandoned tenement a dozen small children sat at the feet of an old man, listening intently to his story. The youth were dressed in what passed for holiday attire downslope, their usual rags overlaid with flowers and garish dashes of colour. 'In the days long ago, before your mother was born, before your grandmother knew your grandfather, before your great-grandmother's first name day; when the mountain was still unbroken, when the sun was fresh and sweet in the sky; we laboured beneath the ground. We hollowed out the stone, we built the slurps to carry water up to the summit. For years and years we laboured, whole generations born and died without ever seeing the light. This is a story of the days before the Founding, of the Time Below.'

Tipple had seemed ancient when Thistle had been one of the children listening to this story, though the years since hadn't done much to age him – as if, having reached venerable, his body found itself unable to wither further. His white hair had gone unwashed so long that it clumped together in peaks and crests atop his head. He had blue eyes that looked clouded even when he wasn't drinking, filmy and pale above a sharply beaked nose. Most days he was a bum, no different to any of the other decrepits too lazy or old to make a living as porters. But on the half-holidays allowed to the humans of the Roost he managed to shake himself back to some semblance of coherence, and regale the youth of the neighbourhood with the pleasant lies they recited on the Fifth.

'Everyone knows that Fink Jon was the cleverest of those who lived below, and Garnet his brother the strongest, and Saffron, whom they both loved, was the fairest. But do you know of Calf the Steadfast? Firm in the cold and the heat, unblinking in the dark, whose strong back bore the sins of his fellows, whose endurance is our deliverance?'

'No,' chorused the assembled children, though of course they did.

'Those Above came first, and never forget it, because they will not. In the time before time when we Five Fingers came on our endless journey from the west, we found them waiting for us, perfect and beautiful and terrible. And though the land was theirs, theirs since before stone was stone, they allowed us to live in the forests and the fields, to seek shelter beneath the trees, to hunt the beasts that ran and swam and wriggled. And for endless days beneath the sun things continued thus, with the children of the west living beneath the protection of the Wellborn.

'But then came the cursed generation, and the Transgression, the crime for which we have not yet paid, the crime which we can never repay. And so terrible and so heinous was the Transgression that the Wellborn decided to extinguish the very line of man, to proscribe it entirely, from the child still at suck to the oldest greybeard. And so the King of the Birds brought all of the children of the west together, and prepared to execute this terrible and just sentence.'

A vendor passed by hawking sausages, street meat speared on a length of branch. Thistle handed him one of Shrub's coins and waited while the man slipped a link of pork onto the small brazier he carried, watching the skin crisp while Tipple talked nonsense.

'And then a man came out from among the Five-Fingered, and his name was Calf, and he was a son of those that had been cursed. And Calf went to the King, though to look upon him was as to look at the noonday sun. And he said "Give us leave and we will labour for you, we and our children and their children after that, until the very sun ceases to give light, and the land grows dark and cold."'

The vendor picked the sausage up in his oily hands, blew on it and passed it over. Thistle bit into it, feeling the juice run down the scruff of his not quite beard.

'And the King of the Birds asked Calf, "How can you make this promise for all of the children of the west? For I know you to be a false people, and breakers of oaths, a people that cannot be trusted." And Calf said to the King of the Birds, "Their sins will be my sins, and their punishment mine." And so the King of the Birds led Calf and the people down into the mountain, where there was no light and no breeze, where rivers ran that had never known the sight of the sun. And the King of the Birds told the people to hollow out the mountain, and to make the waters reach up into the sky.'

It was the same story that Tipple had been telling for years, the same one that Thistle had heard when he was a boy. Thistle had hated it even then and sure as the pit he hated it now, hated the thought of his sisters mouthing the words that he'd once repeated.

'And though the task seemed mad, and impossibly cruel, still Calf led the people in their labours. And there was neither sun nor moon beneath the earth, and time went on for ever. And at the end of the day that was not a day the King of the Birds called Calf to come to him, and he said, "There was one among your people who did not labour. There was one among your people who remained false." And Calf bowed his head. And the next day which was not a day, when it was time again to delve the stone, Calf did the work of two, and carried the burdens of that child of the west who would not labour.'

Suddenly Thistle wasn't hungry, the sausage in his mouth a reeking mass of fat and oil and probably consisting of no small portion of rat meat. 'Birdshit,' he said, loudly enough that the flock of seated children turned their eyes on him, forced a sudden sense of shame atop the rising tide of anger. He tossed the half-stick of meat onto the ground and stomped off.

It was a bad day to walk around angry, what with the whole Rung drunk and laughing, looking to kiss or screw or at least dance. Rat and Felspar and the rest of the boys would be down at the pumps, getting a buzz on before the main event, expecting him to swing by. So Thistle didn't go down to the pumps, instead swapped an inebriate one of his nummus for a half-empty bottle of rotgut and headed east, settling himself atop a quiet stretch along the Sweet Water canal, quiet in the sense that it was not thronged with revellers.

This year he wasn't going to watch it, he told himself. He told himself the same thing every year, but this time he really meant it. The music coming in from the docks was getting louder, the kind that made you want to shake your hips, or stand in the back and watch some pretty girl shake hers. Thistle realised he was bobbing his head, scowled and willed himself into stillness.

The bottle was empty. Thistle tossed it into the water, watched it float towards the docks. Then he sighed, and stood, and followed it downslope.

When the canal intersected with Bright Street, and a snaking line of laughing, hooting festivalgoers, Thistle took a detour atop one of the pipes, balancing himself on the narrow length of metal. The pipes had come first and the city had been built around them, iron arteries threading their way through narrow lines of tenements and across tiny plots of broken land. At some points it rose a few dozen links off the ground, and a fall would leave you with a broken arm next to a stranger's back door – but Thistle had been doing this since he was younger than Apple, and moved swiftly and without much conscious thought. His pipe ended at the very crest of the small ridge that overlooked the quay. Thistle dangled his feet over the ledge and started rolling a smoke.

Most days the docks were busy as hell, ships coming in and going out, porters lined up like ants. But even in high season the port wasn't busy anything like it was during the Anamnesis. The entirety of the Fifth crammed itself along the piers, wandering joyfully, or at least aimlessly. Each of the guilds set up elaborate pavilions with games and prizes, vying with each other in friendly rivalry. The Society of Toters, by far the largest, offered Salucian fighting fish to any child under twelve who could lift the pack of a full man, as much a recruitment tool as it was recreation. Beneath a sign that read 'Fifth Rung Traders' Affiliation', members of the Brotherhood Below passed out cups of grog and twists of rock candy for the children, thieves and killers forgoing their usual trades. The Association of Inkers set aside protocol to offer all comers temporary tattoos formed of some sort of plant dye that would start to run as soon as it got wet. For a few happy hours the penurious children of the Fifth Rung could pretend they were goldsmiths from the Third, or the scions of merchant houses quartered, so high as to be almost unimaginable, on the Second. Of course, there could be no question of these faithful artists conniving in the creation of a brand appropriate to those happy humans at the summit – there are limits to fantasy, as to everything else. Clowns juggled, minstrels sang, hawkers hawked, whores hung bare-titted out of windows, everyone danced. In the centre of a ring of laughing drunkards a Parthan held a chain leash attached to the neck of a black bear, led the beast in an awkward, shuffling step. Its fur was mottled and one of its eyes was dead. Onlookers laughed and threw coins. Thistle wondered where they went to celebrate on the Fourth, or the Third, if their festivities were as pitiful and pointless, if the people there enjoyed them as much as they did down here.

The Submission was the high point of the proceedings, when the neighbourhood children, weighed down by beads and tassels and bits of ribbon, would make their way in a slow processional down to the docks and offer themselves to Those Above. Of course no Four-Finger had been seen at the docks in generations beyond counting, and in their stead the neighbourhood had taken to choosing as a replacement the prettiest almost-virgin the Fifth Rung could provide. This year's Prime sat on a small platform jutting out from a cupboard three times as tall as a man and equally wide. On it had been painted a scene from the Time Below, dark and cavernous, hellish looking, inspiring feelings of gloom and dread. Meant to inspire those feelings at least. Thistle didn't know how long ago the cabinet had been created – long enough for the paint to start to fade, and the wooden facade to rot and crack. One day soon the workings of the machine itself would fail, and the whole ceremony would have to be reimagined. A happy moment that would be, Thistle thought, though presumably it would not come this morning.

The girl sat cold and imperious – part of the ritual, though looking at her Thistle didn't think she had to put any great effort into faking it. Thistle had never seen a Wellborn, but he was pretty sure that none of them looked anything like the costume she wore, a long, flowing headdress of multicoloured streamers, ugly blue robes and a set of four-fingered gloves. Even made up so foolishly, she was stunning as a strand of sunlight. It made Thistle angry, that there were such things in the world, that they would be dangled in front of you just to be snatched away. A girl that pretty would find a match upslope, get an apartment and a few women like Thistle's mother to take care of the household. Thistle hated her in that moment, hated and wanted her all at the same time, almost loved her.

The hour of the Eagle chimed loudly, the sun high in the sky, and the crowd started to quiet. Children shook themselves out from the mass and formed a line in front of the false Prime, the very young carried by their mothers or older siblings. The foremost child wore breeches and a coat with little brass buttons running up the front. Thistle wondered whose son he was, what he had done to earn the front spot. That little outfit must have cost half a solidus, maybe more. Whoever he was, he had clearly been made to practise his speech before this moment – Thistle could imagine him at some dinner table close to the Fourth, a fat mother rapping his knuckles after each error. 'For the crimes that we have committed,' he began, then corrected himself, 'that I have committed, I ask forgiveness. And if it is given, I will swear myself in service to you, and labour . . . and labour all my life to repay the debt.'

'The wrong you have done is terrible beyond imagining,' the Prime said. She had an ugly voice, Thistle discovered then – Thistle and everyone else in the crowd – a squawking, hectoring thing, without dignity or purpose. 'But we are a people kinder than we are just, and we will accept your worship.'

Thistle heard the grinding clockwork gears twist into motion, watched as the cabinet unfolded around her. The small dais on which the Prime sat was pulled inward, the cavernous backdrop replaced by a depiction of the Source itself, the wings stretching to reveal rows of happy-looking human caricatures, an awning spreading out to offer the Prime shade. 'And we will repay your service with protection, today and until the end of days. And we will feed you and clothe you, and give you law, and shelter you as a father does their children, today and until the end of days.'

Thistle's fists clenched at his sides. Every fucking year he did this to himself, every gods-damned, every worthless, misbegotten, cunt of a year. And it was always the same and every year he swore he wouldn't do it the next and then every year he did.

The Prime opened her mouth to continue, bright-eyed and beatific. A drop of red bloomed suddenly on her forehead. When she looked skyward the entire crowd joined her. Dangling from the roof of the chamber was some sort of a bird – not a pigeon or a gull, but a proper raptor, an eagle maybe, or a hawk. Whoever had hung it had slit its throat before doing so, and thick beads of blood dripped down from the wound.

The Prime screamed then, silenced only when the slow leak of red fell into her mouth, went gagging and stumbling off the stage and into the crowd. As if infected by her terror the masses began to scream as well, first the adults and then the children. The Cuckoos milling about the area seemed as helpless as the throng, stared wide-eyed at the bird, holding their cudgels tight in their fists.

The dead raptor swung back and forth like a pendulum, drops

of crimson leaking from its severed neck. Behind it, imprinted clearly against the faded vellum, were five-fingered handprints done in red paint.

In that very moment Thistle didn't know what he felt, couldn't have said for certain. But he knew that it wasn't what the mob of people below him seemed to feel, that sudden squirt of fear that was swiftly overcoming them, that would soon turn their celebration into something little short of a riot. To kill a bird was a crime on a par with holding a weapon, though one that was a good deal less frequently committed. To murder an avian in public like this was a species of madness that Thistle had never seen before, hadn't imagined possible.

Everyone was screaming by now, though Thistle suspected it was mostly in demonstrations of innocence rather than true horror. The Cuckoos were in the same boat as everyone else, half drunk and confused and having no clear idea how to handle what was happening. Distantly, Thistle realised it was a good thing he wasn't in the middle of the scrum. Pretty soon the Cuckoos would move from confused to violent; it was all they knew. Best to leave before then.

But still it was a long time before Thistle managed to break himself away from the scene, climb up the pipe and head back the way he came. From the main thoroughfare a block over he could hear the crowd frantically trying to flee, though from what and to where? What had begun here would echo out in the weeks and months to come, there would be casks of blood to add to what the bird had given, Thistle was as certain of that as he had ever been of anything.

It wasn't till he had got home that he remembered Shrub, and the beads. What with all that had happened, however, no one was in any particular mood to ride him about it.

12

It was Phocas who had taught Eudokia the nuances of *shass*, in those first halcyon days after their marriage. A game of strategy and high cunning, an import from the Others in fact, one of the many traditions that the Commonwealth had quietly adopted. Phocas had been fifteen years her elder, perhaps the most revered man in Aeleria. Second only to Jon the Sanguine in military fame, descendant of one of the oldest families in the Commonwealth. Handsome, rich, recently widowed, young Konstantinos the fruit of that previous union. Eudokia had been twenty, and if she had not been beautiful her wealth and lineage would have been enough to make a wise suitor pretend otherwise. But she *had* been beautiful, as well as charming as a budding rose, and their wedding had been the most celebrated event of the year, a love match between two of Aeleria's most prosperous and noble families. Happiness seemed assured.

And indeed, for a time it had been. They toured his familial estates on the southern coasts, and they toured her familial estates in the foothills west of the capital. They threw galas and attended them, they partook of all the pleasures that could be afforded to the highest Commonwealth gentry. But mostly they fucked, rigorously and with passion, Eudokia a girl discovering the joys of womanhood.

Finally exhausted, he would plead age and insist on a game and Eudokia would laughingly oblige him. It was to his credit that she hadn't felt the need to hide her superiority at it, as she did with most things and for most of the world. Far from it – Phocas revelled in her talent, would brag to friends of her cleverness, insisted that there was no member of the Senate who could match her. She found the admiration flattering, though foolish – why give anyone warning?

'Do I go too slowly, Auntie?' Leon asked.

They sat over the wooden board at a stone table in a distant corner of her garden, enjoying the autumn sunlight, the bowed trees slowly shedding their colour. 'The point of the exercise is to focus narrowly on a particular problem. Whether or not you come up with the correct solution determines whether your time has been well spent.'

'The winner isn't always immediately apparent.'

'Clarity comes quicker than we sometimes expect,' Eudokia said, advancing a wren.

Soon it wasn't *shass* alone at which Phocas recognised her talent. He was Consul at the time, his first office in the civil rather than military sphere. One rises to the position of one's incompetence, as they say, and Phocas's was a case in point. A striking talent on the battlefield, in the Senate and the parlours he proved surprisingly maladroit – in his heart of hearts, there was a certain innocence to Phocas, an inability to understand the weakness in his fellow men that left him barely more than competent in the internecine feuding at the heart of the Aelerian political machine. It was this sort of optimism that she had come to love about the man.

Though, needless to say, it was not a burden beneath which she herself laboured. If Phocas wasn't sure who to trust, the answer was altogether clear to Eudokia – no one, ever, only her, and only because he had to. She already knew everything that happened in Aelerian society; it was a little thing to transfer her network of gossips to a more practical purpose. Soon she had realised that the habits and customs which had brought her to the forefront of feminine society were not so very different from what was now required of her. One did kindnesses for one's friends, injury to one's enemies, quietly acquiring more of the former and fewer of the latter. With her silent assistance, Phocas proved as astute and capable a politician as the capital had ever seen. There seemed no heights to which he could not ascend, no honours or powers that would not, with time, accrue to him. Who knew? The Empty Throne had not always been so.

'Do you imagine I've failed to identify your stratagem?' Leon asked, ignoring the piece she had presented and moving forward on the other end of the board.

'Do you imagine I'm only operating the one?'

'I hear that Andronikos's last speech went strongly with the Senate. A protest has been voted, to be sent to the Salucian Emperor, demanding a change in the status of the free city of Oscan.'

Eudokia sighed dramatically, swapped an eagle for a hawk. 'What a lovely day it is, and how pleasant the company. And why would we want to spoil it by discussing the Senate, when we could be enjoying the game?'

'Are they really so different?'

'Politics has fewer rules.'

And then Phocas had died, the victim of a devil's lance at Scarlet Fields. 'I'll be back before winter,' he had told her, and she had seen in his eyes that he had even believed it, though of course she had not. The Seventh Other War, what foolishness! To have learned nothing from the first six, to have played according to the devil's rules, as if it were a game of *shass*! The Senate drifting slowly and inexplicably towards conflict, one moment desperate for bloodshed, the next as unprepared and frightened as newborns. If only the moment had arisen five years later, she would have been in a position to direct it. But she had been too young, too weak, and the Commonwealth had suffered for it. She had felt no twist of shock when the news returned, only a dull despair, as though the world had been repainted in griseille.

Phocas had acquitted himself magnificently, she had been informed months after his death by one of the survivors, kneeling at her feet and all but weeping. It was very like a man to suppose that this last would be of some value – a noble death, and a name that lives on afterwards. Whatever lies a man might spew, it was for themselves and themselves only that they conceived such acts of self-sacrifice. A woman knows the truth – there are the living, and there are the dead, and what good is a name without arms to hold you in the evening, without seed for children? How pointless and futile and foolish it was, to lose. Inexcusable.

Leon moved, finally. Eudokia advanced with her eagle.

'Are you sure you want to do that?' Leon asked.

'I don't know what bothers me more – that you'd think I would make an error, or that you'd be so slow to take advantage of it.'

'All right, all right,' Leon said, snatching at the piece.

Eudokia advanced her wren another step. Leon pursed his lips in thought.

It was not revenge, or at least it was not primarily revenge. The men charged with overseeing the Commonwealth had proven themselves incompetent to do so, Scarlet Fields had demonstrated that amply enough. Even sweet Phocas, for all that she had loved him, had been unfit for the task. Eudokia Aurelia did not take her responsibilities lightly, had not sought them out of vanity. There were none better able to guarantee Aeleria's well-being. It was more than destiny which had thrust her towards power – it was common sense.

Slow going at first, but then she had time. It was ten years before Konstantinos could be put into play, and she had spent the time consolidating her rule, accruing wealth and saving favours, putting her friends into positions where they could repay her kindnesses, ensuring that her enemies found themselves broken or corrupted. By the time her stepson had been old enough to accept his first commission, as a tourmarches in Dycia, she had quietly become the lynchpin of the second largest faction in the Senate. The years since had only seen her grow stronger, Konstantinos replacing his father in the people's affections, her own stratagems continuing with silent certainty. She could look everywhere upon her successes, and anticipate greater victories in the future.

Still, in her unguarded moments she found herself thinking of Phocas, of the life they might have led, of children and grandchildren. Five times since in her life she had found her menses interrupted, five times she had gone to the white-robed priestesses of Eloha, drunk their vile concoction, taken to bed for a week and risen again empty. She would have Phocas's seed quickening in her belly or she would have none, and so none it had been. Besides, was she not now the Revered Mother, matriarch of all Aeleria, her provenance every man and woman in the Commonwealth – the Commonwealth and what might one day become so?

Eudokia's steward broke her out of her reverie with the sort of natural-seeming cough that seemed the inheritance of those bred to serve. 'Phrattes is in the study, Revered Mother.'

She pursed her lips and stood. Leon did not bother to look up from the board. 'If you decide to capture with that hawk,' Eudokia said, 'you can assume my next move will be to retake with the falcon and proceed accordingly. Otherwise, you'll have to await my return.'

'Don't hurry yourself,' Leon said.

Eudokia had nothing against the Salucians particularly, except in so far as they were people, and thus dishonest, venal and weak-willed. Also they dressed strangely and tended to smell of cardamom. Most Aelerians held Salucians in contempt for being callow and licentious, though Eudokia thought that of all the vices that could infest a population, an exaggerated regard for pleasure was hardly the most objectionable.

Phrattes was a sterling specimen of his race. The chief broker in one of the innumerable counting houses and banking firms that gave the Salucians their wealth as well as their national reputation for being obsequious, double-dealing and slothful. Of no very distinguished birth, still he had managed to attain some rank in his home country, the Salucians being practical people, inclined to see public honours as goods to be bartered like any other. With wealth and rank had come something that nearly resembled power, and it was understood that he was a man who could get things done within the Salucian capital, a power broker of sorts, sharp-witted and calculating.

In fact he was not many of these things, or perhaps it would be better to say that he was many of these things only in a spectral fashion.

'Your Worship,' he said, and all but collapsed to his ankles in executing the bow.

'Revered Mother will do fine,' Eudokia said, taking a seat in her chair. Phrattes she allowed to remain standing. 'We Aelerians are a humble people,' she lied baldly, 'and have no need for the grand forms of address that bejewel the nobility of other lands.'

'Why be jealous of title, when your own quality is so manifestly evident to all the clear-seeing and right-thinking?'

Eudokia couldn't help but be impressed with the flattery – she rarely heard praise executed so well. 'Sit, please.'

Phrattes made sure to lift his robes before doing so. 'The great man has been approached,' he said simply.

It was another mark in Phrattes' favour that he knew to wrap up his pleasantries swiftly. 'And?'

'The great man is interested in peace, as are all right-thinking people.'

'A blessing to be reckoned above all others,' Eudokia agreed. 'And what would the great man want in return?'

'He has let it be known that he would accept forty thousand in exchange for his support.'

Forty thousand meant that Phrattes had been asked for thirty and thought to pocket the rest. She noticed the gold sheen of his belt buckle and revised her estimate. Phrattes had been asked for twenty-five. 'And what has he promised, to expect such honey?'

'The great promise little to the small, as Her Worshipfulness well knows. And the small know to insist on nothing, when invited to the tables of the great.'

'It is wise to keep one's sense of scale,' Eudokia agreed. 'But we are in Aeleria, which sees distinction only in merit. And in Aeleria, we consider it unwise to purchase a thing without seeing it.'

'With the coin in his account, I think the great man would be willing to put something in writing.'

Eudokia thought this over as she finished her tea. 'Thirty-five,' she said, setting aside her cup and standing. If Phrattes was clever he would know to accept his honorarium with the same grace that he had exhibited throughout the rest of the conversation.

As indeed he did. Phrattes put his cup on the side table and rose with a grace and speed admirable in such a heavy man. 'It will require the most delicate negotiations,' he said, bowing neatly, 'but I shall see that they are performed.'

Eudokia gave him a kiss in farewell, tried not to wrinkle her nose at the cardamom.

Back at the table, Leon had decided to take back with the hawk, and had made her next move as instructed. 'Have I told you yet,' he asked, hesitating between two pieces, 'how little that ribbon suits you?'

Eudokia wore a stretch of bright crimson over her forearm, an accessory that had gained favour across wide swathes of the city's population in the last month. 'Red is not my colour,' she admitted. 'But when national honour is at issue, vanity needs go by the wayside.'

'I hadn't realised that you felt such passion on the subject of Oscan.'

Oscan had been Aeleria's outpost in the north-east, the boundary between the Commonwealth and Salucia. As part of the indemnity that had been forced on Aeleria after the Others had intervened between the two nations, it had been made a free city, no longer part of the Commonwealth proper. Meant to punish Aeleria for its belligerence, it had ended up as a perpetual source of conflict between the two countries and a wellspring of discontent to the Aelerian populace.

'The plight of our beloved countrymen, split from the bosom of the Commonwealth by an unjust peace, is always in my mind. I spent three weeks in Oscan, as a girl, during my first tour of the Aelerian lands. A beautiful city, white stone and green gardens.' Of course Eudokia had never come within five hundred cables of Oscan, but she wished her nephew luck in proving it.

'Senator Gratian said something very similar, not two days past.'

Appropriately enough, as she all but wrote the man's speeches. Still, it was a good reminder to be less free with her talk in the future. It would hardly do to make people think that she was cribbing her best lines from that halfwit. 'A man of great wisdom, the senator.'

'You should try not to smile when you say that,' Leon said, moving an eagle.

Eudokia stole one of his wrens. 'Duly noted.'

He hadn't seen that coming, which disappointed her, but what disappointed her more was that he let her see it on his face, and allowed it to affect his next words. 'All the pith and genius of the senator notwithstanding, I fear that his side will be disappointed. Scouring the Baleferic Isles of pirates is one thing – it costs little, people enjoy easy victories and public festivals. But the people haven't quite forgotten what happened the last time we feuded with Salucia, and the heavy, four-fingered hands of their protectors.'

'They haven't forgotten at all,' Eudokia said. 'Which is why you're wrong.'

'War with Salucia will hardly sit well with the merchants.'

'Salucia won't be going anywhere. For a season the trading fleets will be sent south rather than north. When next they return, the markets will be rich with silk and spices, and the native traders desperate for our steel and slaves – the only difference is they won't need to pay a tariff to sell them.'

'You expect the moneychangers to see beyond their interests?'

'I rarely expect anyone to see past what's immediately in front of them. Which is why it's really best that those rare few blessed with vision make a point of exercising it. We call that leadership,' Eudokia said, pushing her wren forward innocuously. 'In truth, you overcomplicate everything. The people dislike Salucia because they have always disliked Salucia, because their parents did and their parents before them. Oscan is a poisoned pill; if anyone in that misbegotten swamp had a lick of sense they'd never have accepted it. It would not require coal oil to start a conflagration.'

'And the Others? Do you rank them so low, as well?'

Eudokia smiled but didn't answer. In the long silence, Leon turned back to inspecting the board, seeking some way out of his predicament. He was a tenacious sort, her nephew, and it rankled him to be beaten so soundly.

But even the most bull-headed of men will face the inevitable, given enough time. 'The game is lost,' Leon said.

'For the last three moves.'

'Perhaps even sooner.'

'When you sat down.'

Leon smiled. 'I should have taken that wren, shouldn't I?'

'It is not enough to be intelligent,' Eudokia said, setting up the pieces for a second game. 'One must also be vicious.'

13

The Source was the most singular engineering feat that had ever been attempted. To create it had required the labour of a dozen generations of humans, two dozen, perhaps more, perhaps many more, slaving away in the dark, hollowing out the mountain and crafting the vast system of pipework that pumped water from the Bay of Eirann to the summit of the Roost. The Conclave, as the structure surrounding the Source was called, was a budding flower of white marble and pure gold, with its face half open to the sky. There were humans throughout the world who would have drowned their children to get a look at the facade, and cheerfully made the rest of the family into corpses at the thought of taking a peek inside. Here the official policy of the Eldest was hammered out. Here, today, at this very moment, the destiny of a dozen human lands was being written. It was no exaggeration to suggest that Calla was standing at the very navel of existence.

All this being true, Calla strained with every fibre of her not inconsiderable will to stifle the yawn that had been working its way up through her diaphragm over the course of the last five minutes. Her legs ached and her mouth was dry and she had a desire to urinate that was rapidly moving from irritant to a source of major concern. Most of the rest of the Eternal seemed to regard the affair with a similar lack of interest, at least in so far as they had chosen not to attend this month's gathering. The great amphitheatre was half empty, vacant benches outnumbering the full. In Calla's memory, admittedly very brief by the standards of the High, she could not recall it ever being otherwise.

For their part, the servants in attendance also seemed uninterested, though at least they had incomprehension as an excuse. It was an open question, the degree to which her fellow seneschals understood the High Tongue. Certainly, even the least accomplished among them could claim a basic understanding of the language, the greetings and honorifics, simple articles. Sandalwood and some of the cleverer ones no doubt understood more than that, though being clever they were loath to show it.

But no human could claim anything close to her own degree of competence, Calla knew this as a fact, as she knew that her fluency owed nothing to her own ability, or at least not much, and everything to the book. In the distant memories of her childhood she could see it clearly, her father at his desk, studying it with one eye always on the door. Twelve generations it had been handed down, from her many-times grandfather Felum, who had been seneschal to the Aubade's father, impossible as that seemed. Hundreds of years of effort into understanding the language of Those Above, effort that would have been repaid with the severest cruelty had it ever been discovered. 'Read it every day,' her father had told her when finally giving in to her demands to study it, 'but only add when you are certain. And for the sake of everything, never, *never* speak of it.' Calla had kept to these commandments even as a child, and doubly so since the death of her father had made the book her own exclusive charge.

'Then we're agreed,' the Prime said, jolting Calla back into the present, 'the tithe from Salucia to be set at seventy slate of iron, forty slate of silver, and three hundred of grain?'

There was no official response to her query, but then the rules of procedure in the Conclave were curiously informal. There were no votes taken, and any High was allowed to speak for as long as they wished, whenever they wished. Decisions were reached as part of a broad consensus, after every participant felt that they had expressed themselves as fully as they desired. Among humans it would have been a recipe for anarchy. That it had endured since the Founding was evidence of how different the Four-Fingered were from the Five.

'That settles external business,' the Prime said. 'Now to move on to the Roost itself—'

'If you would excuse me, Prime,' the Aubade interrupted, 'in fact that is not quite all of it.'

The Aubade was dressed in emerald silk robes tight enough to show the muscles of his chest. Round his neck hung a chain of sapphires, like the petals of an orchid. Calla had had no inkling that he was going to speak, all of a sudden her great swell of boredom receded with his first word.

'If my siblings have read the most recent dispatch from the Sentinel of the Southern Reach, they know that in the last six months alone, the Aelerians have established themselves as the dominant power in the Baleferic Isles and won a signal victory in the Western Marches.'

Calla supposed with something resembling certainty that the majority of Those Above had not read the most recent dispatch from the Sentinel of the Southern Reach. The machinations and manoeuvres of the human nations to the west were of less interest to most of the four-fingered inhabitants of the Roost than the latest bit of steamwork, or the day's carnal gossip. It was an attitude that had trickled down towards the Roostborn humans as well, who often had only the most distant idea of what lay beyond the boundaries of the Fifth Rung. Calla herself, if she were to be honest, would have to admit that she had only the faintest notion of what exactly the Western Marches were, and none at all as to the location of the Baleferic Isles.

The one exception to this rule was of course the Sentinels themselves, the seven Wellborn who oversaw the human nations, and who were the source of the often-ignored intelligence that returned to the Roost. It was not a coveted position. A Sentinel held their post for twenty-five years, a quarter of a century in exile. When they left, a stalk of their hair was ceremonially removed and burned, never to grow back, a mark of pride – or of shame, it was unclear. Upon their return a Sentinel was required to spend another five years in a special demesne in the east of the city, in quarantine lest their pollution spread.

'I thank our sibling for bringing this fact to our attention,' said the Lord of the House of Kind Lament. Quietly, and not to his face, the Lord of the House of Kind Lament was known among the Roostborn as 'the Glutton', for the love and dedication he showed towards his table. Though, in truth, like all the other Eternal, there seemed to be no excess flesh anywhere on his person, and he stood in the Conclave long-limbed and beautiful.

The Aubade continued as if he had not heard the interruption – even by the standards of his species, the Aubade had a magnificent talent for disdain. 'She furthermore informs us that their Senate has been making worrying claims upon the former Aelerian city of Oscan – which, my siblings will recall, was the price that we demanded twenty-five years ago for their temerity in advancing on Salucia.'

'We are all well aware of the Roost's recent history,' the Glutton said.

'And yet you seem to learn so little by it,' the Aubade replied.

'I have perused the Sentinel's missive,' the Prime said, in an attempt to check the growing dispute, 'and wonder what point the Lord of the Red Keep wishes to raise regarding it?'

'When we smashed the Aelerians, we did so to check their continued northward expansion, and to ensure that they failed to become the dominant human power on the continent. Only the first was realised. Though they have turned their attentions on nations to the south and west, away from our own interests, the naked ambition remains unchanged.'

'My sibling's dislike of Aeleria is well known,' the Lord of the House of Kind Lament said. 'His vision on this matter is not unclouded.'

In the time of her grandfather five steps removed, the Aubade had spent his quarter-century as Sentinel of the Western Reach, in Elsium by the Sea. It had been during his tenure that Aeleria had begun their first wave of expansion, sacking and destroying the city. He seldom spoke of it, though it was said by the other Eternal that his experience there had changed him, imprinted the curious, melancholic character that was now his hallmark.

'I, for one, appreciate the Lord of the Red Keep bringing this subject to our attention,' a voice said.

As it was impossible in theory, and unwise in practice, for a human to speak the true name of Those Above, an elaborate system of nomenclature had developed, every Eternal in the Roost having at least one nickname and often two or three. Sometimes they referred to some quirk of their physical appearance, or the castle in which they lived. Sometimes the names were in affectionate admiration, or recognised some extraordinary deed. Sometimes they referenced an event that had long since passed out of human memory, descended down through the generations without the accompanying story – thus the Lady of the Immaculate Safehold was known as 'Hibiscus' for reasons no one living could even begin to guess at.

But everyone knew why the Lord of the Ebony Towers was the Shrike, and not simply because he was young for an Eternal, perhaps not so much older than Calla even, and had been given his sobriquet by the humans of her own generation. All of the High were alien, unknowable, sometimes terrible the way a storm is terrible, or the grip of winter. But there was something in the Shrike that was more than alien, more than indifferent – most Eldest did not look at you when they spoke, seemed barely able to distinguish a human from the scenery around them. But the Shrike saw you, saw you the way a cat sees a limping mouse. His household humans were equally foreign, did not eat or drink or play where the other humans of the First Rung ate and drank and played; did not, so far as Calla could tell, ever leave the estate, except when accompanying the Lord himself. But all the same, strange rumours sometimes slipped out from within the confines of the Ebony Towers, nasty things, things that Calla could not help but believe.

The Shrike was also said to be among the finest musicians on the First Rung, and one of the most talented draughtsmen. It was broadly agreed that there was no more beautiful male of the species – except for the Aubade himself, and of course it was obvious enough where Calla's sympathies lay in that contest.

'By what right do these . . . Aelerians go to war without our say-so?' The Shrike always attended the Conclave but almost never spoke – and when he did, what he said was short and sharp and ugly and often true. He wore interlaced robes of black silk, and his face was covered with white powder like a porcelain mask. The two humans who accompanied him seemed more than usually silent. 'Are they not our bondsmen? Have they not sworn obedience to the Roost, and are their tithes not proof of this?'

'The Five-Fingered are fractious and violent creatures,' the Glutton explained, as though he were talking to a child. 'There has never been a period in their history when they were not killing each other. It would be waste and folly to attempt to police every individual act of violence that these . . . animals perpetrate.'

'You've made an impressive virtue of apathy, sibling,' the Shrike said.

'No doubt this is all very exciting to the Lord of the Ebony Towers,' the Glutton said, after a moment lost in silent offence, 'but to those of us who have spent more than a Locust's age here in the Conclave, the manoeuvrings and diversions of the petty human provinces to the west are not of such overwhelming interest as to demand the entirety of our attention.'

'I have spent longer than that observing the musings of the

Conclave,' the Aubade intervened. 'And longer still studying the behaviour of Those Below. And if you confuse the Aelerians with the trumped-up princelings of the southern kingdoms then you have mistaken a broadsword for a butter knife.'

'The Lord of the Red Keep has the truth of it,' the Shrike said. 'Perhaps the Aelerians require another lesson in that respect. Perhaps it is time we reminded them of their proper place. It has been too long since Those Below have heard the beating hooves of our cavalry.'

'Perhaps if my Lord of the Ebony Towers had ridden out to face them,' the Aubade said, 'he would not speak so casually of their spears.'

'Regrettably, my youth made it impossible for me to take part in the conflict,' the Shrike said, 'though my understanding was that we emerged victorious.'

'Indeed – we crushed the flower of their army beneath the hooves of our stallions. And three years later they were marching west to the plains, and south to Old Dycia. The Lord of the Ebony Tower might take a moment to meditate on the lessons of that.'

'I think the Lord of the Red Keep makes too much of slaughtering Locusts,' the Shrike said. 'While I recognise the renown he has earned in battle, I do not feel the need to brag every time I step on an ant.'

'What a handsome quality is arrogance, especially when paired with youth.'

Here the Prime broke in smoothly. 'Would it satisfy the Lord of the Red Keep if we were to indicate to the Sentinel that the Aelerians must cease their efforts against Salucia, or risk incurring our displeasure?'

Calla got the distinct sense that this did not satisfy the Lord at all, but it was clear the mood of the room was against him. The Aubade had his supporters among the Wellborn, others who thought, like him, that the Roost was insufficiently active in policing the human nations, but they were in the minority. 'I think it in the best interests of the Roost,' he said.

'For our next order of business,' the Prime continued, 'the Conclave shall hear the words of Cormorant, Chief Constable for the Fifth Rung, to explain the disobedience his people demonstrated during the Anamnesis.'

There were more humans in the Roost than could ever be overseen by the small core of Eternal that lived on the First Rung – devolving some of the levers of power was a practical necessity. As a result the greater part of the Roost was overseen by the humans themselves. The custodians maintained order and punished crime, bureaucrats collected taxes and oversaw commerce. In this it was much like any other city – except that all true decision-making power remained in the hands of Those Above. Mostly, they cared little enough what went on beneath them, and a position within the civil order was a lucrative and easy sinecure. On those rare occasions when the Eldest decided to take an interest in the bottom four-fifths of their city, however, the position got a good deal more stressful.

No doubt the Chief Constable for the Fifth Rung was thinking something along those lines just at that moment. He was a handsome man run to fat, dressed in a tasteful set of robes that were just the slightest bit too small for him, and he had been sweating through these at a greater rate than the material was prepared to accept, splotches of wet appearing beneath his arms and at his neck. The Chief Constable for the Fifth Rung, needless to say, did not live on the Fifth Rung, and was certainly not born there. Probably he managed to find his way down there on occasion, though Calla found it hard to imagine these were very frequent.

At least he managed a competent greeting, bowing low in the traditional fashion, his hands behind him. 'As the Conclave is no doubt aware, on the afternoon of the last Anamnesis, the Fifth Rung's celebrations were interrupted by a heinous act of terror. A small group of miscreants, acting stealthily and without the connivance of the performers, killed and hung an eagle from inside the steamwork chamber that is the centrepiece of the ceremony. The custodians, acting swiftly and with certainty, tracked down and captured the responsible parties. Their guilt being impossible to deny, they admitted their involvement unreservedly. Given the nature of their crime, the gravest possible consequences were seen as not inappropriate. The convicted were drawn and quartered, with a limb sent to each corner of the Rung, to remind the people of the swiftness of justice and the continued assurance of order.' Speech completed, the constable bowed again, as low as his age and weight would allow. It was rare for a human to testify in the Conclave, but he had managed himself competently. He seemed for a few brief seconds like a man relieved of a great burden.

'What motivated these men to their act of disobedience?' Another interruption from the Aubade.

Calla suspected the better part of the Conclave could have lived without it. She was positive that, for his part, the constable would have preferred his interview long finished. 'Who can understand the acts of a deranged mind, my Lords? There are many among the lower portions of the Roost for whom sanity is not a given.'

'You say they confessed to the deeds?'

'Yes, my Lord.'

'And in their confession gave no explanation?'

'What exactly is my brother's concern in this matter?' the Wright asked in his native tongue, the first time he had bothered to speak. 'Surely you cannot feel that the sentence was less than rigorous?'

'My concern, sibling,' the Aubade answered in human speech, still staring at the constable, 'is that an act of rebellion has been committed against the Roost, and the reasons and perpetrators remain unknown.'

'The constable has reported that the perpetrators have been found and punished,' the Wright said.

'And what evidence has the constable presented?' the Aubade asked.

It took a long time for the constable to realise this was a question directed at him, and longer still for him to answer it.

'As I said, my Lord, the suspects confessed openly to their involvement.'

'Was torture involved in soliciting this confession?'

'My Lord?'

'Torture,' the Aubade explained, 'physical force applied against the body. Blows to the face and neck. Edged weapons. A razored lash. I'm told an open flame is effective.'

'I believe they were, my Lord, as is protocol.'

'I would think that, beneath such tender ministrations, one could get a Five-Finger to confess to nearly anything.'

The constable had nothing to say to that – was saved, if saved could be the word, by the Shrike himself. 'I would take the opportunity to second the Lord of the Red Keep's concern,' he said. 'The punishment meted out to the Locusts responsible for this atrocity seems ludicrously lenient.' He spoke now in the human tongue, and turned his eyes towards the unfortunate constable. 'You say that those who have sinned have been punished – what about the collective sin of your species, who allowed these traitors to nurse at their breasts, who sheltered them, and who are thus every bit as guilty as those responsible for the deed itself?'

'You find a weed, and you'd burn the field?' the Aubade said crisply. 'What magnificent gardens you must possess.'

'If the Lord of the Red Keep has quite finished sharpening his nails,' the Wright interrupted, 'perhaps he might clarify his point? Should my brother feel the constable to be incompetent to hold his position, I hardly suppose the Conclave will resist him in appointing another.'

'And replace him with whom? Another, equally incompetent? The issue at hand is not with the constable, who is no better nor worse than any of his colleagues. The issue is that we have forsaken our responsibility to govern the entirety of our city, have abdicated the duties demanded of us so long and so thoroughly that they have devolved onto an individual such as this.' The Aubade gestured at the unfortunate constable, who, despite having no idea what was being said, seemed to have some sense that it was not complimentary.

'And does the Fifth Rung so often enjoy the presence of the Lord of the Red Keep?' the Glutton asked.

'Your blow is well aimed – I am as much at fault as any among you. And we can well see what effect this neglect has had. Those Below look to us to guide and teach them, to watch over and protect them. We have failed to do so, and the result is violence, anarchy, disorder. My Lord of the Ebony Towers speaks of collective responsibility, but he has confused the guilty parties. Each and every one of us stands condemned – it is to us that the governance of the city has been given, and it is we who bear the weight for the misery of its inhabitants.'

Looking about the Conclave, Calla hardly had the impression that the collected Eldest were overwhelmed by their sense of shame.

'And what is it you would have us do, then?' the Prime asked finally.

'I propose that the Conclave send a committee to the lower Rungs, to determine what grievances have caused this act of rebellion, and to determine what means are required to satisfy those grievances.'

'You meet antagonism with an open palm?' the Shrike asked. 'Would one train a raptor in such a fashion, or discipline a dog?'

'My sibling is welcome to visit my aviary whenever he wishes a lesson on proper husbandry,' the Aubade said smoothly. 'And it speaks ill of his wit that he can imagine no way to change a thing's behaviour save by beating it.'

'Who among us would make up this commission?' the Prime asked quickly.

Since the Founding, when Those Above had foresworn the wandering of their ancestors to create and populate the Roost, to leave the summit of the city was considered, if not quite blasphemous, at the very least extremely distasteful. The Eldest lived in the sky, or as close to it as they could reach, and in general left the First Rung only to make war.

'Myself, of course,' the Aubade said. 'And also my Lord of the Sidereal Citadel, if he were so inclined. I would hope that the Prime herself would appreciate the gravity of this situation, and act accordingly, though of course I do not presume to speak for her.'

The Prime stood silent for a moment, though it was impossible to read anything of her thoughts on her perfect, immutable face. 'I shall accompany you,' she said simply.

The Wright agreed as well, though he looked less than pleased about it, and it was starting to seem that the Conclave might finally come to an end when the Shrike spoke up unexpectedly. 'I could hardly allow my esteemed siblings to undergo the discomfort of a descent without agreeing to share their sufferings.'

The Aubade stared stiffly at the Shrike but said nothing. There was nothing to be said – the Shrike had as much right to join the committee as anyone, could not be kept off it. The Prime nodded and declared the Conclave over, and the meeting broke up like a rain cloud burned off by the noonday sun, the Eternal disappearing through the great white-gold doors that led to their pleasure craft. Even after a lifetime of observing them, Calla found herself in something like awe of the matchless synchronicity, each individual moving as smoothly and exactly as if they had been a flock of geese turning in flight. Of course, their human servants mucked up the gears some, bumped into each other or teetered down the stairs, but still – one had the sense that if it were not for the humans, the few thousand Wellborn present could have evacuated the building in a flat half-minute.

Calla could appreciate the viewpoint because, alone among the assemblage, the Aubade did not bother to move, remained watching the Source long after the rest of the Conclave had disappeared, staring into its waters without comment or motion. 'And so they scatter back to their games, even as the very thing starts to blaze,' he whispered in the High Tongue, after many moments had passed.

For once even Calla had the good sense to pretend she hadn't heard anything.

14

Bas stood in a vast and sumptuous hall, overly vast and overly sumptuous by any conceivable standards, let alone the rustic ones to which Bas held. He was watching the crowd and resolutely not playing with his collar, though it was an act of will to resist ripping off his stiff, hideous robes and running out into the bushes, naked and screaming.

An inappropriate coda to the gathering, which after all had been thrown in his honour, as part of the general revelry accompanying his ascension to Strategos. Nominally, at least, though it did not seem to Bas that the hundreds of strangers surrounding him needed their arms twisted to attend a party.

He had reached the capital two days before, spent the better part of the interim being gawked at or fed, something between a circus freak and a pig being fattened for slaughter. That afternoon he had received the medal of Blessed Terjunta, official emblem of his promotion. He had thought that would be the end of it, which in retrospect was clear foolishness. Nothing in the capital happened without a gala to celebrate it.

Bas noticed the senator who had given him his honour approaching out of the corner of his eye, steeled himself for the conversation as he had in the past prepared for a cavalry charge. On the senator's arm was one of that staggeringly beautiful race of courtesans the capital bred like cattle, round-chested and hollow-eyed. Accompanying them was a small pack of very important people whose names Bas had not bothered to learn. He'd have been grateful if they'd been willing to offer him the same courtesy.

'Hail Bas the Caracal, executor of justice, the shield behind which Aeleria flourishes.'

The day had been filled with these flourishes, each new inter-locutor vying to cover him in panegyric. It had become quite winding. 'Senator Gratian,' he said.

Bas would have preferred to look at the senator and feel nothing – it wasn't his business to feel anything for the senator. But were he to have been honest, Bas did feel something, and that thing was not kind. A fat man, was the senator, though no doubt he would have called himself stout or hardy or some other word clever men invent to make white sound black. The senator couldn't have carried a pack for half a day's march, let alone stood shoulder to shoulder with a pike in his hands, but at his order tens of thousands of men would launch themselves across the map, death and terror trailing close behind.

'Long years it's been since I've seen you, old friend. Not since the fall of Dycia.' Gratian had been the ambassador to that nation in the days just before it fell. Fell was the wrong way to put it – was pushed, one had to acknowledge, and Gratian had done quite a bit to set the thing teetering. 'Fifteen years, and it's as fresh in my mind as the morning's rain.'

To whom was he speaking? The big-titted bitch on his arm? Presumably her presence in Gratian's bed was a guarantee. Or was it the other senator in sackcloth standing beside him, who reeked of sweat and self-importance, and who Bas felt fairly certain was trying to manoeuvre himself in such a fashion as to have Bas's shoulders brush against his chest? Certainly he wasn't talking to Bas. 'My memory isn't what it was,' Bas said, turning to the drink in his hand, a too-sweet summer wine that he didn't care for but finished anyway.

Gratian began to speak to his woman with the awkward deliberateness of a theatre aside. 'The Caracal is modest, as is proper for a soldier. But a politician is bound to no such code, and I can tell you that nothing could be more calculated to inspire awe in the heart of any true-born son of Aeleria than the sight of our victorious forces bringing the Dycian menace to heel. The Caracal carried the battlements all but single-handed, his great red blade singing a song of terror among the hordes.'

How the senator could see any of that, having been a good cable back from the front lines, ensconced in a tent that could have comfortably fitted half a thema, Bas was not sure. In fact Bas could remember very little of it himself, the taking of Dycia having been lost amidst the innumerable scenes of bloodshed clotting his memory. 'Singing a song of terror', by the gods.

Bas noticed he was holding on to an empty glass, took it as an excuse to absent himself. Gratian didn't seem to much mind – greeting him had been a way to remind everyone of how important he was, and of his long history, perhaps even friendship with the Caracal, and there was no point in Bas staying around to spoil the myth.

Bas flagged down a house slave, let him pour some of what everyone else was sipping into his cup.

Issac was sitting at a table drinking very heavily and staring out at the assemblage, the red ruin of his ears clear in the lamp-light. Theophilus had been quickly stolen away by a mass of young men and women, friends from a youth that seemed far removed. He had his arm round a very pretty girl but Bas could see by his expression he wasn't listening to whatever it was she was saying. Bas wondered why the very pretty girl was unable to discern the same at so much shorter a distance.

Hamilcar was the only one enjoying himself, taking up a

place by the bar and holding court with a cast of inebriates thrilled at the novelty of speaking to a black man. Hamilcar had found the approach to the centre of Aelerian civilisation to be an unalloyed pleasure, thrilled at each stuttering step away from the plains, from the public baths to the improved quality of whoreflesh. He had also somehow managed to acquire what he insisted was the costume native to his people, a leopard-print robe and a strange, brimless hat. It was almost indescribably ugly, and in all his time in Dycia Bas had never seen a man wear anything of the sort. But it was what the crowd seemed to want, and Hamilcar enjoyed living down to the expectations of his audience.

'A charming city, your capital,' he was saying. 'Though I'm afraid it's got nothing to match Old Dycia. The water warm as the air, the little gardens of palm and avocado and pineapple, the ladies in their gossamer, light as perfume.'

'I've heard it's a lovely climate,' said a busty woman with enough make-up round her eyes to be mistaken for a badger.

'It is said the weather breeds the finest roses, and the most potent men.'

Hamilcar's soon-to-be lover made a little tittering laugh that Bas found to be just the wrong side of vile. Presumably Hamilcar felt differently. What her husband thought – or so Bas assumed the perfumed sot holding her arm to be – Bas could not say.

'Hamilcar,' Bas interrupted. 'A moment.'

'Please do excuse me,' Hamilcar said, smiling at each member of the couple in turn. 'The Strategos calls, and it is not for us mere mortals to dispute the will of the Caracal himself.'

The halfwits that Hamilcar had been overawing looked at Bas with something more like bewilderment than curiosity, the same look he'd been getting since he'd left the Marches, as if he had a second head growing next to his first. Bas took Hamilcar by the arm and walked him over to a corner.

'Watch yourself,' Bas said. 'These bluebloods love an excuse to stab a man with a sword. I saw two senators kill each other the night before Scarlet Fields because one had said something disrespectful about the other's boots. You'd think they could have just waited twelve hours, let the demons save them all the fuss.'

'You underestimate the depravity of our surroundings,' Hamilcar said, 'if you imagine infidelity to be a duelling offence. The Third Consul just finished offering me his wife, on the condition that he be allowed to watch.'

'Really?'

'Not in so many words. But one knows these things. Besides, the day has not yet come when one of these silk-wearing tarts can best a Dycian with a length of steel.'

'They'll hang you if you win,' Bas said. 'That's the other thing I learned during our campaign against the demons. The nobles don't play fair.'

Hamilcar smiled. 'Neither do I.'

Bas shrugged and let the matter drop. You could only warn a man so much. And Hamilcar could handle himself, even amidst this nest of vipers. Bas had only really broken him out of his group as an excuse to speak with someone he didn't despise. Maybe Hamilcar even realised that, because he didn't make any effort to leave.

It had not taken Bas long to realise that, though this particular celebration was nominally in honour of his recent promotion, and though he had not been in the capital for decades, he was at very best the second most-looked-at person there, and perhaps even the third. Taking primacy of place were a once-beautiful woman and the still-beautiful man who held her arm, the two of them surrounded by a knot of courtiers as thick as flies on fresh shit.

Bas paid little attention to the subtleties of Aelerian internal politics, but then again, one did not need to be a priest to have heard of Enkedri. And, so best as Bas could figure, Eudokia Aurelia held a roughly similar position within the capital to that which the Self-Created was said to enjoy on a larger scale. The Revered Mother, the Spider Queen, the Imperial whore. The conservative black dress she wore seemed out of keeping with her last title, though the sharp blue of her eyes spoke strongly to the one prior.

Next to her was the man who, if rumour could be credited, was to take charge of the expedition that – anyone with eyes in their head could see – was going to be launched against Salucia. Konstantinos, son of Phocas the Beloved, lost at Scarlet Fields during the great charge that had settled the Seventh Other War.

'He dresses very well,' Hamilcar said.

'You'd know better than I.'

'They say he smashed the Baleferic pirate fleet all but single-handed, a masterpiece of strategy and manoeuvre.'

'That's what they say.'

'There were no pirates on the Baleferic coast, back when Dycia still had a fleet.'

'You didn't appreciate the competition?'

'It's not a game for amateurs, and the pirates were just that. You'd see them plying the straits in these rickety dhows, a hundred of them stuffed into a space unfit for half that, not ten decent swords between them. Never sure whether you should sink them or give them food.' He finished off what was left of his drink. 'We'd sink them, of course. But we didn't feel the need to make such a display of it afterwards.'

The pack of people surrounding Konstantinos laughed uproariously, their bright garments and untanned flesh momentarily shielding the hero from view.

'The greatest victory against the Marchers since the death of Jon the Sanguine, the whole of the west open up to their pillage, and the capital creams itself over a boy with his hair all a-bowed. We'll see what that pretty hair does against the Salucians.'

'Or the Others.'

Hamilcar nodded, poured himself another glass of wine from a flagon resting on a nearby table, then topped up Bas. 'Or the Others,' he agreed, and the two drank. 'Does it gall you – a lifetime in their service, killing their enemies, making them rich and free of fear, and still you will never be anything more to them than a tool?'

'Not particularly.'

'You really mean that, don't you?'

Bas shrugged.

'Is there nothing that you want, Caracal?'

'I'd like this evening to be over,' Bas said.

Hamilcar laughed and drank the rest of his wine in one fierce gulp. 'If you'll excuse me, then. I imagine I'm going to take the Third Consul up on his offer.'

Bas watched Hamilcar slip back into the party. In the far corner Isaac was rapidly turning the corner from drunk to stupefied. He'd need to be taken away soon; it wouldn't do to have his second in command vomiting on the silverware. It would be a good excuse to leave, one that Bas had been looking for all evening. Off to his right he could see a group of gallants gathering up the courage to approach him, and with the same instinct for self-preservation that had seen him survive a lifetime on the Marches, he slipped quickly and silently out of a side door and into the gardens beyond.

The evening was colder than he had thought, too cold to be standing for long in what he was wearing, though in the first moments it was a desperate relief. Belatedly he realised he had drunk too much of the sugary swill that they'd been passing to him since he'd got there; his stomach was a hard knot of misery. Bas leaned against the wrought-iron railing and looked down at the gardens below, rose bushes and coloured ivy, and thought about the pleasure to be had in vomiting on them, the sour stink of his insides bringing honest taint to something beautiful.

'If you would excuse my interrupting,' said a voice from behind him, atonal and sharply staccato.

Bas tensed unconsciously when he heard it, reached down for a weapon that wasn't there, remembered where he was. Then he pulled himself up to his full height and turned round to face the devil.

He hadn't expected it to be a woman. Not a woman, he reminded himself, a female. There were few enough differences between the sexes – at least they both killed as well, riding into battle perched on their massive horses, pronged lances shining.

'I am the Lady of the Ivory Nest, the Sentinel of the Southern Reach. The Roost's liaison here in Aeleria. You are the one they call the Caracal? You will tell me if you are not. I have little skill in distinguishing between Dayspans.'

Bas had known that the Roost kept an Other in each of the capital cities of the continent, half as evidence of their superiority, half to act as spy. But that had been a distant sort of knowledge, something that he had never imagined would play any active role in his life. 'Some people call me that, I suppose.'

She cocked her head, flickered her eyes over him, swirling pools of silver. 'I had thought you would be larger.'

'Sorry to disappoint you.'

'It is not disappointment I am expressing,' she said. 'It is interest.'

Bas almost smiled at that. There was no shortage of humans in the capital, and weren't none of them so very different. It occurred to Bas that this was the first time he'd got a look at an Other who wasn't dressed in plate and trying to kill him. There had been plenty of time for inspecting corpses, of course, but a corpse wasn't the same as a living body. In this at least, the two species resembled each other.

He took a moment to look at this one. She was as tall as Bas, which would have made her something like a giant had she been a human, though for an Other it seemed to be more or less the norm. Her proportions were slightly off, her arms a tic longer than her frame ought to have allowed. Her hair seemed less that than a cluster of thick stalks, like the roots of some massive oak, though there was an absence in the centre of the tussock where one of the strands had been removed. What breasts she had were hidden beneath the folds of her robe, which was loose and dark and made of some material Bas had never seen before.

'It is true that you were the victor in single combat against one of my kind?'

'True as anything.'

'How it was done?'

'He wasn't your father or something, was he?'

She cocked her head at him again – in a human this would have expressed surprise, or confusion, but Bas was quickly coming to realise that their mannerisms did not align with those of his own species, and was unsure what to make of it. 'We had no direct relation as you understand it.'

'Then why do you care?'

Her eyes narrowed. 'Care?'

'Why does it matter to you? Are you interested in evening up the score?'

She took a long time before speaking, as if thinking carefully through each sentence – though whether that was because of her difficulty with the Aelerian tongue, or because she did not have an easy answer, he couldn't say. 'I believe you would say that I am curious? It was not a thing thought possible, that a Dayspan could defeat one of my kind. Some still do not think it really happened.'

Many, many people asked Bas about the battle that had given him his name. Very few had ever got an answer. 'A hammer,' he said. 'A war hammer, flat at one end with a spike on the other. It's good against armour, splinters bone right through metal. I don't think your people use them. At least, I never saw one of you carrying one.'

She seemed to think that over for a moment. The wine had well and truly caught up with Bas now, overtaken him on the road and thumped him into submission. His head hurt – and his knee of course, but only the head could be blamed on drink.

'What is the meaning of your sobriquet?'

'A Caracal is an animal that lives on the Marches – a large cat, like the leopards of Dycia. It hunts birds.' It also rhymed with 'devil's fall', which, if Bas had to guess, was the main reason that some nameless minstrel had decided to brand him with it in the days after the battle at Ebbs Field had turned him from anonymous ranker to the most celebrated warrior in the Commonwealth.

She gave no indication that she had understood, or even heard, but after a moment she began to speak again. 'The colour of your hair indicates you are old, yes? And the lines in your face.'

Bas laughed, an ugly bark. 'I'm not young.'

'Despite that, I think you would be a difficult man to kill.'

Things seemed less funny, all of a sudden. 'No one is that hard to kill,' he said.

'Yes,' she agreed. 'That is a very good point.' She took a moment to consider it, and then said, 'I hope very much that I get the chance to murder you on the field of battle.'

If she had been human it would have been a threat, but she wasn't human, and it wasn't. In fact, Bas got the sense that she had meant it as something of a compliment. 'It isn't called murder if you do it in war,' Bas said, though he'd never been sure why.

15

When Thistle saw Rhythm double-timing it down Talc Street at four in the afternoon, he knew something was going to go down. Because Rhythm generally didn't leave his hole till after dark, and he never ever hurried. Rhythm was the Brotherhood's representative in the neighbourhood, not just an affiliate but a full member, with the burn scars to prove it. And that made Rhythm the man in the Barrow, and the man don't need to hurry.

And yet there he was, undeniably on Talc Street, undeniably in the daytime, and undeniably bustling. Sweat puddled on his thick bald head, dripped down over the scar tissue of a nose that had been broken more than once, was licked off swelled lips by a pink tongue. Rhythm was a big man, dark-skinned, fierce-looking and sharp-eyed. He was dressed in Salucian robes; they didn't look good on him, but that was because he was ugly, and not the fault of the clothes themselves, which were tasteful if not elegant.

Thistle was sitting alone on his steps, the rest of the crew having absented themselves for the afternoon. Rat and Treble were down at the docks watching the ships unload, Felspar was at the Straits, continuing his ceaseless quest for upslope pussy. Thistle had seen almost as many cargo ships as he had apathetic girls, wasn't interested in making the walk to catch a glimpse of either. The sun was warm on his skin and the red brick he sat on warm against his arse. He was debating whether or not to roll a smoke. He only had enough tobacco left for one good cigarette or two weak ones, wanted to save something for after dinner. Would one half-cigarette be enough, Thistle wondered? His future self was an avaricious motherfucker, like his predecessor.

And then Rhythm walked by, and with him the sudden potential for excitement, like light leaking through cloud cover. And even though Thistle had never said a word to Rhythm, and even though on some distant level he was aware that he might be jumping in on more than he could handle, still as soon as he saw the man walk past he knew he would try to speak to him. Thistle was too young to be smart all the time.

''Ey, Rhythm,' he said.

Rhythm stopped walking, swivelled his bull neck over at Thistle.

'Everything all right?' Thistle asked, almost losing his nerve beneath the man's stare. 'I mean, you need anything doing?'

You heard lots of rumours about Rhythm, growing up in the Barrow, and if most didn't contain a grain of truth, that still left plenty to be worried about. They said he'd worked his way into the Brotherhood on account of being untouchable with a shiv in his hand, said he was worth two hundred eagles easy, said he'd sent more men down the pipes than turds. They said a lot of things about him, but the one fixture in this constellation of bullshit, the accepted fact of the matter, was that Rhythm had spent three years labouring in the dark, slaving away below. Anyone who came out of the pit and could still walk, talk, fight and fuck was a man to be feared, respected. A man to turn away from, when he stared at you.

Thistle didn't, though, and finally Rhythm said, 'Thistle?' Half a question.

'Yeah.'

'You Granite's brother.' A statement.

'Yeah.'

'You the one that got into trouble up at the Points.' Another statement.

Thistle shrugged. 'Yeah.'

'Come over here,' Rhythm said.

Thistle stretched himself up from off his steps, trying to look casual and mostly failing. Rhythm looked him over silently a second time, but it was clear whatever was going down he didn't have time to burn. 'You know Isle's tavern?'

Isle's tavern was downslope about half a cable. It was more expensive than the average neighbourhood alehouse, and Thistle didn't have enough money to drink at any of those, so he had never been inside. But he knew where it was, of course – partly because it was supposedly where Rhythm and his boys hung out, and by the prostrate standards of the neighbourhood that made it a little bit famous. But mostly just because Thistle knew where everything was in the Barrow, every gutter and rat and scratched line of graffiti.

'Yeah,' he said.

'That's where I'm going, and that's where you're going too,' Rhythm said. 'Except that you're going to walk a hundred paces ahead of me and you're going to sing out if you see any Cuckoos. A quick holler and then you disappear, you got it?'

'I got it.'

Rhythm leaned in closer to Thistle, and suddenly their differences – in age and size and strength, in experience, wisdom and ability – seemed more distinct than when the boy had been seated. 'And you ain't going to fuck up,' Rhythm said.

'You want to take Cross Keys, or should we just stroll down the boulevard?'

Rhythm almost smiled. 'Stick to the side streets.'

Thistle nodded and started off.

It took fifteen minutes to make it down to Isle's, and if they weren't the best fifteen minutes of Thistle's life he couldn't volunteer any better. Since the Cuckoos didn't make an appearance Thistle's duties consisted of nothing more than putting one foot after the next, and the occasional passer-by didn't have any idea he was holding something down for the man. But Thistle knew, and it brought an added bit of weight to every step, kept his spine upright like a hook.

Thistle stopped in front of the entrance to Isle's, took a backwards glance for the first time since he'd started off from his house. Rhythm was where he was supposed to be, and didn't so much as glance at Thistle as he passed him, slipping out of the sun and into the cool dark of the bar.

Rhythm hadn't told Thistle to come in – but then again, he hadn't told him not to. And Rhythm hadn't told Thistle to call out to him neither, and that had gone well enough. And there was no way in hell that Thistle was going to let this chance slide past him, head home, wait for Rat and the boys to show so he could brag about the little taste he'd got before slinking away.

Thistle followed Rhythm into Isle's, and he held his head upright.

It was dark and dirty and cramped. Rhythm had crossed swiftly from the entrance towards one of the busy back tables. Five men were sitting there, but three of them got up as soon as Rhythm had made his appearance, found seats out of earshot or seemingly so. The two that remained had reputations within the neighbourhood, and not for untoward amiability.

Spindle was a big, dark-skinned Aelerian-looking bloke, with a scar that ran from just below his eye down through his top lip, and biceps the size of ripe melons. The tattoo on his wrist marked him as a permanent resident of the Third, though Thistle could not speak to its authenticity. It was rumoured that the Brotherhood had an arrangement with the Inkers, one which allowed them to acquire brands that they were not technically allowed. Next to him, Chalk sat hunched over his glass of beer as if expecting someone would try and steal it from him. He was the sort of person that adjectives slid right off, you could sit across from him all day and that evening be unable to offer a description. Not tall but not short, not dark but not light, not anything, but sure as hell not decent.

Chalk was speaking when Thistle approached, though Thistle could only make out the last few words: '—as soon put the two of them in the drink.' He cut himself short once Thistle got close, snarled and shifted over to him. 'Fuck you doing? Ain't clear enough we're busy?'

Rhythm turned and noticed Thistle, narrowed his eyes but didn't say anything.

Thistle said something for him. 'Just wanted to see if there was anything else I can help out with.'

'He on the payroll, now, is he?' Chalk asked.

'Who's the mutt?' Spindle asked, cheerier.

'Granite's little brother,' Rhythm answered.

'Granite?' Spindle asked. 'Shit, I used to work the dock with Granite, back in the day. I heard he packed off to the plantations. How's he doing?'

But Rhythm interrupted before Thistle could answer. 'Granite ain't the point right now, and neither is his brother,' Rhythm said, and he put enough on it to bring both subordinates to attention. 'I told you the situation, so I can't for the life of me figure out why the hell y'all are still sitting.'

'Shit, Rhythm,' Spindle said, rising to his feet. 'No need getting sharp about it.'

Chalk didn't say anything, just finished off what was left in his glass and stood. He didn't seem happy to be moving, but then Chalk didn't seem like a happy person generally. As the group passed towards the exit, Thistle tried his best impression of casual. 'Where we headed, boss-man?'

Rhythm smirked but didn't look at him. 'Hadn't thought I'd need your services any more.'

But that was less than a dismissal, and it would take an outright command to shake Thistle off the only interesting thing that had happened to him since – well, a long damn time. And once they got outside Rhythm pulled a cigarette from one of his pockets, lit it against the wind, puffed twice and turned to stare at Thistle. 'You know Sweet Opal's place, off Craw Street, beneath the sign of the blue lantern?'

'Yup.'

'Same deal as last time. Keep your eyes up and shout if you see a Cuckoo. You get there, knock twice, tell Opal we're a minute behind you and make sure there's no one waiting there for us who shouldn't be.'

Thistle nodded and pulled ahead of the party, had to remind himself not to sprint. Instead he stuck his hands in his pockets, bulled his shoulders forward and wedged a sneer onto his face. It was his usual pose when he walked, but he put more into it this time. Appearances to keep up, after all. He wasn't just thugging for his own benefit – he was on special commission, deserved a wide berth.

Sweet Opal ran the best whorehouse in the Barrow, the top two floors of a three-storey tenement not so far up from the docks, catering to a couple of the neighbourhood big shots and any sailors that managed to make it that far upslope. If Thistle had saved up all the money he'd begged, borrowed and stolen for a year, he might have been able to rent a bed there for an hour. Even in the midst of pretending to be hard, he was excited to get a solid look at the place.

He was to be disappointed. Thistle knocked twice on the door below the sign of the blue lantern. It opened almost immediately, and a woman who could only be Sweet Opal looked out of it. Maybe she'd been pretty once, or maybe Thistle didn't have an accurate idea of what men considered beauty. She seemed more like a sketch of a woman than a woman, breasts large as fresh hams and an arse to match. Her face was painted in a garish imitation of an upsloper, itself a garish imitation of a seed-pecker, pancake blush and bright blue pigment on unsmiling lips.

'Get the hell out of here, kid,' she said. 'You're too young to come inside, and even if you wasn't you'd be too broke, and even if you wasn't we ain't open right now.'

Thistle put his foot in the door before she could close it. 'Rhythm's behind me.'

A wave of relief dripped through the paint and Opal put one fat hand on Thistle's shoulder, pulled him into the corridor quickly. 'Hell, why didn't you say so?'

Thistle found himself wedged face first into Sweet Opal's tits. She had liquor on her breath, and something below that – a hot, humid smell, strangely familiar.

'What's your name?'

'Thistle.'

'You working for Rhythm, now?'

'Yes,' Thistle said, the lie sweet in his mouth.

A knock on the door interrupted the dialogue, Opal pulling it open and gesturing Rhythm and his boys inside. 'Tin's upstairs,' she whispered. 'Second room on the right.' Her eyes were different colours, Thistle noticed all of a sudden, one green and one bright blue. Both had been crying.

'Anyone else in here?'

She shook her head. 'We had two other guests, but I hustled them out. They didn't say anything but that don't mean they didn't hear something – there was some screaming.'

Rhythm nodded, brought a hand up to the old whore's face. 'You done fine, Opal. You done good. Go back to your room, stay there until you hear otherwise.'

Opal nodded, opened her mouth, closed it, opened it again and said, 'Currant was a good girl.'

'I know she was.'

'Three years she's been here, never once made any trouble.'

'She was a good girl,' Rhythm reminded her.

'Fucking upslopers.'

'Enough now,' Rhythm said. 'Into the back with you.'

Opal nodded and did as she was told. Even one short, the corridor was cramped and hot as hell, not a place for parley. Rhythm was quick to leave it, heading up the stairs behind Spindle and Chalk, stopping at the second door. Spindle banged on it, his fist bigger than Thistle's head. He didn't seem to put any particular effort into it, but the door bent all the same.

'Who is it?' a voice said from inside, one close to breaking.

'If it was the Cuckoos, you wouldn't get a knock,' Rhythm said.

The door opened quickly. The man standing there – Tin, Thistle assumed, though he wasn't greeted by name – was fat and mottled and largely naked, the last throwing the first pair into sharp relief. He wasn't from the neighbourhood, Thistle knew that right off, and not only because Thistle knew everyone in the neighbourhood. No man in the Barrow could afford to grow man-tits, and no man in the Barrow could keep his skin that pale. He bore a brand that Thistle had never seen before, two shadowed triangles stretched nearly illegible by the dimpled excess of his flesh.

He looked to Thistle like someone about to fall from a great height. 'Come inside, quickly,' he said, his voice all vibrato.

'Get the fuck out of the doorway, then,' Chalk said.

Tin flinched and disappeared back into the room, Chalk and Spindle after him. Thistle had the vague hope that he might slip in as well, but this time Rhythm didn't forget him, turned quickly and made a cutting movement with his hand. 'Wait downstairs,' he said. 'And hoot if you see anything.'

Thistle knew well enough not to argue, especially since he wasn't planning on obeying. He nodded and headed down the steps, waiting to hear the door close before sneaking back to Tin's room and putting his eye to the aperture between the hinges and the wall.

Tin was speaking. 'Enkedri's bloody hand, I'm glad to see you.'

'Given the situation,' Rhythm said, 'I'd be careful about drawing the Law Giver's attention.'

'It was an accident.'

'She got her head bashed in by accident?' Rhythm said. 'That's some bad luck – for the two of you.'

Spindle was bent over in the corner, and he lifted what Thistle took to be the bed sheet off what Thistle was certain was the woman. 'Fuck's sake,' Spindle said.

Rhythm came over, obscuring Thistle's field of vision. 'What did you hit her with?'

'I'm not sure,' Tin quavered.

'The candlestick,' Chalk said, voice like lamp oil.

'Fuck's sake,' Spindle repeated, tossing the sheet back where it had been.

'It was an accident,' Tin said.

'You mentioned.' Rhythm uprighted a stool that had been knocked over in the tussle, put it in front of where Tin sat on the bed, dropped down onto it.

'What are we going to do?' Tin asked.

'About what?'

'About what? About the girl!'

'Currant, you mean?' Rhythm said.

Tin didn't say anything.

'We wouldn't have to do anything about Currant, if you hadn't beaten her face in.'

'I woke up and she was picking through my purse! When I tried to take it away from her she fought me. Far as I'm concerned this whole thing is your damn fault. Opal's your creature, yeah? This is your house. If you were keeping the girls in line like you should, none of this would never have happened.'

Rhythm didn't say anything. Spindle didn't say anything either. Chalk snickered.

Maybe if Tin had been wearing his upslope clothes and sitting in the top seat at one of the warehouses by the wharf, he'd have looked like someone important, but naked as an animal, cock bent below his fat belly – well, Thistle wouldn't have chosen this the moment to start playing the heavy. 'It was her fault, damn it.'

'I guess she's paid for it, ain't she?' Rhythm asked.

Tin didn't answer.

'When you woke up she was rifling through your shit. You told her to stop. She didn't stop, so you grabbed the candlestick up

from off the table and you decided you'd make her stop.' Rhythm
let a moment elapse, as the nonsense spread into the firmament.
'How long you been coming here, Tin?'

'A month or two, on and off. When I needed a hitch on my
lunch break.'

'Currant was your regular?'

'Yeah.'

'So you been coming here for two months, good and steady,
and this is the first time she ever tried anything like this. I tell
you, Spindle, all the time I've spent in a whorehouse, I never had
anything like that ever happen to me.'

'Me neither,' Spindle agreed.

'What was it, Tin? She tell you your rod wasn't quite what
you'd thought? Maybe you couldn't get it up, and she started to
snicker? You don't pay a whore to snicker, maybe you said. And
then the candlestick was in your hand?'

'She was just a whore.'

'And you're just a fat bastard from upslope, likes to beat on
women. And Chalk's just a savage likes to carve up strangers.
And I'm just the man settling it between the two of you. So
maybe you oughta tell me something that'll make me more
likely to judge things in a way won't get you leaked.'

'I bring three ships in a week for you people, three ships on a
slow week, three ships a week for fifteen years. You have any idea
how much coin that is? How much money I put in your pocket?'

'In my pocket?' Rhythm asked.

'Shade's pocket is your pocket.' Shade was supposed to be the
man Rhythm reported to, though he'd never been seen downslope.

'Shit,' Spindle said. 'I wish that were true.'

'I done good for you,' Tin said. 'I done good for all of you,
you know that. No point in letting something like this spoil a
good working relationship.'

Rhythm was nodding at that, not like he agreed, just like he
was marking time. When he didn't say anything Tin got nervous
and started talking again.

'So what are we going to do?'

'Right now I'm thinking about calling the Cuckoos,' Rhythm said. 'Let them know what happened, pass you over as a goodwill. I figure they won't give you more than . . . what, thirty, forty years in the pit? Or, hell, maybe do you ourselves, have Chalk put something sharp just below your ear. Cause it's a funny thing about the Cuckoos – they don't like finding one body, but they don't have no problem if you give them two.'

'Shade wouldn't like that.'

'Shade trusts my judgement,' Rhythm said. 'I tell him you in the pipes, he won't be shedding any tears over it.'

'Shade sounds awful quick to be giving up a hundred eagles a year in contraband.'

'You think you're the only official working the docks we keep in our pocket?' Rhythm asked. 'You are not. Just the only one who gets his jollies killing my girls.'

'It was an accident!' Desperate this time, desperate or getting there. 'I was just trying to scare her!'

'Give him one that won't show,' Rhythm said.

Flesh struck bone. From his limited vantage point, Thistle wasn't sure whether it had been Spindle or Chalk that had hit him. Probably Chalk – he seemed to like hitting people, and Spindle being as big as he was, if it had been him Tin would be laid right out. There was a lengthy intermission in which no one said anything, though Tin wept some.

'I say we bleed him,' Chalk said. 'Wrap him and the whore in the bedroll, pitch them both into the slurp.'

The man began to weep louder. Rhythm didn't say anything.

'I said I say we kill him,' Chalk said. There was a certain breathless quality to Chalk's voice that let you know he didn't find this set of circumstances at all unfortunate, that this was his idea of a good afternoon's entertainment, watching a fat man break, maybe even getting to off him.

'I heard you,' Rhythm said; then, to Tin, 'Where are your clothes?'

'There was blood on them,' Tin said, recovered enough from the hit he took to speak. 'I had to take them off.'

'That's fascinating,' Rhythm said, and he sounded tired. 'Where are they now?'

'They're in the corner.'

'Chalk, run back to your house and get a set of clothes for the man.'

'I dont want this dogshit motherfucker wearing my silk!'

'Chalk.'

Chalk spewed a long string of curses in Salucian.

'Here's how it's going to work,' Rhythm said. 'Chalk's gonna come back with some clothes, and you're gonna clean yourself up as best you can and put them on. Then you're going to head back to the docks and hire a palanquin to take you home.'

'And what then?'

'Nothing then. This is the end of it as far as you need be concerned, a bad dream that you get to wake up from. I'd expect to discover that whatever cut you get from Shade, you're going to start getting a hell of a lot less – but that'll be settled between the two of you.'

Tin didn't say anything for a while – doubtless it was enough trouble to keep from crying again. 'All right.'

'And Tin . . .'

'Yeah?'

'I ever hear of anything like this happening again, I'm going to let Chalk take care of you, and I won't be particular about how he does it.'

Thistle did not imagine this would be a problem.

'Spindle, you're on clean-up.'

'Take her to the bay?' Spindle asked.

Rhythm scratched his chin, shook his head. 'Best put her in the pipes.'

'Not the pipes, man,' Spindle said. 'This is my favourite shirt. You know you can't never get the smell out, once you go down there.'

'I know,' Rhythm said, slapping the bigger man on the shoulder. 'I'll cover it.'

Thistle hustled back down the stairs, making sure to keep quiet. He kept going when he reached the bottom, couldn't stop himself, out the door and into the afternoon. The sunlight did nothing to pierce the sense of unreality that had descended ever since he'd first met Rhythm, the feeling that what was going on wasn't quite happening to him, was a dream or a story he was being told.

Rhythm came walking out a few moments after, but he didn't say anything, just blinked at the light for a while and took off round the corner. Thistle followed him, cause why not at this point? The tenement back-ended against a canal, one of the endless arteries of the Roost's waste, draining slowly out towards the sea.

Rhythm rolled a cigarette and lit it. Thistle did the same. After a moment of smoking and staring out at the draining water Rhythm made a sudden and unexpected motion, reached over and relieved Thistle of his shiv. 'What's this, then?'

Thistle shrugged, looked down at his feet, feigned guilt he didn't feel. In fact he was half happy that Rhythm had seen it, the blade speaking of his strength and seriousness. 'Protection.'

'You mean it's so you can put the slant on somebody, knowing you're carrying weight in your back pocket.'

Thistle shrugged. 'You never carry a knife?'

'Not to sit on my porch. Not to buy a dozen eggs. Not because I like the feel of it dangling next to my cock. You know what happens if the Cuckoos find this on you? What they'll do to you?'

'Cuckoos don't mean shit to me,' Thistle said.

One quick motion and Rhythm had tossed the thing into the water, and on his return stroke he gave Thistle a good backhand, hard enough to knock Thistle's cigarette out from its perch in the corner of his mouth.

Blood on his tongue, Thistle brought his head back round to face Rhythm, made sure he stared at him straight on.

'I can't quite make up my mind about you, boy,' Rhythm said. 'Are you stupid or just playing at it?'

Thistle didn't answer. Maybe he didn't know. After a while Rhythm turned away, looked out over the canal. They watched the current slide past, fresh turds and slick lines of grease and endless bits of detritus.

'I guess you caught an eyeful in there,' Rhythm said. 'Maybe two.'

'I can keep my mouth shut.'

'I've heard loud men say that.'

'Then I guess Spindle will be putting two bodies into the slurp.'

Rhythm rolled another cigarette, lit it and handed it to Thistle. It was the best smoke Thistle had ever had, and not only because Rhythm used better tobacco and had a smoother roll.

'Why'd he do it?' Thistle asked after a while.

'The same reason anyone does anything,' Rhythm said. 'Because he knew he could get away with it.' Rhythm reached into his purse, pulled out some metal and handed it to Thistle. Thistle held it in his palm but didn't look at it. 'You ever need work, stop over at Isle's and ask for me,' he said, before heading back towards the main road.

When Rhythm was out of sight Thistle looked down to discover that he had two gold solidus in his hands. It was more money than he'd ever seen or expected to hold, more than his mother made in a half-year of washing, more than he'd have made in three months as a porter.

And it wasn't nearly enough.

16

To become the Archpriestess of the Cult of Enkedri had cost Eudokia dozens of favours passed and taken, hundreds of hours of political manoeuvring and ten thousand solidus in bribes. In return, she had been granted the rank of 'Revered Mother', an annual stipend of two hundred solidus – she only had to live another thirty-five years to break even – and the right to be present at the selection of her male counterpart. This meant as a side benefit that Eudokia, alone among the women of the Commonwealth, was allowed entrance into the Senate Hall, those hallowed corridors in which the policy of the nation was theoretically hammered out.

As it turned out, the Hall's facade, which she could view any day of her life and had on many, was far and away the most impressive thing about the building. The inside itself was draughty, strangely designed and not nearly as clean as she imagined it ought to be. Built some three hundred years prior, it was designed in imitation of the Conclave, the centrepiece of the Roost.

Eudokia had never been to the Roost, so she could not say with absolute certainty, but she suspected that it was a very poor copy indeed. Or perhaps the Others' reputation for engineering was, like so many other things in these sad days, no more than myth.

To Eudokia's eyes, the only bit of the panorama that could have any claim to grandeur – and she included the participants in this – was the Empty Throne itself, which had priority of place in the centre of the building, on a raised dais that no one seemed ever to go near. It was a magnificent thing – polished ebony twice the height of a man, straight-backed with golden trim and inlaid with precious gems. In the three hundred years since the last king had been slain, he and all of his line, it had remained vacant. Supposedly, at least – though you had to figure after three centuries one of the cleaning slaves must have worked up the nerve for a brief lounge.

Regardless, it was empty now, and Eudokia stood at the foot of it, dressed in the ceremonial robes of her office, which were ugly and cumbersome and immensely uncomfortable. There were many reasons that Eudokia had decided it was to her advantage to become head of the Aeleria's official cult, but a love of the accoutrements had not been one of them.

The last Archpriest had been the son of one of the Commonwealth's oldest lines, a bloviating, tiresome windbag. Already ancient when Eudokia had first taken up her mantle fifteen years past, she had enjoyed the dubious pleasure of watching his onward march into senility. During the last decade of their partnership he had become consistently incapable of remembering her name, calling her Euphemia or Eilexia or even, occasionally and for no reason she could perceive, Dafne. Beyond that he had the unfortunate habit of passing wind during the more elaborate portions of the ceremony, and falling asleep during the quieter bits.

Which was to say that Eudokia had not greatly mourned her partner's death, a sentiment that seemed to be shared by the larger portion of the gentry. Not that this lack of despair was to any particular degree a consequence of his incompetence.

Rather, as Archpriest was a position elected by the Senate, every member of that august body could look forward to a healthy gratuity passed their way by one or more of the claimants.

This time, at least, the outcome seemed all but certain. It was well known that Senator Manuel had set his eyes on the office long ago, the result of the strong sense of piety that the rest of the Senate feigned but that he seemed actually to possess. You couldn't tell it from his robes, but Manuel had as much money as anyone in the kingdom, though in fact he hadn't needed to spend much of it to secure his position. Manuel was a valued part of Senator Andronikos's coalition, and no one would be fool enough to go against the two of them. For almost ten years effective control of the Commonwealth had been split between their faction and that collection of politicians, soldiers, bankers and merchants who were, unbeknownst or not, Eudokia's own. A balance had long held; for her part, Eudokia encouraged Aelerian expansion towards Dycia and the Marches. Andronikos and Manuel had encouraged peace with the Salucians, which meant peace with the Others, and left her designs on the outskirts of the Commonwealth more or less unhindered.

One might have thought it a curious marriage: Andronikos, the man of culture and learning, a gallant as a youth, a libertine in old age; Manuel, austere and humourless. The curious constellation of beliefs and policies that had led to their coalition seemed ramshackle at the very best. But then, all alliances are ramshackle, and built upon convenience.

All alliances are also temporary, a fact of which Eudokia was doubly aware, and which explained her attendance at the Hall that day, and much of her work before that.

The ceremony itself was not due to begin for another few minutes. Manuel himself was standing amidst a crowd of admirers, and Eudokia crossed the floor to add her premature congratulations to those he was already accepting.

'Revered Mother,' Manuel said as she approached, and he even managed something like a smile, the joy of the day enough to overpower his traditional misogyny. 'How blessed this must be for you, to stand for the first time at the very altar of freedom, the heartbeat of ancient and noble Aeleria.'

'I confess to mingled feelings of awe and discomfort,' Eudokia answered, bowing deeply. 'Truly, Honoured Father, it is every bit as majestic as one could ever hope.' She put her hand to her mouth as if she had made a slip.

If she had, it wasn't one that offended Manuel. 'Not quite yet, not quite yet.'

'Forgive me, of course. The announcement has yet to be made. All the same, if you would allow me to say what a joy it will be to give worship to the divines in the company of a man whose piety and wisdom are a byword across the Commonwealth.'

'I can only hope that the gods see fit to grant your prayers,' he answered, though his smile expressed confidence in their favour.

And why not? If there was one thing Eudokia had learned about the gods, it was that they could be expected to side with whoever carried the heaviest purse, or the largest stick, as the case might be. Manuel was the second most important member of the Senate's leading political coalition, and had spent no inconsiderable fortune on bribes and gifts assuring his ascension. If under such circumstances a man could not have some hope of reward, then what was the point of righteousness?

At that moment Eudokia caught sight of Gratian out of the corner of her eye, standing alone in another part of the hall and looking somewhat the worse for wear. She excused herself and went to make sure he wasn't about to embarrass her.

He looked pale as wax, and there was the sour scent of sick on his breath. Eudokia managed to keep herself from grimacing as he gave her a kiss of greeting, but it was an act of will.

'I hope you know what you're doing, Revered Mother,' he said as he pulled away.

'I always know what I'm doing. And when I don't, I fake it very competently.'

'Manuel is a bad person to get on the wrong side of.'

'Who speaks of sides? Of factions? Of camps, cliques or circles?

My sole concern is for the future of the Commonwealth, and the betterment of its people – I would never think of insulting Senator Manuel by suggesting he feels differently.'

'If you imagine sweet words are enough to make the man ignore the injury you're about to do him, then you're not who I took you for.'

Eudokia adjusted Gratian's robes, speaking only when she was close enough to ensure that her words would be lost before travelling past his ears. 'I am exactly the person you took me for, and you'd be wise not to forget it.'

Gratian went from looking like a man who had just been sick to a man who was about to be so. It wouldn't do to have him vomit here on the floor of the Senate, and Eudokia moved quickly to try to calm him. 'Be easy, old friend,' she said, resting her hand on his. 'Things will work out as we've planned.'

'They'll see our fingers in it.'

'It's not the first time I've slipped one on a scale.'

'This is not a provincial governor we're appointing, or a stolen consulship. This is the highest religious office in the land, and one Manuel has been lusting after for the better part of his sixty years.'

'If you had such concerns you'd have been better off airing them when there was still some hope of altering our course.'

'I did air them – vigorously, and more than once.'

Eudokia sighed, removed her hand. There was no point in trying to grow a man a backbone through reason. A coward's motivation was fear, and that meant you needed to be the thing that he feared most. 'Then I suppose I must have ignored them, as I'm doing now. You don't need to have an opinion on what I do – you don't even need to know why I do it. All that's required of you, at the moment, is to smile when it happens. So . . .' she traced an upturned semicircle in the air in front of them, 'smile.'

The grin Gratian managed held very little in the way of jollity, but it was the best of which he was capable. One of the priests was signalling to her from the foot of the Empty Throne. It was time to get started. 'And for the sake of the gods,' she said, turning one last time to Gratian, 'have something to drink. You reek of vomit.'

The ceremony took the better part of an hour, lengthy invocations to each of the high gods, jugs of wine decanted in libations, silent moments lost in prayer. Eudokia had very little to do except stand silently and occasionally hold aloft some relic or another, and she managed to fulfil her role adequately. Throughout it all she kept an eye on Manuel, who was perhaps the only person who actually seemed to be paying any attention.

Though if the remainder of the congregation seemed to be only very casually involved in the proceedings, who could blame them? The fix was in, there was no mystery or surprise to any of it. In solemn procession that morning each had cast their ballot in the brass cask that had been preserved since the very birth of Aeleria. From there, following ancient practice, it had been carried into the chambers beneath the hall by the black-robed acolytes of Tolb. Safe from foreign eyes and outside intrusion, they had carefully tallied the votes. A centuries-old tradition, upheld when the Empty Throne was filled, inviolate since before the birth of the Republic.

Not that there was much need for such secrecy. Only Manuel had made any serious attempt at winning the position – no other counter-claimant had arisen, and it would have been impossible to mount a rival campaign without drawing attention to the fact. As for the acolytes themselves – cloistered members of one of the holiest and most ancient religious orders, sworn to silence and poverty – how could one even dream of corrupting them?

To do so would have required a silent, tireless campaign, years and years in the making. One would need to have been quietly inserting or twisting personnel for decades, introducing candidates as apprentices, shepherding their promotions through the ecclesiastic ranks, ensuring that these men, who had made devotion to the gods their life's work, put their loyalty to – or fear of – you above even divine mandate. Who was capable of such foresight? Of such intricate and subtle planning, of silently building contingencies without any certainty that they would ever be of use, just one of a thousand, thousand, malfeasances, subversions set aside for a rainy day, tendrils stretching throughout the body politic? Who would be capable of accomplishing such an immense task, or be audacious enough even to consider it?

Finally, mercifully, the ritual came to an end. A blank-eyed acolyte brought Eudokia a clay vessel, which she broke against the base of the Empty Throne. From the wreckage she drew a small slip of vellum, stared at it, blinked twice and brought her head back, as if having difficulty making out the words. Finally, she announced in a voice loud and sonorous, a voice that echoed out to every corner of the great hall, 'Senator Andronikos Narses.'

Manuel managed not to cry or break into a rage, but his eyes expanded to twice their usual size and he turned a distinct shade of pink, neither of which she thought sat well with his reputation for unflinching stoicism. It took the new Archpriest a few seconds to adjust to the unexpected honour. He blinked several times and looked about the audience, as if supposing a second Andronikos was about to leap up from his seat and claim the honour.

When that didn't happen, however, he managed to get to his feet and cross over to the dais. Midway his expression changed from shock to good humour. He had not sought the office, but since it had come to him of its own accord, who was he to deny the will of the Senate? Clearly the representatives of the people, in recognition of the great love their constituents felt for him, had decided to do him this honour. It is an easy thing for even very clever men to believe better of themselves than they warrant.

Eudokia embraced him, watching over his shoulder as Manuel simmered, twisting at the end of his worn robe as if he meant to tear it off and run screaming naked through the hall. 'My congratulations on your assumption, Honoured Father,' she said quietly.

To make Andronikos Archpriest of the Cult of Enkedri, and to do it quietly, had taken Eudokia twenty thousand solidus in bribes and a far more sustained and subtle campaign than she had been required to wage on her own behalf. To judge by the smile that she wore while greeting her new colleague, she seemed happy to have paid the price.

17

Calla was quite sure she had never seen an individual as terrified as had been the Marshal of the Seventieth District when late that morning the Aubade, the Shrike, the Wright and the Prime herself had appeared suddenly on his doorstep. There had been no warning of their arrival – on that point, the Aubade had insisted. He wanted to see how the Roost's administration ran under normal circumstances, rather than be presented with any artificial pageantry. Two hours previous, Calla and the Aubade had embarked on one of the swift oared vessels that Those Above used to traverse the city's waterways. They had met the rest of the party at the intersection to the south canal, and begun their long, slow descent. It was a strange and uncomfortable journey – though the waterways across the city were reserved exclusively for the use of the High, in practice few Eternal ever bothered to venture below the First Rung. At the boundary to the next the ancient but still functioning system of locks had lowered them twenty links to the Second

Rung, and after that they had been alone. Alone on the estuaries themselves, though the unexpected passage of an Eldest downslope drew the attention of innumerable humans, standing and gawking in wonder.

Calla thought it was wonder, at least, though certainly by the time they had reached the Fourth Rung those humans who had bothered to halt their bustle for a moment and take a look at the assemblage seemed distinctly more terrified than enraptured.

'The festival was continuing as normal until the trunk was opened, yes?' the Prime asked.

'Well, that, that was when we noticed the . . . the . . .'

'The dead bird,' the Aubade supplied.

The marshal flinched. 'The carcass, yes. That was when we noticed the carcass.'

Unlike the Constable for the Fifth Rung, the Marshal of the Seventieth District seemed to be a native of the territory that he nominally controlled. An old man, light-skinned, though at the moment he maintained a rose colour that Calla did not suppose a sign of good health.

He was wise to be nervous. The interview had not gone well.

To begin with there had been some difficulty in arranging seating for the four High and their human companions – apparently there were not twelve functioning chairs in the whole of the building. Calla found herself wondering seriously if there were twelve functioning chairs in the entirety of the Fifth Rung. That matter had only been settled by bringing a bench in from a different room and stuffing Calla and Sandalwood and the rest of the humans onto it.

It was an inauspicious opening, and things improved little once they were all seated. The marshal had never spoken to an Eternal before, struggled to understand the strange tempo and style of their speech, a task made no easier by the fact that he seemed little brighter than a radish. For Calla's part, she was hoping simply to get through the morning without falling asleep upright. She had spent the previous evening at Bulan's, and she was avidly regretting her nocturnal recreations. Foolish to have slept anywhere but her own bed what with all there was to do that day, but lately Calla had become a bit of a fool for the Chazar merchant, found he occupied her spare thoughts – jokes he had made, evenings they had shared, a peculiar trick that he had learned to perform with his tongue.

'And what was it that led you to your suspects?' the Aubade asked.

'Well . . . they confessed, didn't they?'

'But before they confessed – what was it that tailored your investigations in their direction?'

'They was . . . they was just the sort of people that liked to make trouble, like that,' the marshal said lamely. 'Troublemakers, they were.'

'Not any longer,' the Shrike said in the High Tongue. For all he had insisted on being a member of the commission, the Shrike had so far treated the entire episode as being unworthy of the time and attention required.

'Who had access to the cabinet?' the Aubade asked.

'Supposed to be just the mummers themselves,' the marshal said. 'But they didn't know anything about it. The casket is kept in storage during the rest of the year.'

'And these . . . mummers,' the Shrike broke in, deigning to use the human tongue, 'what form has their punishment taken?'

Calla felt confident that if the marshal could reverse time by eight hours he'd visit the most heinous and unpleasant torture upon the unfortunate mummers, so as to have an answer to this question. His salvation came from the Wright, who had not yet spoken. 'Surely, sibling, you don't imagine that these men would be so foolish as to commit a crime which would leave them the prime suspects whilst simultaneously ruining their livelihood?'

'I put nothing beneath the intelligence of a human,' the Shrike responded, using human speech.

'And the marks inscribed beneath the dead bird?' the Aubade continued, as if the Shrike's aside had never happened. 'These five-fingered prints? What do you know of them?'

'The Rung has no shortage of graffiti, my Lords,' the marshal said. 'It would be an impossible task to run down every symbol and picture.'

'How like a human, to desecrate their own nest,' the Shrike said.

'Your contention then, Marshal, if I understand it correctly, is that a group of troublemakers decided to commit blasphemy of the sort which they must have known would result in a death most terrible, and they did this because, being troublemakers, they like to make trouble? Does this seem credible to you?' The Aubade asked.

The marshal took a very long time to answer. 'Yes.'

'Do you not suppose it more likely that this is the work of some faction within the Fifth Rung? One that works against the harmony and order for which we strive, who saw the trouble on the Anamnesis as a way of spreading their cause?'

'I wouldn't know anything about that,' the marshal said, too terrified to be lying. 'I wouldn't know anything about that,' he repeated, assuring them or perhaps only himself.

The Wright was staring at a small yellow jacket withering out the last of its life in a nearby dustbin. The Shrike was inspecting his nails, which were long and sharp and painted black. The Prime was looking at the Aubade in her vague but benevolent fashion. Only the Aubade himself seemed to be paying any attention to the proceedings. 'What I'm trying to understand,' he continued, 'whoever was responsible, is what grievance would drive your people to this act of rebellion? What have we done to earn their enmity?'

If the Aubade had made the calculated decision to reduce the marshal to a mewling ball of fear, he could not have been more effective. It must have seemed a cruel attempt at humour to the poor man, a set-up, because who would be foolish enough to tell the High themselves of their failure? In any case, he could not find it within himself to answer, though he opened his mouth once or twice as if he might make the attempt.

'We will get nothing more from this man,' the Aubade said in his native tongue, then stood and left the building.

'Finally,' the Wright said, following him out. The Prime and the Shrike joined them, and then it was Calla's turn, and the turn of the other humans in attendance. The marshal did his best to compose himself and give some sort of an appropriate farewell, but between the breakdown he seemed on the verge of having and his ignorance of protocol, this ambition remained unrealised.

Outside it was cold and wet and the sky was grey, though you could see very little of that last, the horizon being broken almost immediately by the endless line of tenements. A dozen custodians stood at what they likely imagined to be attention, having been pulled together frantically after the Eldest had already arrived. The custodians on the upper Rungs served little more purpose than to guide the flow of pedestrian traffic, but so far downslope Calla surmised that they probably played a more active role. In truth they seemed not so very different from criminals themselves, their uniforms patched and faded, with scruffy hair and unpleasant eyes.

Those Above did not seem to mind the rain, or even much notice it, though they loved parasols for their beauty. They continued their conversation as if beside a roaring fire, or a sunlit field.

'That was quite substantially pointless,' the Prime said. 'I hardly think that Dayspan could have been less helpful if he'd been trying.'

'Perhaps he was,' the Shrike said quickly. 'Perhaps his ignorance was a cover for nefariousness.'

'Perhaps the mud conspires to ruin your shoes,' the Aubade said. 'Perhaps the clouds collude to hide the sun. That man is innocent of everything but cowardice and stupidity. Though it hardly says much for the quality of our administration if someone so incapable is put in charge of an eighth of a Rung.'

'It goes along well enough,' the Wright said, leading the way towards the canal and the ships waiting there for them. The return trip would be longer than the journey down, the oarsmen forced to beat their way upcurrent, the long wait at the locks that would allow them to ascend from Rung to Rung. But at least they would be out of the rain, beneath the comfortable awning of the ship. There was a little brazier in the back, and they would warm themselves beside it while a pot of mulled wine did the same.

Except that the Aubade remained standing, rather than follow the remainder of the party, and of course Calla did the same. After a few paces the Prime realised that the Aubade was not following, and turned back to look at him. 'Are you not returning?'

'I'm going for a stroll,' the Aubade said.

'Excuse me?'

'You three are welcome to return, of course. I'm going to take a walk downslope, perhaps take a look at where the crime occurred.'

'The marshal said it had been cleaned up weeks ago,' the Shrike said. 'What do you seek to accomplish, apart from dirtying your robes?'

'I won't know it until I see it,' the Aubade said. 'And I certainly won't find it without looking for it.'

It was clear that the Shrike saw little purpose in the errand, and for once Calla found herself in agreement with the Lord of the Ebony Towers. The expedition had thus far been unpleasant and rather useless, and she saw absolutely no need to extend it out any further. Unlike the Shrike, Calla of course had no choice in the matter. She steeled her shoes for ruin and her soul for hideousness, and followed her master downslope.

Their too-thick escort hurried after them, beefy, frightened-looking men carrying cudgels with noisemakers attached to the handle. It was clear that this was not an activity with which they had much familiarity, because they seemed confused at how to go about executing it. Were they to walk in front of the Wellborn, and clear the way? Or would that be a sign of disrespect, to stand forward of Those Above? They seemed finally to decide the latter to be true, and took to trailing behind with Calla and the rest of the humans.

'What in the name of the Founders is that?' Calla asked the

leader of the guards, a portly fellow whose main concern seemed to be standing very quietly and not drawing attention to himself.

They were the first words she had spoken and they seemed to take the poor fellow distinctly by surprise, as if he had thought her mute or tongueless. 'What are you talking about?'

'That sound,' Calla hissed, 'that awful, incessant, sucking sound. I can't possibly be the only one who hears it.'

'Of course I hear it,' Sandalwood said. If anything, Sandalwood seemed to be enjoying this trip even less than Calla. 'Like a falling turd.'

'Oh,' the captain said, and he wrinkled up his nose in something that seemed like contempt, though whether it was for the setting or their ignorance of it, Calla wasn't sure. 'That's the slurp.'

'The what?' Sandalwood asked.

'The pumps,' the custodian explained. 'Where did you think your water comes from? You stop noticing them, eventually.' He shrugged. 'Or at least you try to.'

Calla had never been below the Third Rung before – she did not think she knew anyone who had ever been below the Third Rung before, for that matter. The general consensus was there was nothing to see near ground level, except perhaps for the docks themselves, which were reputed to beg too dangerous and nasty an area to warrant a day trip. It did not take five minutes' proximity for Calla to recognise that, if anything, the common wisdom was too kind. It was not simply that she had not seen such poverty, misery and filth – in truth she had never even imagined it, could not entirely fathom how any creature could allow themselves or their homes to be reduced to such a state of decay. Everything that could be broken was broken; windows and road signs and wooden walls and stone walls as well. There was nothing that did not seem to be in an advanced state of dilapidation, nothing that was not dirty or chipped, nothing that seemed fully functioning. The houses were grim and tiny and either sagged noticeably sideways or hung down over the street itself, like a pigeon pecking at garbage. Long stretches of pipe wove through and around the tenements, and omnipresent was a damp and unpleasant scent, as if turning over a wet rock. The roads were – as the Shrike had noticed – small rivers of mud, though it had only been raining a short while.

Atop all of it was the *slurp-slurp-slurp* of the pumps, the sound growing louder as they descended. As with every other human in the Roost, the exact functioning of the great machine that took up most of the mountain below was a mystery to Calla. Water came up, water went down – this was as much as she knew of it. Above the Fifth Rung the apparatus that controlled the flow was contained entirely within the mountain itself, and the only traces of its existence were the public fountains and the canals and the little lakes and ponds that dotted the city, artificial but formed so long ago that entire ecosystems had sprung up inside them.

Of course, the environs had nothing on the inhabitants. They shifted about in the alleyways, aimless in the late afternoon, staring sideways at you when your attention was elsewhere, looking away if you focused on them. There were children everywhere, thin and dirty and seemingly identical. Two old women sat in the dust of the road, heavy woollen cloaks patched like mottled skin, staring up slack-jawed as they passed, eyes seemingly unconnected to any internal process. A crooked man leaned out from the shadow of a crooked doorway, spat a line of tobacco into the dirt, muttering to himself in a fashion that did not smack strongly of sanity.

And though Calla would wish to feel empathy, in fact mostly what she felt was disgust. How could one allow oneself to live like this, she wondered? Poverty did not revert one to such a state of barbarism. Did it? It was not pity that these vague semblances of humanity inspired, it was revulsion, and after revulsion, bitterness. How could you think yourself a decent person, when there was such misery in the world waiting to be alleviated? Waiting and waiting and waiting in vain. Their misfortune made a mockery of her pretensions of decency, and she resented them for it.

'I can never understand,' the Shrike said, 'what it is you imagine that you see in them.'

'Best not strain yourself,' the Aubade responded.

A pair of young children standing on the steps of a tenement watched the procession wide-eyed, barely old enough to stand upright but old enough to know fear. A woman appeared suddenly from the doorway, raced over and pulled them both inside.

'Pitiful creatures,' the Shrike said. 'See how they turn their eyes from us as they would the naked sun.'

'One basks in the sun, sibling,' the Aubade said quietly. 'One does not hide from it.'

'Who can be sure of how these things think? Or if they do? As soon see into the mind of a fish, or a stag beetle.'

'Our sibling has always had a fascination with the lesser creatures,' the Prime said. 'As a hatchling he was famous for the affection that he lavished on his charges. When we came back from the last war and he discovered his prized eagle had died, he was inconsolable for more than a year.'

'It was a falcon,' the Aubade said, 'and I still regret its loss.'

'Why compare a raptor to a human?' the Shrike asked. 'You might as much compare steamwork to a lump of mud. We'd have been better had the ancestors stepped on them outright.'

'You think yourself wiser than the Founders, sibling?' the Aubade asked, and even Calla knew enough to recognise the danger in this question. Those Above had no gods and offered no prayers, but they did have one commandment – the Roost was perfect, and those who had created it, the first generation, were sacrosanct.

'You take offence too easily,' the Shrike insisted, 'seizing on a fragment of speech in hopes of showing me a fool.'

'You prove yourself one without any help of mine. Who do you imagine farms your food, mines your ore, cooks your dinner and cleans your toilet?'

'Bees make honey,' the Shrike said. 'It hardly proves them sentient.'

'Another thing about bees,' the Aubade answered, 'is they sting.

There's a reason, sibling, that we do not build apiaries in the bedroom.'

They had come to a fork in the main road, interrupted a procession of young adults. Calla had heard their laughter twinkle its way upslope from the docks, but it ended as soon as they saw the Eternal, replaced with wonder or horror or some combination of the two.

'Then it is there that the comparison breaks down,' the Shrike said. 'The humans might be better equated to grasshoppers – though somewhat less numerous, they share the same pointless love of procreation, the same lack of purpose.'

'They have the same purpose as everything else that flies, walks, digs or swims,' the Aubade said. 'They survive. That there are so many of them is proof of their success.'

'They survive because we let them,' the Shrike said. 'And I do not count *our* forbearance among *their* virtues.'

'Your father thought similarly – I wonder if he changed his mind, when the Aelerians pulled him from his horse and speared him through the throat.'

'I doubt the circumstances allowed much time for reflection,' the Shrike said, leaping gracefully and without pause over a puddle. 'Had they, I would presume his thinking would have come to align neatly with mine. Order amongst the Dayspans is best kept with closed fist, and stained lash.'

'Order? You've no more notion of order than a dog gone mad in the high summer heat. The blood alone is what interests you, savagery your only end.'

'Your affection for the Locusts leads you to discourtesy against your own kind. I am the Lord of the Ebony Towers, and unused to being spoken to in such a fashion.'

'I am well aware of your seat, sibling, and of the shame you bring to it. Your father and I were cohort-mates. I sang the song of loss at his death, I laid the wreaths, kept silent for six turnings of the moon. Would to the Founders I could have warned him to cancel you before your quickening, rather than watch you bring dishonour to his line.'

Calla looked down at her feet, tried to keep her breath steady and even. Though the Aubade and the Shrike were a hair's breadth from mortal conflict, there was no physical sign of it, at least not one perceptible to the human eye. Each insult was exchanged in the flat, emotionless monotone that Those Above always spoke in; both parties stood ramrod straight and stared at each other unblinking, though again this was the standard pose of their species. An observer ignorant of the Eternal tongue would have no idea how thickly death hung in the air.

But Calla was well aware of the humiliation the Shrike was enduring, the tremendous sense of shame that would be heightened a thousandfold were he to gain any inkling that the humans in their midst were a party to it. Calla took a quick look at Sandalwood, could see he was not unaware of the danger.

After what seemed a very long time, the Shrike lowered his eyes from the Aubade, who allowed his shoulders to slump almost imperceptibly downwards, and the moment of tension had passed.

One of the boys across the street broke the silence with an awkward cough.

The Shrike moved so suddenly that Calla barely had time to turn her neck before he had reached the group. For a curious fractured second the Shrike was standing in front of the boy who had coughed, and then the Shrike's hand was through his skull, and all that Calla could think of was a ripe melon dropped from a great height, flesh rupturing and bone shattering into a sheen so fine it might as well have been liquid.

It took a few seconds for the youths to start screaming. Even the other Eternal seemed shocked, struggled to decide how to react. The mass of civil guards dashed across the street, interspersed themselves in the group, though to Calla's eyes the children seemed more horrified than infuriated, more likely to weep than fight. At least they made no effort to defend themselves, and soon the three boys still living were face down against the mud, and the girls were shuffled off to the side, one shrieking all but uncontrollably, the other catatonic with fear or rage or despair.

The Shrike turned his back on the chaos, sauntered over to his party, stood in front of the Aubade for a long moment before speaking. 'I beg pardon, elder sibling,' the Shrike said, and it was not the red stain dripping down to his wrists that made Calla struggle to choke back vomit, it was the little bits of pink, pink like well-chopped meat, that covered his chest and his shoulders and his face, a trail of sinew or brain that had stuck to his cheek and that he made no effort to remove. 'I beg pardon, for one who has forgotten themselves, and their line, and who requires more instruction than he had realised, and who is grateful for your offering it. I beg pardon, elder sibling, and hope that in the future you take pity on my foolishness, and continue to offer your wisdom so openly.' The Shrike stretched himself in the pattern of atonement, left hand over his heart, right hand extended, dripping fresh blood onto the ground. The Prime positioned herself nearer the two of them, as if hoping to ward off a confrontation.

Though Calla knew that none would be forthcoming. Killing a human was not a crime, not an unattached human like the boy whose brain and skull were now decorating the Shrike's chest. It was not even not a crime – it was not anything, it was not mentioned in the codes of law at all, any more than the annals would need to explicitly state that there was no injunction against swatting a fly, or crushing an ant.

Finally, impotently, the Aubade turned his back on the Shrike, and on the screaming children, and on the whole Fifth Rung, and began to walk back towards his launch. Calla followed after him, silent as well. It took three blocks before the screaming of the boy's people was drowned out by the slurp, though it echoed in Calla's mind far longer.

18

The first week Thistle worked for Rhythm he was given three Salucian drachms, a month's salary for a bonded porter. Thistle had spent some of it that night getting Rat and Felspar drunk on corn mash at one of the bars on Bristle Street they'd never had the balls to go to before, and spent most of the rest the next morning on a brimless hat that the tailor told him was all the rage upslope. What was left over he'd given to his mother, told her he'd been doing odd jobs around the neighbourhood. She'd looked at him long enough to let him know she knew he was lying but not long enough to make an issue out of it, then patted him on the head and secreted the coins away. That night they'd had a hock of ham in their stew, and Apple had sat at the table and laughed some.

This had remained, roughly speaking, the ratio by which his wages were spent. A third for revelry, a third for dress, a third for home. Wasn't long before he had acquired a costume that anyone who'd ever had the money to develop taste would recognise as unbelievably garish, and his sisters had put on enough weight so as to obscure the outline of their ribs.

In exchange for his three drachms, Thistle was required to keep himself on hand at Isle's from mid-afternoon to late evening, and to carry things that Rhythm wanted carried, and run the occasional message, and now and again to spend the day keeping an eye on someone Rhythm wanted an eye kept on. Watching the army of porters wind their way upslope every morning, Thistle found it very difficult to call what he did work. Not that he felt guilty – the way he saw it, any of those unfortunate beasts of burden could have had his position, if they'd been possessed of a little more by way of balls. A man had to go out and seize his fortune in this world, not just wait around hoping that it would pluck him from obscurity. Thistle had come to a lot of these insights recently, along with his weekly three drachms.

His friends were in no hurry to call him on it, however, because if he was more generous with his newfound wisdom than he was his hard coin, still enough of the latter got passed around to satisfy Rat and Felspar and the rest. That was what they did most of that winter, drank their way through Thistle's money. That was what they were doing that afternoon, when things all went to hell.

They were at the pumphouse, waiting for him to get out of work with his coin, and they made quite the show when he did. Treble was up quick from his seat, passed over a bottle of potato liquor that Thistle obligingly nipped from. Rat slapped him on the back and Felspar complimented him on his new coat and even the younger Calc brother, who had never liked Thistle and never made much secret of that fact, all the same admitted the cut to be very fine. The two girls in attendance did their best to remind Thistle of their presence, though Caraway had been Felspar's lover since before the first snow, and Timbre was just about the most aggravating resident of the Fifth Rung, and hefty to boot.

'You speak to him about me yet?' Felspar asked, before Thistle had even taken off his new coat.

'No,' Thistle said, slipping the cigarette Rat had just finished rolling and putting it to his lips. Though they had never actually set it down and made it official, the rule since Thistle had started bringing in coin was that he paid for tobacco but didn't roll anything himself. Part of the shifting dynamic that had taken place in the last three months, along with Rat wearing Thistle's cast-offs and Felspar desperately trying to get Thistle to put a word in with Rhythm for him.

'Why not?' Felspar asked, and he leaned one hand on his hip in a theatrical demonstration of challenge. 'You don't think I can hack it?'

Thistle smoked his cigarette and didn't say anything. In fact, Thistle figured Felspar probably could handle his current slate of labours, simple as they were. Mainly what Thistle did that he knew Felspar couldn't do was to hang around Rhythm all afternoon without driving the man to violence. Rhythm was an all right sort but he didn't like big talk, didn't make it himself and didn't see why he had to hear it from underlings, and when you looked at it from that perspective he had a pretty good point. With the mouth Felspar had on him, he wouldn't last an afternoon before Rhythm bopped his head against a wall.

Besides, Thistle knew that what he was doing right now wasn't what he would be doing for ever. Already there had been talk of sending him out on collections, and that could include more than just picking up a bag. In the evening, in the small backyard of Isle's, with the door locked, Spindle would put a long knife in Thistle's hands and run him through his paces. Not a pig-iron shiv like the one he'd been so proud of, but a real weapon, double-edged, the length of Thistle's arm from elbow to wrist. And though he insisted Rhythm was better with one, Spindle seemed good by Thistle's standards, damn good, demonstrating each motion in the moonlight, how to hold it and how to parry with it and how to thrust it into some poor bastard's resisting flesh. Thistle watched him carefully and mimicked each move as best he could, practised the same every morning with a stick on his roof beside his dormant coop. And he thought about the day when Rhythm would give him something real to do, something that might earn him the star that would be burned into his shoulder, that would mark him for ever as a member of the Brotherhood, that would set his future in stone.

But until that day came there was consolation in dressing the way he dressed and walking the way he walked, watching Felspar fall all over himself begging favours and girls blush when he walked in the room.

Thistle took a seat on one of the broken pipes, and Rat sat on one side of him and Timbre sidled up on the other. With a few swallows of liquor in him Timbre seemed even tolerable – she had a voice stolen from a barnyard animal, but she laughed often and had a pleasant smell to her, and from Thistle's position he could stake out a pretty good view of her cleavage, and to judge by her smile, she didn't seem to mind him looking.

Still, you couldn't spend all evening staring at Timbre's tits, and they were nearly out of whiskey, and it was clear that an expedition needed to be agreed on. In the old days it would have been an easy thing – drink until you found that happy line between energetic and uncoordinated, walk a few blocks in one direction or the other and take your alcohol-fuelled aggression out on some group of unlucky bastards.

But the one downside of working for Rhythm was that it meant Thistle had to absent himself from the internecine feuding, the quick slashing raids back and forth that had all but defined his adolescence. It had been one of the points that Rhythm had made absolutely clear to him, after that first week when Thistle had picked up his pay. 'There's a man upslope that I answer to, once every couple of weeks. There's a man upslope from him that he answers to also. And up and up and up. Way of the world. I'm the man you answer to, and so long as that's the case the only violence you do is on my word.'

So far Thistle had managed to keep out of trouble, though it made for some boring evenings, and occasionally Felspar would lead Treble and the rest on a sortie that he couldn't take part in, had to listen to their war stories afterwards with a sense of shame that made him want to retch. Mostly it was made up for on days like this, when he stood head and shoulders above his old friends, and everyone strained close to hear what he had to say. Thistle was the most important person in the Barrow, and every joke he made was just shy of genius, and he was as handsome as a Four-Finger, and all it cost him was a drachm a week in drink money.

The weather was too miserable for a stroll to the docks anyway, cold and wet like winter always was. Easier to walk to Talc Street and get tight. Rat led the way, playing the jester and playing it well, the whole group having to stop every few minutes to laugh uproariously. After a few blocks Thistle curled one arm out round Timbre and she nestled against him and he could feel his breath start to go shallow. Mind occupied on matters other than the road, Thistle was the last one to notice things had gone quiet. But Timbre was apparently less taken with him than he was with her, because she saw them and stopped moving.

There are many things to be said about love, but one of them would not be that it is marked by its constancy. For immutability, for abiding and continued passion, one must turn to love's less cherished sibling, hatred. Thistle had brooded, meditated, obsessed over the Four-Fingers for the entirety of his life, since he was old enough to arrange a thought. He could remember spending hours as a child trying to form some mental picture of these creatures that lived above him and somehow ordered his life. Did they have feathers? Could they fly? Mother insisted they could not, but then Mother had never seen one. In time Thistle had settled on a vague set of abstractions, of size and wealth, of power like the rush of the water through the pumps. Perhaps it was the fact that the group of Eternal standing on Talc Road that afternoon did not correspond accurately to this image that made Thistle take so long to realise what he was staring at. But it clicked into his mind finally, the answer to this question that had plagued him even in his earliest memories.

And his first reaction – though he would never have said this out loud, though even thinking of it made him furious to the point of self-harm – was awe. Awe, and that was the only word for it. They were just enough like him to make him feel shame – two arms and two legs and two eyes – but each superior to his own. As if Thistle and the rest of the group had been a poorly crafted first draft, the Birds' the revised copy. One of them was female, and looking at her and then looking at Timbre he felt a great and terrible sense of shame. The other three were male, and Thistle knew he suffered no less by comparison.

It was not right, Thistle thought, for the gods to come down and walk with men. To give knowledge of beauty unattainable.

They were accompanied by a half-dozen human servants, notable for the exquisite make of their outfits, for having all their teeth and for their general cleanliness – though this last had been little improved by the jaunt they'd taken through the Fifth. Escorting them were a dozen Cuckoos, but Thistle had seen plenty of Cuckoos before, and didn't bother to pay them any attention.

There was a strange rustling sound that Thistle took a moment to recognise as the Birds' speech. It was utterly alien in pitch and tone, more like the babbling of a stream or the movement of the breeze through a garden. And they spoke without facial tic or hand gesture, seemingly without giving vent to emotion at all. Perhaps they didn't have them, or had them only in a distant and incomprehensible fashion.

Felspar shot Thistle a questioning look, but the exact degree to which Thistle was in over his head had been hammered home concretely. There wasn't anything to do but stare until they went away. And certainly they would go away soon enough – how long could anyone stand on Talc Street getting rained on? Hell, if it was up to Thistle he'd have split the hell out of here long since. They would leave and there would be nothing left but the memory, this horrible, tantalising, hateful memory, this memory that would keep him awake and furious that night and long nights to come.

He was right about that, though not quite in the way he supposed.

Thistle was staring at one of the humans when it happened – a pretty girl, well built, dressed exquisitely – and so all he saw was a sudden flash of movement and one of the Eldest was not where he had been a moment earlier, and then neither was Rat's skull.

In that fraction of a second between the Bird moving and Rat being dead, Thistle felt a fear so intense that it seemed to rob him of all conscious thought – the fear of a squirrel for a hawk, a mouse for a snake, a gnat for a hummingbird. Later that night Thistle would realise he had pissed himself, crumple up his trousers and throw them in the canal.

It happened too quickly for Rat to make a sound, but Felspar and the two girls made up for it with formless exhales of breath, like putting your hand on a stove. Treble was too shocked to yell at first, slow in this like everything else, though after a moment he started to mutter, 'Fuck, fuck, fuck,' again and again, unceasing until long after the thing was over.

Thistle didn't scream, though he very much wanted to, especially when he realised all of a sudden that what he was tasting was Rat's brain and blood. A bubble of anger broke through the fear just then, and perhaps the Bird sensed some flicker of motion on Thistle's part, or perhaps it was coincidence, but at that moment he turned his eyes from Rat's corpse. He gazed down at Thistle from what seemed like an immense height, and again Thistle was conscious of nothing more than the terror that was like a weight on his chest, and of the perfect eternity contained within the Bird's eyes.

And then one of the Cuckoos sapped him from behind, and Thistle was on the ground with a pain in his head that promised a happy few moments of insentience. Thistle couldn't even exactly blame them, they were as shocked as he, and being shocked they were just doing what came naturally to them. Thistle went loose and let it happen, for once in his life didn't bother to struggle. On some level he was happy that the Cuckoos had intervened – at least this way he had an excuse for not doing anything to avenge Rat.

There was one image that stuck with Thistle through the beating he took then, through the pain that wrapped his skull in wool, through the rest of that horrible night and the days to come. From what little he had seen of them Thistle had supposed the Birds were emotionless, or at least that they displayed no emotion. But Thistle now knew this to be a lie, because in the brief moment after killing Thistle's best friend – his only real friend, he saw now – and before returning to his own group, the Eternal had looked straight at Thistle, into Thistle, and he had smiled, white teeth stained with Rat's red blood.

19

Looking at him leaning back on the windowsill, the winter sun playing on his flat chest and dark black hair and still-turgid member, Eudokia could almost imagine that she cared for Heraclius. His smile might have been winning instead of spoilt, his eyes innocent rather than stupid. It was a rare thing indeed, especially at her age and in this stage of their relationship, for Eudokia to find herself being fucked in the late afternoon. But the Revered Mother had a policy about vice, which was to indulge it quickly and without reservation, then move swiftly on to more important matters. And so after a fruitless half-hour of going through her correspondence, during which she realised her budding lust would allow for no work, she had sent swiftly for Heraclius, who had been out at one of the clubs doing whatever it was he did when they weren't coupling.

He had, it was only fair to say, performed admirably. Men took such absurd pride in these matters, would trade half their wealth for another third of cock, went mad if they thought they hadn't satisfied you. The woman's role in the exercise was quickly disregarded, as it was in most other matters.

'Do you think I ought to purchase a larger palanquin?' Heraclius asked now, without preamble.

Eudokia sighed. Between ejaculation and aggravation was a scant five minutes. What he of course meant to ask was whether or not a carriage ought to be purchased for him, and Eudokia had no doubt where he would settle on the matter. It was not the avarice that bothered her – she had little enough right to criticise, given that from her end the relationship was entirely an issue of physical desire – it was the naked manner in which it was expressed, and the fact that if she did give him money for a carriage he would use it on the ugliest rig imaginable, garish and cumbrous and altogether awful. Like many naturally handsome people, Heraclius lacked the most basic appreciation for beauty, had never needed to cultivate a proper sense of taste or style.

'If it pleases you,' was what she said, deciding then that she would need to get rid of him, in the short term rather than the long. For some reason this thought sparked a renewed sense of lust, wanting instinctively to take advantage of this body that would not for ever belong to her. Heraclius noted her change in posture and breathing, rose from his spot and took her in his arms.

A knock on the door interrupted their play. Eudokia recognised it immediately as Jahan's blunt and loud and lacking any of the usual submission of a house slave.

'Away, damn you,' Heraclius half yelled, but Eudokia was already pulling away from him. She stood quickly from the bed and grabbed a bathrobe hanging on a hook by the night table. Jahan did not bother her meaninglessly, and duty trumped pleasure.

After their time together even Heraclius had come to recognise that he stood a distant second to Eudokia's work, though he was not altogether clear on what exactly that work entailed. Still, he put on an exaggerated frown, like a child's, which contrasted unpleasantly with his erect penis. 'You would leave me unattended?'

'I won't be long,' Eudokia said, pinning her hair back neatly. 'Surely you can keep yourself entertained, in the meantime.'

In fact Eudokia wasn't certain how long her business would take – but ten minutes or an hour, Heraclius could wait. It was not as if he had anything else pressing to do. Eudokia put on her house shoes and slipped into the antechamber adjoining her bedroom. 'Yes?' she asked.

Her bathrobe displayed more of her than was appropriate, but if the show of flesh meant anything to Jahan, he made no sign of it. 'The Salucian is here,' he said.

'Which one?'

'The smelly one.'

Eudokia sighed.

'The merchant.'

'Send him in,' Eudokia said, taking a seat beside a small tea table.

Phrattes seemed much the same as when last she had seen him. He bowed very low, and on his way back up he didn't bother to look at where her flesh was peeking through her robe. Was he a practitioner of that brand of eroticism for which his country was famous, or was she no longer very much to look at? With nothing more to go on either way, Eudokia decided to believe the former.

'Sit, please. May I offer you something to drink? Tea? Mulled wine, perhaps?'

'A glass of mulled wine would be much appreciated, Revered Mother. There are many lovely things about your country, but I confess that I do not find winter to be one of them.'

Eudokia nodded to Jahan. His scowl deepened a tic – he disliked leaving Eudokia alone and unprotected. A second nod sent him scuttling on his way. Eudokia appreciated the concern, but she appreciated good service more. And while Eudokia was always willing to believe the worst of anyone, even the most jaded pessimist would have a hard time seeing Phrattes as being the sort to make a suicidal attack on her person.

'Soon your work here will be completed,' Eudokia said, 'and the wide thoroughfares and ancient markets of lovely Hyrcania blessed once again by your presence.'

Phrattes accepted the compliment with a nod that was closer to a second bow.

'Your work *will* soon be completed, yes? And the wide thoroughfares and ancient markets of lovely Hyrcania blessed once again by your presence?'

Phrattes laughed. 'Indeed, Revered Mother,' he said. 'It was that very eventuality that I had arrived to discuss with you.'

'One might almost imagine now would be the time for that conversation.'

'The great man has accepted the first instalment of our money.'

Eudokia's money, he meant, though there was no reason to point this out. 'The specifics of the transaction?'

Phrattes reached into the folds of his robe, handed over a tightly bound roll of parchment. 'A note of credit has been exchanged from the Slate Bank of Chazar into the great man's personal account, as you wished. He was willing to accept the funds direct – indeed, I daresay his concerns were centred around the rapid arrival of the coin, rather than obscuring his involvement in the transaction.'

Jahan returned while Eudokia was looking over the figures, walked over and set a cup in front of Phrattes in such a way as to spill most of it.

'I must admit, Revered Mother,' Phrattes said, 'that your reputation for cleverness does you less justice than you deserve.'

'Have I that reputation?'

'Too cunning by far, is the mind of the Domina, if she supposes that her humble servant is capable of deciphering her enigma.'

'I assure you, she does not suppose anything of the sort.'

'To succour an enemy, in his moment of weakness? This is no winning stratagem of which I am aware.'

'You have made your first mistake already, Phrattes, if you think the great man my enemy. Circumstances have clouded his judgement, and I anxiously look towards the moment when I might bring clarity to this unfortunate soul.'

'And when do you imagine that moment will come, Revered Mother?'

Eudokia had a certain smile that she gave sometimes, a smile that was the full stop at the end of the sentence. She gave it to Phrattes then, though for once in his life the Salucian seemed slow to grasp the subtext.

'If I had a better understanding of our destination,' Phrattes said, all smiling teeth and hungry eyes, 'I could be of more help as a guide.'

'Is that your position?'

'What does one call someone who runs ahead of you, mapping out the path – who pursues your quarry relentlessly and with cunning, who tracks him and sets him up for the kill?'

'We call that thing a dog,' Eudokia answered sweetly.

Phrattes laughed at the insult, but he couldn't quite make it reach his eyes. That was fine. Eudokia did not require masochism in her servants – they need not enjoy the whip, so long as they knew enough to pretend.

He left shortly thereafter, and Eudokia returned to the chamber, slipped her shoes off and put her robe back on the hook. Heraclius had taken her injunction too literally, was standing at the door stroking himself. The last spur of appetite was gone now, her mind taken up with plots and stratagems. How foolish the motions of lust seem when unaccompanied by the spirit! Like badly done pantomime.

But at this point there was no way out of it barring a fight, and so Eudokia slipped herself beneath the covers and allowed him his pleasure, nodding along at his exhalations. It said little for Heraclius that he seemed unable to distinguish between the actual enjoyment he had given her earlier and the simulacrum she was currently performing. At least it ended quickly enough. Heraclius slipped into slumber, she slipped into the adjoining bathroom to wash her thighs before returning to bed. You couldn't really blame them for the trouble they made, it was in their very nature – from the first, the gods had decreed that men were ever to make a mess without being called upon to clean it.

She'd need to find something for him, Eudokia was thinking as she got back into bed, now that she knew she didn't want him any more. If he was tougher she could have got him a post in the army – but he wasn't tough, he was just big, and she didn't imagine it would take any longer for the hardbitten men of the thema to come to that discovery than it had taken her. Perhaps a vice consulate in one of the coastal cities, something to get him far enough out of the capital that she wouldn't need to worry about his making any awkward scenes at social gatherings.

Not that it could do much to injure her reputation among that half of the city who had long ago decided on her as the embodiment of all of their fears and fantasies, the 'whore-bitch of Aeleria' and whatnot. She took a sort of perverse pleasure in cataloguing the innumerable rumours, exaggerations and falsehoods that fluttered around her bedchamber like cherubs – the extra-species dalliances, the stud farm of young men she kept locked in her basement, stealing away their vitality along with their fluids. All nonsense, sad to say. One slow afternoon Eudokia had spent a few minutes backtracking through the history of her bedchamber, had come to the pleasant-sounding number of twenty-and-two. She'd known senators to reach twenty-and-two in a lost week of revelry, stumbling from whorehouse to whorehouse along the Way of Silk. Twenty-and-two didn't seem so vast a sum for a woman of fifty, who had lost her husband against the Others. You'd think they expected her to pine endlessly for Phocas, let dust gather between her legs. Well – it would spread quickly enough over her corpse. Until that day came, Eudokia would take what enjoyment the world offered her.

Jahan interrupted her meditations with another knock on the door that very nearly removed the thing from its hinges. Heraclius snorted at the disturbance, pulled the blankets closer around him and rolled towards the wall. Eudokia envied him his torpor – how easy a thing being a fool must be, she mused, as she wrapped her robe round her and went to check on the disturbance.

Orodes was dressed as an Aelerian tradesman, breeches and a billowy shirt, and he had that curious pallor and ambiguous set of features that might reasonably be attributed to any of the nations running along the Tullus Coast. His body gave an impression, if not of fitness particularly, than at least of strength and mass. He had beady little dagger-prick eyes, and though Eudokia could see he was working hard not to sneer, his efforts were not entirely crowned with success. Eudokia did not like him. Eudokia thought that perhaps no one had ever liked Orodes, that his mother, taking her first look at the boy, still covered in her own fluids, had thought to herself, 'Eh.' Orodes was a man who existed by being useful, rather than because anyone particularly enjoyed his company.

Jahan farted loudly in the corner, drawing Orodes's attention away from Eudokia, a reminder of the Parthan's presence, a veiled if graceless threat.

'How good of you to make the visit,' Eudokia said, nestling into her chair. She could feel him watching her flesh hungrily, was happy to see him doing so, and not exclusively out of a sense of vanity. A man is controlled by his passions, and the stronger and more obvious those urges, the easier he is to herd.

'Domina,' Orodes said, and bowed awkwardly before taking the seat opposite her.

'And how is the Badger?'

'Busy, Domina, busy.'

The Badger ran a bar near the docks in Hyrcania, and the neighbourhood that surrounded the bar, and some of the neighbourhoods that surrounded that neighbourhood. Eudokia only ran the Badger, which from her perspective was much easier. Whenever possible Eudokia preferred to work with criminals and kingpins, who could be relied upon to look after their own practical interest, rather than politicians, who sometimes got their pretensions of morality confused with the real thing.

Five years the Badger had been her stalking horse in Salucia,

or one of them at least, and so far had proven himself as competent as he was greedy – which, to Eudokia's way of thinking,
was all you could ask of anyone. She had never met the man in
person, of course. That was why Orodes existed, to serve as
go-between.

'I have delivered your message,' Orodes said. He spoke Aelerian
with only a very slight accent.

'Marvellous,' Eudokia said. 'And?'

'My employer foresees difficulties.'

'Your employer?' Eudokia crossed her eyes in an exaggerated
show of confusion. 'But I am your employer, and I most certainly
do not anticipate any problems as regards my orders.'

'My immediate employer, I should have said.'

'Indeed, you should have said that. Is this a question of money?
I hardly think you have anything to quibble about, when it comes
to funds.'

'I'm afraid it is not a question of compensation. You are asking
the Badger to go against the interests of Salucia, to make himself
a traitor to his nation.'

'Nations, countries, cities, species, races, tribes.' Eudokia held
her hands open, as if to suggest how little weight she gave them.
'There is one universal division, written on the heart of all living
creatures – there is you,' Eudokia said, making a short cutting
motion with her hand, 'and there is everyone else. I cannot
imagine the Badger has come so far in the world and not struck
upon this truth.'

'Would the Domina feel the same way if it was Aeleria that
she was being asked to betray?'

'But it's not the same thing at all.'

'No?'

'No – because, of course, I run Aeleria, while you and your
master are slaves in Salucia. What is well for the Commonwealth
is well for me. The same cannot be said of your position.'

'There is more to it than patriotism. The Badger is . . .
concerned at the wisdom of your proposition. He thinks perhaps
you underrate the dangers.'

'Is that what he thinks?'

'Public discontent is easier stoked than extinguished,' Orodes said.

'What a lovely epigram. You've a bit of the poet in you.'

'You'll be a thousand cables away from the conflagration when it starts,' Orodes said. 'We will remain very much in the thick of it, then and in the days to come. The Badger fears that the trouble you wish to make could well spread out of hand.'

'Sneak a look at my breasts another time, and by Enkedri and his children, I will have Jahan remove that portion of your body which leads you unto distraction.' Offered in so sweet a voice that Orodes didn't realise he'd been threatened until some seconds after Eudokia had ceased speaking. When he did he blushed with shame, but the red bloom faded to a pale pink as he took in the rest of the Domina's words.

'And not with a blade, either,' Eudokia added.

Jahan shattered a nut in his left hand.

'You were speaking of fear,' Eudokia added. 'A topic, I admit, of great interest to me. What a valuable thing dread is, how wise the gods were to implant it in our souls! Can you imagine a world in which we had not been gifted so vigilant and attentive a ward? The species wouldn't last a day, we'd all be leaping off cliffs and sticking our hands into hot coals just to see what it felt like. Truly, fear is the better part of human wisdom – one might say that the whole of prudence consists of ranking our fears appropriately, and dealing with each according to the severity of the danger represented.'

Jahan cracked another nut, slipped the meat into his mouth and let the shell remnants fall onto the carpet.

'And if I may say so, Orodes, both you and the Badger seem to have got your priorities of terror confused, like a man dying of famine worrying about next year's seed! Because whatever pitfalls are inherent in the design I have outlined, they are not equalled, they are not approached, by the absolute certainty of punishment that hangs over your head, if you make the irreparable error of refusing to obey my orders. I pay the Badger to eat the people that I tell him to eat. Does he imagine himself the only carnivore on my payroll?'

At that moment Orodes seemed to be incapable of imagining much of anything, save how dearly he counted his manhood.

'Tell your immediate employer that if he finds himself unable to fulfil my request, I'll turn to one of his rivals – perhaps the Chimerae, or the Blue Serpent – so many vie to do me favours. But whomever it is, their first task, by way of demonstrating fitness for the occupation, will be to kill the Badger, you, and all of his people, in a fashion as painful as it is imaginative.'

'Domina . . .' Orodes began finally, so pale that Eudokia worried he might mess on the carpet, 'please, I . . . I'm not—'

'You're not much of anything, Orodes, but we must make use of those tools available to us. And the best service you could render me would be to etch this moment indelibly into your mind. So when next you stand in front of the Badger, and he objects to the course of action I have prescribed, and provides the same excuses that you have just offered – you will know for certain how little any of them will satisfy me, and of the severity of my displeasure made manifest.'

For a man who made some part of his living with a knife, there was very little choice left for Orodes. He nodded and looked down at his boots.

'I offer no empty threats,' Eudokia said, standing smoothly. 'If you can convince our friend to stick to the agreement he long ago made with me, all to the good. And if you cannot,' she leaned forward, still smiling, 'if you cannot, then you would be wise to remove yourself from Salucia at whatever speed can be managed. Go to sea, take up service with a crew of mercenaries, join a mummers' band and travel the length of the continent. It will not stop my vengeance – though it may delay it, for a time.'

Eudokia returned to her bedroom, brushing aside the open door. Heraclius was awake and sitting upright. She disrobed, watched his eyes widen as the robe struck the floor. 'I find myself requiring your services once more,' she said.

20

Bas woke up just after the dawn, coming to quickly, alertly, pointlessly. He stared at the ceiling until well after the sun had dragged a line of shadow past his bedpost. Occasionally he scratched himself. Mostly he lay very still.

Eventually he pulled himself upright, leaked last night's liquor into the bedpan. Then he pulled his trousers off the bureau, sniffed at them uncomfortably. He visited the public baths every day, sometimes twice a day, sometimes for hours each time, but still the scent of the city seemed to have worked its way into him. Bas had no exaggerated regard for cleanliness – on the plains he had often gone weeks without bathing, dirt and sweat and sometimes blood accumulating till it was visible on his skin. But that was the honest odour of labour and perhaps death, not the fetid swelling of the metropolis, of too much flesh packed too closely together, of faeces and urine distributed inconsiderately beside cooking meat.

It had been two months since he had entered the capital, and Bas had spent most of it trying not to rot. The forces being accumulated for what seemed the increasingly inevitable war with Salucia were still filtering in from throughout the Commonwealth, and even after they arrived it would be several months of training before they were even capable of marching across a parade ground without accidentally spearing one another.

He dressed, he went to the kitchen, he ate a few pieces of dried jerky and a half a loaf of day-old bread, masticating grudgingly. He drank three cups of tepid water and stared out of the window at the alleyway that back-ended against his house, a little trickle of raw waste running down the middle, plump turds drying in the morning sun. He pulled his boots on and walked outside, squinting against the light.

Bas hadn't known much about the capital when he'd chosen his quarters, and given that fact he supposed he could have done worse. If his neighbourhood had nothing to particularly recommend a visit, at least it seemed to have a slightly higher percentage of tradesmen and workers than it did pickpockets, broken-down drunkards and painted-up whores. No one had figured out who he was yet, or if they had they kept quiet on it. No, they hadn't figured it out – there wasn't anyone in this thrice-damned city that could keep a secret. If anyone had known who he was he'd be getting mobbed by attention-seekers and unexpected friends.

A twenty-minute walk east along the Way of Gold would take Bas to the centre of the city, to the shining monument to civilisation that was the Senate Hall, to the high white temples and squat grey offices that surrounded it. Bas did not walk east. Bas had not walked east one single time since moving to the capital. Some days he walked west, along the Way of Stone out towards the outskirts of the city, though you could perambulate until evening and never lose sight of the sprawl. Some days he walked north, on the Way of Timber towards the low rung of hills where the lesser nobles had their estates.

Today he walked south. It had been an easy winter, the ground was unfrozen and the road upturned mud, made worse by the endless procession of carts and palanquins. But still it was better than ducking through the alleyways, piles of refuse like caltrops, thoughtless housewives slopping buckets of shit out of second-storey windows. Or maybe it wasn't better, because at least on the side streets you could avoid some of the hawkers and the vendors, the thieves and the conmen and the whores and the endless, faceless lines of beggars.

One of these grabbed at Bas's sleeve as he walked by. 'A bronze nummus, a single bronze, for a man who lost his sight in service of his country!' His voice was plaintive and desperate and carried the stench of alcohol. 'I served in the Eighth Thema under Phocas himself, when we marched against the Birds! Took a blow at Scarlet Fields, I did, and haven't been able to see since!' He pointed at the dirty gauze wrapped round his eyes.

But this last must not have been very thick, because when Bas turned his gaze on him – an unfriendly gaze, since Bas well knew that the Eighth Thema had not left the capital during the war against the Wellborn, had been garrisoning the city for half a century – he shivered back into his ditch.

The Marchers were masters of subterfuge, double-talk and outright dishonesty. Theirs was a culture that held that a man's only purpose lay in the conquest of other men, mental victory being preferred to physical as it left your victim alive to bear scorn. Bas had spent many an hour warming himself by a counsel fire, getting drunk on some chieftain's liquor, swearing friendship and loyalty, only to find a week later that selfsame chieftain had gone ranging, taking scalps and women. Duplicity was not the sole province of the capital, Bas knew, but the honest inheritance of the entire species. Still, there was something about that partic-ular brand of falseness as was practised in the capital that set his teeth grinding against each other and turned his hands into fists. At least on the Marches you might knife a man for lying to you – here it was the coin of the realm, and you were the odd one for not accepting it.

He walked on, and around him the city got nastier and dirtier, got grimmer and greyer and duller. Hard men, and boys striving to be so, eyeballed him, but none for very long, not even the crews of adolescents that lazed in the afternoon sun, mean and scrawny and looking to make a meal of anything. A big man, and not particularly well dressed, and did you get a look at his eyes? Flat and empty and unblinking, and how much you think he could have on him, not more than a couple of tertarum, and you won't be getting those without a good fight. No – this one was not prey.

So Bas spent his afternoon, as he'd spent many such since returning to the capital of the Commonwealth whose standard he had planted atop the burnt-out remnants of a half-dozen lands. At nightfall he found himself near the docks, in one of those neighbourhoods that rarely saw anyone lucky enough not to reside within its confines, where even the most virgin traveller would quickly realise themselves unwanted.

He could have walked into any tavern in the area and it would have been the same. The bartender looked up, narrowed his eyes, went back to doing nothing. The space he owned, or at least managed, bisected the bottom floor of a larger building, narrow and long and dark. There were tables, and chairs for those tables. There were holes in the walls for the evening to leak through. There was a fire in one corner, but it wasn't big enough to warm the place.

Bas took a seat at the bar. One leg of his stool was shorter than the others. 'Whiskey,' he said.

The bartender gave him a look like he'd have preferred to serve Bas a few strong fingers of hemlock, but then he reached beneath the counter and pulled out an unlabelled bottle and a dirty glass.

'Leave it,' Bas said.

If the bartender hadn't already been scowling, he would have started then. 'Let's see your coin first.'

Slowly, deliberately, Bas loosed his purse from his belt, dropped it onto the counter with a thump and a jangle. The bartender's face flickered all the way from contempt to avarice. Bas pulled a silver tertarum out and placed it next to the bottle, making sure to open the drawstring wide enough for the publican to get a look at the solidus that remained behind.

After an hour the bottle was empty and the place had started to fill, with dockworkers and sailors and anyone else who had a few bronze nummus to rub together and a desire to forget themselves. Labourers trying to wash away the day's sweat, men enjoying their narrow window of freedom. Bas did not like them.

He got up from his chair and made his way towards the back. A longer walk than he would have thought; the bar seemed to stretch on and on, the flickering candlelight rendering the patrons wall-eyed and slack-jawed and chinless. Perhaps that was not just the flickering candlelight.

Bas watered the little patch of dirt outside, then returned to his seat. In the interim three men had slipped in and taken up a position at the opposite end of the counter. In the interim lots of people had probably slipped in, but it was the three men that Bas marked out as being worthy of notice. The first had a Salucian-style dagger at his hip, and he kept resting his hand on it, like he was afraid it might run away. The second was a fat man who thought himself a big one. The last was dressed well, better than he should have been, better than anyone working an honest job in this part of the city could hope to dress.

It took a longer time to get the second bottle of whiskey than the first, not because it was busier, though it was, but because the bartender was pretending he didn't see Bas waving. But he brought it over, finally, and Bas pulled out his purse and gave over another tertarum, though the first should have covered it.

Bas left his purse on the counter after he'd paid, sitting next to the whiskey. Halfway through the bottle he pulled out a small pile of solidus and started to play with them, stacking and restacking them, shuffling them through his fingers absentmindedly, or perhaps purposefully. Bas could feel the tension growing just behind his eyes, like a bad headache. It had been building for days, a background hum at first but getting louder and louder until now it seemed to drown out even the nearby conversations, not that Bas imagined any of these to be worth listening to. Bas wasn't sure if he was drinking whiskey to try and quiet the sensation or to bring it to a head, but either way he kept on drinking.

At the other end of the counter the bartender and his three friends were conversing quietly and shooting Bas sidelong stares of indeterminate enmity. Bas ignored them, shuffling the thick octagonal solidus, letting them ring out against each other. When he'd made a ghost of the second bottle Bas turned it on its side and stood up from his seat. He wasn't sure if the stumble he took while leaving was deliberate or feigned.

Outside the air was cold, would be unpleasantly so in a few minutes, but overheated from the whiskey and the fetid air of the bar Bas enjoyed it, wrapped himself comfortably in the evening. The moon hung so low that he worried it might scrape its belly raw on the chimneys and steeples of the skyline. He heard them coming out of the tavern behind him, but still he waited a few seconds before turning, savouring the night, anticipating the moment to come.

There were four of them, they had picked up an extra hand before they'd walked out of the bar. That was smart. Smart of the three that had been watching him, Bas meant, not smart for the one who had joined up belatedly. Maybe not smart for any of them. Bas had been planning on leading them into an alleyway, making them come at him one by one, but in the end he didn't do that, perhaps because he didn't want to leave the moonlight.

The four men who were coming to hurt Bas aligned themselves in a semicircle in front of him. The one with the dagger pulled it out and pointed it at Bas and started to say the things one says in that situation, but Bas didn't hear or wasn't listening.

There came a moment when the speaker with the nice-looking dagger realised all a-piece that Bas was bigger than he'd thought, bigger or perhaps just more frightening. And his eyes went wider, just round the edges, but Bas was waiting for it, had seen it on a dozen-dozen men across the length of the continent. And Bas smiled on the inside and struck out with his hand, going for the man's knife – which wasn't a smart move, really, wasn't the sort of thing any master of arms would teach, try to disarm a man barehanded. But foolish or not, all of a sudden the knife was spinning out into the ether, a quick flash of moonlight against steel and then it was lost in the muck.

The speaker stopped speaking then, except to make a sort of grunting sound when Bas broke most of the teeth in his jaw and left his nose a mass of raw pulp. If the other three had moved on him just then they might have had a chance, especially as one them was flourishing a boot knife. But that isn't really the way it works, not in this sort of a situation at least. The most important thing in any fight is to get the other man thinking about what will happen if he loses it, because once that fear sinks in he already has.

Bas caught the second thug with a shot on the chin that was as close to perfection as you'll find this side of heaven, or hell, the ideal punch, a punch that sent the unfortunate recipient comatose before he had hit the ground, eyes dull and senseless. He landed badly, Bas heard a sharp crack that was probably the man's neck, though he wasn't certain and anyway didn't really care.

The one who had been speaking and had been holding a knife but was now not doing anything but bleeding tried to run away then, run away or maybe try to retrieve his lost weapon, Bas wasn't sure. In the event it didn't matter – Bas grabbed him by the scruff of his long hair and jerked back sharply, and some of the hair came out but not all of it, and what didn't come out was attached to the unfortunate man's head, as hair often is, and then the man was lying on the ground. Bas gave him a short, savage kick against the temple and he stopped moving.

Bas took a strong shot to the skull then, hard enough to send his vision blurry. The fat man had thrown it, though Bas had to admit that looking at him closer there was some muscle beneath all that flab. Bas had met a few men in his life who were stronger than he was, stronger like they could take him arm-wrestling or carry a heavier load, but a fist-fight wasn't either of those things, and what counted more than anything was hand speed and ferocity. When Bas had been a young man he'd been marvellously fast, had performed feats of agility that had, quite literally, been immortalised in song. He wasn't fast like that any more, hadn't been fast like that for ten years at least – but for a person his size he was still quick as all hell, and certainly he was much quicker than the big man, who had probably been getting through fights his whole life by bearing up to a guy and falling on him. That was what he tried to do then at least, and it wasn't a bad bit of strategy, wrap Bas up so his friend with the boot knife could get a lick or two in.

Bas's first jab tapped the man's eye closed, and his second rang the man hard enough that he dropped his guard, and the third jab you couldn't really call a jab, in so far as it broke the man's cheekbone and a wing of his teeth and probably a few other bits of his face – Bas couldn't say for certain in the bad light.

The last one was still holding that boot knife, and Bas laughed at him, not because it was so funny really but because Bas was filled up with the spirit of the thing, overcharged with energy. And he bore down on the man who, knife or no, was backing away as quickly as a person can go back, which is not as fast as a person can go forward, as Bas proved just then. And Bas put his hands round the hand that was holding the knife, and he twisted, and the man screamed and dropped the knife, and then Bas put his hands up round the man's head, and he twisted a second time, but this time the man did not scream and what fell in the mud was not a knife.

And then it was done, and Bas could breathe again, and he did, long, slow, deep breaths. One of the men was dead and another was well on his way to joining him, and wherever they were going or had gone Bas thought probably neither was enjoying the moonlight, not as Bas was doing. The remaining two were unconscious or wished they were, insentience a reprieve from the misery plaguing them.

Bas payed no mind to any of them, not to the corpses nor to the men who would have made him one. He felt like he always did after a good scrap, focused and clean, though there was blood on his shirt and also soaking into his hair. And behind it that dull sense of sadness, as after a birthday, or a sunset, or an orgasm.

It would be an exaggeration to say that Bas's re-entry brought the bar to a complete halt. Some of the men didn't see him and some of the men who saw him hadn't been paying attention to him earlier, had no foreknowledge of the attempted ambush. The bartender knew though, slunk lower the closer Bas got, until they were in front of each other and his neck reached barely above the counter.

Bas looked at him for a while. Then he slapped a solidus down on the bar, hard enough to set the wood shaking. 'I forgot your tip,' Bas said.

The bartender's jaw was fluttering up and down, and his eyes seemed slowly but surely to be forcing themselves out of his head. 'Thanks,' he said finally, though he left the coin where it was.

21

Calla sat at a corner table in the Falling Dew, one of the many bars running along the easternmost edge of the Second Rung. Across from her Bulan rested in a wicker chair, framed by broad glass windows pulled tight against the winter's chill. In the twilight beyond, custodians lit the wrought-iron street lamps, the flickering orange throwing relief on the modest limestone houses, on the squares and promenades, on happy-seeming workers making their way back to their families; and past them, the edge of the Rung, a sheer rock face, the bay below rendered silent by distance, the crashing waves muted, the cries of the seabirds inaudible. From where Calla sat it might have been possible to imagine that this was the entirety of the Roost, a populace well provided for and content, and beyond them the ocean. Possible for someone, perhaps, though not for Calla, at least not any longer.

'Magnificent view,' Bulan said, the way one says something to interrupt a silence.

'Magnificent,' Calla agreed, or at least echoed.

In fact the view was nothing like the one Calla enjoyed from the summit of the Red Keep, or could be afforded from many of the other small drinking houses and eateries sited across the First Rung. But it was almost the hour of the Woodcock, before the sounding of which all non-resident humans atop the summit of the Roost would need to find themselves below it, or face unpleasant consequences. Bulan's bracelet, acquired at immense expense, allowed him to roam the public areas of the First Rung in the daylight hours, but offered him no protection from evening's fall. By contrast a quick glance at her own brand and the custodians guarding the gate to the summit would fall over themselves ushering her upslope. It was one of many privileges that Calla had only lately found herself reflecting on.

Bulan finished packing his long-stemmed pipe, lit it with the beeswax candle that dripped bright rose onto the willow table, settled it into a contented smile. They had spent the afternoon in a frantic bout of lovemaking, hours lost to the thrust and pull, hours that Bulan no doubt took as evidence of his own amorous abilities. Calla was happy to let him continue under that misimpression – it was best to allow a man his illusions, it did no harm to anyone. But in truth her fervour for copulation had very little to do with the Chazar, though he was reasonably skilled and not untender. Calla had found within herself these last weeks a passion that she could not previously remember possessing – a passion that was as much manic as erotic. Pinned by Bulan's arms, beneath the broad swell of his chest, grunting in unison, there were long moments when she was free of any thoughts beyond the immediate. Others might turn to drink, or one of the many narcotic powders and philtres that were popular on the higher Rungs, but Calla's responsibilities were such that she was unwilling to fog her mind, even briefly.

She imagined she had carried off the facade competently enough, until Bulan leaned forward and set a hand atop hers. 'Will your troubles spoil the moon's arrival, as they did the sun's departure?'

It was her first real smile of the day, and the day was almost over. 'Am I read so easily?'

'It would speak little of Bulan if he could not decipher the mood of a woman who has shared his bed.'

'You seemed obtuse enough while lying in it.'

'At the time I had practical motivations for feigning ignorance.' Bulan's hands were large and strong-seeming, though with a pleasing softness that spoke of long hours holding a quill or sifting an abacus. 'But they are spent now, unless . . .' He drew half-jesting eyes towards the doorway, laughed when she blushed. 'No? Then it is pointless to maintain the charade any longer. Pass your burden to one who would help shoulder it. It is said that there are seven hundred and seventy-seven names for the One God, and that the last and holiest is "He who listens".'

'Is that true?'

'You would need to come to Chazar to prove me a liar, and there seems little enough chance of that,' frowning as he said it.

Calla sighed, slipped one hand free of Bulan's, gulped down some of her wine. 'It's nothing you haven't already heard,' she said.

'The boy's death?' Bulan asked, knowing the answer. It had been a month since that hellish descent to the Fifth Rung, long enough for a bruise to fade, a wound to scab over, a blister to burst. And Bulan had done his best to play chirurgeon, especially in the first days afterwards – held her close, given attention to her venting. To little enough avail.

'Of his life as well,' Calla said. 'The poverty and the decay, the stench and sound of the pipes, the sheer misery . . .'

'Is he so different to any of us? What is life but an accumulation of troubles too soon ended?'

'Your words are glib,' she said, 'and lack merit. Ennui is not despair, nor melancholy destitution.'

Bulan's pipe, jaundiced meerschaum carved in the shape of a Catoblepas, had grown cold waiting on the table. He brought the wick of the candle against it a second time, took a few shallow breaths, releasing soft clouds of scented tobacco. 'I have stood in the slave markets of Partha, where mothers sell their children into short lives of servitude, where the handsome and pretty are made into chattel, where young boys are culled for the chop. Where misery is bought and sold, a commodity as any other. I have smelled that filth, I have heard their desperate cries. If you imagine that the Roost has some monopoly on misfortune then you are a fool.' His eyes softened. 'Though I know otherwise.'

'Perhaps I am a fool,' she said. 'Twenty-nine years atop the Roost, and I barely gave thought to what went on below me.'

'And what would you have done had you known? How would you have remedied the misfortune of so vast a swell of strangers, you without power or influence? Pain is a well without a bottom. Were any of us to understand, in full measure, the depth of the world's suffering . . .' He shook his head. 'Indifference which hews near to cruelty – this is an essential quality of our species. And perhaps not of our species alone.'

'The Shrike is an . . . abomination,' Calla hissed, surprised at her own sudden rush of fury. 'His actions cannot be held against the rest of the Wellborn. He is mad, but there is madness among humans as well.'

'And yet your lord did not stop him.'

'He could not, I told you. He did not have the right.'

'One does not codify insanity into law – perhaps the Shrike is not so unique a specimen as you might prefer to believe.'

'Your tongue is sharp, as ever. But your eyes have failed you, as they sometimes do. The Aubade is as distant from the Shrike as the sun is the moon.'

Bulan swallowed that without reaction, drumming his fingers aimlessly against the table. 'Have you ever raised a dog?'

'The Aubade possesses an esteemed bestiary, though canines are thought too common to occupy it.'

'I have owned many. To protect my property and to chase rats and for company. Some are clever, some foolish. Some large, some small. Some will roll onto their back when they see you, some will bite your hand should you try and feed them. But they are all dogs – their variations do not obscure this essential fact.'

'Busir was your father's name – and his father? And his father before that? How far back does your knowledge go? I can recite my lineage for three centuries, and for all that time, the Aubade has watched over us.'

The first hint of annoyance seeped into Bulan's oaken baritone. 'Such studious shepherding, and with no hope of gain! I have misjudged the High entirely.' Their table was in the corner, and the bar was not busy, but Calla swivelled her head round nervously all the same – it was unwise to speak so loudly of Those Above. 'I had been under the impression that you were his servant, responsible for seeing that his wants are swiftly fulfilled, but perhaps I am mistaken.'

At some point, without entirely realising it, they had shifted positions – in Calla, pride ran stronger than guilt. And not in Calla alone. 'It is only four-fingered hands that drip with blood? In Chazar no one is impoverished, nor brutalised? There is neither desperation nor vice?'

'I have already said otherwise. You may be sure of this, Calla of the Red Keep – in all the world, should you see anything of grandeur, of artistry, of beauty, you may know that it is built upon the bones of one man, the flesh of another, the misery of a great many. The Roost is not unique in subjugation – though, as in everything else, the Eldest manage it with a skill no human can match.'

Calla bit her lip and fell silent, as much because she was afraid the other patrons might overhear the conversation as because she could not, in that moment, think of a retort.

Bulan seemed not to take any great joy in his victory. 'The tide rolls in, the tide rolls out. The moon wanes and waxes. Man lives and screams and breeds and dies; the One God alone knows the why of it.'

'I do not believe in your One God,' Calla said petulantly.

'Then no one knows,' Bulan said. 'Or at the very least, I do not.'

Calla did not know either. Her wine glass was empty, as was the pitcher the waitress had drawn for them what seemed only a short while ago. A steady rain had begun to beat against the windowpane, a hard, cold rain. The sort of rain that made one grateful to have a roof to shelter beneath, and a fire to keep warm beside, the sort of rain that reminded one that not everyone had either of those things.

'The boy is dead, Calla. Regret will not revive him. There is cruelty in the world, yes. There are miseries uncountable. But there is the moonlight,' he said, gesturing towards the evening. 'There is wine, and music, and the feel of flesh against flesh.' He proved this last by leaning forward and caressing her cheek. 'Bitterness avails no one.'

But Calla had spent her life enjoying the moonlight, and wine, and music, and the other pleasures of which Bulan spoke. She had never been unaware of the sparkling joys that infused her existence, had relished them, had followed the practice of her masters in setting, if not hedonism, then at least beauty, as the purpose and cornerstone of her existence. 'Perhaps I am new to the novelty,' she said, slipping away from his touch, 'but the taste is yet strong on my tongue.'

'You will have long years to grow used to it,' Bulan said, tapping out the ash from his pipe in too forceful a fashion. 'Despair is a common garnish.'

They ordered another flagon of wine, drank it in a silence that seemed loud. At one point Calla opened her mouth as if to say something, but after a moment her lips closed round it. From the First Rung Calla could hear the chiming of the hour of the Woodcock, signalling the firm arrival of darkness.

'It grows late,' Bulan said, finishing what little was left in his own glass. 'Shall I arrange you a palanquin back to the gates of the First? Or perhaps there is somewhere else you'd like to spend the remainder of the evening?'

Calla thought about Bulan's apartments, his warm bed, wanted to find herself in it, and not simply as recompense for using him as a convenient if unwarranted target of her anxiety. He smelled of rosewater, and beneath that of his own musk, ripe but not unpleasant. His eyes, unaccustomedly hard these last moments, had reverted to their canny softness. Calla saw herself once again lost in his embrace, solving, however briefly, in sweat and seed, that equation which had bedevilled her ever since visiting the Fifth Rung a month prior.

'There is no need for a palanquin,' Calla found herself saying. 'I can make the walk.'

'As your preference,' Bulan said, frowning, one more unfortunate amidst the multitude.

22

When Andronikos finished his wedding toast the whole party, five hundred souls at two tiers of long, wooden tables, erupted into applause, Eudokia first among them. It was far and away the best speech that she had ever heard him give, pithy and funny and even faintly insightful, qualities he had never previously demonstrated in his past pronouncements. But then, love is a more interesting subject than politics, if equally treacherous.

Andronikos's daughter sat hand in hand with her husband, blushing and smiling. Prisca looked beautiful, and very happy, though the former was much the product of her dress and the light and the singular, shining moment, and would be gone by morning. The latter wouldn't stay much longer either, if Eudokia had to make a guess on the subject. Because Galerius was every bit as pretty as Prisca, and perhaps a bit more so, and though he had so far managed not to offend etiquette by outright flirting with any of his wife's handmaidens, nor was he able to keep himself quite as focused on his beloved as one might hope in a man who had been married all of three hours.

But tomorrow was tomorrow, and tonight no one with a claim to honest speech could say anything other than that the gala was magnificent. No expense had been spared in celebrating the marriage of Andronikos's only child. The leading lights of the Commonwealth had been invited to the senator's country estate to bear witness to his majesty, and to celebrate the continuation of his line.

From Andronikos's wit they moved on to more substantial fare. The house slaves who brought dinner were dressed in finery that would have shamed a provincial noble, and they did their duty with grace and speed. For the first course they served leg of duck and roasted rabbit and some sort of animal from south of Dycia that looked like cow and smelled like cow but was called something different. As it tasted like cow also, Eudokia wasn't sure she saw the point in having it imported across the continent, but the rest of the guests seemed to appreciate the novelty more than she did. After a brief interlude of sherbert and fresh fruit, they were back to flesh, roasted turkey and golden-crusted pies stuffed with chicken and partridge and groundhog and pig liver and pig heart and a number of other cuts of meat that Eudokia couldn't distinguish. Eudokia had been going to this sort of feast since she was a child, found the gluttony absurd. How much did anyone need to eat? Why not just throw it directly into the trash heap, save the middle step?

As to everything else – the silverware, the decor, the sweet, soft music wafting in from the band – no, one could not deny it: Andronikos had taste, and the celebration was a demonstration of that. He also had, somehow, acquired a great deal of money – and the celebration was a demonstration of that as well.

Eudokia allowed a passing servant to refill her wine glass, thanked the girl and brought the cup to her lips. It was an excellent vintage, and well paired to the course. It must have cost a solidus a bottle. Eudokia smiled to herself, drank it quickly and motioned for more.

Eudokia was seated one over from the main table, but she caught Prisca's eye easily enough, the girl blushing and smiling and seeming as though she might burst from happiness. From Prisca's pride of place Eudokia had to run her gaze a long way down the table to find Manuel, looking small as well as small-minded, shovelling a titbit of meat into a grimace.

It had been an easy thing to get Prisca to sit Manuel at the second tier of tables, the least recompense given what Eudokia had already done to ensure her happiness. Eudokia had asked that the bride might make a point of keeping the two of them apart, claiming a longstanding dislike for the senator – which was true so far as it went, though if Eudokia was to have the deck cleared of every member of the party who she disliked, there wouldn't be enough guests left for a cantra dance. Regardless, Prisca hadn't seen any harm in the matter, was just as happy to keep his homespun robe and his body odour as far away from all the bright young things as possible. Andronikos had probably not noticed, his attention being focused on the multitude of small tasks required of him as founder of the feast. But Manuel noticed, his usual look of sober superiority replaced with one of undisguised bitterness. And for a man who claimed drink was a refuge of the weak and enfeebled, he was obliging himself with Andronikos's wine at a rate which would impress a sot.

It was shaping up to be a wondrous evening, Eudokia thought, nibbling at a flaky crust of bread. One to be remembered for years afterwards.

Dinner lasted on and on and on, and though the Domina herself barely swallowed a mouthful of pudding, the arrival of each new course brought a wider and wider smile to her face, until she seemed almost giddy. It was two hours after Andronikos had finished his speech when the final course concluded and the rest of the evening's revelry began; though after the marathon of consumption in which they had all just taken part, few seemed enthusiastic to take to the dance floor.

Eudokia noticed her handmaiden holding court in one corner. Irene had somehow only got prettier, which hardly seemed to be fair to Prisca, nor any of the other women at the party. Her hair was up in a beehive, her black dress was short above the bust and long down to her ankles, albeit with a slit in the side that showed no small dash of skin. The cadre of gentlemen standing in a semicircle around her didn't seem to mind, laughing at gags that Eudokia suspected weren't quite as clever as their behaviour suggested. She had to clear her throat twice before any of them noticed her, which was ungallant but not unexpected.

'Revered Mother,' Irene said, kissing her in greeting.

'Cruel to shame the bride on her wedding night,' Eudokia said, taking her handmaiden by the arm and walking her away from her suitors.

'Was I to come dressed in rags?'

'I doubt it would make much of a difference for your catch.'

'What do you think of them?'

Eudokia looked back at the group of men pretending they weren't watching Irene walk away. 'The Third Consul is as devoted a practitioner of the Salucian vice as one is to find – he's probably more interested in finding out the name of your tailor than getting into your dress. The Dycian ambassador has the pox, I have that from an unimpeachable source. Tiberius is such a well-known frequenter of dockside brothels that he almost certainly has the pox also, though I confess that to be an educated guess and not the product of certain intelligence. Maurice is rich and not altogether unattractive but he has that habit of snorting every time he makes a joke, which I would find intolerable were he seated on the Empty Throne. And Zeno is as handsome as any man in the Commonwealth, but he barely has the wit to sign his name. So, all in all, my dear, I'd tell you to throw them back, and see what else your nets can fetch.'

Irene laughed. 'As always, Revered Mother, your insight is rather too keen. Though I think you are too quick to dismiss Zeno – I've always thought wit to be an overrated quality, in a man. Certainly Heraclius has served you well enough.'

Eudokia wrinkled up her nose. Heraclius's rank was not, in and of itself, sufficient to have earned him an invitation to the wedding and, as Eudokia had explained, it would hardly be appropriate for her to insist on the presence of her nominally secret lover. That he wasn't here was a good part of the reason she was finding the evening so enjoyable. 'I do not require cleverness in Heraclius any more than I require my pastry chef to play the flute. One chooses a servant for their competence in a particular task, and avoids putting them in a position that requires skills they have no hope of developing.'

'My point exactly.'

'But a husband is not a servant,' Eudokia continued quickly. 'More is expected of him, or more should be. Nor can a husband be dismissed quite so easily as a valet.'

'You are thinking of dismissing Heraclius, then?' Irene asked.

There was no particular reason to remain silent on the matter, but Eudokia did not need one. Privacy was second nature to her and she had already gone further in discussing the matter with Irene than she had intended. 'I think those prawns were the best I ever had,' she said. 'I might have to find a way to steal Andronikos's chef.'

'He's all but wasted among these churls,' Irene agreed smoothly.

'I do wish you would allow me to find someone appropriate for you,' Eudokia said.

'I wish very much the same, Revered Mother, though it seems we have a different notion of whom that might be.'

Eudokia took one of Irene's hands between the two of hers. 'You are a sparklingly beautiful creature, and short on neither charm nor intelligence. But Konstantinos is as far beyond you as an oak is a weed.'

'He seems to think differently.'

'Like the greater portion of his sex, dear child, Konstantinos doesn't think. He feels, and he speaks, and sometimes he follows my advice closely enough that if you were to watch him from a distance you might be forgiven for supposing that the outcome of his actions are the result of planning. But you would be wrong – and whatever sweetness he may whisper to you in the still hours of the morning, you will find them insubstantial against the day's harsh light. He will take you to bed, and perhaps even to his heart – but you will never marry him.'

'Surely you would not stand in the way of true love?'

Eudokia thought it inappropriate to express to Irene exactly what she thought of that hallowed ideal, given that they were at a wedding. 'I have been grooming that boy for greatness since before your first blush,' Eudokia said. 'If you think I would allow his destiny to be derailed because your arse looks magnificently fetching in that dress, you know me less well than you suppose.'

One of Eudokia's elder brothers, now long dead, had been given a dog one year for his birthday. Big-headed, stupid-seeming with a grin made of tiny, sharpened teeth, teeth that had never done anything worse than gnaw at the furniture, teeth that one day, without explanation or warning, had suddenly gripped onto Eudokia's brother's arm so swiftly and so tenaciously that one of their house slave had needed to beat the creature's brains in with a stool to gain its release. It was a lesson Eudokia had received ample reminder of throughout the remainder of her life: there is nothing on earth that loves you so much it might not one day hurt you.

Eudokia thought about that dog, as she watched Irene force a smile and return to making her assembled coterie of suitors miserable.

Eudokia drank more of Andronikos's very expensive wine and thought over this new development. There were times when she wished she could castrate her stepson, though that would do poorly for his masculine image, as well as any future hopes she had for heirs. No, severing his testicles might be too strong a measure, under the circumstances. A firm conversation should be sufficient to remind her nephew of his responsibilities. So far as Eudokia was concerned, Konstantinos could go ahead and dip his cock in a hornets' hive if for some reason he was so inclined. But he would marry who she told him to – yes, by the Self-Formed, there could be no doubt about that.

She'd talk to him tomorrow, and decision made she felt better about the subject, and even less disposed to wound the genitals of her adopted son.

The older generation – those that could admit to it, and weren't hanging around the dance floor in a shamefaced attempt to pretend they had not yet exhausted the greater portion of their virility – were standing on Andronikos's small enclosed patio. Eudokia saw Andronikos, Manuel and a number of other senators of their clique. It was bad form for a woman to approach such a gathering of grandees, she knew; her feminine aura might well wither in the face of such sheer masculine force. But Eudokia was not one to hold too dearly to convention, at least not unless it suited her.

'Honoured Father,' she said, addressing Andronikos by the title she had arranged for him to receive. She said it loudly enough for Manuel to take notice, and was gratified to see his sneer stretch. Rumour held that relations between the two senators were worse than icy, that only the most desperate pleading had been sufficient to convince Manuel that his being passed over for the Archpriesthood had not been Andronikos's doing.

'Revered Mother,' Andronikos said, made happy enough by the evening to eschew their traditional antagonism.

'You'll excuse my interruption, I can only hope,' Eudokia said. 'But I wanted to offer congratulations on this auspicious union, as well as to comment on what a magnificent and beautiful occasion it has been. One worthy of the ancestors – don't you think, Senator?' Addressing the last question to Manuel.

'I think the ancestors would find much in today's Commonwealth to be wasteful and extravagant,' he said.

And if Andronikos had had any sense at all he would have allowed that one to pass, because it was the sort of thing Manuel could be expected to say whenever offered the opportunity, and perhaps even less foul than usual. But strength rarely breeds magnanimity, Eudokia had found. The higher a person rose, the more bitterly they raged against any blot or stain on their eminence. 'By Enkedri, do you set out every morning to be the worm in the apple? Is there no moment of joy that you can't find yourself tainting?'

'I simply believe that life's happy occasions are best celebrated modestly, without any unnecessary indulgence.'

'Of course you do,' Andronikos said. 'That's why I ate dried cod at the wedding of your son!'

Andronikos and the rest of his senators laughed, and to Manuel, who did not laugh, it must have seemed that the entire party was enjoying themselves at his expense. And though Andronikos, made exuberant by the levity and his daughter's seeming happiness and the concrete manifestation of his own self-importance, did not notice the way Manuel's little black eyes swelled in his head, Eudokia took notice of it most clearly. And as happy as Andronikos was in that moment, Eudokia was happier – because what is more congenial than the sight of a plan fulfilled, of a scheme brought to fruition?

23

Bas stood outside his tent, watching their approach. Watching her approach. It was early afternoon and it had been raining for much of the morning and Bas was not wearing a cloak. Bas had discovered since returning to the capital that what the Aelerians called midwinter the Marchers would have called early autumn or, more likely, nothing, since the Marchers were hardy folk and the vague dampness that passed for cold here in the east would not have warranted their notice. He told himself that this lack of clothing explained the chill, but despite Bas's many other talents he had no gift for rationalisation, or at least less of a gift than most.

It was a modest-sized group that traveled the great northern road leading out from the city and up to camp, but only one of them could possibly be the Sentinel of the Southern Reach. Her horse was black as a night beneath ground, and bigger than any such animal he had seen since the war. She rode the monstrosity smoothly and her escort, a silk-clad courtier and a half-dozen savage-looking Parthans, struggled to keep up.

She swung down from the saddle before she had brought her animal to a full stop, a demonstration of agility that would have impressed a March lord, but which she did with a distinct suggestion of casualness. Bas had heard that the Eternal trained their horses to hate the smell of man, and perhaps this was the case, because the Sentinel's animal seemed agitated, tossing its great thick neck back and forth. The Sentinel brought her head up against it, whispered strange-sounding words. Enough to quell the thing's fury, though even still it carried a clear hint of menace, as a sheathed sword or a naked woman.

By then her lifeguard had arrived and dismounted. The Parthans were as black as Hamilcar and seemed far meaner. Each carried a talwar and any number of small, sharp, curved metal things hanging in their loose robes. Bas would not have backed any three of them against the Sentinel, perhaps not any five, perhaps not all of them together. But the Senate, in a rare display of good sense, had determined it would be unwise to allow the Roosts ambassador to wonder about the city unattended. That they had felt the need to compose her lifeguard of foreigners spoke to the consensus of Aelerian sentiment towards the Four-Fingered.

As this animus was shared to no small degree among the themas, Bas had some concern about the Sentinel's visit. At this point the camp was skeletal, the huge masses of raw recruits he'd been promised slow to arrive. There were probably not twenty men among the few hundred sitting about in the barracks and waiting for something to do who had taken part in the last war against the Others – which was, admittedly, closer to thirty years back than twenty-five, and had ended with few humans left alive to swear vengeance.

But still, Aeleria had hated the devils since the last king and all his line had been killed at the Lamentation some three centuries past. Bas wondered if the Sentinel had taken part in that as she had in the Battle of the Scarlet Fields, if the human blood on her hands dripped back through the centuries, if locked somewhere in that head of hers was the memory of a man who looked distantly like Bas being pushed to the ground and dispatched with no modicum of grace nor dignity, of his wife and mewling children sent to join him. It didn't matter to Bas, but he knew it did to many of his countrymen.

The point being that he was perfectly happy to have the Sentinel surrounded by a number of large, violent, well-compensated men who had no particular affection towards Aeleria and could be expected to cut down a couple of raw recruits if that became necessary. Bas was less than pleased to see the one remaining member of the Sentinel's entourage arrive then, a man named Kantoleon, the chief liaison between the Other and the nation in which she resided. Quite apart from his tardiness he gave the impression of being no very competent horseman, and the ride out from the city had left him winded and dishevelled. He dismounted awkwardly, and after a long moment savouring the dirt beneath his feet, he bowed to Bas and began the formal introductions.

'Strategos Bas Alyates, the Caracal, this is our emissary from the Roost, the Sentinel of the Southern Reach.'

'We have met,' she said, as if to remind Bas of this fact.

'I recall.'

Kantoleon was still struggling to regain his breath – you'd have thought he'd sprinted out here, rather than ridden – and Bas took the opportunity to inspect the Sentinel once again. You would not quite call her beautiful – too alien, too foreign, despite her long hair and fair skin – but perhaps something close. Her violet eyes were impossibly strange and he noticed now, as he had not before, that her fingers had one more joint that did his own.

'I would like to take this opportunity to thank you, Strategos, for taking a few moments out of your busy schedule, to escort us on a tour of the camp,' Kantaleon said.

Bas grunted. He supposed that what was primarily required

of a man in Kantaleon's position was oily obsequiousness, but still he couldn't help but feel he was carrying the point too far. It had been Kantoleon who had approached him a week earlier, tried to explain the situation, though his speech was so labyrinthine, so choked with excuses and subterfuges that it had taken Bas half an hour to figure out what was being asked. The Sentinel wished to inspect the training of the new thema, and had requested that Bas be her guide. Would the Caracal consent to act as such? In theory the Sentinel could go anywhere and do anything she wanted, or very nearly so, but it seemed that in practice she rarely left the sizable hunting preserve the Senate had granted her a half-day's ride out of the city.

Bas supposed he could have said no, and what would they have done about it? And he was going to say no, had planned to say no. So it had come as something of a surprise to him when he ended up saying yes, and he had spent fully the rest of the day trying to figure out why he had done so. Boredom was a great part of it – by Terjunta, he was bored, that sort of boredom in which he had come to recognise the seeds of potential madness. And certainly she was a magnificent thing, and just to be able to look at her for a few minutes was a source of what in another man you might have called happiness.

As to why the Sentinel had asked for him specifically, Bas could not possibly explain. Bas had little enough understanding of what motivated the actions of members of his own species, would not have begun to guess at what drove something as foreign as the Sentinel. Perhaps, at bottom, it was simply that Bas did not fear her, did not feel uncomfortable in her presence, or at least not any more than he felt uncomfortable around everyone.

It was a rest day; the hoplitai-in-training were killing the slow hours in their barracks, or inside the city if they had been lucky enough to get a day's pass. But still there were no few of the Commonwealth's children milling about, hoping to catch a look at the new arrival or simply having nothing better to do. Parthans were not very highly thought of among the Aelerians, and the Others even less so. Bas did not imagine there were any among his ranks so mad as to want to fight their way through a well-armed bodyguard to earn the right to be killed by the fists of the Sentinel, but the bristling stares she received from most of the passers-by would have wounded anyone capable of normal human empathy.

A characteristic that seemed entirely absent to the Sentinel. After a moment inspecting the scene she walked swiftly into the heart of the camp, Kantoleon and her lifeguard following after. Bas was taken by surprise, had to hurry a bit to catch up with her long, graceful steps.

'How many men are in a thema?' the Sentinel asked, turning to Bas.

'Ten thousand, my Lady,' Kantoleon answered.

She looked at Kantoleon curiously, as if she had just met him, as if his existence at this moment was a source of utmost confusion to her. Then she turned back to Bas. 'How many men are in a thema?'

'In theory, ten thousand, though I've never served in one that was up to full strength. You have to assume a twentieth of them are sick at any given time, more if you are in garrison, far more during a siege. There's a somewhat smaller number of deserters, or dead men kept on the rolls so their comrades can have a few more cloves of bread.'

'And how many themas does Aeleria count?'

'Fourteen, my Lady. Fifteen when this one comes to full strength.' This from Kantoleon again.

'I was not addressing you,' the Sentinel said, as if she were supplying information, rather than offering rebuke.

'Fifteen,' Bas confirmed, 'once this has come up to strength.'

'And where are they located?'

'Most are scattered about the Marches,' Kantoleon cut in, 'and the rest are garrisoning other posts throughout the Commonwealth.'

'You may leave now,' the Sentinel said, her eyes still on the camp set up before her.

'Forgive me, my Lady?' Kantoleon asked.

'You and the lifeguard,' she said, 'may return to the manor. I have no need of you.'

Kantoleon was a man who made his living with veiled suggestions and half-truths – blunt speech left him uncomfortable and faintly ashamed. He hemmed and hawed for a moment, but without forming a clear sentence. Then he performed a curious, mincing sort of motion, like a bow but with several awkward hand gestures, and fell back the way they had come. After a moment the Parthans did the same, though before they left, the leader, or at least the one dressed most garishly, gave Bas a long, slow look. Bas ignored it. He didn't need to be reminded of what would happen if the Roost's emissary was murdered in the heart of an Aelerian camp.

'I cannot tell if that man is deliberately trying to infuriate me,' she said, after they all had gone, 'or if stupidity is a customary part of officialdom in your country.'

'Both,' Bas said, turning and walking down towards the armoury.

With Kantoleon no longer around to hamper their conversation, the Sentinel could give full vent to her curiosity. She asked about everything, a constant stream of questions, queries and interrogations. Whether or not she was putting the information together in a coherent way, however, Bas could not say. Each question seemed to exist as an autonomous and complete thing, having no relation to its predecessor. One moment she would be demanding some piece of information that seemed relevant – how long were the pikes used by the themas, and were they all the same size – and then she would move on to something that seemed to Bas utterly trivial – how many nails were used in shoeing a horse, and why had the third cohort chosen the wolf as its figurehead?

He could not say that he found it unpleasant. True, she was brusque, had little understanding of the conventions of human speech, but this did not bother Bas, who was himself no very polished conversationalist. 'Surely you must know some of this,' he said, after she had spent a quarter of an hour asking Bas to describe the process by which a pentarche is promoted to tetrarche. 'How is the army organised by your people?'

'The Roost has no need of an army,' the Sentinel said, as if surprised at the very concept. 'Why would it? The Roost is the Eternal, and every Eternal would sacrifice themselves in its defence.'

'All of them?'

'Not the hatchlings – what you would call children, I suppose. Nor the very aged or infirm. But everyone else. The last time we rode against you, there were not fifty of my kind left within the city.'

Bas was struck by her curious lack of guile. Was she so innocent as not to understand that Bas had been and might again be her enemy? Or was she just too arrogant to imagine that he'd ever be able to take advantage of this information? And if it was the latter, was she right? For surely, the last time the demons had ridden out against Aeleria, they had been equally certain of their superiority – and had not at all been proven wrong.

'And among your people? Why have these men decided to enter into the Commonwealth's service?'

'Not all of them did. Some are convicts who thought a stint in the thema better than death on the galleys. Many are second or third sons with nothing to inherit and no trade to take up. Some of the very foolish ones might even have had some notions of heroism or love of country, though we usually break that out of them after a few days.' Bas shrugged. 'Who can say why a man does a thing?'

'And why did you choose to serve?'

'I was born into the thema,' Bas said uncomfortably.

'You did not indicate that this was a possibility.'

'It usually isn't.' Bas said. And this would normally have been enough for him, not a man much given to discussing the past, or at least his past, but then for some reason he ended up adding, 'I was born outside of a garrison on the edge of the Marches.'

'But the females of your species are weak, and do not fight in your armies.'

'They do not fight in our armies, that is true,' Bas said. Then, after a moment, 'She was a camp-follower.'

'Where did she follow the camp?'

'Wherever it went, I suppose. She was a whore,' Bas clarified, or thought he clarified.

'A what?'

'A woman who sold herself to men for money.'

'And your father?'

'Was her client.'

'Yes,' the Sentinel said, 'that makes sense.'

'My mother died when I was a child. A man of the Thirteenth took me in, made sure I had something to eat and wear until I was old enough to join in formally. Armies breed bastards like rotted meat does flies. I was luckier than most,' he said, meaning it. The lot of the Commonwealth by-blows in foreign lands was not a kind one, and it was worse, as most things were, on the Marches. A whore did not need a child, for all that her profession seemed likely to make one. Those that weren't exposed to the elements one evening would likely as not die within the first year anyway, of cold or from lack of food or from one of the illnesses that arise when one is freezing and hasn't eaten well. An orphan, without even the limited protection that their mother might provide – well, they were as worthy of pity as any other living thing.

The thema had proved Bas's salvation. The Thirteenth were a pack of savages, but they'd seen to him just the same, fed him from their own stores, let him sleep at their fire, given him cast-off clothes, even once found milk for him when he'd grown sick. At five he'd been a mascot, marching along with them, singing their fighting songs, the old hands laughing at his stumbling grasp of profanity. At eight he'd been an extra set of hands, carrying supplies, foraging for wood and food, performing what small tasks he'd been capable of. At twelve they'd started training him with a sword, not training him as you would a child either, but real practice, with blunted blades and light padding. At fifteen he'd taken the oath – three years younger than the law demanded, but he was big enough to shoulder a pike, and as far as the men of the Thirteenth were concerned their job was to spread the law of the Commonwealth more than to follow it.

'And you?' Bas asked. 'Why are you here?'

She had a way of speaking as if everything she said were as obvious and unquestionable as dirt. 'Since the Founding, the Wellborn have posted Seven Sentinels across the lands, to ensure the human nations operate in harmony with one another.'

Except that the Founding of the Roost, so far as Bas understood it, had taken place closer to three thousand years ago than two, when the greater part of the continent would have been no more than old-growth forests and untamed plains. What had the job been like, back in those distant days, he wondered? There were still towers scattered across the continent that were said to have been the product of the ancient Sentinels, strange and wondrous things, crumbling but still beautiful.

'And why are you one of those seven?'

'Is it not a thing to be proud of, to uphold one's duty to one's kind and country?'

'It depends on the kind,' Bas said, 'and the country.'

'No,' she said after giving it a moment's thought. 'I do not think it does. And I do not think that you think that, Strategos.'

Bas realised he was smiling. 'Call me Bas.'

'Bas,' she repeated, or acknowledged.

'And what am I to call you?'

'Here I am called the Sentinel of the Southern Reach.'

'That's a title,' Bas said. 'Not a name.'

'Is a thing not named for its purpose?'

'If that were the case,' Bas said, 'very few of us would be named anything.'

'The name I am known by among my people is private. In any case, you would not be able to understand it, nor to pronounce it. No human can.'

'And the humans in your charge? They must call you something.'

'Of course. They call me Lady,' she said, as if this were the most obvious thing in the world.

Bas did not want to insult her by laughing. 'And what if you and another of your kind were standing together, and a servant needed to draw your attention?'

'My humans are far too well trained to interrupt a conversation between two of the Eternal,' she said. 'I suppose if there were some sort of emergency, they would refer to me by my full title.'

'Which is?'

'I am the Lady of the Ivory Estate.'

'I've never been to the Ivory Estate,' Bas said.

Another stuttered pause while she tried to understand why this was relevant. 'It's no longer Ivory,' she acknowledged. 'But it was in my grandmother's day, when it was first built.'

'I see.'

'Now it's mostly blue.'

'The Lady of the Ivory Estate,' Bas repeated. 'It does not trip lightly off the tongue.'

'I suppose . . .' She fell silent for a moment, then another one, as if working through some complex problem in her head. 'I suppose you might give me a name.'

Bas wiped a drip of sweat from his forehead. 'I'm not sure that I could do you justice.'

'I won't be able to tell either way.'

This time Bas did laugh, but then he gave the matter a few seconds of thought. 'Einnes?' he ventured.

'What does it mean?'

'It doesn't mean anything,' Bas said. 'It's just a name.'

The Sentinel of the Southern Reach, or the Lady of the Ivory Estate, or Einnes, could not possibly have known that this was a lie.

She repeated it several times, slowly, as if tasting each syllable. 'Einnes I am, then. At least among the humans of Aeleria.' She took a look up at the sun, which fell swiftly so early in the year. 'It grows late,' she said, 'and I had hoped to get a hunt in before supper.' Bas found himself escorting her back to her great black mount – which, he now realised, had remained standing where she had left it for the better part of an hour, without fetter, rope or chain. Isaac and Hamilcar and some of the other officers sat silently nearby.

Einnes swung herself up onto the beast with the same ease that she had displayed upon dismounting. 'Farewell, Bas.'

'Farewell, Einnes,' Bas said, and found himself choking back a smile.

Hamilcar waited until her horse had carried her out of earshot before commenting. 'She is a beautiful creature, is she not?'

Isaac spat on the ground, turned his broken teeth to a sneer. 'I'd sooner set my cock in the mouth of a rabid dog.'

If Bas heard any of this, he gave no sign. He was watching Einnes gallop away on her magnificent, strange, wondrous steed, and as he did so he made sure to keep his face as blank and unreadable as a bluff overlooking the sea.

24

Thistle and Spindle and Chalk and two other men were playing Rag-a-Jack at a back table at Isle's. Chalk was the worst Rag-a-Jack player Thistle had ever met, threw away his high cards without giving it any thought, acted proud as a seed-pecker when he was bluffing, shrunk in his shoulders on those occasions when he had a decent hand. The rest of the table weren't anything much to speak of, and for that matter, Thistle couldn't claim any great mastery – but Chalk was on another level of incompetence altogether.

'I'll up you a tertarum,' Thistle said.

Chalk stacked and restacked the few coins he was still holding on to, spent a few seconds trying to read Thistle's mind. 'Do you have it, or are you just trying to make me think you have it?' When Thistle didn't answer Chalk threw the rest of his coin into the pot. 'Because I've got four blues,' he said, flipping over his hand to prove it. 'Which means I'll be drinking off you tonight.'

'Six reds,' Thistle said, turning the cards over one by one, slowly, deliberately, rather nastily.

Chalk didn't say anything.

'Six is more than four,' Thistle explained. 'Feel free to count off your fingers if that'll help.'

Five months working with Chalk had rubbed off most of the fear he'd once had of the man, leaving a patina of contempt. Chalk was ugly and Chalk was mean, and Chalk could hit a target with a thrown knife nine times out of ten, but apart from that there seemed to be very little that Chalk was capable of accomplishing. Even Spindle, with his slow way of speaking and empty eyes, was smarter, smarter and more reliable, which Thistle supposed was the reason he'd been made a full initiate, a star branded onto his shoulder, while Chalk remained hired help. 'I guess I wasn't bluffing, was I?'

Thistle thought maybe there was something wrong with Chalk, something more than the obvious, that is, because when things got tense he had this unbecoming habit of blinking repeatedly, almost uncontrollably. 'You got a big fucking mouth, for a little bitch ain't yet stuck a man,' Chalk said. The two players at the table that weren't Spindle, loose affiliates of the Brotherhood but nothing more, looked very deliberately towards the wall.

'I've been sticking you all night, Chalk,' Thistle said. 'Or hadn't you noticed?'

Chalk's left hand began to shake vigorously. Chalk's right hand eased its way into Chalk's jacket, towards one of the many pieces of sharpened metal that Chalk strapped on to himself before he walked outside in the morning. And now Thistle started to wonder if maybe Chalk was crazier than he had previously credited the man, crazy enough to try and murder him in a crowded bar, blood on the floor and damn the consequences.

The answer to that question should have worried Thistle, but for some reason it didn't, he was too full up with rage to feel anything else. Rage at Chalk for being so fucking stupid and at Spindle for being friends with Chalk and at himself for spending another night sitting at a table with halfwits, especially when it looked like one of those halfwits might kill him.

'Thistle,' Rhythm said, the door to the back opening and his square, bald head appearing from it. 'Back room. The rest of y'all, cut out.'

Thistle pulled his sneer up into a snarl, then pointed at the money lying on the table. 'This better be here when I get back.'

'No cause for that kind of talk, Thistle,' said Spindle, and he shook his head sadly, and Thistle knew he had pushed things too far. Still, there was nothing left but to keep his glower stitched onto his face as he walked into the big man's office.

'Take a seat,' Rhythm said, circling around to the back of his small desk and dropping into his own.

Thistle followed his suggestion, or his order, depending on how you looked at it.

'You think it's wise, making an enemy out of Chalk?'

'I can handle myself.'

'You wouldn't last thirty seconds in a room with Chalk. That man was a killer straight from the womb.'

'And what am I?'

'You?' Rhythm leaned back into his seat. 'You're just angry. Anger ain't shit.'

'Fuck him,' Thistle said. 'He can't afford to lose, he shouldn't play.'

'You talk nonsense like this, I hear my knife sing,' Rhythm said. 'Makes me want to pull it out and hear the tune proper, hum along while you bleed out. It'd piss Chalk off, not getting to do you himself, but I think it might be worth it all the same.'

Thistle knew that if a man was going to put a hole in you, he wasn't going to warn you about it beforehand. But he couldn't pretend he didn't leak a little sweat sitting there, the most dangerous man on the Rung threatening to end him, in his steady equanimous rasp.

'Two months you've been like this,' Rhythm said, apparently deciding to let Thistle live a few sentences longer. 'Going around looking for walls to kick, ever since that Four-Finger did for your boy. Yeah, I heard about that. I hear about everything.'

'So?'

'Exactly – so? So what? You think he's the first of us ever been offed by a Bird? You think his mummy's the only one ever cried? You think you're the only person ever been done wrong?'

Thistle didn't say anything to that, just simmered quietly.

Rhythm undid the clasp on his cuff, rolled the white silk sleeve up to reveal his biceps. Even in the dim light Thistle could make out a row of puckered scars, each about the length of his middle finger. 'You see these?'

'Yeah.'

'One for each year below. One for each year I never saw sunlight, never smelled grass, never drank water didn't taste like metal. How many I got on me?'

'Three,' Thistle said.

'Three,' Rhythm confirmed. 'Three fucking years. I went to the pits at seventeen. Was walking out of a bar when a pack of Cuckoos mistook me for someone else, and I was young and full of liquor and I decided to act the big man, ended up touching one of them. Of course he'd put hands on me first, but the magistrate didn't think that part of the story relevant. Didn't even let me tell it, just listened to that lying fuck talk about how I was drunk and violent, and then he shook his head and said, three years. And when they say it, it happens right then, not like you get to go around saying goodbyes. That morning I gave my mother a kiss on the cheek and went out to work, and that was the last I ever saw of her. She was dead by the time I came out. You think you got more right to be angry than me, Thistle? You think you got more right to your hate?'

Thistle didn't say anything.

'Ain't much to think about down below. No way of marking time except by when they feed you, and they weren't so regular about that. You dig and you think, and you dig and you think. Some guys thought about their women, though you'd have to be an awful fool to imagine she'd wait it out for you, especially since not one in five comes out alive at the end.' He tapped loudly on the table, as if to make sure that Thistle was listening. 'Not one in five. Some guys – a lot of guys – all they think about is the wrongness of it, the unfairness. When they get out they're so full of bile they spew it at everyone they find, end up back below sooner rather than later. That's what their anger gets them.' Rhythm stood up from his chair and opened a window. The winter chill came in with it, but Rhythm didn't seem to notice, or didn't seem to mind. He leaned his head out and took a deep breath of evening, then sat back down behind his desk. 'Three years I was down there, Thistle – three long years. And you know what I thought about?'

'No.'

'Never going back in. Spending every morning afterwards greeting the light, and maybe doing it in a decent house next to a decent whore. A man like me, he doesn't get to be angry, he doesn't have that luxury. A man like me needs to survive. When I picked you out, I thought maybe you were a man like I was, like I am now. Was I wrong in thinking that?'

Thistle didn't answer.

'Get out of here,' Rhythm said. 'And don't show up for a few days. Make sure you want to work for me. Make sure that you aren't just sprinting into the darkness yourself. I don't pay you to carry a chip around on your shoulder. You can't brush it off, you'd best find yourself a new line.'

The money was waiting on the table. Outside the weather had turned from cold and dry to cold and wet, tendrils of sleet curling down from a dark sky. Thistle watched them fall from the shelter of the doorway, tried to figure out somewhere to go.

Home he dismissed without consideration. The boys would be down at the pumphouse, drinking themselves friendly. But Thistle wasn't in a friendly mood, didn't feel like having to dodge Felspar's constant begging or Treble's stone-eyed stupidity. Thistle never seemed to want to see the boys these days, spent most of his nights drinking at Isle's or sitting by the canals. Rat had been the centrepiece of the whole thing, though Thistle had only realised it belatedly. Thistle had made the decisions but the only reason there was anyone to listen to him was because they all liked to be around Rat.

So Thistle wandered aimlessly upslope, which was a good way to get your head broken, as he well knew. He was dressed pretty enough to draw the attention of any sharp-eyed hard-boys he might pass, twins to Thistle in all but birthplace. Maybe Thistle was even hoping to attract a few, give himself the opportunity to skin a knuckle, lose himself in the rush of speed and violence.

Lucky for someone, what with the weather the usual packs of scavengers had scattered, and there was no one around to take Thistle's open challenge. Flakes of snow collected on his dense locks, melted and dripped down onto his jacket. The mud pulled at his boots, seeped into his stockings, left his toes numb. In time he found himself on a part of the Rung he'd never been to before, right up close to the boundary with the Fourth. The blocks of tenements were larger and slightly better kept, though you'd need to be something of an expert in slum architecture to see the difference. The pipes were less oppressive upslope, their sucking sound more restrained.

Thistle noticed the three men because they were trying so hard not to be noticed, keeping the loudest silence Thistle had ever seen. They gave all evidence of being engaged in some sort of organised mischief, though Thistle struggled to determine the particular species. Closer to middle age than youth, too old to be amidst some errand of casual tomfoolery, but dressed too poorly to be affiliated with the Brotherhood. Porters, probably, not even foremen, though what they would be doing out so late on a night like this, and with such conspicuous secrecy, Thistle had no idea.

He followed them because he had nothing else to do and because it was fun practice, feeling a professional among amateurs, a wolf among sheep. Spindle had given him some lessons in shadowing, and though Thistle lacked Spindle's experience he had the advantage of not being noticeably larger than average. For all their pretence of wariness Thistle had no trouble following along behind them, even with the streets all but empty in the dark and cold.

After one final spasm of pointless caution, they turned quickly down a side street and disappeared into one of the endless crush of warehouses that stacked this portion of the Fifth. Thistle found a spot in the shadows and spent a while looking at the building they had walked into. Two men stood outsidef it in big black cloaks that obscured most of their other details. They didn't seem unfriendly enough to be engaged in a crime, nor did Thistle notice they were carrying weapons.

Thistle found himself approaching them, couldn't exactly have said why. 'Good evening, brother,' one said. 'How can we help you?'

Thistle nodded inside. 'I'm here to see the show.'

The first guard smiled at the second guard, who moved aside to allow Thistle to pass.

The warehouse smelled of fruit. A crowd of twenty or twenty-five men of distinctly the cheaper sort half filled three ranks of overturned crates. The men he'd been following were sitting up at the front, and didn't turn round to check on the newcomer. Thistle took a seat on a box at the back – strawberry, to go by its scent – and waited to see what he was waiting for.

'First time, brother?' the man next to him asked, white-haired and lean, his clothing worn but well repaired.

Thistle grunted non-committally.

The man took this as a yes. 'You'll remember tonight for ever, brother,' he said. 'You'll remember tonight for the rest of your life.'

Thistle thought he was going to say more – old men who start talking are generally loath to stop – but instead he turned to face the stage and left Thistle to his thoughts.

After a few minutes the two guards from outside came in and closed the front door, took up a position beside it. The atmosphere was excited but not at all unpleasant. Still, the sound of that door closing got Thistle to worrying, this whole escapade being ill-considered, pointless at best and possibly more dangerous

than he had anticipated. He was kicking himself for his reckless-
ness when the man who had saved his life six months earlier
walked in through the back door.

It was a small stage but he took up all of it. The great sweep
of his white hair looked every bit the crown. He wore the same
costume Thistle had seen him in the first time, a strangely formal
version of the uniform forced on men working below. His eyes
were bright blue and he had big, gnarled hands, like a smith or
a brawler.

'Everything that you know is a lie,' he said simply.

'Your name is not your name. Your history is false, your myths
doubly so. Your words are the words of another. Your labour
feeds the belly of a stranger. You sire children to be chattel. Your
breath itself exists in the service of beings to whom you are of
less interest and import than an insect. Truly, in all the world,
there are none who can claim such abject misery, such utter lack
of purpose, such profound and absolute misery, as yourselves.
Everything that a man can lose, you have lost.'

Thistle realised he had been nodding along in rhythm, and
that his heart was beating very quickly in his chest.

'Who has done this to you?' the man asked, still speaking in
his steady baritone. 'Who is at fault?'

'The Four-Fingers!' yelled a man behind Thistle, a man who'd
had something to drink before the meeting, if his slurred words
were any indication.

'False!' the speaker roared suddenly, a clap of sound that echoed
through the small enclosure. 'False!' he roared again, and the
man who had spoken shrank his head down into his shoulders
and looked less than proud.

But when the orator continued it was in the same easy tone
as before. 'The Birds are no more responsible for your decline
than the grapevine is the drunkard's. It is you and you alone who
must be held responsible – you and you alone whose complicity
in this injustice demands reproach. You have allowed your memories to be forgotten, you have bent knee to demons. You have
accepted your subjugation without complaint, without reproach,

without rebellion. Do not look to the Four-Fingers. Do not look to those upslope. You and you alone are responsible for this calamity, and you and you alone have the capacity to remedy it.'

Thistle could hear the man clearly but found himself leaning forward all the same.

'The Four-Fingers put us beneath the ground – we forgot the light. The Four-Fingers gave us names – we were fool enough to accept them. The Four-Fingers called themselves gods – we chose to worship them. You sit with your hands unfettered, with strength in your arms, with the ancient blood of the west in your veins, and you complain of oppression. Freedom is in your grasp, if only you would take it.'

One of the men in the side corner, thickly muscled and poorly dressed, had begun to weep, deep-chested sobs of a kind Thistle had never heard a man make before. With one thick fist he beat at his breast in time with the words, not lightly either, an ecstatic act of masochism. His fanaticism fell like seed on fallow earth, and soon half the audience was engaged in similar displays, pulling at the roots of their hair, shaking back and forth.

'No Four-Finger can claim your inheritance. And no Four-Finger can redeem you from bondage. You and you alone must make that choice, must make it again and again, every morning, every evening, every waking moment of the day. I am Edom, First of His Line, chaplain of the Five Fingers,' he said, holding one hand aloft, each digit splayed wide. 'If you are unwilling to remain amidst the squalor of your birth; if you demand a right to the wrongs that have been done to you before your grandfather's grandfather was pulled forth from the womb; if you would rather die than see another generation of our kind be robbed of the future the gods have decreed for them; then you are already one of us, and must but say the words.'

It was only then that Thistle made the connection between the man who had saved his life a half-year earlier and the disturbance at the Anamnesis that had so excited him, that he had thought about secretly for weeks and months afterwards. Thistle felt as if Edom were looking directly at him. Everyone who heard

Edom speak thought that, but in Thistle's case it was actually the truth.

'A new world is coming, my brothers,' Edom said, after a long pause. 'Will you be a part of it?'

There couldn't have been more than thirty men in attendance that night, but if you had heard the roar that erupted in response, you'd have thought there were far more – five hundred men, a thousand, ten, the entirety of the Rung. An explosion of passion the likes of which Thistle had never seen, sufficient to reduce the hardened porters and dockworkers and cheap thugs in attendance to a state of near mania. The man next to Thistle grabbed him suddenly and pulled him into a bear hug, and it was only after a moment that Thistle realised he was hugging the man back, and that the wetness he felt on his cheeks wasn't perspiration, or at least not entirely so.

Thistle shoved himself free of the man and sprinted for the exit. One of the guards said something as he broke out the back but Thistle couldn't hear him, heading swiftly into the night air. The sleet had turned to snow and now stuck heavy on the ground, thick as cobwebs and white as fresh milk. It disappeared near as soon as it touched him, thawed by the heat kindled inside his chest.

25

The citadels of the Roost were as varied and diverse as the menagerie of creatures that blessed the Lord's gardens. The Haunt of Stars was silent and subtle and ineffably quiet, brought a sense of composure and peace and faint sadness. The Red Keep was like a ray of late-afternoon sunlight crystallised into one towering and magnificent edifice, warm and welcoming and noble. The Prime's demesne was a vast and infinitely mysterious creation, with things strange and beautiful hidden beneath every stone and behind every redoubt, a tableau of perfection carefully delineated over the course of the epoch.

But even among this extraordinary collection, one could not help but recognise the Sidereal Citadel as being unique. The Wright, as his name would suggest, was famed among Those Above and Below for his genius in the creation of steamwork, curious mechanisms of metal and glass that walked and danced and performed many other sorts of wonders. During the course of his long life – for he was quite a bit older than the Prime even, had, in fact, stood as guardian for the Aubade himself in that impossibly distant period when the Lord of the Red Keep was still a hatchling – the Wright had rebuilt his manor according to his predilections. Everything that might be powered by water or steam rather than human muscle was done so: doors opened seemingly of their own accord, bridges between the towers dropped at the turn of a crank, awnings and balconies appeared unexpectedly from hidden indentations. Sterling orrery corresponding to no celestial pattern of which Calla was aware hung down from the ceilings, and the walls were adorned with automated tapestries depicting mounted Eternal riding into combat, or the cycle of a flower from bud to blossom.

It was to see the newest of the Wright's creations that the Aubade, the Prime and their respective entourages were standing on the top of the highest tower in the Sidereal Citadel. Like the Red Keep far to the east, the Wright's castle was located at the outermost edge of the First Rung – but whereas the Red Keep stood overlooking the bay and the ocean beyond, the Sidereal Citadel lay suspended above the Second Rung and far below one could watch the humans go bustling about their day.

Not that anyone was actually watching them, not with the strange splendours on offer at eye level. The Eldest loved flying things of all sorts, kites and fluttering pendants and the air-filled sacks that had become all the rage in the last few years, heated pouches with little baskets held beneath them that Those Above would use to flit undirected across the city. The Wright's new craft, however, was in a class entirely of its own. The largest part of its bulk consisted of a half-dozen great packets, each slowly swelling with smoke from oversized silver braziers set beneath them. They were strung to the hull of a canal boat composed of interwoven willow, with a bronze beak at the front. But sliding out from the sides of the frame were two sets of wings like those of a dragonfly, purple silk stretched over metal wires. Eight stout men, two to each side, sat crammed onto narrow benches, waiting to turn their muscle towards the contraption. If they were frightened of their imminent sojourn into nothing, they didn't show it, smiling and whispering to each other, reckless and without fear, like their lord.

Inside the hull Calla could hear the sound of metal pushing against metal, and swarming in and out of it were the Wright's servants, humans wearing plain working clothes, checking screws and bolts and the endless minor details that would mean the difference between glorious victory and a fiery death below. The Wright was explaining the inner workings of it to the Aubade, elaborately and in great detail, though between translating it mentally from the High Tongue and the sheer complexity of the conversation, Calla understood very little.

In fairness, the Aubade seemed to be in little better shape. First in nearly every other task to which the Eternal set themselves, he had no head for steamwork, nor much understanding of its intricacies. What he did possess, however, was a keen sense of etiquette, and he had graciously spent the past half-hour listening to the Wright's explanations of the contraption he had built.

'In principle, of course, it's a relatively simple variation on the classic system of air-bladders to provide lift, merged with wings to provide forward movement. Where my genius comes into play is that I've miniaturised the essential components, creating a vehicle capable of guided flight in a fashion never before conceived.'

'Can you call it genius before the thing's flown?' the Aubade asked. 'If it drops like a stone, wouldn't the quality be more accurately called madness?'

'I suppose you would have to call it both. Some of the rudder problems, in particular, I had to solve were quite taxing. Even if it fails overall, the specific advances I've made are definitive evidence of brilliance, speaking objectively.'

'It won't fail,' the Aubade assured him, 'and you are quite the cleverest thing the Roost has ever produced.'

'Perhaps not ever,' the Wright said, after giving the question some thought. 'But certainly contemporaneously.'

The Wright pulled his sibling aside to explain some or other feature of the craft and for a moment Calla was left alone with Sandalwood. It was the first time they had spoken since their visit to the Fifth Rung months earlier. Part of that was because of Bulan, who had gradually gone from being an occasional dalliance to something more serious. But more of it was that seeing him served as an unpleasant reminder of that horrible morning and, illogical and unjust though it was, Calla found herself resenting him for it.

Though today, at least, that memory seemed attenuated, unfocused. Early spring but the weather was already warm, and all across the summit of the Roost shoots of green could be noticed, the first scent of flowers lingering in the nostrils. It seemed a day for renewal, for casting away burdens.

'May the sun shine bright on you, Calla of the Red Keep,' Sandalwood said with mock formality.

'In a few minutes you should be able to make that request of him directly,' she said.

Sandalwood smiled. 'I am not sure that the Lord's expedition will carry us quite so high.'

'Perhaps the next time. It is an extraordinary thing you have created.'

'I think, as I had so little to do with its construction, it might not be too immodest of me to suggest that you do not truly understand the truth of those words. The Wright is . . .' Sandalwood fell silent. 'It is a privilege.'

'A vice can be made of modesty, as of anything,' Calla said brightly, slipping one arm beneath his. 'And today's victory is nearly as much yours as your master's.'

He blushed and began to answer, but the Wright called out to him then, needing his input on some or other aspect of the craft, and he smiled and dipped his head. She watched as together they inspected the array of machinery, talking quietly and making small adjustments. If it was the Wright's child, then at least Sandalwood had proven instrumental in its delivery. He looked handsome, sharp and focused, and happy the way someone is happy when they are performing a difficult task with skill. Once

he looked over to see if she was watching him, and he smiled to
see that she was, and she smiled to see that she had made him
smile. Afterward, with the Aubade's permission, she might take
the evening off, invite Sandalwood out for a celebratory libation
and perhaps even take him home after. Bulan wouldn't like it,
but then Bulan would never know, and anyway Calla felt more
than confident that she was not the only woman privileged to
grace the Chazar's bed.

Lost in thought, Calla had not noticed the Aubade drift away
to speak with the Prime. The two of them conversed quietly at
the outermost reach of the precipice, their beauty a palimpsest
against the endless blue of the afternoon sky. Their liaison
continued with all the haste of a fleeing tortoise, a pace that
might well see Calla's children dead before flowering. He had
sent an etching two weeks earlier that might have been of her
face, or of the sky before a winter storm, and she had responded
with a special blend of joss that still lingered happily in the
corridors of the Red Keep.

Alas, it seemed this was not the time for love. 'The reports
from the Sentinel of the Southern Reach are that the Aelerians
continue their preparations,' the Aubade said. 'And that the war
party is ascendant.'

The Prime was staring out at the Wright's masterpiece, and
seemed less than thrilled to have to turn her attention away from
it. 'With all there is to see today, can't we speak of something
else?'

'I take no joy in politics, nor of turning our talk towards them.
But the Aelerians are a threat that needs to be taken seriously.'

'Those Below are never happy except when they're killing each
other,' the Prime said. 'I have stood beneath the sun for two
hundred turnings, and there have not been ten when the Dayspans
were not at war.'

'You do not need to tell me of the Five-Fingered,' the Aubade
said. 'I've spent as much time observing them as any of us.'

'Experience does not necessarily lead to understanding,' the
Prime said. 'There are many in the Conclave who would say that

your time as a Sentinel has tainted your judgement – that the destruction of Elsium by the Sea rendered you antagonistic towards the Aelerians, and over-willing to intervene in human affairs.'

It was to the Aubade's credit that he could consider this suggestion without rancour. He deliberated for a time before speaking. 'In truth, I think of my years outside the Roost but rarely. My memories of Elsium by the Sea are faint and ill-preserved. Though there are times when I can recall the sound of the water lapping against the sands, and am filled with the most terrible sense of despair, as if there were nothing in the world for me but to hear that sound again.' He fell silent, and despite his words seemed very much lost in memory, blinked twice to shake himself free of it. 'But that is not to the point – my past history is used as a comfortable excuse to ignore me, to continue blind to the truth.'

'Which is?'

'That the humans are a threat to us. That we have thought too long of them as chattel, and must readjust our understanding.'

The Prime turned her gaze away from the airship and onto the servants who were running over the top of it. 'They seem quite threatening.'

'You look at your house servants and the people of the First Rung, and you imagine them to be representative of the species. But you are wrong, as wrong as you would be to call a wolf a dog. They are clever, and they learn quickly, and they are cruel, terribly cruel. You imagine their short span is a weakness? I am far from sure of that – their nearness to death makes them mad to leave something of themselves behind. They do more in a day than we do in a month, and with lives so brief can barely give a thought towards the future.'

'One wonders why they have not sacked the city and killed all of us.'

'I ask myself that often,' the Aubade said. 'Once they were too fractious to turn their attentions towards us. Now I imagine they simply overrate our strength.'

'There is as much danger in fearmongering as in complacency. I rode beside you the last time we met the Aelerians, and well remember your blade among them. If the Locusts are so desperate to meet their death, then it will be no very great struggle to bring it to them.'

'I suppose it is a factor of our span, that makes it so difficult to adjust to time's passage, to imagine that there might yet be things that we have not seen, that tomorrow might not arrive identical to yesterday.'

'Does life bore you so, that you need make monsters out of shadows and demand that we all follow you in pursuit of them? Or is it sheer bloodthirst that would have us descend upon the Aelerians with fire and sword? I had not thought that you and the Lord of the Ebony Towers would have so much in common.'

For a moment the Aubade seemed bright and terrible as the noonday sun, the mention of the Shrike leading him towards fury. 'I would think you know me better than that.'

After a moment the Prime dipped her head. 'Yes,' she said, which was no very great apology but it seemed it was all he would get.

Calla thought they both looked happy to see the Wright waving over to them, bringing their conversation to an abrupt end. The expected moment had finally arrived. The Wright bowed to the Prime and then to the Aubade, pulled his robes tight about him and in one easy leap cleared the gangway to land upright. He gave a signal to two of the house servants still standing on the tower, who swiftly released the ties that anchored the ship.

The assembled crowd held its breath in wonder and terror. The strange, hulking, absurd contraption, freed from its bounds, rose slowly up into the air. Sandalwood called the beat of the rowers, *one-two one-two*, and the ship lurched forward, making its way out into the naked air. The Wright stood on the bow, enjoying this moment that his long months of labour had created. You could not quite call it graceful – the craft bobbed violently, could be no very comfortable berth for those ensconced inside. But, awkward or not, the thing flew! It did not float or glide – it flew as a bird, wings humming in even but rapid time, the balloons a bright burst of colour against the azure sky. Calla laughed and clapped her hands in sheer wonder, and she was far from the only one.

Who, looking at the craft, would have doubted the truth of the Prime's words? Calla had heard that the humans on the lower portions of the Roost, and those benighted souls beyond it, credited the High with all sorts of supernatural abilities, said that they could read minds and call down lightning with a word – nonsense, of course, though she could understand how such stories had begun. For were they not worthy of myth, these creatures among which she lived? Were they not legends, though they stood and walked as men?

Calla was looking at Sandalwood, who was standing beside the Wright with a smile to match his lord's, and so she didn't see whatever it was that exploded actually explode, only heard the sound and felt a sudden wave of heat and force that knocked her to the ground, head turning tortuously, a drone in her ears that was more like a pain than a noise.

It took Calla a long time to stand; her arms wouldn't do what she told them to and her legs proved similarly rebellious. When she finally managed it she discovered the front of the craft was thick with smoke, and the chittering left wing that had so amused her a moment before was gone completely, bits of falling debris the only evidence that it had ever existed. One of the rear sacks had burst and the ship listed vertically, the humans manning it tumbling towards the prow.

The buzz in her ears died enough for her to hear the chorus of five-fingered screams. The explosion had knocked the Wright to the deck of the ship, but he was back up swiftly. He grabbed the nearest human, one of the rowers, a man bull-necked and stout, and threw him over his shoulder as if he were a sack of wheat. Then he sprinted across the deck and made a smooth leap onto the dock.

Calla was so focused on the Wright's escape that she did not realise the Aubade was making the reverse journey. Without preamble and seemingly without consideration he tore across the deck, building up speed for the jump. Calla's heart was in her chest and then her lord was in the air. The ship hung some far way out from the precipice, and the Aubade barely made it, catching the tip of the bow with one hand. Calla screamed then, adding her voice to the crowd, but the Aubade continued on unflappable, swinging himself up and darting straight into the hull.

The fire had spread so rapidly that this was now obscured entirely by black smoke, and what happened next Calla couldn't make out clearly. The rest of the assemblage, human and High, had been reduced to chaos, the Wright's servants shrieking and running back and forth along the quay. One of the unfortunate crew members came sprinting out from inside the hull, engulfed in flame and shrieking so loudly and so terribly as to drown out, for a moment, the rest of the cries. Then he was over the edge and falling and his voice soon lost. Another eruption of sound and the side air sack was gone as well, and the weight of the ship began to pull unceasingly downward.

And then the Aubade came out of the smoke, a human slung over each shoulder. There was an instant when he stood unmoving on the trembling deck of the ship, marshalling his energies for the task in front of him. Calla was screaming at him to stop, that he could never make it, that he had barely made it the first time. Later she would realise how mad this was, since of course staying on the ship was suicide, but in the moment somehow she did not realise it.

Perhaps the ship had drifted closer to the tower, or perhaps the Aubade's first leap had been below his normal standards, because this time he cleared the distance easily, landing, by coincidence or design, just in front of Calla herself. Midway through his leap the final air sack popped desultorily and the craft plunged like a stone, dropping so rapidly that Calla barely had time to mark its descent before she heard – no, felt – the impact below, a caterwaul of crushed steel and wood and flesh that seemed to shake the very foundations of the city.

The Aubade set the two humans he had saved down in front of her, then allowed himself to be led away by the Prime. One of the humans was breathing shallowly, but the other was quite terribly burned, flesh blackened and blistered, and Calla knew that he was dead, or would be dead very soon. The smell was appalling, made Calla want to weep even if she hadn't wanted to weep anyway. A swarm of servants were quick to reach them, offering what aid could still be offered, and Calla happily vacated her spot near the carnage.

The Prime was inspecting the wounds that the Aubade had received, steam burns along his arm and a cut that wept crimson just above his forehead. It was a task made more difficult by the fact that the Aubade seemed as jubilant and energetic as a child. 'What a splendid show!' he insisted, struggling to rise. 'Did you see that leap?'

'I saw, I saw,' the Prime said, putting her hand on his shoulder and settling him back onto the ground. 'You were magnificent – now please stop moving.'

The Wright had been quite ill-treated by the fire, though not to such a degree as some of his humans. His robes were tattered and torn, his skin was bruised where it was not covered with soot and the flesh of his shoulder was a charred and unappetising red. He seemed to notice all of this very little, however, over-looking the sight of the crash and speaking animatedly to himself. 'The third gear, it must have been the third gear. It caught loose shifting and tore out enough of the air sack for the gas to leak out, and then—' He rose quickly from where he was sitting and switched to human speech. 'Sandalwood? Sandalwood?' He turned his neck back and forth sharply, surveying for his lost man. 'Where is Sandalwood?'

'I'm afraid he's dead, my Lord,' one of the workers chimed in, a thickset young woman who had been standing near the edge when the craft had gone down. Her face was streaked with ash and a section of her long hair had been burned away.

The Wright leaned his head back over the precipice and stared at the wreckage below. Then he turned back to the woman who had spoken. 'Evergreen, you are now Chief Seneschal. Congratulations.'

'Thank you, my Lord,' the woman said after a stuttering moment, though she seemed less than thrilled at the promotion.

The craft lay far below, a peculiar and ungainly cenotaph for a man who had been her friend and lover, as well as for many people who had no doubt served the same function for others. It had fallen, Calla could see now, in the midst of a crowded thoroughfare on the Second Rung. Humans swarmed around it, and it was not hard to imagine their shock and horror at this catastrophe that had, quite literally, tumbled down upon them from the skies.

'The first thing to do, of course, is inspect the wreckage,' the Wright explained to his new seneschal. 'Some of the bladders are likely still good, and perhaps one of the rudders. Remember – there is no such thing as a failure. This is but a setback, and one which will make our eventual triumph all the more thrilling.'

26

Eudokia followed Andronikos out of the main chapel, down a long, narrow set of stairs and into the small room that had been set aside for the refreshment of the Archpriest and Priestess of the Cult of Enkedri. In contrast to the gilded grandeur of the cathedral, the antechamber was small and dark and unprepossessing. It was quiet though, at least, and after half a day of ringing gongs and endless chants that wasn't something to dismiss casually. Laid on a table were an amphora of table wine and a few vittles, and Eudokia poured two glasses and brought one over to the senator, who had collapsed into a chair almost as soon as he'd entered the room.

'It was really quite an improvement on last month, Senator, you should feel proud.' Andronikos snatched the glass out of Eudokia's hand and downed it in one swoop. Eudokia ignored this coarseness and continued. 'You'll have mastered it completely with a few more years' practice.'

For some reason this thought seemed not to bring the senator any great sense of comfort. He took off his headdress and laid it on the table next to them. Technically speaking, this was a violation of the sacraments, but Eudokia found it within herself to be magnanimous.

'Bugger the ritual,' Andronikos said unhappily. 'And bugger Enkedri.'

'A portion of the liturgy with which I'm unfamiliar,' Eudokia said, taking the seat beside him.

Eudokia had got Andronikos elected high priest to fracture his coalition with Manuel, but it was a pleasant upside to see how incompetent he was at his duties, and that he clearly loathed discharging them. He couldn't get through a prayer without stumbling over the words, and his voice, so forceful and persuasive in the Senate Hall, turned weak and quivering when reciting scripture. Midway through the service he had spilled the sacrificial wine, necessitating the repetition of a lengthy portion of the prayer, and Eudokia had managed to rein in her good humour only by reminding herself that levity was beneath the dignity of her office.

Of course she found the whole thing as pointless and absurd as did Andronikos. Eudokia thought it spectacularly unlikely that Enkedri and his siblings existed, but if she was wrong, then what horrible, grasping little pedants they were! Had Eudokia been granted divinity she'd have found something better to do with it than watching two old farts in ugly robes mutter gibberish over summer wine.

All of that notwithstanding, however, it was widely agreed that Eudokia performed her service masterfully, in a voice near sonorous, with a sense of piety at once reserved and distinct. Eudokia was a performer, among her many other roles.

It was the day of the Ascension, when Enkedri revealed himself to his siblings as being supreme among them, a day for putting on masks and throwing them off. Across the city the different guilds and neighbourhoods would immerse themselves in elaborate pageantry, trying to outdo each other in displays of garishness and frivolity. Here in the cathedral, things were less exciting – though they were about to get more so.

The ceremony had been meant to last three hours, though with Andronikos's various missteps it had taken more than four. They would need to repeat the service in only a few short minutes and Eudokia hoped that, with his first failure behind him, Andronikos might prove more competent the next time round. But she would not hold her breath.

He certainly wouldn't do a better job if he kept drinking so heavily. Having downed the proffered glass he was quick to pour himself another, and quicker still to drink it. 'How you must hate me, Domina, to have imagined so torturous a punishment.'

'What a strange thing to say! Of course I have nothing for you but the utmost respect and affection – feelings no doubt shared by your colleagues, which is why they decided that you were the only man capable of fulfilling the office of Archpriest!'

Eudokia's kindnesses seemed to do very little to assuage Andronikos's temper. He must really loathe ritual, Eudokia thought – or perhaps it was the recent news of Manuel's defection, the speech he had given two weeks earlier claiming that the honour of the Republic was impossible to rectify with the continued occupation of Oscan by Salucian forces. That the blood of all true Aelerian patriots cried out to be unified with their brothers, and that if war was required to satisfy that end, then it had best come sooner rather than later.

The sudden destruction of that coalition, which had seemingly run the Commonwealth for the better part of ten years, had been a dramatic and unexpected reversal – unless you were Eudokia, of course. With Manuel and his supporters having crossed lines, Andronikos found himself desperate to cobble together what support he could from the rest of the Senate, marshalling all his rhetorical abilities and calling in every favour he had earned in twenty-odd years of corrupt dealings. Even so he had only managed to avoid outright war by by enacting a measure demanding that the Salucians attend a conference to discuss the issue. It had been a clever ploy, an attempt to co-opt the people's fury without actually doing anything.

'For my part,' Eudokia continued amiably, 'I can't begin to express the joy I take in performing the rituals at the right hand of so upright and pious a compatriot. I daresay if I were here with any of the other contenders, our interaction would be a good deal less enjoyable.'

'Manuel? If I never again am forced to smell his unique melange of sweat and self-righteousness, it will be too damn soon. You know that rumour everyone tells about him is true.'

'Really?'

'I don't know,' Andronikos said. 'Probably.'

Eudokia made a clucking sound in the back of her throat that could have indicated anything, and took the opportunity to scan the room for any stray servants or minor officiants who hadn't slipped out. Comfortable with their isolation, she smiled and turned back towards the senator. 'A trying time for you, these last few weeks, I'm sure. Still, no one could say that your attempts to avert conflict with Salucia were anything but considerable. Phrattes must be very pleased.'

His cup stalled midway to his mouth, and a few drops of red graced the carpet. Apart from that, Eudokia thought he dealt with the shock admirably. 'Excuse me?' he asked.

'Phrattes, the Salucian merchant you've been taking money from.'

Andronikos was not a fool, for all that Eudokia had played him for one. He didn't rant or rave, at least not at that moment. He even set aside his cup and smoothed out the wrinkles in his ceremonial robes before continuing. 'I'm afraid I've no idea what you're referring to.'

'Perhaps I've been confused. When I return home I'll make sure to take a second look at those payment slips from the Slate Bank of Chazar. They seemed awfully definitive, but then, it would not be the first mistake I've ever made.'

Andronikos's eyes were very wide. He drank until he discovered his glass was empty, then he stood up and carried the amphora of wine back to his seat.

'Now, now, Honoured Father – if you continue like this, I'm

afraid you'll be no good at all for tonight's ceremonies. And I can't very well be expected to run everything by myself, can I?'

'He's your creature, then?'

'He's well rented,' Eudokia said, 'though I think we both know the man sufficiently not to overrate the strength of his loyalty.'

'Everything I have done has been in service to Aeleria,' Andronikos said angrily. 'War against Salucia would be a disaster, would lead us to another war against the Others, another Scarlet Field. I have always, and will always, put the good of the Commonwealth above all else. If Phrattes wanted to pay me for something I was going to do anyway, the least I could do is let him.'

'I'm not certain your fellow senators will feel quite so liberal about the matter – it's been some time since I've examined the relevant portions of the code, but I imagine they might see your recent financial arrangements as high treason.'

'How long have you been planning this? Certainly it was before you convinced my idiot daughter to marry her idiot husband. The Spider Queen, indeed. By the gods, is there nothing you wouldn't do to ensure my destruction?'

'Let's not regard ourselves too highly. You're a means, not an end.'

'And what is that end?'

Eudokia smiled, apple-cheeked and fetching. 'I want the same thing that you want, of course. The health and strength of Aeleria. Its enemies scattered, its people prosperous and happy.'

'I don't see how it's in the interest of the Commonwealth to have twenty thousand of its sons run down by the demons. What could possibly make you think the outcome will be any different than it was last time?'

'Because,' Eudokia began, as if the point were obvious, 'last time Aeleria did not have me to lead them. I have been planning for the Eighth War since we lost the Seventh. Every step the nation has taken for twenty years has been in service of that end. We took Dycia to have a springboard for our campaigns against the Marches, and the Marches to ensure the stability of our flanks. When we march on the Roost we will do so with the strongest army in the history of the world, and we will lay it to waste. You and the rest of the Senate may be content to bend knee to the demons, to rest with their boots upon your neck so long as you are allowed your privileges, but I am afraid I am not so naturally submissive. It is Aeleria's destiny to overthrow the Others, to rule the continent. It is the destiny of Eudokia to rule Aeleria.' Eudokia's voice had grown cold, and her eyes savage, till Andronikos began to feel fear worm its way through his cocoon of wine. 'And by the gods whom we both serve, that destiny will be fulfilled.'

'You would drown the world in blood, in service of your ambition?'

'How rigid a code of ethics you profess, what an uncompromising morality. Tell me, when exactly did you discover this steely resolve? This morning? Before lunch? Thirty seconds past? Certainly it wasn't when you were selling yourself to the Salucians, trading the Commonwealth's security to swell your purse.' Andronikos's cheeks were reddened by shame and wine. He opened his mouth to speak, but Eudokia waved him silent. 'In fact, Father, none of this is a concern of yours any longer. You've been freed of the burdens of leadership, and how happy you must feel, how relieved.'

'And what role do you intend me to play?'

'The one you've been angling for, of course. I mean to make you the head of the embassy we're to send to the Salucians. Who better than the great peacemaker himself to ensure that any recent difficulties are made good?'

'You'd . . . you'd make me ambassador to Salucia?'

'It's near as done. Tomorrow, Gratian will announce the reconciliation between your two parties – an emergency measure, day-to-day politics put aside in the greater interest of the Commonwealth. You'll leave shortly. A grand parade is already in the works; I can assure you the pageantry will be stunning, will be all that the moment requires.' Eudokia took a moment to stare off into space, as if imagining what was in store for Andronikos. 'Of course, no one expects you to work miracles. And if, despite all of your best efforts, the warmongering Salucians, thinking themselves impervious in their alliance with the Wellborn, force our nation into war . . . well, you can be assured of my continued support there as well.'

'You . . . you . . .' Andronikos's face had gone from red to purple, as if his rage were a solid thing and had stuck midway down his throat. He finally managed to eject it, along with a spray of profanity: 'Scandalous fucking cunt!' He stood up like a shot and shattered his glass against the wall.

The insult passed over Eudokia like a gust of wind, failed to tilt the axis of her smile. 'I'd thought you too decorous a man to resort to such vulgarity,' she said sweetly.

Andronikos's burst of rage, or perhaps the shift in his circumstances, had left him breathing heavily and thick with sweat. It took him a long time to sit down. 'You've made a stronger enemy today than you suppose.'

'I'm made of sterner stuff than the wine glass,' Eudokia said. Then she gathered up her robes and stood. 'Enough of this back and forth,' she said. 'It ill-befits two such colleagues, allies and friends, to be feuding.'

Before answering, Andronikos brought the amphora to his lips, guzzling from it like a babe at suck. An undignified activity given the man's rank, but then these were trying circumstances. 'Yes,' he said finally, his eyes empty as the jug.

'Excellent,' Eudokia said, smiling. 'And I'm afraid there is one other thing – with your duties taking you out of the capital, it seems a shame to let the services of your head cook go to waste . . .'

Andronikos groaned and rubbed little circles into his temples. Eudokia took the headdress from the table and set it on his skull. He sat motionless as she adjusted it carefully, making sure what hair remained to him was covered beneath the silken cap. 'We'll talk about the specifics later,' Eudokia said. 'Best put it aside for now. Remember – today is a celebration! You'll call down the gods disfavour, looking so miserable.'

Andronikos stitched a smile across his face and let Eudokia lead him back into the chapel.

27

Bas was not happy, you could see that from an arrow-shot away, a storm cloud trailing behind him.

'Shoulder!' Isaac yelled and five hundred men put their pikes against their right shoulders with one rapid movement, ready now to walk forward in lockstep. In theory at least. In actual fact, if Bas had had to put a guess to it, he would have said that perhaps a hundred men shouldered the pike with one rapid movement, these competent few unevenly distributed amidst a far larger mass who had taken Isaac's command as exhorting them to move their pikes to their left shoulder, or to try and bring it forward, or simply to do nothing at all.

'First ranks, front!' Isaac yelled, at which point the first three lines of men, preparing to receive a hypothetical charge, turned their weapons to horizontal. This went little better – if any of the men had been given real weapons, as opposed to comparably sized wooden sticks, a good many of them would be wounded or dead. If they had attempted such incompetence in the face of an actual enemy, Bas suspected, then all of them would be.

For all his long experience with war, this task was a new one to Bas. The Thirteenth had been in existence for nearly a century before he had joined their ranks, and even after the most terrible defeats – at Pawn's Ford against the Marchers, at Scarlet Fields when the demons had ridden them down like sheaves of wheat – still there had been enough remnants to reconstitute the group. Replacements trickled in at all times, of course, but their training was the responsibility of their pentarche. They'd pick up the duties required of them soon enough, what with the alternative being the contempt and perhaps the cruelty of their fellows.

What was being asked of Bas now was the creation of an infant fighting force, to make an army of this ragtag band of recruits, here because they were too poor or too stupid to avoid being conscripted, or perhaps as an alternative to civil punishment. Ex-criminals made the best soldiers, Bas had found, though also the worst. The good ones were mean and tough and liked to kill things, and all you had to do was break their spirit firmly enough to make them take orders. The bad ones were idiots and children, and no amount of corporal punishment would turn them into soldiers.

At this point, few of them were showing much talent for anything. The pike was a simple weapon, when compared with the sword or the bow. The range of movements required of it was limited – over your shoulder when you walked, up in the air when you stood stationary, in front of you when it was time to shove it into someone. The trick was that each motion needed to be performed in unison with the men behind and beside you, or else you started to stab your own people. Which, with his long experience, Bas knew to be an ineffective tactic.

'You are the most incompetent pack of fuckwitted peasants I've ever had the misfortune to endure!' Isaac yelled. 'I'm tempted to march you all out into the river, watch you drown beneath your packs.' Isaac's merits as a subordinate were many; among them were the fact that he could yell louder than Bas, and that he was more creative in his displays of contempt.

But still, Isaac was not the Caracal, and on occasion Bas felt it necessary to make his presence clear. He strutted forward suddenly and stopped face to face with one of the men in the front ranks, grabbed his pike and righted it. The unfortunate victim of his instruction seemed about to vomit from the attention. 'You will keep this pike straight if I have to shove it down your throat,' Bas said.

The hoplitai nodded and started to stutter.

'That did not require a response,' Bas said.

The hoplitai seemed happy to hear that, kept his weapon upright while Bas returned to his perch.

That they all seemed to be in mortal fear of him was not an altogether good thing. At the moment it made them compliant, but ultimately it would just make them stupid. In truth, it was not the hoplitai that worried him. Anyone could be taught the basics of drill, virtually anyone at least, and the true imbeciles would be weeded out soon enough. But an army lived or died on the strength of its petty officers, its pentarches and tetrarches, bitter, scarred veterans whom no one liked and everyone listened to and who inevitably died standing. Those weren't bred in three months of training, Bas knew, nor in three years.

'Enough,' Bas roared, the front-line hoplitai flinching at the volume. 'If tomorrow is this bad, I'm going to break out the whip. We'll see if you learn any quicker with your backs cut to ribbon.' Which sounded rough, but wasn't any more than hot air. Bas wasn't actually going to lash anyone the next day, nor the day after. Feared was one thing, hated was another, and judicious use of corporal punishment was how one stayed on the right side of that line.

Isaac dismissed them in detail, and Bas marked their retreat with an expression that would have withered a daisy or broken a length of iron.

'Well?' Bas asked, after the task was completed.

'They ain't the Thirteenth,' Isaac said. He took a flask from one of his pockets, offered it to Bas, drank from it unsparingly after the Strategos turned him down. It was not the first time he had nipped from it that day, if his breath and conduct were any guide. The themas contained few teetotallers, and Isaac had always been the sort who more needed than enjoyed a drink. But this was the first Bas had seen of this new development, and he liked it less than he did his new crop of soldiers.

Problems atop problems, but at least he was doing something now, rather than burning away the days in the city. Bas walked over to a nearby rain barrel, cupped his hands and drank until his stomach was full, then dumped a quart or two over his head, matting his long hair over his eyes.

'The Caracal is disappointed?' someone asked during this moment of blindness.

Bas didn't recognise the voice, which was like silk or a whore's perfume, but he was reasonably certain he wouldn't like whoever it belonged to. He looked up to discover Konstantinos holding a towel out to him, and after a moment Bas took it, tussled it though his hair and hung it round his neck. 'They're green as saplings,' Bas said.

'We'll have time to season them,' Konstantinos said.

Bas wasn't sure who 'we' were in that sentence, but regardless, he did not think it true. A soldier was not truly that until he had survived his first battle, felt death in his bowels and overcome it, seen his comrades do the same. All the pike practice in the world wouldn't prepare them for shoving a piece of metal in the wriggling flesh of a fellow human. Though this in no way invalidated the necessity of more pike practice, else the first person these virgins would kill was likely to be on their own side.

'Besides,' Konstantinos continued, smirking like a youth, 'they hardly need to be crack fighters to take up a spot in a garrison in Dycia.'

'Is that what they'll be used for?' Bas asked.

Konstantinos shrugged in a fashion he might have mistaken for sly, happy to be asked and happy not to tell. 'That's the official word,' he said.

Bas didn't push him, in part because he didn't want to give him the satisfaction, but in larger part because he felt a queasy sort of certainty that Konstantinos did not really know either, only thought he did. This suspicion was confirmed a moment later when Konstantinos leaned in close and whispered, 'I would not want to be a Salucian come next summer.'

Konstantinos smelled of cinnamon, Bas noticed, better than a man ought to allow himself to smell. He was also wrong, or at least not altogether right.

Bas was a man with a keen understanding of his own qualities. He was a fine soldier, a competent tactician, a mediocre strategist and no sort of politician. But it hardly requires genius to predict the progress of a wheel, and Bas had watched this game play out once before. The Salucians had never been any good at soldiering, but then again they hadn't needed to be, because behind the Salucians, with their silk brocades and lisped voices and cleft arse-holes, there were the Others, and the Others were very good at soldiering, very good indeed. That Aeleria not be allowed to consume Salucia had been the official policy of the Roost for half a century, they had gone to war over it twenty years earlier, and Bas had little hope that their feelings on the subject had since changed. Aeleria would march north, burning as they went, and they would enter Salucia like it was a virgin's bedchamber – and then? Then?

'Then they'd best be prepared,' Bas said, hoping that it would be enough to get Konstantinos to leave.

Konstantinos took his hand off Bas's shoulder, but kept his bright blue eyes on him. 'How could they not be,' he said, 'with the Caracal training them?'

When Bas didn't respond long enough for the silence to become awkward, Konstantinos laughed in his stead and trotted off towards the rest of the officers. By Enkedri, but he looked the part. Tall and broad-shouldered and the sort of handsome that suggested intelligence. And he had none of the aristocrat's typical disdain, or if he did he managed to hide it competently, glad-handing each man in turn as if for that moment the whole of his world resided in them.

Bas had served for eight long years beneath perhaps the greatest military leader Aeleria had ever possessed, Jon the Sanguine. Jon had looked nothing like he should have, a small man with a big head, tiny, ugly, beady eyes, bow-legged with an ungainly roll when he walked. Jon had a high-pitched voice, like a woman or a eunuch, and a sharp tongue that he used liberally, to anyone who had earned his displeasure and a good many who hadn't. Jon took offence easily, was over-conscious of any perceived slight, put far too much stock in medals and honours and had a sense of discipline that bordered on the sadistic.

Jon had a mind like a steel trap, knew the name of every officer in the army down to the level of pentarche and a good many of the hoplitai as well. On campaign he slept for three hours a night, awoke as if his cot were covered with fire ants, fiercely impatient with any subordinate who might be feeling the strain of eighteen hours in the saddle and six months at war. Jon could dictate a dispatch to the Senate while planning the next day's route, sniff out a falsehood before it was uttered, look into a man's eyes and delineate the contents of his soul. Ever shrewd, always prudent, never risking anything except when it needed to be risked, but then tossing everything in the pot, Jon had snatched victory from the certainty of defeat with such frequency that it had become all but commonplace, had left a monument to his own greatness in scorched earth and weeping widows from the Pau River to the Dycian Sea.

Of course, even Jon the Sanguine hadn't been enough against the demons. Looking at Konstantinos, Bas wondered why exactly this uptrussed popinjay imagined himself to be capable of what had been beyond the powers of the Blood-Letter himself.

'I knew your father,' Isaac was saying. 'Not well,' he was quick to add, as if fearful of seeming bothersome, 'but I was a subaltern in the Thirteenth, during the last dust-up with the Birds.'

'The Thirteenth? Then you would have been at Scarlet Fields, when he fell.'

Bas had never seen Isaac duck his head before, and he didn't like seeing it now, not before this blueblood, no matter who his father had been. 'Yes sir, I was there. They held up the Birds for an hour, Enkedri as my witness. I never saw a man die so well. The Strategos was there too, he saw it same as I did.'

'I have a bad memory,' Bas said pre-emptively, hoping not to be dragged into the conversation.

Actually, he remembered Konstantinos's father quite well – had been there to watch the man's death, as Isaac had said, though he'd been busy enough trying to avoid his own to pay too much attention. Phocas had been handsome, like his son, and well-muscled, like his son, and gave off a strong impression of confidence, a lack of which Konstantinos clearly did not suffer from.

He had also been a fool, a quality that Bas strongly hoped had skipped a generation. Phocas had been in charge of the right wing of the infantry, and he had positioned it badly – even Bas had been able to see that, and him only a tetrarche. Taken up a line with a steady sloping hill behind them, nowhere to run when things went bad, no chance of a fighting retreat. Bas did not think that anything could have won them victory against the Others, but he was certain that Konstantinos's father had not helped the matter. True, when the day was lost he had played his role out in full, hadn't run when many men would have, had seen to it that his men conducted themselves similarly. No doubt they had accounted for some few of the Four-Fingers. Unquestionably they had found a place in the national myth.

Isaac was right, Phocas had died very well. What of it? The man had had no monopoly on bravery, which was, as far as Bas was concerned, an overrated virtue, indiscriminately distributed. For sheer furious courage, for that disdain for mortality that was effectively indistinguishable from a suicidal tendency, there were none to compete with the Marchers. How many battles had Bas seen them hurl their massed cavalry against the Aelerian line, how many thousands had he watched expire with a line of steel stuffed through their intestines, how loud their screams and how desperate their courage? And what had all that dying gained them? Their country lost, their children enslaved, their holy places desecrated, their existence all but ended.

Dying did not impress Bas, he did not see the point of it. Any fool could die, and most did.

'If you were at Scarlet Fields, then you must also have been at Ebbs Wood,' Konstantinos said, turning his eyes from Isaac to Bas.

Isaac nodded more vigorously than was needed, the result either of the drink or of his unprecedented slavishness. 'Yes sir, I was there as well.' Bas looked over at Isaac, hoping to halt his friend's descent into foolishness. But either he didn't see it or he chose not to follow. 'It was the grandest moment of the war,' Isaac asserted passionately. 'They were always sending out champions before the battles, like the Marchers do, and of course none of us was ever mad enough to go out and meet one, especially after Scarlet Fields. I was holding a pike in the front line that morning when they sent theirs riding across, big as two men standing atop each other, like they all are. And then the Caracal – I suppose he wasn't the Caracal yet – broke out from our lines, pretty as you please, went out to meet the man.' Isaac shook his head back and forth, as if he still couldn't quite believe what he had seen, even all these years later. 'I know there are men who say it's a myth, who cannot imagine that a human could defeat an Other, not even the Caracal. But you can look at his weapon and know it's the truth.'

'I'd like to see this fabled sword,' Konstantinos said.

Bas didn't answer for a while. 'The Marchers have a tradition,' he said finally. 'A drawn blade is not to be sheathed dry.'

Konstantinos took no offence, or at least showed none. 'A wise people, the Marchers,' he said. 'Shame we had to kill so many of them.' Then he smiled and dipped his head to Bas before slapping Isaac on the shoulder and strutting off, ready to spill his beneficence further down the line.

'Twenty years I served on the Marches,' Isaac said, 'and I've never heard of that tradition.'

'Stop drinking before sundown,' Bas answered, softly even though he was confident no one was in earshot.

To his credit, Isaac didn't argue or bluster, just dropped his eyes and nodded. 'I don't like it here,' he said, finally.

'There'll be another war. There's always another war.'

Bas wasn't sure why this seemed a source of comfort to Isaac. He wasn't sure why it seemed to be a source of comfort to him, either. Lately, Bas found himself unsure about a great many things.

28

The Roost was the largest and most prosperous port in the world. The goods of a hundred lands washed up on its shores, silks and slaves and raw ore and dried onions and salted cod and powdered ginger. Bales of sweet-scented cloves and packed casks of honeycomb with bee corpses drowned in the sweetness they had made, and books in every language and of every description, and straight-edged Aelerian blades – though these were less common than usual at the moment, as if the Aelerians were holding on to their weapons. Collections of exotic wildlife, trapped and caged and transported from across the seas in hopes of finding a place in the menagerie of an Eternal, hooded raptors swivelling their heads blindly, pink squid puckered tight against great glass tanks, fierce tawny cats the size of ponies pacing back and forth in iron cages. Here and there, kept behind double-locked glass and watched over by scowling guards, one could even find scattered pieces of High work, filched by an unscrupulous house servant or sold by some desperate seneschal to pay off their lord's profligacy. Not more than toys, really: spinning gadgets of metal and steam, wild-maned horses that galloped about in circles when you wound them up – the sort of thing a hatchling might play with in the brief period of innocence before entering their ageless maturity.

Only a fraction of it would be sold within the Roost itself. For the human civilisations of the surrounding lands, and even those far distant, the Roost operated as a great way station, goods unloaded and bought and sold and then repackaged and shipped off to some distant corner of the continent. And the heart of this tremendous engine of commerce was not the docks, which after all were too far downslope for any respectable citizen to venture, but the Perennial Exchange, a vast and labyrinthine market that took up much of the Third Rung. It was justly famous the length of the continent, one of the wonders of the Roost, to be compared – if found wanting – with the Source itself.

And today's visit from the Aubade would be the first time, to the best of Calla's knowledge, that any of Those Above had bothered to take a look at what was one of the great economic engines of the world, taking in more in taxes and tariffs than most nations produced in sum.

She had accompanied Bulan on a visit one afternoon, so he could show off his prowess as a trader and the respect that he was granted by the petty merchants who occupied the market – as if Calla, living among gods, would be impressed by the pretensions of the Salucian silk trader trying to undercut Bulan on his next shipment. But still, Calla had to admit, it was a marvellous place, a microcosm of every land and language, reckless men with more to win than lose yelling at one another in the pidgin tongue they had developed, a language ideal for barter and insult. Fortunes were made and lost, dreams fulfilled and shattered, a swirling morass of glorious anarchy, ever-changing, perpetually unsatisfied, mad with desire and ambition. What was greed and vanity in one person became, by some curious bit of algebraic chicanery, something almost like a virtue when practised by the surging masses, a liveliness and voracity that one could not help but find invigorating.

She had mentioned her visit off-handedly to the Aubade upon returning to the Red Keep. He had listened carefully and then shocked her into silence by informing her that he would be visiting it come the morrow, and that Bulan would make himself available as escort. Calla had managed to convince the Aubade to give Bulan more time to prepare a proper reception, had pushed back the date a week, but his mind was set on the project and to try to dissuade him would be pointless and insulting.

Calla was nervous. She had arranged to meet with Bulan before the Aubade's arrival; they were standing at one of the many small piers set along the canals that snaked through the Rung. The market, which grew faster than a glutton, had long since expanded to overtake this pier, though this seemed no very great problem, given that the Eternal never used it. Or at least had not used it in a long time, such a very long time that weeds the size of men grew out of the water and the quay was buttressed on both sides by food stalls.

Bulan was nervous also, but he was doing a better job of hiding it. Not a man unused to strain, indeed seemed to be one of those rare few who thrived upon it, who swallowed toil and trial and grew stronger from it. But still, this was not some trivial bit of barter, or a long con he was trying to pull on a rival. On the one hand, there was the great renown to be had in escorting an Eternal out among humans, even the possibility that the Aubade might be so impressed as to grant him some access to the infinite fortune it was believed, not entirely falsely, that all Eldest possessed. On the other hand, it was a widely known bit of Roost lore that any Eldest might kill or wound a human without punishment or penalty.

So Calla could appreciate that Bulan might be feeling some flutter of agitation before his meeting with the Aubade. He was dressed in an elaborate suit of robes that he had bought for this occasion, or at least that she could not remember seeing before. They were made from the skin of a spotted animal native to

Bulan's homeland, and they were quite beautiful – though they had been more so before Bulan had sweated through them. 'In Chazar,' he said, turning towards her, 'it is the custom of a man who makes an appointment to show up for that appointment at the time he has made it.'

'In the Roost – which, perhaps it has escaped you, is where you currently reside – it is the custom of the Eternal to do whatever they wish, at whatever moment they wish to. Happily, the Lord of the Red Keep was never one to hold too strongly to tradition, and is generally known to be punctual.' She slipped her arm underneath his, allowed him to pull her tight. 'Worry not, Bulan, son of Busir.'

'Worry?' he said, as if the word was unfamiliar and he hoped to commit it to memory. 'I am not a man who has ever been troubled by that particular emotion. I am a man, however, who has other things to do today besides squire around your lord.'

'Then a happy day this is for you,' Calla said, disentangling herself from him and smiling cruelly, 'because he swiftly approaches.'

Calla could hear the Aubade before she could see him. A spindly youth came sprinting down the banks of the canal, or at least as close to a sprint as he could manage in such close environs, yelling, 'A High! A High!' Pedestrians stopped to watch; even the mad press of business seemed to ease for a moment, the brokers and merchants taking a scant few seconds away from making money to gape in awe at the craft and the thing that rode atop it.

The ship arrived, finally, the Aubade himself at the prow. Looking at him standing there, his hair-stalks dyed rainbow and cascading down nearly to his ankles, thin robes of silk and samite and silver, three heads taller than the tallest man on the Rung, Calla could hardly condemn the crowd for their rapt attention.

He alighted from the craft almost before it landed, his leap so smoothly executed that a rumbled gasp made its way through the horde. The Aubade seemed not to notice. 'Greetings of the sun to you, Calla,' he said, then turned to her companion. 'I am correct in believing you to be Bulan?'

Bulan had been anticipating this moment for a week, and still his courage almost failed him. But he smiled through his awe and dropped smoothly into the Wellborn greeting, performing it with an excellence that spoke of long practice. 'Good day to you, my Lord of the Red Keep,' he said. 'I hope the light finds you well.'

The Aubade took a long look around at his environs – not a casual glance, but a slow, penetrating gaze, a sincere attempt to grapple with what was in front of him. 'This is the Perennial Exchange,' he said, self-evidently.

'It is indeed, my Lord,' Bulan said. 'The beating heart of the Rung. Every moment we are speaking a fortune is made or lost, a man thrust upwards to the spiral of his ambitions, or brought crashing down towards disaster and despair. Bulan bids you welcome to his home.'

'The Roost is not your home,' the Aubade said.

'But the Exchange is not quite the Roost, as you shall see,' Bulan said, smiling. 'And anywhere there is money to be made, that place is Bulan's home, as surely as once was the belly of his mother.'

The Aubade made no comment, except to motion to Calla, and Calla turned and nodded at Bulan, and Bulan bowed again and walked deeper into the thick of the market. He was an excellent guide, it soon become clear, offering a running commentary on the stalls that they passed – what they sold and to whom they sold it, the origin of their goods and their likely final destination. To hear him speak there was no trader, merchant, exporter or vendor who Bulan did not feel to be running his business with at least partial incompetence. Everything was an opportunity to Bulan, every sale made was one that he could have handled more skilfully, were he not already busy with his other labours.

'Tell me, Bulan,' the Aubade began while looking through the stock of a bead merchant, twirling his hands through the long strings of multicoloured shell and glass that hung down from the awning. The owner was a Dycian woman, or at least she looked Dycian, dark and heavy; and unlike more or less everyone else that they had seen on the Third Rung, she did not seem particularly impressed by the presence of the Aubade in her establishment. 'You are a man well travelled, yes? You have seen something of the diversity of your species?'

'If I would be too polite to claim such, I am not so humble as to refuse it if offered.'

'What do you think of the Salucians?'

'Rich,' Bulan said. 'Rich from their plantations and their ore. And cunning – everything they say has two meanings and both are likely to be lies. But they lack courage – or perhaps they simply have faith in their friends.'

'The Dycians?'

'Clever,' Bulan said. 'Sharp traders and good pirates. Arrogant as well, unbelievably arrogant, given that they live with the Aelerians' boot on their neck. Though if you meet one, you'd best avoid mentioning that fact unless you are very quick with a knife.'

'And the Aelerians?'

'They are loud, and boastful, and often speak nonsense, and soon you come very close to discounting them altogether – but then they do something so clever that you begin to wonder if their earlier foolishness was not a feint. They cannot haggle, but they have more of everything than everyone else, and can sell it cheaper, so it doesn't matter. The wharves of their capital are flooded with the furs and amber of the March lords, and now the fruits and spices of the Baleferic Isles. Behind all of their demands is a naked pike, and the hard men who carry them. And they are proud – by Enkedri, how they are proud. They accept no insult, brood upon every injury until they can repay it tenfold.'

'And Those Above?' Calla asked.

Bulan smiled but did not answer, and they walked onward.

There seemed neither rhyme nor reason in what caught the Lord's fancy, or least none that Calla could detect. He would pass rows of stalls selling the most exquisite silks or jewellery, only to spend half an hour inspecting a butcher shop. Twice he instructed Calla to purchase the entirety of a store's stock, glorious, shining days for the owners, the sort of windfall that one might dream of but would be a fool to expect.

After they had bought out the contents of a small glassware dealership, the Aubade halted abruptly in front of a squat, wooden building with a sign displaying a fat man holding a bag of coin and a flagon. 'This is what you would call a bar?'

'Or a tavern, or a public house.'

'Are these part of the Exchange?' he asked.

Bulan laughed. 'They are the very heart of it! These hand-to-hand transactions, these petty vendors –' He made a dismissive gesture. 'The real money is made wholesale, not a half-dozen necklaces sold to passers-by, but the raw silver ore to make them. And what better place to discuss the specifics of a deal than a tavern? If you come away victorious, you are only a few steps from a celebratory libation; but should success fail to crown your efforts, you are no further distance from succour.'

The Aubade listened to Bulan finish his speech, and then without saying anything to indicate his intentions walked quickly inside. Bulan and Calla followed swiftly.

The restaurants and drinking establishments that Calla usually visited were on the First and Second Rungs – quiet, well stocked, beautiful little places, where a few glasses of wine could be consumed quietly by soft candlelight. The Fat Man, or the Happy Sot, or the Banker's Draft, or whatever this bar was named, was of an entirely different sort. It was large enough to hold a hundred people comfortably and had no doubt often held far more than that, alcoholics and lechers and happy-seeming whores. At this time however, just after the hour of the Kite, it was mostly empty, a few hardened alcoholics waiting in the wings, the single employee a smiling man behind the counter who nearly went into fits when the Aubade made his appearance.

Calla whisked the Lord away to one of the far tables and Bulan ordered a flagon of red wine and a few skewers of grilled meat.

It was impossible for the Aubade to consume anything that had also been prepared for the consumption of humans, even had the quality of the fare approached his standards – which of course it did not. But he seemed to be enjoying himself all the same, inspecting the environs and watching Calla and Bulan consume their order. At the very least he did not seem bored, which was rare for an Eternal.

'Tell me, Bulan,' he said, 'of your homeland.'

Bulan smiled, poured himself some more wine. 'She misses me,' he said. 'From across the eastern sea, I can still hear her call for my return.'

'And you? Do you not miss it as well?'

'I miss her every day, my Lord,' Bulan said, no longer smiling. 'I miss the blossoms in the springtime, and the prayer calls that go out from the temple of the One God. I miss the food, for there is much to say of this city but honesty bids me add that there is not a single soul living here who is capable of correctly cooking lamb. I miss hearing the words of my own tongue spoken, and I miss my sisters and my mother, who weeps for me every evening, and prays for me at daybreak.'

'Then what is it that has brought you so far from Chazar?' the Aubade asked, with what seemed to Calla to be true interest. 'What has brought all of you, this vast assortment of the human species, from the joys of hearth and home?'

'Yes, Bulan,' Calla said, having drunk enough at this point to be feeling cheeky. 'What could possibly tempt you to remain so far from the pleasures of your country?'

Bulan was as quick-witted a man as ever she had come across, cleverer even in speech than in thought, and he was not at all a dullard. But he waited for a time before answering. 'The fifth ship.'

The Aubade thought this over for a moment. 'A curious answer.'

'I am here in the Roost to set up a factor as a clearing-house for my own goods, so that I don't have to pay one of the larger interests a gods-damned third, which is what they charge.' He looked bitter for a moment, then shrugged. 'What I will charge also, once I am up and running. And when it is in place I will be able to send my small fleet of trading vessels further afield than ever before, and have a place to store my stock until it has reached its peak price.'

'But still I have not heard tell of this fifth ship,' the Aubade said.

Bulan smiled. 'Next year I will have five ships making the western run – down to Aeleria, then out to old Dycia, then back to the Roost, then the long voyage home to Chazar.' He held up five fingers, each ringed and manicured and slightly plump. 'A pair of these will never return –' he bent two digits down into his palm '– lost on the shoals or taken by pirates. I have a full bond on all of them, ships and cargo, though of the two I will lose, only one will ultimately pay out. Of the remaining three ships, one will meet with foul weather off the coast of Calabar, have to spend the winter in port, won't return until the summer after next. And I'll have to pay the crew extra for their time, and some of the stock will have rotted, and I'll be lucky to make a profit of two against five.'

'Are you sure you would not do better as a porter?' Calla asked. 'I could arrange something for you, if you'd like.'

'That was three,' the Aubade said, uninterested in Calla's attempt at humour, if he was aware of it.

'Then one sunny afternoon in mid-autumn, when I am growing very worried that perhaps this year the One God has forgotten my piety, and the sacrifices I have made to him, and will not even allow me my two ships safe – on that afternoon a boy will appear at the front door of my office, excited near to death, and I will give him a silver without even letting him speak, and bet him another that I'll be the first to reach the docks.' He closed his hand and slammed it against the table. 'And though my feet touch wharf stone ahead of his, I'll pay up all the same. And with that one ship, *Fortune's Smile*, perhaps, or the *Lover's Breath*, with the goods in her belly – fistfuls of black pepper from Dycia, furs from the Marches, metalwork from Aeleria – with these I will have enough to recoup my losses in their entirety. To pay off my men, to refurbish my ships and replenish my stocks.'

'And the fifth ship?' Calla asked.

Bulan leaned towards Calla, took her hand with the one he had been using to count imaginary caravels. 'With what I make on the fifth ship, dearest, I will buy a sixth ship. And next spring, when the great harbour at Atil is filled with our vast merchant fleet, and the high priest of the One God comes to bless our fortunes, and the scions of the great merchant families – the Slate Bank and Blackrose and Ieseph's Sons, and the Chazarian branches of the Dycian counting houses – when they tour along the wharves they will see what I have built, from one rickety dhow that my father nearly sold for drink. And they will nod to me, and comment on the weather, and I will return their pleasantries in kind, and pretend I have forgotten all the insults they did me when I was too small and weak to return them. And they will pretend that they have forgotten offering them as well, and vie with each other to compliment my business acumen, though my fleet of six will yet be nothing compared to their vast resources, and my income barely a trickle against their river. And do you know why?'

'No,' the Aubade said.

'Because I hunger. Because their appetites were sated before ever they were born, by their father or grandfather before them, while I sprang from the womb ravenous, a cannibal, with no thought for anything but my own fortune. And in the year after that I will send out eight ships, and the year after that twelve, and then fifteen. And soon I'll have enough capital to give bond on the voyages of others, and to trade in hard currency. To build a mansion in the western hills, and to marry my daughters off to foreign princelings.' For a moment Bulan was lost in dreams of wealth uncounted, of thick golden ingots and eagle-headed coins. He shook that away and turned back towards the Aubade. 'But first,' he said, 'comes the fifth ship.'

'And will that be enough?' the Aubade asked. 'When you have your fifth ship, and your sixth ship after that, and your trading house, and your mansion in the western hills, will that be enough for you?'

'Nothing will ever be enough for Bulan, son of Busir,' Bulan said, and whether it was the drink or the conversation, he seemed to be enjoying himself a great deal. 'I will heap stone atop stone until the end, I will build until I can draw breath no longer. And if the One God is good, I will pass it on to my sons, who will be fierce and bright as Bulan, though as beautiful as their mother.' He shot a sidelong glance at Calla that made her heart skip, but then continued. 'And they will go forth full of fire to make a mockery of my efforts, that they may say to themselves, as all men wish, that their father was no better man than they. And the house of Bulan will grow and grow and grow, until it is a byword, in every port in every country in the world, for wealth and for style and for excellence.' Then he smiled, shrugged, finished off what was in his goblet. 'Or perhaps they will squander my fortune on women and strong liquor. I will be dead by then, and not likely to care much either way.'

The Aubade did not say anything for a long time. The Aubade did not say anything for such a long time, in fact, that had he not been the Aubade one might have interrupted his thoughts, or at least fidgeted in one's seat. Calla kept absolutely still, of course.

'I would give you something, Bulan, son of Busir,' the Aubade said finally. 'For your story.' From inside one of the pockets of his robe he pulled out a brooch. The outside was pure gold, which would have made it valuable enough on its own, but the crux of the thing was the elaborate clockwork centrepiece, which showed a ship sailing across the waves. The background changed gradually, noon to night-time, and the waters went from turbulent to calm, but still the ship moved forward. It was clearly Eternal craftsmanship; no human could have hoped to create such a masterpiece.

Calla had seen enough of their like not to gasp at its beauty, but she did not blame Bulan for his lack of similar composure. 'I assure you, my Lord, that neither thanks nor reward is necessary. It was an honour to have shown you more of your domain.'

'That was not a request,' the Aubade said.

Bulan needed no further persuasion. He ducked his head low, took the brooch from the Lord's hand. 'Thank you, my Lord,' he said, staring at the clockwork ship as it struggled its way through the waves. 'I will treasure it always.'

'It is no less than your services merit,' the Aubade said. But despite the gift, the Lord's good humour seemed to have evaporated, and it was not long afterwards that he stood abruptly and walked out of the bar.

Calla still had half a glass of wine to finish, but of course she stood up also and went to follow after the Lord. 'Speak soon,' she said to Bulan.

Bulan had not yet bothered to affix the brooch, which he stared at for a moment before answering. 'Until then, Calla of the Red Keep.'

Despite having been run in rings for the last few hours in a territory he had never before seen, the Aubade knew exactly where his ship lay. They did not speak, not until they were both seated beneath the back awning, their rowers marking time ceaselessly upstream. 'Was the afternoon a success, my Lord?' Calla asked.

'It taught me much about your species,' the Aubade said. He turned back to watch the Exchange for a moment. The coming of evening had slowed the place only very slightly; no one was yet bothering to break down their stands, and the press of the crowds seemed almost as mad as ever. Young boys carried trays of tea and sweet pastries, moving through the mob deftly and with speed. Men yelled and thrust their chests forward into each other until violence seemed certain, and then one would shrug and they would shake hands in agreement. Everything seeking to eat or be eaten, ever moving, ever changing, at once unsure of itself and certain of its future.

'Much indeed,' the Aubade said.

29

Eudokia had been late at work, as she was most nights, and like most nights she hadn't got to her chambers until the moon was past its zenith. Alone, as usual. There were two activities best enjoyed in bed, and Heraclius was only a competent partner at one of them. She had too much to do the next morning to spend the hours preceding it with a pillow over her ears trying to block out his snoring, or being poked awake by his elbows, or quietly contemplating whether, if she were to murder the man with her fingernail scissors, she'd be able to hide the body before the servants came awake. Yes, was the answer she had come to some weeks earlier when he had last managed to plead his way into her bed, and since then she had thought it better for everyone if she was never again offered the opportunity.

Eudokia had changed into her shift and turned off the lantern and fallen swiftly asleep. She made it a point not to toss and turn, not to eat up the few hours she was able to allot each day towards unconsciousness. Sleep was like any other activity, in so far as Eudokia saw no point in doing it half competently.

She woke dazedly some hours later from a heavy slumber. There had been something in her dream, something she was worried about or needed to do, but it was gone now and trying to recall it only made it dissipate more swiftly. Eudokia yawned, stretched, peered her head out of the window next to her bed. Spring had been slow to arrive, but these last weeks the first buds had started to form, and the soft breeze tapping at the window frame wasn't at all unpleasant.

The mansion was three lines of a square overlooking gardens that became fields if you walked through them for long enough, though Eudokia rarely did. Her suite of rooms was on the top floor of the main building, offering the crowning view of the estate. A view that, as Eudokia took a moment to indulge in it, seemed too clear for so early in the morning, as if illuminated by some source other than the moon.

'Fire,' Eudokia realised, and at that exact instant she heard the clanging of the bell that was meant to warn the staff of just this state of affairs. Excellent, Eudokia thought. Now I don't need to waste my voice with screaming.

Eudokia walked over to her wardrobe, pulled on a cotton robe and a heavy wool one over that, spent a few seconds wondering if she should take anything else but decided against it. What few papers she hadn't destroyed on principle were locked tight in a safe below the desk in her study, an iron monstrosity that should survive the inferno. Or perhaps it would all burn up together, Eudokia had no idea really, and there was nothing for it regardless. Her jewellery was worth a small fortune, as were her clothes, but she owned too many to go picking through them in the dark.

The door leading to Heraclius's quarters swung open and the man himself came sprinting into the bedroom naked, penis flapping back and forth like a caught fish. He leaned in close enough for her to smell his sleep-breath and screamed, 'Fire! There's a fire!'

She pushed him back to an appropriate distance with one

hand. 'That would seem to be the case,' she said, then sat back down on the bed and pulled on her shoes.

'What are you doing?' Heraclius asked, still yelling.

'I'm not going to sprint outside barefoot,' she said. 'And speaking of which, you might want to put on some trousers.'

Heraclius looked down at his nudity, up at her, down at his nudity. Then he ran back into his room.

'I'm not waiting,' she informed his back.

Theodora was just about to knock on her door as Eudokia opened it to leave, which Eudokia found to be a touching bit of loyalty, if pointless. 'Mistress, there's—'

'A fire, yes, thank you Theodora. Where is Jahan?'

Jahan had a small suite of rooms some distance from her own, though he seemed rarely to use them. Thinking about it now, Eudokia realised this was the first time in years that she had opened her door and not seen him standing outside it.

'I'm not sure, mistress. I haven't seen him.'

Eudokia took note of that. 'Make sure the rest of the servants' quarters have been alerted, and assemble in the back gardens. Hopefully someone will have done something about bringing us water by that point.'

Theodora nodded and sprinted down the hall. Eudokia herself headed down the main stairs, and her steps were light as a child's and she had to stop herself from smiling. 'Enkedri the Self-Created, whose eyes are the sun and moon, whose hands shape the star fields, whose heartbeat anchors the world,' she prayed silently, 'please destroy the east wing. If you destroy the east wing and leave the rest of the house undisturbed, I'll sacrifice ten red heifers in your honour, and I'll wield the blade myself.' She thought about it for a moment, weighing the theoretical. 'If you destroy the whole lot of it, however, you'll only get five.' That seemed a more than reasonable agreement, though it did assume that Enkedri had a particular love of heifer corpses, which was a sentiment as popular as it was unproven.

Reaching the ground floor she noticed a smell of smoke and a faint uptick in temperature, though that last might have been

Daniel Polansky

just her imagination. The fire bell echoing loudly throughout the grounds was very much reality, however. Eudokia felt – and there was no other word for it – giddy. Hers was a realm of long-laid plans and silent traps, of slow strategy and delayed gratification. She found it rather thrilling to be in the midst of an immediately dangerous situation, one that required speed and surety. She had always thought she'd be good at it, was pleased to have the opportunity to test herself. Then again, Eudokia had always thought she'd be good at everything.

She was making for the back gardens when a house slave she had never noticed before came running towards her, flapping his arms. 'We can't go out that way, mistress,' he said. 'The fire has spread.'

Eudokia could see a faint glow further down the corridor, and she knew the man was not lying. 'What do you propose?'

'We can cut through the servants' quarters and come out through the front – won't take but a moment,' he assured her.

Eudokia nodded and waved her hand at the man, and after waiting a second to make sure that she was following he took her round the back of the staircase and into a small corridor leading towards the kitchens. He was tall, with a long scar running down his cheek, too ugly to be serving as one of the front help, though he was dressed in her livery rather than as a groundskeeper.

The back kitchen was set up for the slaves' breakfast, the big round table taking up the centre of the room covered with half-eaten plates of food. They'd even left a pot of what Eudokia took to be porridge bubbling away on the stove nearby.

'It's just through this way,' her guide was saying, 'we're almost there.'

The pot was a heavy thing and, needless to say, quite hot, so Eudokia made sure she had a firm grip on its handle before calling the attention of the house slave and tossing the contents into his face. He dropped as soon as it hit him, his screams deafening, then curled up into a ball on the floor, rubbing his melting face with melting hands.

Eudokia could understand now why it had become traditional to drop vats of boiling things on people during sieges. She could also understand why the gods, in their infinite wisdom, had provided human beings with skin. Absent it and she could see the pink of raw flesh and something white that she could only assume was bone. 'I certainly hope I got that right,' Eudokia thought to herself, though she took some comfort in the knowledge that if she had just thrown a pot of boiling porridge in the face of an innocent servant, his body would be consumed in the coming blaze, and she wouldn't hear any more of it.

Still, Eudokia wasn't altogether heartless, and she couldn't help but acknowledge the man's screaming as quite the most terrible thing she thought she had ever heard. It was some relief when she noticed the hilt of a knife peeking out from his breeches.

'I'm fairly certain we don't provide those for staff,' she said aloud.

But her would-be assassin didn't hear her, and his screaming only got louder. The water had burned away his eyelids, or at least he couldn't bring himself to close them, and his eyes were red as pulp.

Eudokia looked around for a moment and grabbed an iron griddle that was hanging from the wall. The man was dying but not fast enough, and she didn't suppose he had come alone. She lifted the skillet above her head and brought it swiftly and without hesitation down against the top of the man's skull. He went limp as soon as he'd been struck, but Eudokia gave him two more, just to make certain. Blood splattered onto the floor and onto the walls and onto her robes.

Clang, clang, clang went the fire bell.

Eudokia pulled the dagger out of the man's belt, held it in her palm for a moment, getting used to the balance. She took a quick look back down at the way they had come, but it had filled up with smoke. This would explain the fire's rapid spread, and Jahan's unexpected absence as well. She grabbed a lantern from the wall and headed onward.

From the servants' quarters Eudokia moved swiftly towards the main hallway, hoping to escape out of the front door and then make her way around the grounds to find help. This was the plan, at least, though it derailed quickly enough when her lantern caught the movement of a man ahead of her. A moment later and the illumination was sufficient to show he was not one of hers. Though dressed in a reasonable approximation of a servant's outfit, he had a small sword as his side and his eyes had the blank look that you'd see in a smith at the forge or a carpenter at his table – a professional engaging in his chosen occupation.

'Whatever you are being paid,' Eudokia said coolly, 'I am in a position to pay you more. And you are in a position to ask for it.'

Either he was too stupid to answer or smart enough to know that nothing she said in the moment would be held to come the morning. Eudokia still had the dagger in her waistband but she didn't bother to do anything with it. Knife work was no speciality of hers, as she imagined it was of this man's.

He moved swiftly towards her, weapon half drawn, then stopped and turned his head back to look the way he had come. Whatever it was that had grabbed his attention, Eudokia couldn't hear it, couldn't hear anything in that moment but the rushing of blood in her veins, and couldn't think about much more than the idea of it splattering on the walls. But then there was something protruding from her would-be assassin's breast, something that glinted in the light of her lantern. And then he was sliding to the ground, and behind him stood her nephew, naked to the waist, his small sword slick with blood. 'We've been attacked!' he said, a child's response to the situation, though there was nothing childlike about the red that covered his hands up to his elbows.

'We're being attacked,' Eudokia corrected. 'Now hurry to the stairs.'

'Is it Andronikos?'

'There'll be time enough to determine the culprit,' she said, 'and to arrange a fitting punishment. Or at least, there might be, if you stop talking and hurry to the gods-damned stairs.'

Though they weren't so very far up those when Eudokia heard a commotion that could only mean her pursuers had found her. When they reached the second floor she pointed down the hallway. 'Hide until they come after me, then double back the way we came. Find Jahan, if he hasn't been killed. Otherwise find anyone, and have them meet me at the main door.'

'I'm not going to just leave you,' Leon said.

How much better a place the world would be, Eudokia thought then, if people would just do what she told them. How much better for everyone. It was probably the single most frequent thought that Eudokia had, but she was thinking it particularly strongly just at that moment. 'They're not after you, you silly little child. You don't matter at all. Listen to me and we might have some chance of saving the both of us.'

She all but knew this was a lie, wondered if he did. Probably not – otherwise, he would have stuck around out of some ingrained sense of gallantry. This tendency towards purposeless heroism was something she would need to shake out of him, assuming she survived till morning. Eudokia grabbed him and held him tight, then released him, put both hands against his chest and propelled him down the hallway. He stared at her for a long second, then turned and ran as she had instructed. Eudokia did the same in the opposite direction.

She moved down the darkened hallway at a rapid pace, but not so quickly that the men following her wouldn't notice her lantern. When she could hear them distinctly she ripped open a side door and threw herself inside. It was one of the dozens of spare guest rooms, hadn't been used for years, sheets still covering the furnishings. The key was in the lock and the lock still worked, thank the gods, and she turned it quickly and then broke it off. She inspected the environs for a few swift seconds, then made her way over to the window.

Here she found her first bad luck of the day, not counting the fire or the group of men trying to kill her. The window was warped into the frame. She shoved the tip of her knife into the bottom crack, began to work to loosen it, actively but not frantically.

Eudokia hadn't really supposed that she had lost her pursuers, but she had been entertaining the notion that they might take a while to narrow down her location. A vain hope, she realised when she heard the sounds of footsteps coming down the hallway and then hands futilely trying the knob.

'Domina,' a voice said. 'Open the door, for the love of Enkedri! The fire is spreading, we don't have much time.'

'Come in then, quickly!' Eudokia said, still working at the window.

'The door is locked, Domina.'

'Just a moment,' Eudokia said, 'I'll open it.'

After a few seconds during which Eudokia did nothing of the sort, she heard a soft chuckle waft its way inside. 'Open the door, Domina.'

'I can't be certain that would be beneficial to my health.'

'If you let us in, I promise, we won't harm you.'

'Quite a lot of trouble to not make any trouble for me,' Eudokia thought to herself, but she answered in a quivering voice, 'You swear? Upon Enkedri and his children?'

'Upon Enkedri the Self-Formed, and Siraph his consort. On Terjunta who watches over soldiers, and Eloha who sprung from the depths.' He was speaking loudly but in the pauses Eudokia could hear them working at the hinges of the door.

'And the minor ones as well?' Eudokia called back from the window. 'On bright-plumed Avas, and Kairn the dicer, and on Tolb who lives among the low?'

There was a pause on the other side of the door. 'On all of them.'

'And on the demigods? On two-headed Amphisbaena, and Catoblepas, and the Skolopendra herself?'

'Open the fucking door,' the voice said.

'That friend of yours in the kitchen died in as much misery as any human being has ever endured, and I confess that murdering him gave me no small thrill.'

A nasty chuckle sneaked in through the keyhole. 'Why do you suppose we got into this business?'

Eudokia broke open the window only a few seconds before her assailants managed to do the same with the door. She shoved the dagger into her belt and threw her lantern back into the room, and the burst of heat gave her a moment to scamper outside. Eudokia hadn't climbed anything since her first bleeding, but there was an old trellis next to the ledge and one hardly needed to be a squirrel to go hand over foot. She reached the roof as quickly as she could, swung herself on top of it. It was formed of hard red clay tiles, and Eudokia loosened one with the point of her dagger and waited silently for her pursuers.

'Get back down here, you withered old cunt!' the face from the window yelled.

Eudokia couldn't quite make out the trajectory of the stone she dropped, though she took the scream that followed to be a positive sign. It wouldn't be enough to keep them off for long, and the trellis was too firmly attached to the wall to do anything with, but at least it would delay her pursuers, beyond being thoroughly enjoyable in and of itself.

She forced herself to her feet, saw, for a moment, her estate stretching out beneath her, made clear by the light of the moon and the light of the fire they had set, and felt a moment of dizziness from the height or the smoke or from being pursued by men hoping to kill her. But she shook through it, began to make her way forward as best as she was able. A short way down she slipped and felt her ankle do something that it wasn't supposed to do – it was close to agony but she did not scream, indeed barely slowed, steeled herself and rose quickly, ignoring the pain shooting up her body. There would be time enough to bandage it, she consoled herself, or it wouldn't be an issue long.

The roof was shallow and went on for ever, and Eudokia moved across it as swiftly as she could make herself, which she knew was not nearly swiftly enough. When she reached the top she dropped onto her arse and slid down the other side, careful to catch herself just before the edge. Thirty links below – she hoped it was not more than thirty links – a balcony stretched elegantly over the front gardens. She didn't give herself time to think, just pushed herself over, and when her ankle gave out as she landed she didn't make a sound either, or at least not very much of one. She did rest on the balcony for a few seconds after, however, breathing shallowly, the pain in her leg as bad as anything she had ever felt.

Eudokia didn't remain motionless for very long. The banisters in the balcony were wide and she slid through one, hanging by her fingertips, feeling the nothingness below. She had meant to rest there a moment, but made the mistake of looking down and found herself falling.

Eudokia had never stinted on upkeep – it was one thing to let an unused wing lie fallow, quite another to allow the magnificent gardens that surrounded it to degenerate. The hedge tore her robe apart and scratched her deep enough to draw blood and did not entirely stop the pain of her landing, but it almost certainly kept her from breaking her neck.

For a time it was impossible to move; all breath was lost to her, she had to count to thirty just to bring her heart down to a twice-normal beat. It took longer for her to dislodge herself from the indentation she had made in the broken bush. By that point she could hear them from the roof, yelling back and forth at each other and trying to figure out where she had gone. Forcing herself out of the indentation she had made, she crawled along in the shadow of the shrubbery. She was close to the main door, perhaps she could hide long enough for assistance to arrive.

But the moonlight ruined any chance of subterfuge; one of them spotted her and gave a yell. Eudokia pushed herself to her feet, screamed at the pain, felt a hot flicker of shame at her weakness, forced herself onward. A few steps forward she took a quick look behind her, saw two of her pursuers leap straight from the second storey, out over the balcony she had clung to and into the bushes below. The third was not so lucky; jumping a second or two later, he swivelled in the air as he fell and landed awkwardly, groaned loudly and then went still. Her second one tonight, Eudokia thought excitedly – but that still left two, and two would be more than enough to kill her.

If she could have run she might have tried it, just on the slim chance. But she couldn't – indeed she could barely stand, and so she decided simply to stand upright and face what was coming. It seemed clear to Eudokia that she had reached her last few moments above the ground. Well, she wasn't the first person to find herself in this situation. And she would meet it, as she had met every challenge she had ever faced, with the dignity and poise of her ancient line.

'A merry chase,' the first man said. He was the one that Eudokia had dropped a tile on, and it had shattered his nose and most of his teeth, leaving the centre of his face a mass of pulp. He was smiling through it, though. 'A merry chase, but we've come to the end of it.'

'You're bleeding,' Eudokia observed.

He laughed and pointed his weapon at her. 'It's a shame I can't spend any time on you. I like the tough ones. They're more fun to break.'

Eudokia didn't bother to respond – there was no point in wasting any more time on the man, a degenerate and a barbarian, unworthy of her final thoughts. She pulled the dagger out from her waistband, trying to decide whether to aim it at her throat or her chest. She settled on the former – an odd angle, but she wouldn't need to worry about striking through bone.

And then the front door opened and Jahan was there, without a single scrap of clothing, blood on his moustache and his chest and his genitals; whether his blood or someone else's, Eudokia could not be sure. Leon was close behind him, sword drawn and looking quite furious, though in that moment Eudokia's attention was occupied more or less entirely by the Parthan. This seemed equally to be the case for the two men who had been about to murder her, and who would have found the task easily accomplished if they had struck in this brief interlude. But the sight of her naked bodyguard, ichor-covered and furious, was the sort of thing that might give even a dangerous man pause, and her would-be assassins twisted their attentions rapidly towards him, hoping to make some sort of defence against his rage.

To no avail. Unpractised as she was in warfare, Eudokia found it impossible to make out the individual movements by which Jahan subdued her two attackers. All she could say was that at first there were two men holding small swords, and Jahan himself was unarmed, and then there was one man holding a small sword and another on the ground trying to breathe through a shattered trachea, and then the only person holding anything was Jahan, lifting the remaining survivor into the air by the throat.

Phocas had not been wrong, all those years ago, when he had claimed Jahan as the most dangerous person he had ever met. He had proved that by defeating two armed men barehanded in less time than it would take to recite a stanza, but he proved it doubly then when he held back from killing the second, holding him above his head like a helpless babe. 'Leave this one alive?'

Eudokia shook her head 'There's no need. It's clear enough who sent him.'

Jahan nodded, wrapped both hands round the throat of the almost-corpse. Eudokia did not hear the crack, but when Jahan let go of him the man was most certainly dead.

They inspected each other for a moment. Naked, Jahan was somewhat uglier than she had realised. 'There were four of them outside my room,' he said. 'Two of them knew what they were doing. You were gone by the time I could get there.'

'Heraclius?' she asked.

Jahan shrugged. 'I didn't look.'

Leon sprinted down the steps and grabbed Eudokia in a fierce embrace. 'Thank the gods,' he said. Then he said it again.

She let him hold her another moment, then pushed him away. Now that her life was no longer in danger her body had got round to feeling pain, particularly in the ankle she had landed on when falling, which was at once quite agonising and strangely distant. 'Is that a knife sticking out of your chest?' she asked Jahan.

'Yes,' Jahan said without looking down.

'We'd best get that taken care of,' Eudokia said. 'To the back gardens.'

'Do you need me to carry you?' Jahan asked.

'It would hardly seem so,' Eudokia said, hobbling onward.

30

Thistle paced his way upslope, eyes swivelling in the early-evening light, consciously stopping himself from fingering the dagger he had started carrying. It was six weeks since Thistle had made peace with Chalk, and three since Pallor, who was the man forty-five minutes' walk west, had laid claim to a stretch of docks that had traditionally lain in Rhythm's territory; the docks itself and the protection and smuggling money that came with it. At first it had seemed like the usual bluster, the kind of disagreement that would be taken care of by negotiation or appeal to the authorities, those shadowy higher-ups within the Brotherhood who were never seen but whose whisper was law, and who generally didn't like having their cut lessened on account of bloodshed. Then one evening Pallor had smashed up a gambling house Rhythm ran, an act that Rhythm felt required repayment. They'd been going tit-for-tat ever since, broken bones and stolen coin, no corpses but you couldn't think that would last for ever.

Thistle was nervous being too far from his home turf. Mostly these days he did not leave the neighbourhood; mostly these days he barely left his house, had lost his taste for cheap bars and slightly more expensive whores. There did not seem to be much these days that Thistle hadn't lost his taste for. He spent the balance of his time on his roof, looking down and thinking things that he chose not to share with anyone. But one night every week, or at least almost every week, Thistle slipped down from his perch and scuttled his way upslope. He would come back hours later, long after midnight, looking tired and uncertain, and wet if it had been raining.

There were more of them every week, till they couldn't all sit on the fruit crates and had to stand, till they were packed into the place thick as lice. Not all of them from the Fifth either, plenty of well-fed men looking nervous at being so far from home, upslopes creeping down the mountain to hear the word of the new prophet. Thistle would go and sit quietly in the back and leave when the speech was done, didn't stick around to talk to anyone or to let anyone talk to him. Nor did he mention it to any of his people downslope, not to Rhythm or any of the other folk at Isle's, not to Felspar or Treble either.

Thistle arrived early to find the warehouse barred and shuttered, like the rest of its siblings on the block. He had missed going the week before; Rhythm had needed him to ride herd on a crew of porters carrying some illicit goods upslope, holding a head-knocker in one hand and feeling like a phony, wondering if everyone else felt the same. Had the Cuckoos cracked down in the interim? He thought he would have heard rumour of it, but perhaps he was wrong. Looking at his face just then you could not have said with any certainty what it was that he felt. Despair? Relief?

'It's not here tonight,' said a voice from behind him, one that Thistle recognised.

It was the first thing the Edom had said to him since he had saved his life almost a year before. The first thing he had said directly to Thistle, at least, though every speech he gave seemed to have been aimed at the young man from the Barrow.

'We've had to move it to a larger location,' Edom said. 'Do you know the quadrant on the Fourth Rung where the charcoal burners work?'

'Not really,' Thistle said.

Edom nodded, his grand leonine head bobbing up and down. 'Do you still let them call you Thistle?'

'Yeah.'

Edom grunted unhappily. 'Walk with me,' he said and turned himself upslope without waiting to see if Thistle would listen.

Thistle did listen, hurried to catch up and then matched Edom's gait. Edom was taller and walked with a brisk but even pace, like he was hurrying off to fulfil some not at all unpleasant task. Thistle expected him to say something but he didn't, not for a long time, not till they were nearly within sight of the boundary.

'Have you ever been this far upslope?'

It galled Thistle that he had not, but he found he could not bring himself to lie to the man. 'No.'

'Yours is one of our smaller chantries. Most of our members come from the Fourth Rung, or even the Third.'

'I'm not a member,' Thistle said.

Edom rocked his head back and forth, as if the question remained uncertain. 'Do you know why it is you are called Thistle?'

'What my mother named me.'

'And do you know why she named you that?'

'No.'

'Because she knew no better. In the rest of the world a name is a salute to the gods, a tie to the past, a prayer for the future. But the Time Below stripped us of our memories, and our myths, until we could not even recall the names of our ancestors. We returned to the sun amnesiacs, and in our frivolousness we call our children whatever foolish thing meets our fancy. Doggerel, all of it, though on the upper slopes the words are sweeter-sounding.'

Thistle had never before thought to consider the origin of his name, had no idea if what Edom said was true. Though as ever when Edom spoke Thistle had the sense of turning a bend to discover himself atop a high vista, looking down over things he had thought large and solid and finding that they were neither.

They followed the walls east, towards one of the checkpoints leading up to the Fourth. Thistle was starting to get nervous, looking down at the naked flesh of his wrist. He didn't have authorisation to go any higher into the Roost, not the temporary bracelets that guaranteed passage for a fixed period of time, nor the tattoos that marked the owner as being a permanent resident. Without one of them the Cuckoo would never let him through – at best he'd suffer the humiliation of being turned away, at worst they'd decide to shake him down, maybe even find his weapon.

But Edom didn't seem concerned, strode onward casually. The challenge was implicit and Thistle wasn't one to back down. And the truth was, though he wasn't altogether comfortable admitting it to himself, Thistle had come to trust Edom, didn't suppose he'd be leading him into folly.

The Fifth Rung had a gradual upward slope, a few degrees that would find you, after several hours' walk, standing some quarter-cable above sea level, staring at the boundary to the Fourth. Walls thrice the height of a man and formed of solid basalt, the Rung itself beginning atop them, an intricate series of locks allowing for the pleasure craft of Those Above to ascend or descend.

Those Below, of course, made do with stairs. The gate leading up to them was heavy-looking and intricately wrought and seemed not to have been shut in a very long time. It was manned by a Cuckoo, looking much like every other Cuckoo Thistle had ever seen.

'Good evening, Adze,' Edom said.

'Good evening, Edom.'

Thistle had never heard a Cuckoo speak to anyone with respect before, wasn't quite certain how to take it, like a rat standing up on its hind legs and asking for directions.

'And how is the wife? Recovering swiftly, I can only hope?'

'Oh yes, yes indeed. This was an easy one, thank the Founders. Not like the first.'

'And the babe herself?'

The Cuckoo grinned so wide that Thistle thought his head might split into two. 'Oh she's a pip, you can see it already. She stares at you, sir, not something you see so much in newborns, I don't think. Shows intelligence.'

'She gets that from her mother?'

Adze laughed and slapped Edom's shoulder. 'She certainly doesn't get it from me!'

Edom laughed along with him, and it didn't seem to be feigned. Either Edom was an exceptional liar, or he was exceptional in some other fashion. 'I was going to take my friend up to Rose Park, let him get a sight of the new blossoms. That won't be a problem, will it?'

Adze looked at Edom for a moment, smiled and held out his hand. It took Thistle a moment to realise he should grab it, and a moment longer to shake off the disgust of going flesh to flesh with a Cuckoo.

'Adze,' he said.

'Thimble,' Thistle muttered. Adze let go of his hand. Thistle resisted the temptation to wipe it vigorously against his jacket.

'Enjoy yourself up there,' Adze said, waving.

'Best to your wife, and the budding genius.'

Adze laughed. 'Will do, Edom, will do.'

Thistle and Edom ascended the stone staircase and on into the Fourth. The lower portion of the Rung looked very similar to the upper portion of the Fifth. Admittedly, they were some ways above the slurp, which was a point in its favour, but apart from that you would have been hard pressed to mistake the tightly packed tenements for paradise. The people looked like they did around the docks, or near enough – a bit better fed, maybe, but not much, and at one point they passed a number of youths who could have passed for the Barrow boys waiting out another evening.

Thistle might have noticed this if Thistle had been in the mood for noticing things, which at that moment he was not, so comprehensively occupied by rage that he couldn't think of anything else. His vision was starting to blur and there was a copper taste in his mouth like blood.

Edom chuckled. 'You think me a hypocrite?'

'All those big speeches, you dip your head to the first fucking Cuckoo you see.'

'What have you ever heard me say that made you think the custodians were my enemy?'

'Tear down the edifice, you said.'

'And burn it to ash,' Edom agreed. 'But that man is not the system, only a victim of it. You hate him. Why exactly? Because he upholds laws that you find abhorrent, that hold down his fellow man. That newborn we spoke of, that's his third, and what loyalty do you think he ought to have beyond what he feels for them? Should he jeopardise their future for your sake, for the sake of your people? Would you do the same for him, Thistle? This man whom you hated without knowing, without thinking about for more than a moment?'

'You know how many times I've been hit by a Cuckoo?'

'And how many times have you been struck by Adze, who just took your hand?'

'One's the same as the other.'

'No, Thistle,' Edom said, halting abruptly and letting his smile curdle off his face. 'You could not be more wrong, not if you had a week to come up with a piece of foolishness. That is how they think of us, and I will not have you repeat their lies. Adze is Adze, and Thistle is Thistle, and Edom is Edom. What is it that you think I preach, Thistle? Hate?' Edom shook his head. 'You must hate the Four-Fingers, and what they have done to us, as you must hate injustice, as water hates fire and light abhors the darkness. But if you imagine the sole of my message to be hate, then you have received but the least part of it.'

'And what is the greater?'

'Love, of course. These are your people, Thistle – every one

of them, from the boys you grew up with to those poor fools on
the First Rung, slaves to their core and not knowing it. You must
love those closest to the devils most of all, because it is they who
have been most terribly wronged. You, at least, know where you
stand – they imagine cruelty is kindness, and the rough back of
a four-fingered hand a lover's caress. These people know nothing
except what is. It is my task – it is our task, boy they call Thistle
– to show them that there is more yet that could be. But until
that day comes, until the light is brought to that poor man, that
poor man and all those like him, all one ought to feel for them
is pity.'

'I didn't need to hear your speech to hate the fucking
Four-Fingers.'

'Perhaps you have less to lose than he. You do not see it, but
you are blessed, my young friend – the veneer that these unfortunates cling to, the paltry returns they receive for their endless
generations of service, which blind them to the injustice which
they suffer – you never laboured beneath it.'

'Being poor ain't no fucking blessing.'

'Poor in what, Thistle? What are you poor in? Not intellect,
nor strength. Certainly you are not poor in your sense of self-pity
– indeed, by that standard you are as well provided for as anyone
I've ever known.'

'Don't think that costume is fooling anyone,' Thistle said heat-
edly. 'Where you from, Edom? The Third? The Second? I bet you
never went to bed hungry,' he continued, pointing a finger at the
man. 'Not once in your whole damn life.'

'My father owned a general store. I was born a few blocks
from here, in fact, so perhaps I cannot claim this unique grasp
of poverty that you boast of so proudly. And what of it, boy
they call Thistle? Does the place of my birth affect the truth of
my words? Indeed, you were born to misfortune – does that
justify a lifetime of foolishness? A lifetime of squandered potential, inflicting misery for a few bits of silver? You think I don't
know how you got that pretty coat, what you had to do to earn
it? I know better than you, boy they call Thistle – know better

than you just what it is you are wasting, when you consent to carry a knife in the service of some cheap criminal.'

Thistle had been angry before this last retort – before the start of the conversation, before he had woken up this morning, for a very long time before that – but just then his face got so red and his eyes so beady that you'd have been forgiven for thinking he might have grabbed the aforementioned knife and buried it in Edom's chest. Certainly Edom could have been forgiven for thinking that, though to judge by his face, as even and certain as ever, this was not a concern.

'I think you're a two-penny conman,' Thistle said. 'And I wouldn't go to your fucking meeting if I was starving and you were handing out bread.' He turned and started quickly back the way they had come.

'Better than bread! I hand out truth, and I think you have already supped on it!'

Thistle did not seem to hear it, tearing his way back to the Fifth, fire in his eyes – but then again what we seem to be is not always what we are.

31

The gods came first, or at least their altars did, massive statues several times the size of a man, carved from red sandalwood and black ebony. Enkedri the Self-Formed, eyeless and unsmiling, Siraph, his consort, with her folded shawls of bejewelled silk. Terjunta the sun-born, each of his four arms holding a different weapon, loins sticky with sacrificial blood. Eloha thick with lust, Kairn the fortunate, Tolb who shepherds the lost, the entire pantheon bringing blessing to the day's endeavour. Held aloft on ceremonial sledges decorated to resemble clouds, dragged through the main streets of the capital by a flock of pious-mad worshippers, novices and acolytes vying for the honour of staining their robes with upturned mud. In the wake of the divines came a single chariot of burnished copper and gold trim, pulled by a team of stark white horses. Riding atop it and not at all smiling was Archpriest Andronikos, now head of the embassy to Salucia. The altars would accompany him as far as the dock, though it was hoped the gods would continue on with him. As ever, the mailed fist came close behind the silken glove, and the third entrant, riding atop a chariot just a hair's breadth less luxurious than the ambassador's, was Protostrator Konstantinos, the Gentleman Lion, son of Phocas the Beloved. It was down to him that the Baleferic Isles were swept free of pirates, that the Salucians were desperate to make peace, that the demons quaked in their nests. Handsome and broad-shouldered, he made up for the senator's asperity with an open and attentive smile.

And none of them, Bas thought – not general, senator or god – could claim a reception equal to that which greeted the white-haired woman who stood next to him, held upright by an ash cane and her own insurmountable pride.

The roar was deafening. It was louder than anything he had heard before. It was louder than a summer thunderstorm on the Marches, a thousand cables between you and a decent copse of trees, streaks of lightning coming so fast they made midnight seem like noon. It was louder than a battle, than the echo of metal against metal and metal against flesh, than the screams of the wounded and the dying. Bas had once been struck in the head by a slung stone, left an indentation in his helmet size of a duck's egg, left him open-mouthed and stunned, and the crowd was louder than that also. Watching the mob of people try to push through the cordon of guards that surrounded them Bas was put in mind of nothing so much as a pack of starvelings let loose on a slaughtered pig. They had insisted he carry his sword with him during the parade, part of the legend they were ever happy to burnish, and though at first he had thought it an absurd affect-ation, now he found himself grateful to have a length of steel in case the crowd broke free in a moment of misguided passion.

The Domina, by contrast, seemed serene as the hanging moon, a constant and benevolent smile on her face, waving gracefully at her supporters. Of course the Domina had always been a figure of immense esteem, of almost veneration, but the month since she had survived the attempt on her life had seen her fame rise to heights that would have driven a modest man mad with hubris. What exactly they had done to Eudokia, Bas could not have said.

It had not been Bas's idea to ride in a cart with her, nor for that matter to attend the day's celebration at all. There was work to be done at camp, there was in fact a great deal of work to be done at camp. On the off-chance that Andronikos somehow failed to succeed at making peace with Salucia then it would be a good thing if those men tasked with waging war against her could claim some reasonable standard of competence. But Kantoleon had suggested his presence, and hinted that this suggestion could find itself an order of the Senate, if necessary, and Bas had bowed to the inevitable.

Behind him sat a light-skinned Parthan, the sort of fat that would be no impediment to killing a man, scanning the crowd with cool disinterest. Next to him Theophilus remained wide-eyed, bewildered but happy. The Parthan was there to ensure the Revered Mother's safety. Theophilus was there because they had needed someone to balance out the Parthan. In truth Isaac deserved the spot, but to get him on the chariot would have required a direct order and still risked mutiny, and Bas thought it wiser not to chance it. Hamilcar would have been thrilled beyond measure, but even Bas was polished enough to know that it would not do to have a black man riding in the same cart as the Revered Mother.

They turned from the Way of Gold to the Way of Sail, the road growing smaller and the crowd more tightly packed, till Bas fancied he could smell the sour wine on their breath and the stink of damp flesh. Floating above the crowd were a number of effigies, straw figures of Aeleria's enemies. One in Salucian-styled robes was having his tender portions punctured with a pointed wooden stick. Another, larger than the first, with four fingers and a duck-bill made of yellow paper, received continuous and violent attention from the surrounding crowd, raised aloft then pulled back down, the mob thrilled to distribute their cruelties on so deserving a target.

For a celebration of peace it was quite the most belligerent gathering in which Bas had ever taken part. Nor had it escaped his attention that, this recent embassy notwithstanding, there had been no slowing in the recruitment of new hoplitai, nor in his training of those who had already volunteered. Best be prepared for anything, certainly, though it had been Bas's experience that a man carrying a hammer finds plenty of loose nails, and the Aelerian thema was a heavy hammer indeed.

They came finally to the Elon Bridge, stretching above the River Taver, which had been cleaned and garnished with cut flowers; roses and fat tulips, crushed by the previous entrants. A cordon of hoplitai held the crowd back from following them, lest by sheer weight of numbers they send the entire structure into the drink. Above the hard knot of pikemen, swaying like some obscene flag, was a representation of Phalomei, the Queen of Hyrcania. Her tits were the size of melons. 'Whore' was scrawled across her chest.

Bas cleared his throat of dust and dislike, spat into the river below.

Midway across the bridge conversation became possible for the first time since they had ascended the chariot. 'The displays of the people earn the Caracal's disapproval?' Eudokia asked.

'They love war, these tinkers and tradesmen.'

'The gods suit us for different things. Some sow, some reap, some kill and some heal, some serve and some rule. Blessed is the man whose labour matches his skill! Blessed is that nation whose peasants are submissive, whose soldiers are brave, whose leaders are wise!'

'But we are a republic,' Theophilus cut in suddenly, 'and the people choose their leaders.'

Eudokia smiled, turned that smile behind her and onto Theophilus. 'A clever child – you would be of the Opos line?'

Theophilus blushed, looked aside, nodded.

'You are correct, of course. In other lands, in Dycia that was, in benighted Salucia, a random quirk of birth is enough to bring a fool to the very apex of power. We Aelerians are far luckier. Our leaders, if they wish to remain so, must remember always that they are nothing but a conduit for the will of the people. But to say that is only to answer half the question – for what is it exactly that the people want?'

'What they have always wanted,' Theophilus responded, as if he had the words memorised. 'When the demons slew the last king and all his line at the Lamentation, the survivors chose their leaders from among those who survived. Men who had shown bravery in battle, and wisdom in counsel. Who could be relied upon to maintain their privileges, to safeguard the state, to act as a bulwark against tyranny.'

'Those men we just rode past, who were shaming the Queen of Salucia in effigy – do you think they know the name of their consul? Do you think they concern themselves with the rights won by their ancestors, with the privileges of the common folk against the Senate, of the capital against the provinces?'

'Likely they were slaves,' Theophilus remarked uncomfortably.

'You suppose them unique in their vulgarity? Unrepresentative of the nation? A reasonable enough conceit, albeit a false one. Varied when taken individually, in aggregate the underlying core of the species swiftly asserts itself. Every man and woman is distinct from every other. But every mob is the same mob, whether composed of mineworkers or monarchs.'

Following the line of the river into the distance Bas could see the docks, the grand trireme which was to carry Senator Andronikos on his mission of peace, the small fleet of warships that would escort him. Brightly coloured sails contrasted against the blue of the water and the blue of the sky. A crowd swarmed up the pier and all along the quays, part of that line of pink which they had been traversing, as if along some vast oesophageal track.

Eudokia spread her hand out towards the causeway, closed her hand as if to gather up the scattered multitudes. 'This is what you speak of, when you speak of the people. Do not let false abstractions cloud your judgement. This is the foundation of the Commonwealth, these the pillars of the state. As you say, in Aeleria leadership flows from the will of the people. It is their wants, fears, passions that are responsible for the state of the nation.'

'It seems no very stable a thing to build on,' Theophilus remarked.

'An understandable misconception. In fact, the people are as faithful as ever one might wish a lover. They cherish victory and scorn defeat. They worship strength and abhor weakness. They will forgive you malfeasance, greed, corruption and indifference. They require little from their leaders, save that they remain invincible.'

'Not every battle is a victory,' Bas muttered.

Eudokia seemed pleased to be addressing him directly. 'Indisputably a fact – and yet can you blame the people for thinking otherwise? Almost thirty years since Scarlet Fields, an entire generation who have known nothing but triumph. Ought they not to have faith in the path they walk, in their leaders who guide them upon it? The Caracal's unsheathed sword has won them victory across the Tullus Coast, has made them well fed and sleek. War has made them rich, and proud, and happy. They have done well by war.'

'She's a fickle bitch,' Bas said. Eudokia remained comfortably unshocked by his profanity. 'And invincibility is a high bar to set,' Bas said. 'I think it will not take much to make these cobblers turn craven, and cruel.'

'You speak directly to the truth of it,' Eudokia said, though despite the compliment for a long moment she stared out at the great masses waiting to meet them, as if she had forgotten Bas entirely. 'Terrible are the risks a man runs, when he thinks to become a ruler.'

'A man,' Bas repeated, but Eudokia did not answer.

The end of the bridge was in sight, and with it the end of the conversation. In the interim between the passage of Konstantinos and the arrival of their own carriage the mob, overwhelmed with excitement, had swarmed the cordon separating them from the parade route. They clustered around the foot of the causeway, halting any forward passage, so desperate for the arrival of the Domina that they made their own desire impossible.

Theophilus broke the moment of silence. 'And should the people's will be done, Mother, should they gain their triumphs over Salucia and the demons beyond them? What shall be done when there is no one left to war against? When there is nothing more on which the people can gorge themselves?'

'What a strange question, coming from a soldier,' Eudokia

remarked. 'There is always *someone* left to war against. It is nature's first law – eat, or become food.'

The detachment of hoplitai escorting them continued forward, unsure of themselves, and their hesitancy encouraged the crowd into a further frenzy. They began to force themselves onto the bridge and towards the chariot, irrationally, an instinctive reaction to weakness. The soldiers found themselves intermingling with the first ranks of the mob, belligerence coming swiftly on the heels of fear, faces grown vicious. A fat man in the outfit of a dockworker put a hand on one of the soldiers, not quite a shove but close enough to be taken as one by a neighbouring hoplitai, who delivered a blow with his cudgel that sent the assailant into the dust. The mob surged ahead, that spark of violence about to grow into a conflagration.

'Stop! Stop by the order of Domina Eudokia Aurelia!'

Bas had been in charge of men for the better party of thirty years, and he could not remember having ever heard an order given more naturally, or obeyed more peremptorily. The opening strike was not repeated or returned. The pentarche, standing just behind his line of troops, hoping still to maintain some control over the situation, turned his head swiftly back towards the chariot. 'Forgive me, Domina, they will be removed in only a moment.'

'By Enkedri,' Eudokia said, and though it did not seem as if she was yelling her voice could be made out well beyond the first ranks of the crowd, 'the day has not yet come when I will call for the whip against my own children.'

If the mob did not hear the words they at least got the feel of them. And they redoubled their fervour, a hungry wailing, displays of enthusiasm that seemed indistinguishable from despair. Mouths that might have been smiling or weeping, a great beast wavering between love and violence. Bas's knuckles pulled tight round the hilt of his sword, though if the mob turned angry it would be like setting blade against a surging river; he and the hoplitai would bring down a few in the front ranks but would be torn asunder a moment after, some lucky peasant carrying his Roost-forged blade home as a souvenir, a less fortunate one needing to make do with a bloodied swatch of clothing.

'Jahan, if you'd be so kind as to help me alight,' Eudokia said.

For once even the languid Parthan seemed agitated. He leaned forward and whispered a warning into the ear of his mistress. Bas added one of his own, 'I'm not sure that's wise, Domina.'

'Nonsense,' Eudokia said, as her Parthan, obedient against himself, lifted her neatly off her feat, placed her gracefully on to the bridge beneath them. 'What have I to fear from the people of Aeleria?' And indeed the crowd, which had been close to maddened a moment before by the heat of the day and the drink they had taken to withstand it, by the packed dust, by the thrill of the coming war that the announcement of the peace embassy had done nothing to curb, by that instinct for chaos that inevitably arises when men gather in large enough numbers to make individual punishment impossible, grew still. The hoplitai, stunned as much by the crowd's turn as they were by Eudokia's unexpected descent, pulled aside to allow her passage. Before moving forward, Eudokia turned back to offer one final word. 'A conduit of their will, nothing more.'

On the Marches it had been possible for Bas to suppose himself the agent of some impersonal force, no more responsible for his actions than a bolt of lightning or a falling clump of hail. A foolish conceit, one impossible to practise any longer. It had been Bas's sword, his army, his skill that had brought the surrounding nations into the Aelerian fold, or beneath the Aelerian boot. But he had not directed it, had not chosen where to point it. It was clear to whom that distinction must be given, for better or for worse.

Eudokia Aurelia, the Revered Mother, walked slowly into the swarming mass of her followers, into the deluge of meat and sweat and fervour, her head perfectly level, a smile benevolent and imperturbable, soothing them with her voice and very presence – and even Bas could not help but marvel at her bravery.

32

The Aubade had taken particularly exquisite care with his wardrobe this morning, managed, after spending twice as long with his tailor as usual, to assemble a costume that rivalled the sun for grandeur and the stars for subtlety. That was the first sign Calla had that something was very wrong. The second was that they had left for the Conclave earlier than was required, mid-morning, halfway between the hours of the Starling and the Eagle; and upon arrival had remained on the steps of the edifice itself. Not for very long, though, because after a few moments the Prime showed up, early as well, and the Aubade approached her at a rapid clip. 'I would speak with you,' he said simply.

The Prime nodded, as if she had expected just such an occurrence. She and the Aubade walked off a distance, till they were out of earshot of anyone but their human servants. She wore a tight-fitting mantle of pale cerulean that blossomed out at the hips. Her hair was dyed sterling and pinned up like a wasp's nest, showcasing the gem set above her forehead. 'And what is it that my sibling wishes to discuss with me?'

'I will make a request of the Conclave, this morning. I would ask that you support it.'

'I can hardly promise assistance in an endeavour of which I remain ignorant.'

'You know what I plan to ask – or at least you can guess.'

'And you can guess my response. We are paying proper attention to the situation between the Aelerians and Salucia. To move forward at this juncture would be extreme.'

'You remain blind to the rising tide.'

'Is that one of the witticisms that you learned in your time among the humans? We long ago tamed the waters, or had you forgotten?'

'The water claims everything if you wait long enough.'

The Prime didn't say anything for a time, nor did the Aubade, though Calla somehow felt that both wished the other might break their silence.

Finally, the Prime said simply, 'You've had my answer.'

'I have,' he replied, and allowed her to enter the Conclave ahead of him. Afterwards Calla followed the Aubade to his usual spot directly in front of where the Prime sat on her chair of sterling, the silent eruptions of the Source framing her. It was still a few minutes before the hour of the Eagle, and Calla waited while Those Above and their human servants trickled in desultorily, in the same languid manner in which they attended every meeting – those that chose to attend at least.

The hour of the Eagle chimed from the great clocks set across the city, and the Prime called the meeting to order, a brief and formal invocation asking the attendees to display the wisdom of the Founders. By custom it was her right to set the agenda, but she hesitated in doing so, allowed the Aubade his opportunity.

He was not slow in taking it. 'I ask forgiveness of my siblings for interrupting our usual protocol,' he said. 'But at this moment of crisis I believe my haste appropriate.' Everything that the

Aubade did was an exhibition in decorum, in grace and quiet dignity, and the fashion in which he stood and addressed the audience was no exception. 'Our reports from the Sentinel of the Southern Reach are clear and unequivocal – the Aelerians prepare for war. They will find some pretext on which to launch themselves at Salucia, and by the autumn their forces will have marched north to subdue their enemies.'

'Has the Lord of the Red Keep added prescience to his list of abilities?' the Glutton asked.

'No, brother, though I have a talent for logic that some others in this Conclave seem unwilling to display.'

'Should everything my sibling predict come to pass,' the Prime said, even at this last moment pushing for reconciliation, 'there will be time to move against Aeleria, as we have in ages past.'

'I am afraid, Prime, that you too fail to appreciate the gravity of the situation beneath which we labour. If we wait for the Aelerians to arm themselves, to crush the Salucians as they did thirty years past, they will be able to turn the full force of their war machine against us. We do not have the luxury of time. The reports we have received indicate that the Commonwealth will march towards Salucia with thirty thousand men, and certainly by the time they have entered Hyrcania, they will be able to put a far larger number into the field.'

'And what would the Lord of the Red Keep have the Roost do?' the Prime asked, as if laying a trap.

'I would have us send an emissary to the Salucian Empress, arrange a stratagem. While the Aelerians break themselves against the border cities, I would have our armies ride south to their capital, and bring the rebellious humans to heel.'

There was no gasp of surprise from the Eldest in attendance, no shouts or murmurs, nothing to indicate that what the Aubade had just suggested was just short of blasphemy. But Calla knew the temper of the species she had long lived among well enough to appreciate how deeply shocking was the Aubade's proposal. Those Above did not ally with Those Below; they subjugated them, had done so since the first Four-Finger had come from the east, in the forgotten morning of time.

'Join forces with the Locusts, sibling?' the Shrike asked. 'Why not join forces with the rats? Is there no embassy from the cockroaches available to speak with? You shame yourself.'

'There is no indignity I would not suffer, if I supposed it to be in the interests of the Roost,' the Aubade said. He pointed to his missing stalk of hair, penalty or sacrifice for his time spent abroad. 'I have always put personal pride below the future of our nation.'

'We are well aware of your time among the humans, sibling,' the Glutton said. 'Though today you have demonstrated that it has dulled your wisdom, rather than sharpened it.'

'I find myself in agreement with the Lord of the House of Kind Lament,' the Prime said. 'For too long, this Conclave has allowed the Lord of the Red Keep to speak words of agitation and unrest.'

'For too long, the Lord of the Red Keep has allowed this Conclave to ignore the danger that grows daily, and to take the steps required to fend it off.'

It was common custom to rise while speaking, and so the Prime was already on her feet. But she seemed to grow taller then, taller and more terrible. As if you were staring, not at a living being, but at the very essence of some great and arbitrary force, the personification of a mountain, or the wind. 'The Lord of the Red Keep will retract his statement.'

The Aubade stood with his arms folded, gazing at the fountain itself. He did not speak for a time but remained as he was, impassive against the fury of the Prime, and against the waves of contempt that the rest of the Conclave radiated in his direction. 'My sibling knows that I will not.'

'Indeed she does,' the Prime said. For a moment she too seemed to be gathering her strength for the trial ahead, or pushing past some internal stumbling block. 'I accuse the Lord of the Red Keep of acting contrary to the interests of the Roost. I accuse him of ignoring the will of the Founders, of seeking crisis to fulfil his own lust for glory.'

'I accuse the Prime of failing to uphold her responsibilities,' the Aubade responded. Calla felt suddenly as if she were standing on top of the Red Keep and staring down at the sea below. 'I accuse her of ignoring threats to the Roost, of allowing dangers to fester and grow, rather than face them head-on.'

'Siblings,' the Wright said, standing abruptly and gracelessly, perhaps the first physical manifestation of the horror of the events unfolding. 'This rash talk ill-befits both of you. I beg of you, take a moment and consider your words, before—'

But the Aubade continued right over him, a terrible breach of etiquette, one that Calla could not remember ever having seen an Eternal commit. 'The Prime has failed in her trust to ensure the continuance of the Roost, has closed her eyes to the danger that is in front of us. All of you have,' he said, swivelling his eyes back and forth across the assemblage, perfect and terrible, unbent against the crowd's fury. 'But the Prime most of all.'

'I request that my sibling meet me at the courses,' the Prime said, 'that we might arbitrate my failures as in days of old.'

Calla realised then that she was near to weeping; she closed her eyes as tight as she could and bit back down the lump that had risen in her shapely throat. Had anyone cared to look at her then there would have been no doubt that she understood the proceedings, understood and was horrified – but no one did. The attention of the entire hall, four-fingered and five, was occupied exclusively by the Aubade and his lover.

'I accept,' he said simply.

33

Shortly after noon a shooting pain began to develop in Eudokia's left leg, a pain severe enough to contort her thoughts and make work troublesome. It happened every day at about that time, every day since the fire, and like every day she ignored it.

'It would be difficult,' the physic had told her when she'd asked him if she would ever again be able to walk unassisted. He recommended massage and a particular rite of sacrifices to be given to Siraph and Terjunta, respectively. She only agreed on the first – the result of her recent adventure suggested that either the gods were little concerned with her well-being, or alternatively that they had already done more than could reasonably be asked of them, in which case Eudokia thought it better not to push her luck.

The rehabilitation of the estate progressed more swiftly than her own. The main wing had been damaged irreparably by the fire; the greater part had had to be torn down and rebuilt entirely.

Happily, this gave Eudokia an opportunity to indulge her own tastes in architecture, tastes she had been forced to ignore over thirty years of living in Phocas's ancestral home. Unhappily, even with her vast resources the buildings could hardly spring from the ground overnight, and in the interim Eudokia and her household were crammed into the east wing. Eudokia thought rarely of the evening itself, was too busy to allow the events to scar her. Still, when she filed into the east wing in the evenings, with its draughts and vague smell of mildew and absurd, hideous features, she sometimes wished she had not allowed Jahan to dispose of her assailants quite so comfortably.

But mostly, despite the leg, and despite the inconvenience of her new environs, Eudokia felt the attempt on her life to be one of those strokes of luck that occasionally arise as evidence of fortune's favour. Never in her long history had she been more popular, more beloved. People she had imagined her inveterate opponents seeped from the woodwork to ask after her health, to offer their support. Her enemies, even those without any clear hand in the thing, were excoriated, could barely go out in public without being berated. The week before, one of Andronikos's supporters had had his jaw broken by a pack of sailors for making an ill-timed joke about her misfortune. Poor man, she had heard that he would never again be able to speak quite right. A terrible loss for the Commonwealth.

A few words to Andronikos in the days after the attack had withered him away to very little. In fact it was hard to see his attempt on her life as anything but an admission of defeat – having been bested on his preferred battleground, he had been forced into areas of which he was less certain. He had shot his last bolt, would now buckle beneath the pressure she applied against him, fall gently into line. Had he not swiftly shuffled himself off to Salucia, and did not her spies report that he was doing as he was bid, pushing forward intransigently the maximalist Aelerian position? No, Eudokia felt confident that the danger from that quarter had passed – there was nothing more to worry about from Andronikos.

Well, even Eudokia, Revered Mother, scion of the house of Aurelia, was not right all of the time.

She knew there was something wrong when they were announced together. Because there was no reason for their association; they had no connection except through her. Heraclius would have needed to be blind or impotent not to have paid Irene some interest, and while it would not have shocked her to discover that he, being a red-blooded man in the prime of his youth, which is to say a child controlled almost exclusively by the bit of flesh swinging between his legs, had found occasion to supplement the love she gave him, she could not imagine even he would be foolish enough to choose his paramour from within her own household. And even had he been, Irene at least could be trusted to act with more discretion. Besides, she had the pick of the court at her disposal, did not need to go grubbing about with Heraclius.

Of course Eudokia made no show of worry, lounging back in her chair with her leg propped up on some pillows, adding slowly to the scarf she was knitting. Jahan's hooded eyes drooped ever so slightly less than usual, quick to catch trouble.

Irene looked as stunningly beautiful as always, perhaps even more so. Her hair and her eyes were black as fresh coal, a length of green ribbon held up her tresses, a pearl the size of a finger-joint hung down into the cleft of her neck. She was trying, without success, to hide a glorious smile.

Heraclius, by contrast, seemed barely able to hold himself together. It was generally within even his meagre powers to dress himself, but today his sash was knotted incorrectly, there was mud on the cuff of his robes and his hands, normally manicured, were bitten to the quick.

'Revered Mother,' Irene said, leaning down to kiss Eudokia's cheek.

'Darling,' Eudokia said.

'Revered Mother,' Heraclius half stuttered, bending over to do the same.

'Dear,' Eudokia replied.

For a time there was no sound but the soft rustle of thread on thread.

'May we sit?' Irene asked.

'I'd think you'd be more comfortable offering the blow while upright – though of course it's to your preference.'

But they were slow to deliver it, Irene looking long at Heraclius as if for support, though whatever the endeavour in which they were involved, she would find him a weak reed. 'We're worried about your health,' Irene said eventually.

'How thoughtful of you,' Eudokia said. 'I do have a bit of a tickle in my throat – you might fetch me a cup of tea.'

'I think it more serious than that.'

'Indeed?'

'Serious enough that perhaps it would be wise for you to remove yourself from the whirlwind, as it were. I am told the springs at Elfi have wondrous recuperative powers.'

The springs at Elfi were three weeks by carriage from the capital. 'From what sort of ailment do you think me suffering?' Eudokia asked.

'One that will prove fatal,' Irene said flatly, 'unless swift effort is made to correct it.'

Heraclius shuddered, began to stare at the courtyard outside with the sort of longing that suggested he would give a very great deal to be outside among the hedgerows, rather than in here with two she-wolves.

'What have you told her?' Eudokia asked, her voice carefree as a kite on a sunny day.

But Heraclius didn't answer, just kept gazing out towards the gardens. Irene was happy to speak for him, however, which really was all to the good, otherwise they'd be waiting around for the rest of the afternoon. 'Would you like to guess?'

'I'd never dream of spoiling your fun.'

'It would cause quite a scandal, were it ever to come out that Senator Andronikos had been taking money from the Salucians. I don't imagine it would be much less of one if it ever came out that you were giving it to them.'

If this was intended to elicit a response, it was an abject failure. Eudokia's eyes did not flutter, the even set of her mouth did not curl. Perhaps her heart beat a bit faster, but to know that you'd have needed to put your hand against her chest, and no one was doing that.

'The game is up,' Irene hissed, unable to maintain her pose of indifference any longer. 'Heraclius told me about Phrattes, and I told Andronikos. The senator has been in touch with him, convinced him his interests lie in other directions.' Irene shook her head. 'You really ought to know better than to trust a Salucian,' she said. 'They're an irredeemably dishonest people.'

'They've no monopoly on betrayal,' Eudokia said smoothly.

Heraclius flinched, opened his mouth, realised he hadn't yet thought of anything to say, closed it again.

'Surely you don't think to take the high ground?' Irene asked. 'You've been skewered on the same lance you hoped to wield – it's sheerest hypocrisy to pretend otherwise.'

'I had not invited Andronikos to sit beside me at tea,' she said, 'nor to share my bed.'

Irene shrugged. 'I don't suppose I can expect you to be neutral on the matter, though if you made the attempt you'd see that we're the better party. The Commonwealth gets peace, the senator gets out from beneath your thumb.'

'And you?'

'I?' Irene shrugged. 'I get to be you.'

'Setting unattainable goals,' Eudokia said, 'is a sure path to misery.'

Irene laughed. 'I'll never have your wit,' she agreed. 'But I will have money, and status, and power. And I suppose I'll have to settle for those.'

'You'll find that last leaves you little time to enjoy the first two. And you, Heraclius? What is it exactly that you've been promised, in exchange for listening at keyholes?'

Irene was enjoying herself immensely, seemed positively glowing. By contrast, Eudokia thought she had never seen

347

Heraclius look so desperate – though she promised herself that she would not be able to say that for ever.

'You were getting ready to leave me,' he said finally, lamely, the first words he had ventured since his greeting.

'She told you that?'

'No,' he said, than recanted. 'Yes.'

'She was right,' Eudokia said, 'but I'd have taken care of you, as an act of kindness.'

Irene spent a silent moment enthralled by Heraclius's discomfort. How she must hate Eudokia, to have made such an effort to bring the poor fool over to her side! How much it must have galled her to seduce him, to stand his fumbling touch and inane flirtations! 'I admit,' Irene said finally, 'I hadn't thought you'd bend knee so easy. Won't you raise your voice, even just a little? Call me a sluttish little whore, or break a nail on your stolen lover's face? Remind me of all the things you've done for me, berate me for my betrayal?'

'Is that what you imagine strength looks like?' Eudokia shrugged. 'I'm afraid you'll leave disappointed. We're past the point of recrimination. You've made your choice.' The tenor of her voice remained as friendly as ever. 'We'll see what it gains you.'

Heraclius seemed to lose three links in height, and even Irene half shuddered at this last. But she caught herself and came back more forcefully, as if to erase the stain of her fear. 'Empty threats from an old woman. All you've left is a graceful exit, and you've only that because of my kindness.'

'How magnanimous.'

It was an exhausting thing, throwing punches at the Domina. Twenty minutes of beating on her and Irene was ready to go and lie down. 'As always your composure is exemplary,' she said. 'It will be one of the many things that will be missed, after you retire from court. Which, by the way, Andronikos insists you do within the next few weeks. After that, I'm afraid, it will be necessary to force your hand.'

'I see,' Eudokia said.

'Are there any questions?'

Eudokia looked back and forth between them, apparently unruffled, her face a mask of benign indifference. 'One only. Did Senator Andronikos not wish to take part in this discussion? I'd think him loath to miss the opportunity to gloat.'

Irene smiled, happy to see that Eudokia's last card wouldn't ruin the game. 'In fact, he was most unhappy to be deprived of the pleasure. But duty keeps him in Salucia. It's no easy thing, stopping the war you've nearly started.'

Eudokia dropped her head slightly, acknowledging the information though not commenting on it. The sun eased in through the garden windows, along with the soft scent of things growing. A song bird trilled. The breeze blew. Time passed.

'Well, then,' Irene said, 'I'll take my leave of you.'

'A pleasant day to you both,' Eudokia said.

Irene fell into a mocking curtsy and headed out the way she had come. Heraclius followed her, stopping and turning to throw Eudokia one last look – regret or despair, she wasn't sure which – but the door was fast shutting and he scurried out before it closed.

Eudokia picked up the ball of yarn she had put aside at the beginning of the conversation and turned back to her knitting. 'Domina?' Jahan asked, and was it her imagination or was there a bit of a tremor to his voice?

'Instruct Orodes to push the event forward,' she said. 'Everything else remains in place.'

'Yes, mistress,' Jahan said, and this time his voice was settled as stone.

34

Things had got nasty in the Barrow, in the Barrow and up at the Straights and even out towards Seven Points, nasty all over the Fifth. You could feel it come in with the heat and the wet, this sense of fear and uncertainty, like everyone was holding their breath. Two months Rhythm and Pallor had been pricking each other to death, shallow wounds but painful, the two neighbourhood kingpins on a collision course. The normal pace of illicit work had slowed to a crawl, the whorehouses shuttered, gambling dens closed; even the usual constant shuffling of contraband had turned to a trickle. The Cuckoos had stayed out of it so far, but they wouldn't for ever.

Thistle had gone back to sleeping on the roof, and not just because of the change in weather. He had a couple of bricks that he kept near the ledge, had the vague notion of dropping them if someone came by that he thought deserved it. Thistle didn't think that he was important enough for Pallor to bother to send people after, and there was something of an unwritten rule about staying away from a man's family. But then again the thing about unwritten rules is that they aren't written down and there's no one to enforce them, and so in the evening Thistle curled up in his coop, and kept his blade within easy reach.

It was from the roof that he saw Spindle, moving swiftly with two new men as a tail, hard-looking ex-dockers Rhythm had brought in as reinforcements. Spindle himself was wearing a full travelling cloak despite the heat, and beneath it Thistle knew were all sorts of nasty things, throwing-knives and brass knuckles and daggers so long that Thistle was not clear as to why they weren't called swords. He had the hood of his cloak up round his head, but his scowl was visible from three streets away.

They'd caught Chalk coming out of his favourite whorehouse two weeks earlier, and it turned out he was made of flesh after all, as a few pokes with a shiv revealed. Credit due, he hadn't gone easy, crawled for a long time before he died, trails of blood leading downslope a half-cable. It hadn't meant fuck all to Thistle, one less rabid dog in the world, but Spindle had somehow got it mixed up that Chalk had been his friend and had taken the whole thing with uncharacteristic fury. The two of them had been at Isle's when the news came in, and Thistle had grabbed one of the bar backs and sent him straight to find Rhythm, told him to get the boss-man down as soon as he could make it. It was a close thing, by the time Rhythm had shown up, Spindle had worked himself into such a fury that he was ready to march over and knock on Pallor's door that very night, by his lonesome if necessary. It had taken everything Rhythm had to threaten, cajole and beg Spindle into composure, but in the weeks since the big man had lost that good humour which had once been his second most notable quality.

If Thistle didn't lament the loss, nor was he so stupid as to miss what Chalk's exsanguination meant. It had been ten years since there had been open war between the various tentacles of criminality that made up the Brotherhood Below, ten years of easy graft and constant corruption. Thistle wasn't altogether sure what had broken the long period of fruitful malfeasance, or if maybe Rhythm wasn't thinking whether he would have been better off letting Pallor get away with whatever scam he had been running. Not that it mattered now – it was blood for blood, there wasn't any going back.

So Thistle watched Spindle make his way down the street, sitting on the end of the roof doing little tricks with his knife. Letting it tumble between his fingers and swivelling it in the palm of his hand, gimmicks that at first had made him proud as a flush rooster but which now he barely even realised he was doing. He didn't see much of Felspar or Treble or any of the old boys these days, because he didn't have anything to say to them and because he didn't want to bring trouble down on their heads. If he'd saved more of what he'd been making he'd have moved out of his mother's place, but he hadn't and so was more or less stuck. And there was something about the idea of exiling himself from the homestead that secretly made Thistle miserable, perhaps even a little frightened, though he'd never have admitted it.

Spindle stopped in front of Thistle's stairs, then cupped his hands and bellowed, 'Thistle! You up there?'

The two men he'd brought with him stood around trying to look tough, and mostly succeeding. Thistle didn't like either of them. He thought he saw something like water behind their eyes, and anyway if they were worth having around they'd have been worth having around full-time, right? Not just brought in after your first choice got himself dead.

Thistle leaned far enough over the ledge for Spindle to get a look at him, held up one finger. Spindle had never come out to see Thistle personal before, and he had certainly never come with a crew. This was it, Thistle felt with certainty; they were going to do what they should have done a month prior, snap the back of Pallor's organisation. Or maybe Pallor would do the same to them. Thistle didn't imagine Chalk was the only one without an honest claim to immortality.

Thistle had been waiting for this moment for months and months, before things had gone sour with Pallor, as soon as he'd joined up, before that even. The moment when he'd make his bones, prove to Rhythm and everyone else that he was a soldier in good standing, a two-fisted razor-fiend you'd best cross the street before offending. The moment when he'd see whether or not he was really any of those things, if the facade he'd been wearing these last months – hell, most of the last couple of years – went more than finger-deep. And now that it had finally come, what was it that Thistle felt? Excitement, certainly; his nerves jangled unevenly. Fear, some fear, though not as much as he had expected. Mostly what he felt, staring down at Spindle and what was coming for both of them, were mingled sensations of relief accompanied by a strange feeling of boredom – the story wasn't any good, wasn't interesting or special, but at least it was almost over, and anyway there was nothing to do but play it out to the end.

Thistle slipped his blade into his back-sheath and pulled his shirt over it. He walked downstairs with slow, deliberate certainty, made sure to jump over the loose step that he had never fixed. Why hadn't he fixed it, he wondered now? Had he been so damn busy? What had happened to all that time that he had slept and slunk and frittered away?

Mother was waiting for him when he came down, standing in front of their doorway, her eyes shifting nervously between Thistle and her feet.

'Now's not the time, Ma,' Thistle said. In his mind that was the end of it, and he was somewhat surprised when she stayed where she was, had to stop himself short or he'd have run her down. A year ago they'd been the same size or maybe he'd had a few fingers on her, but now she barely came up to his shoulders and he made a point of being careful not to squeeze her too roughly when they embraced. Not that this came up much. 'I gotta go, Ma.'

It always took her so damn long to speak, and then whatever she said was pointless, just something to fill the silence. 'I know what's going on,' she said.

Thistle didn't really think that was true, or at least not very much true. 'All right.'

'I know who you've been working for,' she said.

'It's no kind of secret, Ma. The whole fucking neighbourhood knows.'

'Don't curse in front of me.'

Thistle figured it was pretty late in the day to be talking about profanity, with his knife pressing hard against his spine. 'Sorry,' he said anyway.

'I know you're working for Rhythm.'

'You need to get out of the way now, Mum. I got someone waiting.'

'They can wait a while longer,' she said, and like he'd twisted a spigot she burst into tears, no preamble to it at all: one instant she was sad-looking but steady, the next in full-on mourning. 'He can wait for ever!'

It occurred to Thistle that Spindle and his boys could probably hear his mother shrieking from outside; the walls weren't thick enough to hush a whisper. And though Thistle knew he probably should be past the point where this mattered to him, the thought of the rest of his crew listening to his mother weep caused him a sharp stab of shame. 'It's my job now, Ma. I have to go and take care of it.'

'What would your father think?' she yelled at him, and Thistle thought, by the Time Below, she must be far gone if she supposes that old bastard has any more claim on me dead than he did alive. 'I won't let you go,' she said, and she put her arms round him, somewhere between an embrace and a restraint.

Coming down the stairs Thistle had felt empty and steady and prepared for what was to come, as prepared as he was going to get, anyway. Looking at his mother now, worn lines around her eyes, he could feel himself starting to think again. And that made him angry, angry at himself as much as her, though she ended up getting all of it. 'You took the money easy enough though, didn't you, Ma? You weren't worried when I was bringing home a slab of pork every day, didn't ask where it came from. Didn't wonder about Apple's medicine, or the dresses I bought the girls.'

He regretted it as soon as he said it, not because it wasn't true or because she didn't deserve to hear it, but because she started weeping harder. 'I should have said something six months ago,' she said.

'It's not six months ago, it's now. And this isn't a good time to talk.'

Her hand was wrapped round his wrist, displaying more strength than he'd have thought she possessed. 'Don't go, by Enkedri the Self-Created, who watches over all of us. By Siraph his consort, by—'

'Praying don't work for Apple,' Thistle said, and he threw everything he had into it. 'Why the hell would it work for me?'

She wasn't a strong woman, his mother, except in so far as she had held together a family of six for twenty years. But she couldn't hurt anyone, which the Fifth Rung had taught Thistle was the only true measure of power. She forgot to keep crying in the moment after he had said it, her eyes went wide and she took a deep intake of breath like he had punched her in the stomach.

Thistle took off his purse and shoved it into her hands and hurried down the steps before she could say anything else. Spindle was waiting outside, and if he noticed that there was anything wrong he had the good sense not to mention it.

Rhythm had spent the last month floating between a network of safe houses, corner bars and small tenement rooms, moving every few days or even more frequently when he was feeling mistrustful. Only Spindle knew where he was at any given point, a set-up the specifics of which Thistle knew better than to question. They stopped in front of a random tenement building near the Sweet Water canal, random except that there was another thug waiting outside of it, an ex-sailor by the name of Chestnut. He nodded at Spindle and Thistle as they walked in, nodded at Thistle just like he had Spindle, acknowledging their superiority in the hierarchy. Another day and that would have puffed Thistle's chest, but his mind was still taken up with what had just happened, and what was soon to, and he barely noticed.

Spindle walked them up a set of crooked stairs to the second floor, which was dark and loud and miserable. The building had been subdivided away into almost nothing, whole families crammed into the closets. Spindle walked them through three consecutively smaller cells, tramping across the bedrooms of small children already well versed in despair, past their drunken mothers and squat, waddling grandmothers.

Rhythm was the most important man in the neighbourhood. He made more in a week than a family of porters made in a year, maybe a lot more. He could buy anything he wanted, or at least anything that anyone on the Fifth would want to buy. Men touched their foreheads when they saw him, made sure to speak well of him in public places, well and loudly.

The room he was sleeping in was big enough for a makeshift bed and very small table and an equally sized chair. It was windowless, which seemed like a reasonable security precaution but didn't do much for the heat, which was sweltering, or the smell, which was more than sour. There was a bottle of liquor on the table and a heavy fighting knife beside it. Rhythm had swapped the garish costume that he preferred for worn trousers and a tunic, and he had been wearing them a while, to judge from the stain and the odour. He looked sallow, and anxious and savage. 'Come in,' he said. 'Wish I could offer you a seat, but . . .' He made a gesture at the room that Thistle supposed was meant to indicate that there wasn't anywhere else to sit, though Thistle knew that already.

Thistle wasn't sure how the hell they managed to cram him and Spindle and the three other guys into the room, it seemed like a job for a group of contortionists rather than thugs. But they did, even managed to close the door afterwards, and as soon as it was shut Rhythm started to speak.

'I know some of you have been wondering why we waited to answer for Chalk. I had my reasons. No point in ending trouble in a way that'll bring us more down the line. I needed to talk to some people, make sure hitting Pallor wouldn't upset anyone that matters.'

Thistle imagined this meeting, Shade or maybe Shade's boss sitting upslope a few cables in some well-appointed restaurant, him and a couple of men like him, eating fresh oysters and drinking bottles of wine worth more than a Barrow tenement. Sometime after the meal was over they'd have got round to discussing the trouble their subordinates were making in a part of the city as impossibly far away as the moon, debated the matter half-heartedly a while. And then one of them would've said something like, 'hell, I don't care, let him off the guy if he's so keen to do it.' And then Shade or Shade's boss would've said 'Fine, done, now what are we going to drink with dessert?'

'I got the OK two hours ago,' Rhythm said, smiling for the first time in the conversation, maybe for the first time in weeks. 'Pallor disappears tonight, and we don't need to worry about any older brothers coming to look in on him.'

'Good,' Spindle said. 'Fucking great.'

'Don't get too excited,' Rhythm said. 'We've still got to go out and do the thing.'

'Hell, boss,' Spindle said, 'that's the easy part.'

Pallor hadn't bothered to go to ground, arrogance that would be proved foolishness if Rhythm had his way. Instead he had holed up in the back room of his gambling house and added on a couple of extra hitters, just daring Rhythm to come and say hello.

Well, Rhythm was the risk-taking sort. The six of them – Thistle and Chalk and Rhythm and the three new heavies Thistle didn't give a shit about – were going to go in full force, and make sure they were the only ones coming back out again. The plan was not exactly overwhelming in its complexity, and though Rhythm ran through it twice, they were out of the room almost as soon as they went into it. Which was all well and good as far as Thistle was concerned, since someone – Chestnut, he thought – had his elbow wedged into Thistle's back, and the stench verged on overpowering.

Thistle was the last out, and before he could leave Rhythm put a hand on his shoulder. 'You ready for this?' Rhythm asked.

'Do I look ready?'

Rhythm took a few seconds to answer, but then he nodded brusquely. 'Yeah,' he said. 'You do.'

They moved in three groups so as not to give Pallor any notice they were coming, one of the old guard with one of the new, presumably to make sure that no one scampered off

– though what exactly Thistle was to do if Chestnut decided to do a runner was never exactly clear to him. It didn't happen, anyway; Thistle figured Chestnut was probably too stupid for the possibility to even occur to him. They were the first to arrive, so Thistle took up a position in the shadow of a nearby alleyway.

Chestnut was nervous and jittery and wanted to talk to Thistle. Thistle was nervous and jittery and wanted Chestnut to keep his fucking mouth shut.

'I guess this is it,' Chestnut said.

Thistle thought even Chestnut would be able to figure out the answer to this question.

'How many men you think they got in there?' Chestnut asked.

'Sixty-seven,' Thistle muttered.

Spindle and his partner showed up a moment later, shutting down any further conversation, and Rhythm and his man came by not long after that. No one said anything but Rhythm shot Thistle a look like 'get ready' and then he nodded at Spindle, who nodded back and strutted up to the entrance.

Spindle rapped twice on the door, heavy blows with his huge hand. The door opened and a face stuck itself out and then Spindle's knife stuck itself into the man's throat, a masterful bit of work, the man dead before he could even scream. Spindle clambered over the corpse and Thistle found himself the next one through the door.

Sprinting inside, weapon out, pulse echoing so loudly in his head that it took him a moment to realise he was screaming. But that was fine, surprise was out now, they were going for sheer terror, and if you didn't feel a little spurt of ice in your veins at the sight of Spindle and his bloody knife tearing through the place, you had to be made of stone. Pallor's few patrons that night were not made of stone, it turned out, and they scrambled away from the gambling tables as fast as their stubby little legs could carry them. A towering heavy was standing guard next to a back door, and he yelled a warning at the same time as he pulled his own weapon. He and Spindle circled each other for a swift handful of seconds and then Spindle went at him fast and hard, and Thistle didn't exactly see what happened but whatever it was it left Spindle standing and his opponent dying on the ground.

So far Thistle had not done anything to justify his presence there, or the long hours he had spent practising the knife, but that was about to change. A back door opened and three men came out of it, blades drawn, and they roared and went after Spindle, and Thistle did not think even Spindle could handle three men at once.

On the long walk over, and in the endless interminable hours before, Thistle had developed for himself a simple, thuggish maxim. All he needed to do, he would tell himself, was to take his man – to square accounts, to make certain that one unfortunate counterpart went into the next world before he did. If someone got him afterwards that was all right, that was nothing to be ashamed of, everybody went at some point. Just make sure you put someone there to welcome you.

The thing was that Thistle's man didn't seem to know that he was Thistle's man, hadn't got the message, was focused on Spindle to the exclusion of anything else. The other thing was that Thistle's man wasn't that at all, wasn't more than a boy, younger than Thistle even. And though Thistle knew full well that he had no business thinking about anything in that moment save the moment itself, being as fast and perfect as he could possibly be, the truth was that all Thistle could think about was why in the hell had Pallor brought a boy to something like this? What kind of an asshole, what kind of a worm-souled half-witted scrounging piece of filth would bring a boy to something like this? It made Thistle so fucking angry that he was glad he had someone in front of him to kill.

The knife stole into the boy's ribcage, just to the side of his breast, like Spindle had showed him, easier than Thistle had expected. It wasn't difficult, the blade seemed to yearn for it. Thistle pulled it out and put it back in again, and the boy whose name he didn't know turned towards him, mouth opening and closing like he was trying to tell Thistle something. And in that strange, desperate moment, it seemed the most important thing in the world to Thistle that he find out what it was – he wanted to grab the boy and shake him, demand he reveal his secret, though the boy was already dying and then he was just dead.

It wasn't until Thistle felt a hand on his shoulder that he remembered there were other participants in the drama, and he whirled round with such frantic speed that he nearly cut Spindle with his knife, dripping red onto the floor and all but forgotten.

'Be cool, kid,' Spindle said, 'it's done.'

Some of the blood that was on Spindle was Spindle's, but to guess from the three dead men littering the ground, three plus the one Thistle had done, which made four men, four men on the ground, most of it was not.

Rhythm inspected one of these corpses with an expression of bemusement. 'I can't say I'm surprised to see you like this, Pallor,' he said. 'I always thought you had a little too much bitch to you.' When Pallor didn't answer Rhythm laughed and then kicked the body and then laughed again. 'Hell, boy,' he said, walking over and slapping Thistle on the shoulder. 'You didn't think to leave any for us?'

Thistle looked down at his shirt and discovered it was thick with ichor, all but soaked through with it, and he thought for a moment he must have taken an injury and not felt it in the excitement. He patted his chest, and his stomach, and his arms, and he realised he was unmarked. 'It was all from the boy,' Thistle thought. And then, 'There is so much blood in a person, so much more than you think.'

Rhythm had brought five men with him but in the end it had all really come down to Spindle. Maybe Thistle had done his little bit – certainly the boy he had just killed would have thought that. But mostly it had been Spindle, Spindle who had wanted these men dead perhaps even more than they had wanted to live, Spindle bringing righteous reckoning on behalf of one of the most venal, ill-tempered and stupid men Thistle had ever had the misfortune to meet.

The handful of patrons had taken shelter behind the bar,

unable to flee while Rhythm and the second wave were still blocking the entrance. Rhythm smiled at them and tipped his hat. 'Sorry for the trouble, friends,' he said. 'I'm afraid Pallor's isn't open for business any longer – but if you still fancy a flutter, walk yourself down to Isle's, we'll make sure to treat you right.'

Spindle hooted and beat his chest and laughed.

They paraded back to Isle's, the six of them, first Rhythm, then Thistle and Spindle, stained with blood like they'd been dipped in an abattoir. It was evening and the streets were quiet though not at all empty, and the occasional passer-by made sure to give them a wide berth or ducked down a side alley if they could. Just north of Alcon Street a child started to sprint along after them, acting as tout, calling out their victory for everyone to see. He couldn't have been more than six, and he was bony and unshod, and after they got back to Isle's Rhythm gave him a tertarum and won a slave for life.

Rhythm and the others went inside to get drunk, but Thistle followed Spindle silently round to the back, stripped naked and went swimming in the canal that abutted Isle's. It was too dark by then to see what they were swimming in, and Thistle was grateful for it. Whatever it was it had to be better than what was covering him. He did the best he could to clean himself off, no easy task without soap, rubbing at his forearms and his face vigorously. Spindle got out not long after they'd gone in, but Thistle stayed leaning against the bank, let the canal flow over him.

He did not know how long he spent in there. Long enough to see the moon reflect in the water, long enough for his skin to grow puckered, long enough that he started to feel cold despite the warm summer air. When he finally pulled himself out he found his clothes had been taken away, and a fresh set waited to replace them. Rhythm must have sent someone back to his house, and presumably that person had gone ahead and told his mother that he hadn't been killed. Thistle hoped someone had, anyway.

They all yelled happily when he came in, 'they' being Rhythm and Spindle and the other men who had come along to fight but hadn't really done anything, and also a whole host of hangers-on and sycophants who had played even less of a role in Pallor's end but who seemed more than happy to celebrate it. They were sitting around a centre table and of course they made space for him, space next to Rhythm. Getting to it was no easy thing, he had to run a gauntlet of back-slaps from well-wishers, half the Rung springing up suddenly to remind Thistle of how much they had always liked him, and what a popular boy he had always been, and how everyone in the Barrow had always, every single second of every single day, known he would make good.

Thistle had never seen Rhythm drunk before but he was seeing him so now, and the state suited him no better than it did anyone else who had ever entered into it. He was still wearing the clothes he'd been wearing for days, and he reeked, Thistle could pick out his stink even through the crowd.

'The slayer himself!' Rhythm said. Spindle was sitting on the other side of him; he had a whore on one knee and a broad smile on his face, and he spilled out a quarter of a bottle of liquor pouring a round of shots.

'You did good, kid,' Rhythm said after they'd all knocked it back. 'You did real fucking good. I knew you had it when I saw you eyeballing me back that first day, knew you'd come through when it counted.'

Thistle had hoped to hear something like this for months now, from the first moment he'd seen the man. Now he found it didn't mean very much to him, not very much at all.

'You keep on like you're doing,' Rhythm continued, 'you'll be getting your first brand in no time. Hell, who knows how high you could go? I'm not going to live for ever. Maybe one day you'll be the big man in the neighbourhood.' He laughed and finished what was in his glass. 'The sky's the limit!'

At the right hand of the king of the Fifth Rung, women to be reached out for and caressed, the drink running freely, respected and even a little bit feared. And how low the sky seemed at that moment, and what was the point in trying to reach it?

35

The kitchens in the east wing were, like everything else in the east wing, ugly and garish, gilded as a doll's house. Eudokia sat on a high stool at the servants' table. Jahan was in his usual position in the corner, dull eyes missing nothing. Eudokia's cane leaned against the wall beside him, though for once her leg wasn't giving her any problems. Indeed, when Irene and Heraclius made their way in through the swinging side door, she seemed positively exultant.

'There you are. Come in, come in. Sit down and try one of these appetisers.'

Irene and Heraclius crossed over to Eudokia, though neither of them sat down, and only Irene took the Domina up on her offer. In the distance, past the front gardens and out in the street itself, one could hear the slow, even beat of a tocsin – though only if one was making a point of listening for it.

'Jahan, care for a shrimp croquette?'

'I hate fish,' he said.

'It's not fish, it's shrimp.'

'It's from the water.'

'You don't like anything but red meat and sugar. I can only imagine what your bowels must look like,' Eudokia said ruefully.

'These are from Andronikos's chef?' Irene interrupted.

'The senator realised he wouldn't have any further need of the man, what with his leaving the capital. He was kind enough to allow me his services.'

'I hadn't realised you two were so close,' Irene said, chewing a salmon puff through a nasty smile.

'Oh, the senator's done more for me than I think you can imagine,' Eudokia said, and popped one of the assorted pastries sitting on the small silver tray in front of her into her mouth. She offered another to Irene, who declined with a wave of her hand, then to Heraclius, who was either nauseous or trying to seem imperious.

It had been three weeks since she'd seen either of them. Irene had presumably been spending the time at her mother's house. What Heraclius had been doing now that he was no longer welcome in her home, she couldn't say and didn't particularly care. Whatever it was, it seemed not to have been treating him well. The green shirt he wore was ruffled and clashed unpleasantly with his blue trousers. These last had a stain below the knee, as if he had fallen in a puddle on the way over.

Irene, by contrast, looked positively glowing, as beautiful as Eudokia had ever seen her. Perfidy sat well on the girl. 'The food is marvellous, Revered Mother,' Irene said. 'But I don't suppose you've summoned us out here simply to get my opinion on your newest acquisition.'

'No, not entirely,' Eudokia admitted.

'I have heard nothing of your . . . removing yourself from society,' Irene continued. 'Am I to assume that you're going to take this opportunity to let us know about your imminent plans for retirement?'

'Never assume anything, dear. That's how mistakes get made.'

'I can only hope that you don't imagine me to be unwilling to follow through on my . . . promise.'

'Threat, you mean? Not at all, not at all,' Eudokia said, making a face over the rice ball. 'Ring for the cook,' she said, turning absently to Jahan. Then, back to Irene, 'You've utterly convinced me of your unscrupulousness. I am assured of your complete and total lack of principle. Truly, there is nothing that I would put past you. Absolutely nothing whatsoever.'

'Thank you,' Irene said blandly.

The servants' door swung open, and the head chef entered, flour-stained but looking happy. 'Mistress?'

'The croquettes are divine, Thaddeus. Just divine. The rice balls could do with a bit less salt, however.'

Thaddeus took his hat off, swung it gallantly. 'I'll make a note of it.'

'You can send in the next course whenever it's ready.'

'At once, Revered Mother,' Thaddeus said, but before leaving he turned quickly in the direction of Irene. 'Congratulations,' he said, then ducked back out the way he'd come.

Irene wiggled her nose in confusion. It was a fetching affectation, though inappropriate to the moment. 'I would have thought you'd have more important things to worry about than the menu for your next garden party.'

There was one last pastry remaining on the tray, a morsel of chicken stuffed with almond and honey. Eudokia crushed it daintily between her teeth, then brushed her hands together, scattering powdered sugar into the ether. 'I've never seen the point of insulting a fallen enemy.'

'No?'

'It lessens one's victory. Having reached the summit of a mountain, does one declare it a hill?' Eudokia shook her head. 'A person's strength is judged by the strength of their foes.'

'That's fascinating,' Irene said, 'though hardly germane to our subject.'

'Such impatience. Is the house again on fire? Do you have some pressing engagement to attend? I would think you'd want to savour your moment of triumph as long as possible.'

'Perhaps I want to display that magnanimity you spoke of, to keep your discomfort brief.'

'I don't credit you with such grandeur of character. But back to the point, I hope you won't take what I'm about to say as being bombast, or vanity.'

'One can hardly bask in defeat,' Irene said.

Eudokia smiled, breathed in deeply, as if savouring the scent wafting in from the kitchens. 'You are quite the two stupidest little things that I think I have ever had the misfortune to encounter.'

'Are we?' Irene hissed through a false smile.

'With Heraclius of course, it comes as no surprise – he is, after all, a penis with a man attached. But you, Irene? I confess I thought better. I knew you to be vain, ambitious and narcissistic – the young are all like that, they can hardly help themselves. But such idiocy? It is inexplicable. At the very least I'd have credited you with some basic sense of self-preservation, the same courtesy I'd give to a mouse, or a fly.' Eudokia shook her head. 'Too much, apparently. You've observed me for years now, child, every day nearly. What could you possibly have seen, during that period, that made you think you were my equal?'

'I wouldn't speak to me so, if I were in your position.'

'I can almost assure you that you would.'

'With what I hold above your head?'

'Do you think I'd forgotten your betrayal? By the Self-Made, there are simply no bounds to your arrogance. We've been sitting here chatting for ten minutes and you still don't understand what's going on?'

'You can natter all you wish,' Irene said, no longer trying to hide her anger, 'But it doesn't change your situation.'

'I take it you haven't heard the news, then? Senator Andronikos is dead.'

And now, to the steady beat of the drum on the street outside was added the sounds of the public mourners, the weeping a touch more melodramatic than necessary but impressive by virtue of volume alone.

'Two days ago, though it was only announced this afternoon. Hence the weeping,' Eudokia said.

'Dead?' Irene's skin had gone from clotted cream to corpse.

'Murdered. Tragic, I know. Salucian extremists, from all reports. A mob of them broke into his house, sacked the place.' Eudokia shook her head back and forth sadly. 'The Senate is passing a resolution for war as we speak. We Aelerians are a peace-loving people, but to allow the murder of our ambassador to go unanswered? A man whose lifelong struggle for amity is well known to all, a man whose name is a byword for honesty, virtue and incorruptibility? Surely not. Andronikos's martyrdom will go down among the noblest passages in the annals of Aelerian history, and in a month's time the largest army the world has ever seen will march north to right the savage injustice done to us. The people will demand it. And the will of the people must be upheld.'

'This changes nothing,' Irene insisted. 'We still have Phrattes, and he still has proof of the payments you gave him.'

Eudokia sighed dramatically. 'Yes, poor Phrattes. It seems this ravenous gang of madmen that make up the lower classes of Hyrcania did not stop with dear Andronikos. They were so furious at the merchant's well-known leanings towards peace that they killed him as well. Burned his offices and his estate. I don't imagine that any of his personal papers survived this . . . atrocity, sorry to say. In fact, I can all but guarantee it.' She allowed a moment for the extent of her victory to envelop them, then turned her attentions towards Heraclius. 'You make a poor spy, darling. Next time you go listening at doors, make sure you understand everything you've heard.'

Heraclius had looked far from the picture of health upon entering the room, and now he seemed positively ready to rip the hair from his head and run screaming out into the street. The stain of defeat had slowly but indisputably bled through Irene's triumph, and now she too looked rather more like a beaten dog than was to be expected of so beautiful a creature.

'Normally I disapprove of murder – it's too easy a habit to fall into. A quick splash of blood and all your problems are taken care of.' Eudokia shook her head. 'Rarely that simple, of course. Still, circumstances dictate our course of action. You should never hold so firmly to a rule as not to recognise when it must be made an exception of.'

'You would send the whole nation to war,' Irene said, 'just to save your position?'

Eudokia brought one slender hand up to obscure her eyes. Her mouth set into a hard, sharp line and the barest hint of teeth flashed out from between her lips. She said nothing for a time, and Irene and Heraclius were wise enough to follow suit.

'It is the gall,' she said finally, slowly and with a deliberate lack of emotion, 'that I cannot abide. That you sought profit by injuring me, that you betray my kindnesses – such actions require punishment, but in fact they do not truly wound me. What has, I confess, caught in my throat – what very nearly left the two of you bobbing in the river – is that you imagine your petty intrigues rise to my level. The sacrifice of Andronikos was necessary to spur the nation into action I've been arranging for the better part of twenty years. That his death cleared my slate, as it were, was a happy accident. But never for a moment imagine that either of you were anything but a sideshow to me, a tiring and unpleasant distraction.'

Irene had known Eudokia for years, and Heraclius had known her longer still, and more intimately. Neither had ever seen the Domina angry before, or at least they had never seen her display it. It seemed at once terrifying and unnatural, though it only lasted for a moment.

'Well,' Eudokia said, again to all appearances still as a sunken well. 'It's done now, either way.'

Theodora entered, carrying with her another batch of the rice balls the cook had not quite succeeded in crafting correctly the first time round. She left the tray on the table in front of Eudokia, curtsied to her and then to Irene and Heraclius in turn. 'Congratulations,' she said quietly.

'What are you talking about?' Irene snapped at the girl, who looked flustered and backed out of the room swiftly.

'Don't yell at Theodora,' Eudokia said, wagging a finger. 'She's only being polite. Commendation is appropriate, given the upcoming nuptials.'

'Who's getting married?' Heraclius asked, even further behind the conversation than usual.

'The two of you, obviously.'

No one said anything for a while. Eudokia kept eating, however.

'I had very seriously considered faking your death and selling you to a dockside brothel.' Eudokia stood then, her cane lying unused beside her, and she looked down at Irene as she spoke. 'I had considered it very seriously indeed.' She held her eyes on the girl for a time, watched her wither like a flower in the late summer sun. Then she smiled and continued. 'But that's one of the many lovely things about power – it affords you the opportunity to be charitable. And I do like the symmetry of it. You wanted him so much dear – he's yours.'

Irene's pert lips quivered.

'I've already told your mother. She was surprised at first, never having heard you speak of the groom, but she trusted my judgement. At first she was hesitant about moving forward so swiftly, but when I conveyed to her the strength of the bond between you, the depth and passion of your love, well . . . what sort of a mother would she be, to think to stand between the two of you, to stifle your happiness? It was more difficult to arrange a slot at the temple of Siraph – but then again, there are advantages to being Archpriestess. Of course the reception will be held in my gardens. The leading lights of the Commonwealth will be there, all eager to wish you well in your new life together. It's sure to be a grand affair.' Eudokia popped another rice ball into her mouth. 'If the cook can ever get this batter right. A quick honeymoon, and then it'll be straight off to the Marches.'

'Marches?' Irene asked, almost stuttering.

'My wedding gift to the two of you. A man of your . . . talents,

Heraclius, deserves a position commensurate with them. After our recent successes against the March lords, the Commonwealth has need of capable men, men willing to put aside the pleasures of the capital and take up the duty of civilising the plainsfolk. You're to be governor of the city of Faun's Gate, your term of office to begin six weeks hence. City might be a bit strong,' Eudokia amended. 'Town. Settlement, at least.'

'Faun's Gate!' Heraclius repeated, pale as milk-cheese.

'Yes, it is a bit of a ways, isn't it? Still, in time I'm sure the onward march of civilisation will leave it almost habitable. I'm told they've recently built a public baths.' Eudokia paused, considering. 'Or perhaps it's that they're planning on building a public baths. Yes, I think that was it. Either way, they have water. Of course, the March gets very cold in winter – but you'll have your love to warm you.'

With a sudden cry, Heraclius dropped to his knees, having passed from torpid to hysterical without any of the usual intervening steps. 'It's because I love you!' he said, his head nearly in Eudokia's lap. 'I didn't care about her, or the money, or anything else – I only did it because I thought you were going to leave me.'

Eudokia helped herself to another rice ball while she looked down at him. 'You know, I think I almost believe that.'

But Heraclius was not yet finished with his scene, staggered up from his kneeling position, his face red and hysterical. 'I'll kill myself!' There was a small knife on the table, barely sharp enough to cut butter but it would do for melodrama. Heraclius snatched it up and held it against his neck.

'I'm afraid I don't have a half-hour to spend watching you saw through your windpipe,' Eudokia said.

Jahan snickered.

Heraclius turned his eyes up to the Parthan, brought the knife suddenly up to face Eudokia. 'Then I'll kill you!'

'I would very much suggest you not attempt something so foolish,' Eudokia said. 'Jahan doesn't know you well enough to realise what an abject coward you are, might well take your threats seriously. And it would be difficult to have a wedding with the groom lacking a head.'

Jahan had stopped snickering. The walnut in his hand cracked. He let a few flakes of shell fall to the ground, then popped the meat into his mouth. Heraclius looked at him, looked at Eudokia, looked back at Jahan. Then he put the knife back on the table.

'One thing to remember about your future husband,' Eudokia said, turning to Irene. 'He has a fine cock, but not much in the way of balls.'

36

Bas received word of the death of Andronikos late one afternoon while sitting in the coolest, darkest corner of the neighbourhood bar he had come to occasionally frequent these last few months. The coolest spot in the bar was also the spot furthest removed from the door, so he was ignorant of the rising tide of energy spooling through the city, carrying the citizens of the capital out into the streets, calling for justice, calling for blood – which, as far as the people seemed to be concerned, were the same thing.

A youth in worn trousers came running in an hour before nightfall, said something to the bartender, an ugly, friendly man named Anders whose chief virtue was that he didn't know who Bas was. Anders turned to the bell that hung over the counter, rang it loud enough to get the attention of everyone in the bar. There were only about ten patrons all told, and they'd have listened even without the fanfare, but then Anders didn't have so many opportunities for melodrama, and you couldn't quite blame him for taking advantage of this one.

'Senator Andronikos is dead!' he exclaimed.

There was a long pause, the patrons having only the dimmest notion of who Senator Andronikos was, whether his death was triumph or tragedy.

'Murdered by Salucia,' Anders continued, 'while trying to arrange peace for Oscan!'

The Salucians they knew though, the most hateful and licentious bunch of bastards that had ever had the misfortune to occupy territory adjacent to Aeleria. The patrons being no less fond of histrionics than the owner, there was a sudden chorus of howls, wails and one disconsonant blubber, as the assembled drunks worked through their despair at the death of a man whose existence they had been largely unaware of half a minute before.

The barkeep rang the bell vigorously in an effort to reclaim sole ownership of the stage. 'His soul has been judged by the Self-Created, and will sit at Enkedri's right hand.'

Everyone repeated that last bit. Everyone but Bas, though since he was in the corner, no one noticed his silence.

'The Revered Mother has declared a day of prayer and mourning, in honour of this great man.'

The day of mourning did not, so far as Bas could see, indicate any sort of moratorium on buying drinks. In this Anders was like the rest of Aeleria – his passion for the Commonwealth stopped somewhere short of his purse.

The mood in the tavern echoed through the rest of the city, a certain portion of despair and anger, but mostly just the love of feeling for feeling's sake, the opportunity to vent excess emotion, like a mummers' show. The bars and hostelries and eating houses were packed, everyone in the city wanting to be near everyone else. There was no shortage of opinion, nor of people willing to listen. Every tavern had a man at the counter explaining what this meant for relations between the Commonwealth and Salucia, and every prediction was different. It was a great windfall for that selection of braggarts, blowhards and self-professed experts, a few hours during which the rest of the city offered its interest in their nonsensical wisdom.

It all looked half-play to Bas. He doubted very seriously that tomorrow would see any lines at the thema's recruiting stations, and even that scattering of men whose enthusiasm outweighed their discretion wouldn't be enrolled in time to see combat. Bas didn't trust a man who signed up to kill anyone on account of how much he loved the flag. How long do you think that would last, getting screamed at by some officer, or marching twelve hours in the mud, or watching a volley of arrows descend on you from the sky? The best soldiers were men who could do nothing else, for whom war was a profession and not a passion.

Still, now was the time to claim something off patriotism, and Bas was quick to take his share. His landlord was happy to let him out of the lease he had signed, a service to the Caracal he could now brag of, his duty towards the Commonwealth discharged, all at the cost of a few solidus. Afterwards he insisted on buying Bas a drink, told him to kill a Salucian for him.

The camp was a festival ground, or perhaps a madhouse – everywhere was bustle, commotion, movement, dogs chasing their tails, children spinning in circles till they made themselves sick. Rumours flew like loosened shafts and facts were as hard to acquire as a two-week pass. They were to march for Oscan on the morrow; best get to sharpening pikes. No, the whole thing was a feint, they were to take ship and do an end run around the border cities, cut through Salucia's soft underbelly like a broadsword through a stick of butter. Where was this fleet that could transport thirty thousand men a thousand cables north, and where were the warships that would protect them while they did so? Who knew, who could say? The only certainty was that things were happening and things were happening right now; you had best start swimming along with the current.

Bas managed to keep a somewhat cooler head, but then he had a better insight into the matter than your average hoplitai. It would be a few weeks before they got going, and even then they'd be spending another month or perhaps even two in one of the cities bordering Salucia, gathering men and supplies. No man here would die this week, not unless they were knifed by a fellow soldier or got drunk and drowned in a latrine. But they didn't know that, and not knowing that they were filled with an excitement absent from civilian life.

And why not? The Salucians were a paper tiger. No, not even a paper tiger, a paper jackal. There probably wouldn't even be any fighting, just a quick bloodying to brag about afterwards, and then they'd march into Salucia like it was a whore's bedroom. Konstantinos, the Gentleman Lion, was in charge, the most brilliant strategist since Jon the Sanguine, everyone said, and the things people say are always true. And behind him stood the Caracal himself, there to finish what he had started so long ago, his red sword dripping with the blood of the Eternal.

It wasn't just the neophytes either, though at least they had an excuse. Bas passed Theophilus discoursing loudly with some newly raised pentarchs about the differences between Salucian cavalry and the Marchers, his time on the plains having rendered him expert. Further on, Isaac was giving out orders three at a time, checking on everything that could possibly be checked on, though he must have known as well as Bas that they wouldn't be going anywhere for a while. Bas couldn't quite blame him; he was happy too, or as happy as a person like Bas could ever be. It was the happiness of a tuned lute or an unsheathed blade. It was the joy of having a purpose.

Hamilcar, of course, had to serve as fly in the ointment. Bas found him sitting on an overturned pony keg, watching the hoplitai sprint around camp purposelessly. He held a cup in one hand, and Bas did not suppose it was filled with water.

'Are you feeling swift today, Caracal? Are your claws keen, your teeth sharp?' He raised his cup to Bas, then downed most of it. 'It is quite the crusade your Commonwealth sends you on – the register of her fury, her right hand made manifest.' Bas stood so that he was blocking the sunlight, Hamilcar squinting up to look at him. 'Are you happy now, Caracal, to be bringing justice to so foul an enemy? To repay the Salucians for their relentless and unprovoked aggressions?'

Bas felt nothing for the Salucians one way or the other. He had been in Salucia for eight months near thirty years past, and most of that time had been spent staring at the outside of city walls. He must have spoken to one of her citizens at some point, a whore or a tavern keeper in one of the captured cities, some poor farmer whose goods he was 'requisitioning'. But if so, he could not recall the details with any clarity – they were sunk in amidst a thousand other such encounters on the plains, and in the border states, and in Dycia itself.

'Look at them.' Hamilcar waved his hand to indicate the throng of men bustling about as fiercely as any colony of ants, albeit with less purpose. 'How many of these idiots cheering and laughing will make their way back to their homes? How many will lie in shallow graves before the year is out, wild dogs gnawing at their shin bones?'

Bas shrugged. There was no point in guessing.

'Was I ever so young, Caracal?'

'I don't know.'

'Were you?'

'No.'

'Of course not – you aren't like we mortals. You're a hero, a legend, and legends never die any more than they doubt.' Isaac was a happy drunk, or at least a calm one, getting slower and quieter until he passed out on his stool. But Hamilcar had a seed of melancholy in him, and it grew swiftly when irrigated with liquor. Bas could remember a night years ago on the plains when he'd had to pull a knife out of the man's hands to keep him from turning it on himself. Hamilcar had woken up the next morning with a bruise over his eye and no memory of how he had got it. Or so he had claimed at least, and Bas saw no good in disputing his ignorance.

'Let it lie, Dycian,' Bas said quietly.

'The stories they tell of you, Caracal, of your victories and your accomplishments! And if some of the truth is lost, when the minstrels speak of the ash-skinned bowman who kills as he laughs, and the scarred subordinate, who walks ever beside you, what of it? We exist only to burnish your story, me and Isaac and Theophilus and everyone else in this entire damned camp. How many men have you led to death, do you think, Caracal?'

'Stop fucking calling me that.'

'A hit! A palpable hit!' Hamilcar laughed and drank more. 'I hope every one of these children finds themselves below the dirt before this war is over, Caracal. I hope their mothers weep and beat their breasts. I hope your Commonwealth crashes down on itself, leaves you all to starve among the wreckage.' He finished off what was left in his cup, set it down in the dirt. 'No, I don't,' he said, then, a moment later, 'yes, I do.'

'Get back to your quarters, Hamilcar,' Bas said. 'And sleep until you wake up feeling foolish. That's an order.'

Hamilcar brought himself upright without stumbling, though he went slowly to make certain. Then he gave Bas a salute that was mostly mockery and walked to his tent.

Bas's attention had been sufficiently taken up with the Dycian that he hadn't noticed the commotion spreading through the camp, not until the cause of it dropped off her horse and beside him. Einnes had come unescorted, and his first instinct – one that surprised him, as he examined it later – was fear for her, because with the temper of the thema so high it was not at all difficult to imagine her arrival leading to violence.

They looked at each other for a moment. Having made the decision to trek all the way out here, Bas had assumed that she would speak first, but after giving her a full fifteen seconds to do so he determined it was better to take the initiative. 'Sentinel,' he said.

'Strategos,' she replied. And then she didn't say anything for a while, just looked at him. He found himself, as he had on any number of past occasions, trying to determine the exact colour of her eyes. Were they mostly violet or mostly blue? Did they change, depending on the time of day, or her mood? Bas had never heard of anything like that among his own species, but who could say, when it came to the Others?

'It seems Aeleria will go to war,' she said finally.

'Yes.'

'And you will lead them?'

'I'll be at the front,' he said, though he well knew this was not the same thing.

'Then we'll be travelling together.'

Very little about Einnes surprised Bas, in part because he generally did not find himself getting surprised, and in part because he had learned enough about her at that point not to expect her to conform to any normal standards of behaviour. This proved to be enough, however. 'I don't understand.'

'I am the Sentinel of the Southern Reach. My territory includes both Aeleria and Salucia, and I will accompany your forces as an observer, to ensure that the continued interests of the Roost are respected.'

'And if they aren't?'

'Then the wish I expressed that first night will be granted.'

Bas wanted to say something but he did not know what it was exactly. Perhaps Einnes felt similarly, because she stared at him a long time before leaving. Or perhaps she didn't; it was impossible to say. She was as much a mystery to him as he was to himself.

Einnes was back on her horse and out of camp in the span of no more then a few moments. Bas watched until she had disappeared along the road leading back into the city.

A hoplitai ran past him laughing, slipped a toe in the mud and bumped into him, realised what he had done, apologised so profusely that Bas almost felt bad for the boy. Was this the calibre of men in his command? Children and incompetents? What would happen when he led them to war? Hard to say – he'd have given them no sort of chance against the Marchers, but the Salucians had as little in common with the lords of the plains than perhaps any other group of humans Bas had ever come across. But still, war is not a game, even when the sides are less than evenly matched. Hamilcar's drunken tirades aside, Bas had no illusions of his own immortality, nor that the songs the minstrels had written for him would act as shield against spear, sword or arrow.

That was the last thing that Jon the Sanguine had taught Bas, taught him early one morning beneath a cattle-hide yurt amidst the endless and unchanging plains that only now, after he felt certain he would never see them again, Bas realised he thought of as home. A scream cutting through the air, and Bas sprinting into the man's tent ahead of even Jon's subaltern, and the boot on the ground and a reed-snake with Jon's knife in it, a spectacular throw though it would do no good. Jon looking up at him with eyes full of fear, because he knew as sure as Bas did that there was no cure for what had just bitten him. Waiting for the leg to swell up, Jon becoming less and less coherent and more and more bitter until he couldn't do anything but curse at the men he had spent his life beside, and the sun and the sky and the grass that he was soon to leave. And then even that being taken away from him, till he could do nothing but scream in agony, and then moan piteously. And then nothing, a ditch dug in a trackless flatland and a stone monument that would wear away before the winter.

Jon the Sanguine was a genius, and a legend, and perhaps even a hero, if you had Aelerian blood in your veins and you weren't too careful about how you used the word. But most of all, Jon the Sanguine was dead. Dead in a strange land, dead without anyone to mourn him. A corpse, as Bas would find himself in the not so very distant future.

Well – it was the way of flesh, and in the meantime, Bas had work to do. He grabbed a passing subaltern. 'Get Isaac and the rest of the commanders,' he said. 'Tell them to assemble in my tent in fifteen minutes. We have a war to plan.'

Einnes was to accompany them, was she? At the very least, Bas would make certain she got a show.

37

The morning was overcast and grey, as was appropriate to the mood and purpose of the gathering. Virtually the entirety of the Eternal population of the Roost had come out to watch the proceedings, a greater number than Calla had ever seen concentrated in one place. The atmosphere was one of subdued anticipation; if not quite festival-like, then too close to festival-like given what was to come. The Wright was there, and the Glutton. The Lord Bristle and the Lady of the Azure Seat and the Lord of the Verdant Gardens. The Lord of the Ivory Towers and the Lady of the East Estates sat near the front, twinned together since the night of their union. The Shrike had shown up early, not long after Calla had arrived, anxious to assure himself of the best possible seat. Not for the first time Calla realised how much she hated him, the taste sour on her tongue.

Calla stood on the side of the course, watching the Aubade make his final preparations. He had risen at dawn, as on any other day, eaten a light repast and left quickly for the armoury, a spacious hall located in the east wing. Though he had a reputation as one of the fiercest of all the High, the Aubade almost never visited his collection and had not added to it in Calla's memory. Then again he hardly needed to; there was row after row of elaborate suits of heavy plate and display cases filled with different sorts of weaponry. The armourer was a grizzled man with copper skin and ugly eyes who clearly took the maintenance of the collection seriously. To Calla there seemed to be little difference between one suit and the next, but this she soon realised was sheer ignorance, as the Aubade and his smith quickly became engaged in a running discussion about the relative merits of each, how one would do better against the head of a mace but less so against a sword, and did the Lord know whether the Prime would be using a single-headed lance or one with several points, and she was widely famed for her skill with a flail, and perhaps a wider shield would be better. He had settled finally on one of the less elaborate pieces in his collection, interlocking plates of Roost-forged steel, a bright blue base with golden trim. Attached to the back was a framework of filigreed silver fitted with freshly plucked peacock feathers. His helmet was an unadorned basinet, with a small opening in the back through which his hair would be braided. Still unable to make a decision regarding his arms, he ordered the armourer to assemble a selection of different weapons and to cart them all to the courses.

Then it was on to his stable, to repeat the process with the chief groomswoman and her charges. Though here, at least, the choice was simpler. The Aubade had no particular favourite among his many instruments of death, but he had one horse that he prized above all others, a huge mare the colour of silver. The horses of the Roost were larger than any other breed, larger and far more fierce – the Red Keep had lost three equerries in the past five years to the seemingly random savagery of the creatures, and Calla made sure to stand as far from them as etiquette would allow.

And after all that bustle, they had journeyed by boat to the courses, the equipment and the beast to follow. The Aubade had spent a few minutes investigating the grounds, but then he had retired to a small pavilion at one end of the field. He had shut himself inside alone, and what he was doing there Calla couldn't say. That had been the hour of the Starling, and little had happened since, giving Calla plenty of time for reflection – or at least enough time to exacerbate all of her worries and concerns, though unfortunately not enough to come to a resolution with any of them.

The previous night Calla had seen what she was confident would be the last of Bulan, son of Busir. Tourmaline had knocked on her door well after dinner, when Calla had been released to her quarters. Calla had the book in front of her but wasn't able to work. For once she was happy for Tourmaline's interruption.

'Your sir is at the entrance, mistress,' she explained breathlessly. 'The gatekeeper won't mind keeping it a secret, miss, but you'd best hurry, as he gets off soon and the night man is a drunkard and a gossip.'

Calla wrapped a shawl round her shoulders and went out to discover what it was that had brought Bulan to her home so unexpectedly. 'You forget yourself, sir,' she said playfully when she saw him, standing in the shadow of a side entrance. 'You'll give me quite the reputation, showing up so late in the evening.'

But for once Bulan seemed in no mood to banter. 'Leave here with me,' he said.

'That's very little of a joke, and I am renowned for my sense of humour.'

'Do not pretend you think me such a fool as to have bribed the guards to enter the First Rung after nightfall, then sneaked here like a common footpad out of some misplaced sense of coquetry. I know you find this intrusive. I'm hoping you'll forgive the violation. Indeed, I am hoping you will make a more serious one.'

'Which is?'

'Leave here with me, tonight. Pack no bag and tell no one. Take my hand as if we were to go for a stroll. I have a palanquin waiting to take us to the docks. One of my galleys lies in port at this moment. In three hours we can be at sea, bound for my homeland,' he said, 'our ship piloted by a captain who would die before revealing my secrets, and a crew too ignorant to have any idea who you are. I would rather not speak of the life we might have there – you have known me long enough not to be ignorant of my qualities, good or bad. But if you require guarantees of some sort, know that I would make them without hesitation.'

'What has possessed you to speak such foolishness? I am the Seneschal of the Lord of the Red Keep himself, my home is the stuff of dreams. What could you possibly offer me that could match the splendour that is mine by birth?'

'Survival,' Bulan hissed. 'It is very bright here, and very beautiful. But do not let it blind you to the future, which comes more swiftly than we realise, and which is often more terrible than we imagine.'

'I take it you have heard the results of Conclave,' Calla said. 'And it is true, the Prime is known to be a deft hand with a lance. But there are none to match the Aubade with blade or axe, and I would be a poor servant indeed if I removed myself from his service in the hour of his greatest need.'

'This duel is a pinprick compared to the river of blood that this city will see in the coming months.'

It took Calla a struggling moment to pick her way through this. 'You mean this war that Aeleria has declared?' She shrugged her shoulders. In truth she had all but forgotten the cause of the fight, so absorbed was she in the fact of it. 'What of it?'

'The Aelerians will march into Salucia, and the Eternal will be drawn in against them.'

'Yes, yes, as they did twenty years ago.'

'This time will not be like the last. The Aelerians will shatter Those Above, and then they will take the Roost and everything in it.'

Calla spent a moment reflecting on two unpleasant possibilities. The first was that Bulan was quite irreparably mad, and somehow she had missed the signs during the half-year of their acquaintance-ship, despite the long hours spent gossiping over wine and the longer hours spent cocooned in bed. A horrifying circumstance, because of what it said about Bulan and because of what it said about her. The second possibility, of course, was far more disturbing; that Bulan was as clever as she had always taken him to be, and that his predictions contained more than a grain of truth.

Calla chose to believe the former. 'You speak nonsense.'

'How many Eldest are there in the whole city?' Bulan asked. 'Six thousand? Eight? How many are born each year? There are more men in one thema than there are Four-Fingers above ground. They have not yet reached out and crushed you because they are slow to realise their strength, like a boy just grown to manhood.' He took her by the shoulders and forced her gaze upwards, to his. 'But they will not remain so ignorant for long. The Aelerians will be at the gates of the Roost within two years, mark every word I speak. And they will be inside them soon after.'

She put her hand up against his chest, pushed him away softly. 'No doubt the Aelerians thought the same the last time. But they were wrong then, as now. You have seen them,' Calla continued, as if trying to explain something obvious to a child. 'They are better than us, stronger and more perfect. Who is there to match the Lord in might, in speed, in fierce purpose?'

'No three men alive,' Bulan said confidently. 'No five men. But ten? Twelve? Twenty? War is not a series of duels, is not fought on groomed land as tomorrow's contest will be. There are more Aelerians under arms than there are wasps in a hive, and no wasp has anything on them for savagery.'

And perhaps what he was saying seemed plausible enough to make Calla angry. 'You speak nonsense. No human army has ever defeated Those Above, not in all the time that ever was, not before the Founding or since.'

'Everything is impossible, until it happens.'

'The Roost is more than Those Above. There are hundreds of thousands of humans in this city, countless numbers – do you imagine they will stand idly by while their homes are destroyed?'

'The Roost is the most perfect thing in existence,' Bulan admitted. 'There is nothing that has ever been built to rival it, and I doubt greatly that there ever will be. Built with five-fingered hands, built with their toil, maintained by their labour, their sweat, their blood. Well and good,' he went on swiftly, cutting off Calla before she could object, 'it is the way of the world. My galleys are crewed by debtors and foreign slaves, captives taken in war. But I do not suppose them my friends, or the evil I do to them a kindness. They would have my head if they were able to take it, and I could hardly complain of ill-treatment.'

'Do you think me a slave?' Calla asked, almost startled at the concept. She turned her hand towards the east gardens, the warm spring breeze carrying with it the smell of holly and rose petal. In the distance Calla could hear the soft strains of a psaltery, sweet and faint and desperately beautiful. 'This is paradise, Bulan. This is what you foreign-born would call heaven.'

'And you cannot leave it.'

'I do not want to,' Calla insisted, though she knew this was not quite the same thing.

'Do you think every human in the Roost is the Seneschal of the Red Keep? When the Aelerians come anyone not living on the First Rung will rise up with them, and the fine things you have will mark you as their enemy. The Roost will drown in blood, and you with it.'

'You're wrong,' Calla said. 'The Roost is eternal.'

'Nothing is eternal,' Bulan hissed. 'All that is green will one day grow black. I have heard stories of what the Aelerians did to Dycia, Calla. I would not have you suffer the same.'

And now they were well past the point where Calla could pretend that her lover was a madman, or a fool. What he said made more sense than Calla wished – perhaps even echoed currents of her own thoughts, currents she had ignored or suppressed. She thought for a moment of the boy the Shrike had killed, and then she thought about how long it had been since she had thought of him. Was the whole city like that? A den of animals, made brutal through mistreatment, held at bay only through the naked threat of force?

It couldn't be. She did not believe it. She would not. 'This has been the home of my family since before the Aelerians came from the south. Before the first cornerstone was laid in Dycia, before the Salucians yet knew the working of metal.' Calla leaned in, allowed Bulan to take her in his arms, kissed him smoothly and with all the passion she could summon. He seemed to sense that this would be their last embrace, responded in kind. When it was over she took a small step backwards, stared up into his deep, brown eyes. 'The Roost will never fall,' she said. 'But if it does, I will be buried in the rubble.'

Bulan looked at her for a moment, breathed in deeply as if to continue the argument. But then he exhaled, his shoulders sinking downward, and they stared at each other for a long, silent moment. 'Farewell, Calla of the Red Keep,' he said at last, then turned abruptly and headed back the way he had come.

'May the sun shine on you, Bulan, son of Busir!' Calla said to his back. But he did not turn to look at her, or make any sign that he had heard.

It had been a long night, afterwards. There were many reasons she should be unable to sleep and she counted all of them, staring up at her ceiling until the first flickering rays of light shone in through her window.

Calla brought her mind back to the present, fought through the clinging scraps of memory. It was undignified, a woman of her age being upended by the disappearance of a lover. Who was Bulan, to have affected her so? How many men had she brought to her bedchamber over the years, handsomer and of finer quality? At the end of the evening, there was only so much one could expect from a foreigner.

The Lord had left his tent to inspect the weapons that had been brought from the Red Keep. He seemed to settle on one, said something to the armourer and then moved to approach her. Even clad in his elaborate suit of armour he walked in almost unbroken silence, and Calla was so caught up in her thoughts that she didn't notice him until they were nearly face to face.

'The Lord of the Sidereal Citadel has agreed to take on the contents of the eyrie, animal and human, should it become necessary. The aquatic creatures as well, though he will need to add another wing to his property. I doubt there will be any interest in the apiary. It is not truly first-rate, I suppose, for all that I have worked to make it so. I am no kind of apiarist, if truth is to be valued more than kindness.'

'You have many other qualities to boast of, my Lord.'

'The Prime has of course agreed to take you into her service, should the circumstances necessitate it. I've spoken accurately of your quality, and am sure she will find you a suitable position. She would be a fine mistress.'

Calla would draw a razor across her wrist rather than spend the rest of her life as a toady in the house of the Eldest that had killed her master, though it would be a far easier lot than most of the rest of the Lord's household would enjoy. Without a High to serve they would be banished from the First Rung, forced to seek what shelter they could find downslope. Some of the more skilled might find work on the middle Rungs, but the larger portion, the domestics and the labourers, would find themselves dragged down to the very roots of the city, forced to make ends meet any miserable way they could. The Red Keep would be stripped of what treasures the other Eldest decided to take and then left to rot, another once great estate lost to time. The gardens would be overrun with weeds, the flowerbeds would lie fallow, the animals unsecured. No banners would flutter from the Lord's battlements, no songs grace his halls. The crows and pigeons would make their homes where gods had once resided.

The thought of this, and of the combat soon to come, seemed not to have caused the Aubade any discomfort. His eyes were unclouded; he betrayed no hint of worry or concern. He motioned to the servants who assisted him with his war gear: big men, brawny and dark-skinned. They led the Lord's horse out from its stall, walking it at the very end of a long chain, careful not to get within reach of its hooves or its cruel-looking teeth.

The Aubade vaulted atop it without assistance, though it was even taller at the shoulder than he was. 'Try and find a mate,' he said, leaning down from his horse. 'It would please me to think that your line will continue.'

It wasn't until the Aubade had reached his mark that Calla realised this last comment, uttered quietly enough that only she could have heard it, had been delivered in the High Tongue.

The Wright had been agreed upon as an appropriate arbiter, and he stood on a dais in the centre of the field, to be removed once he had finished speaking. He was dressed plainly, or at least as plainly as Those Above seemed capable, his robes the colour of rain clouds. 'Siblings,' he cried, and his voice was tremendously loud, loud enough to be heard in the back rows and to injure Calla's ears from where she was near the front. 'A challenge has been offered. A challenge has been accepted. Can the challenge be retracted?' He turned towards the Prime.

'It cannot.'

'Can the challenge be rejected?'

'No,' the Aubade answered, after a few seconds' hesitation.

'Then the challenge shall continue. May you walk in the foot-steps of the Founders.'

The Wright dropped from the dais and took a spot among the crowd. A number of human servants, moving swiftly, disassembled the platform, leaving the field unobstructed. The Aubade motioned to one of his assistants, who brought over a shield large enough to shelter a bull from the rain, and an ash-wood spear tipped with glittering red steel. Across the way the Prime did the same. Her armour was one smooth and unbroken sheen of silver, and the diamond that was the symbol of her position perched in the crown of her helmet. Her hair-stalks trailed behind her like the comb of a rooster. Her lance was painted gold, and had three nasty-looking prongs at its end.

They remained like that for a moment that seemed far longer. Then the raven was released, swooped into the sky, and the combatants spurred their horses onward, like an arrow released from a bow. The ground quivered with each step – not exaggeration or metaphor but a literal truth, Calla could feel the stadium shake beneath her. The two riders crossed the distance between them so rapidly that Calla had no time to prepare herself for the impact. The Prime's lance struck one corner of the Aubade's shield and glanced aside, but the Lord of the Red Keep had aimed true, and with such force that the Prime's shield all but shattered, fragments of coloured steel flying off in all directions. The sound was a thunderclap – the great force of their combined charges would have broken the bones of any human fool enough to try to withstand it, would have punctured a stone wall. The Prime rocked back and forth, but she remained in her seat, and by the time she had reached the other end of the course, and her attendants had replaced her shield and weapon, she seemed to have recovered altogether.

Three more lances were broken in turn, each as long as a sapling but a good deal thicker. By the fourth pass one could almost imagine that the two combatants were beginning to feel the stress of the thing, that they had slowed down slightly but perceptibly.

On the fifth pass the Prime demonstrated what had earned her renown for spear work. She began her charge as she had the first four, but in the instant before striking she shifted the point upward so that it caught the Aubade directly on his crown. The force knocked him clear from the saddle, ripped him free of his moorings, sent him careening skyward and then firmly into the dust. The silver frame of his false wings snapped in half, peacock feathers hanging in the air.

Calla screamed.

While in the armoury earlier that day Calla had picked up one of the array of helmets the Aubade had collected, marvelling at the weight of it, almost too much for her to lift, let alone carry atop her head. The entire suit would have weighed twice what she did, but all the same when the Aubade rose he did so with astonishing agility. Two of his house servants came hurrying over from the sides, each carrying one end of a massive broadsword, taller than any human Calla had ever met. They knelt down as they reached the Aubade, and with one swift movement he freed the weapon from its sheath, revealing a shining blade of Roost-forged steel, red-flecked and flared at the tip.

The Prime dismounted, again with a smoothness and dexterity that Calla could not have managed naked. She gave her mount a slap on the rump that sent it galloping back towards the sidelines. Her own servants approached, offering her chosen weapons, and a moment later she was prepared to continue the contest. In one hand she carried a long blade as bright and clean as a ray of sunlight, and with the other she kept the glittering chain links of a morning star swinging swiftly above her head, like a falcon circling a kill.

The Aubade nodded at the Prime. The Prime nodded back. The battle was joined.

Calla knew nothing of swordcraft, though even had she been an expert she would have had difficulty following the exchange of blows, so swift and seamless was each movement. The Prime worked to hinder and trap the Aubade with her chain, in hopes of moving in swiftly and finishing him off with her sword. For his part the Aubade seemed willing to remain on the defensive, dodging out of the way of the fluttering couplings, waiting for an offered opportunity. When he did attack it was with a speed that would have been astonishing even had he carried a much smaller weapon, but which seemed impossible with his blade the length of a young tree. Whatever injuries he had sustained in the fall, he gave no indication that they were affecting him, or no indication that Calla could see. Here and there a strike managed to get through the other's defences, but each time it deflected off the thick plate. For a while it seemed like a game, no different than some of the training matches she had seen the Aubade take part in – so much so that when the end came Calla was utterly unprepared for it, lulled into a false and foolish sense of comfort.

In one instant the two were facing off as fiercely as ever, as if their toil had not depleted their energy one jot or tittle. Then there was a flash of movement, but who had moved, or what that movement had accomplished, Calla could not say.

Then the Aubade was turning away, settling his sword across the wide arch of his shoulders, stalking back to the lines. Calla's eyes turned back to the Prime, upright but standing strangely, stiffly. And then her sword fell into the dust, her silver armour stained a heavy red about the chest, and then Calla caught one quick flash of what had caused it; the Prime's sternum broken, the neck sheared through and the spine laid clear.

The Prime collapsed. There was a gasp from the assembled throng, followed quickly, almost immediately, by vigorous and sustained applause.

Why not? It had been a marvellous display, the finest duel seen in generations, two of the foremost warriors Those Above had ever produced fighting and dying for the diversion of their people. Even those Eldest who had been firmly in the Prime's camp, who had supported her in the Conclave and who were hoping for her victory, could not help but recognise that they had just been witness to a masterful performance, two artists at the height of their craft. And who could grudge the victor his success? Who could fail to recognise the greatness of the Aubade? Was he not the grandest, the most perfect, the noblest specimen, everything that was good and righteous and ideal?

Calla realised that she was sobbing.

Alone among the Eternal the Aubade had not joined the indulgent throng. He was sitting on a stool on one side of the courses, having removed his helmet and breastplate, and two of his household attendants were carefully tending to his wounds.

Calla held her robes up with the tips of her fingers and sprinted over to him. 'It is finished, my Lord,' she said, still weeping, stumbling through her words. 'It is over.'

Dark red ichor leaked down his face, darker than the blood of a human, the same colour as the sword that he had carried. But his eyes were as cool and implacable as ever, and he answered without hesitation: 'It has not begun.'

38

Thistle had been on his knees so long that they had started to hurt and then gone numb and then started to hurt again. He had not eaten anything for more than a day, hadn't had a drop to drink since before midnight, six long hours before. He was in the basement of a butcher shop on the Fourth Rung, a small stone room empty of furnishings except for the small altar at which Thistle knelt. The only illumination came from two flickering candles on top of it, a plain wooden bowl between them. Thistle had been meditating on these lights for hours, until they seemed to encompass within their small, sputtering flames the entirety of the world he had known and was poised now to leave behind.

'Who is this who comes before us?' Edom asked.

Thistle kept his head down and did not answer.

'He cannot tell us,' an unknown voice informed him, 'because he does not know.'

'Why does he not know?' Edom asked.

'Because his name has been stolen from him.'

'Does he consent to take his place among his brothers?' Edom turned his eyes now on Thistle and Thistle felt their weight like a burden, like a porter on a long jog upslope. 'Does he swear eternal fealty to the cause of his species, to their freedom, to their prosperity, to their future unjustly denied?'

Thistle did not speak, but he held out his right hand. Edom made a shallow cut on Thistle's palm, held it in place as it dripped little blooms of red into the bowl. He performed the same operation on his own hand, which Thistle only now realised was thick with scars old and new.

It wasn't much of a wound, but Thistle found himself light-headed after receiving it, some combination of the heat and not having eaten, or perhaps just the unconscious shuddering of an organism about to be born anew.

'What did they call this boy?' Edom asked.

'He was Thistle, the false-known,' a voice answered.

'And who is he now?'

Thistle had been frightened that, weakened as he was, he would prove unable to rise, would dishonour himself at this pivotal moment of his existence. So he threw himself into it, forced his body into motion and rose up quickly, too quickly, almost stumbled before righting himself.

But he could feel the swelling goodwill of his new brothers, steadying him with their own strength. 'Pyre,' he said with a force and confidence that surprised him, that ignored how tired and hungry and weak he felt, that left his body light and his head full of fire. 'Pyre, the First of His Line.'

Pyre raised his hand open-fisted, five fingers above his head, the shouts of his companions echoing in his ears, the death of a nation on his lips.

WANT MORE?

If you enjoyed this and would like to find out about similar books we publish, we'd love you to join our online SF, Fantasy and Horror community, Hodderscape.

Visit our blog site

www.hodderscape.co.uk

Follow us on Twitter

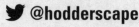 **@hodderscape**

Like our Facebook page

f Hodderscape

You'll find exclusive content from our authors, news, competitions and general musings, so feel free to comment, contribute or just keep an eye on what we are up to. See you there!